THE ALCHEMIST'S RING

JASON LEE WILLIS

THE ALCHEMIST'S RING

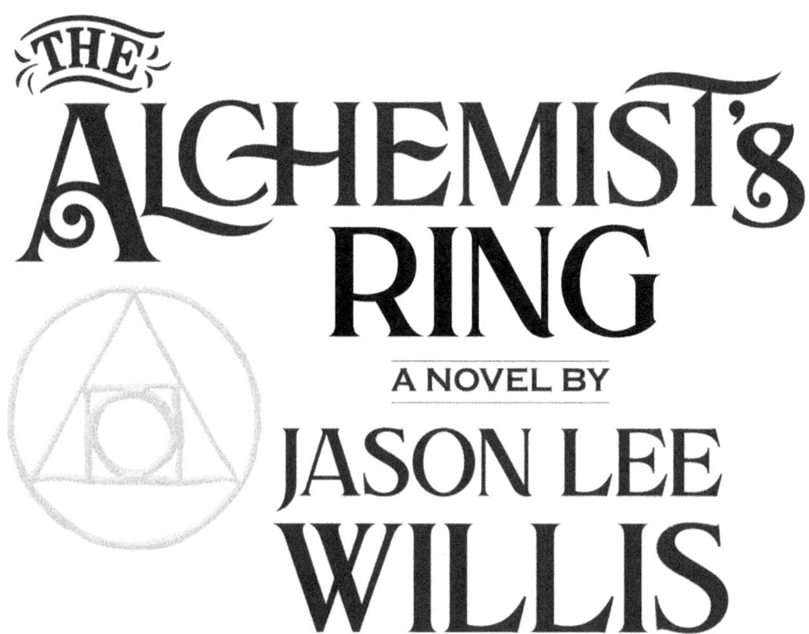

A NOVEL BY

JASON LEE WILLIS

Lura
Publications

Lura Publications
803 Silver Street East
Mapleton, MN 56065
www.lurapublications.wixsite.com/books

Publisher's Note: This book is a work of fiction. Names, characters, places, and incidents are products of the author's imagination or are used fictitiously. Any resemblance to actual events or locales or persons, living or dead, is entirely coincidental.
In 1683, Baron Lahontan arrived in North America and spent a decade upon the frontier. For the next twenty years, he remained a fugitive. The Alchemist's Ring is a fictitious account of these journeys.
During his travels, Lahontan encountered numerous indigenous cultures. Please note that, to remain true to the era, the historic nomenclature for these cultures are used in this novel. Please refer to the index for an overview of indigenous names and terms.

Book Layout © 2024 BookDesignTemplates.com

Library of Congress Cataloging-in-Publication Data
Willis, Jason Lee, author.
Eckman, Raven, editor.
Bunkowske, Caryl, editor
Anderson, Mark, designer.
The Alchemist's Ring / Jason Lee Willis. – First edition.
Summary: A 17th century explorer flees North American upon a pirate ship and becomes entangled by conspiracy theories involving ancient relics.

eBook ISBN: ISBN: 979-8-9903790-1-5
Softcover ISBN: 979-8-9903790-0-8
Hardcover ISBN: 978-1-971362-03-8

[1. Historical Fantasy – Fiction. 2. Maritime History & Piracy – Fiction.
3. Thrillers – Fiction. 4. Action & Adventure – Fiction.]
Library of Congress Control Number: _________

Dedicated to the Kansas City babe.

In 1987, I was a freshman in high school who eagerly agreed to be part of Tri-Valley High School's swing choir. How do you deny a request from upperclassman girls who want to dance with you for hours on end? So not only did I get to dance with real-live girls, but there was also a planned trip to Kansas City where we'd perform at Worlds of Fun amusement park.

In the middle of our performance, my heart skipped a beat. There in the crowd, a babe locked eyes with me. She smiled. She nudged her friend. She waved at me.

When the performance was over, I tried to use my telepathic powers to get her to stay right where she was—leaning against that low wall. I pushed Mark, Shane, and Jason out of my way and ran right past Mrs. Linge to get back to the stage—but she was gone.

Who was she? What was her name? Why did she smile and wave?

Alas, it became one of those great mysteries in life.

Decades later, my brain cells from 1987 can no longer be trusted, but that moment lived on in memory far longer than the length of those two songs.

You are my exotic Queen Rehena.
You are my mysterious Wenonah.

Author's Note

So after spending a whole lot of time on the frontier in *The Alchemist's Stone,* this tale is about to take the reader around the world. The real lives of Pierre-Charles LeSueur and Baron Lahontan led my research right into the golden age of pirates. Like my other novels in the Alchemist Chronicles, this story will be rooted in history with equal parts fantasy.

Think of it this way: I had hundreds of historical stones to help build this structure, and with a bit of mythological mortar, I was able to piece things together. Just like the other stories are inspired by Indiana Jones, the Davinci Code, and National Treasure romps through history, this story followed my love of Pirates of the Caribbean, Master and Commander, Black Flags, and even Treasure Island. Yet my storytelling style requires that the fantasy elements *could* be possible, so that means I enjoy the real history as much as my creative twists.

So have fun, but if you want to learn some lore, check out the index and do your own deep dive into history.

I'd like to thank John and Ron for being sounding boards for my earliest drafts of this story while I was still exploring. Next, Raven rolled up her sleeves to bring a bit of sanity to the story, and after I adjusted the course of the ship, Caryl challenged each comma and clause. I'm indebted to this team.

Special thanks to the Prairie Lakes Regional Arts Council for their support of this project. It's a few months behind schedule, but this larger-than-life tale is possible due to their funding.

PREFACE

Salutations, my old friend and mentor—the humble Doorkeeper.

Oh how I miss our time together drinking coffee at obscure cafes in Rome.

Your wise advice and strategic counsel have been a buoy during my dark days of tribulation. My travels have taken me to the ends of the known world: from the American frontier to distant India and many wondrous locations between. Alas, the path you've placed me on many years ago has still not taken me to my final destination, and without end in sight, I write this brief correspondence to explain any strange reports submitted by other agents stationed around the world. It is my intention to follow where Providence leads, even if it leads to my death.

Should I fall before making a full and complete report of my mission, I have included a list of friends and enemies who might better explain the actions I have taken. The accounts of my travels could hardly be contained within a book, so for now, this letter—and the world—must be enough.

But know this:

You were right about the Magnum Opus, which many call the Philosopher's Stone.

The tales of its creator also seem to be true along with other sinister works his wicked hands crafted. Yes, wise King Solomon's quest for the Magnum Opus failed long ago, but his part in the tale of the ancient alchemist and his foul Stone has entangled me in a great net. Pray for me that I learn from the mistakes of greater men than I.

Your humbled friend,
Louis-Armand

The *Antigua* Crew (1693)
William Kidd—Captain
Gareth LaGrande—First Mate
Hendrick van der Huel—Quartermaster
Richard Barleycorn—Navigator
Robert Lamley—Doctor
William Moore—Master Gunner
Jago Firken—Provisions Boatswain
William Jenkins—Carpenter
Manuel Del Torro—Sail Master
Papa Bones—Cook
Nuno Caverelli—Anchor Boatswain

The *Ganj-i-Sawai* Incident (1695)
Captain Muhammad Ibrahim of the
Ganj-i-Sawai
Captain Corgi Baba of the
Quedagh Merchant
Captain Thomas Tew of the *Amity*
First Mate John Yarland
Captain Richard Want of the *Dolphin*
William May of the *Pearl*
Captain Henry Avery of the *Fancy*
First Mate Patrick Dalziel
Captain Thomas Wake of the *Susanna*
Captain Joseph Faro of the *Portsmouth
Adventure*

The *White Zombie* Crew (1704)
Louis-Armand Guerin—Captain
Charles Johnson—First Mate
Manuel Del Torro—Quartermaster
Naro Bon—Navigator
Thomas Barrow—Doctor
Benjamin Horne—Master Gunner
Drake Murray—Provisions Boatswain
Jimmy Duke—Anchoring Boatswain
Giovanni Naufragio—Carpenter
Papa Bones—Cook

The Flying Sylphs (1701)
Captain Wart Jacobs of the *Phoebe*
Captain Athena McCormack of the *Euryd-
ice*
Captain Archibald Vero of the *Daphne*
First Mate Willow Thomas
Captain Vincent Galloway of the *Meliae*

The Black Fleet (1701)
Admiral Roger Silverthorn
Black Robin Bellomont
George Farrington
Ned Ireland
Richard Cass
Robert Walsh
Allen Bennett

Edward Drummond

The Congress of Pirates (1705)
Admiral Abraham Samuel of Port Dau-
phin
Admiral James Plantain of Ranter Bay
Admiral John Pro of St. Mary's Island
Admiral Pedro Dias
Captain Olivier Lavasseur
Captain Patrick Dalziel of the *Salome* and
later the *Earl Mar*
Captain Robert Culliford of the *Mocha
Frigate* and later the *Lif*
First Mate John Swan and captain of the
Lifrasir

The Free States (1705)
Presider James Morrison
Vizier Denis Falcoa
John Yarland
The Scottish Families: Drummond, Haly-
burton, Pennycook
The French Families: L'Blanc, deVilliers,
Valencourt, Derry
The Portuguese Families: Moniz, Lordel-
lo, Teixeira, Perestrello

The Republic of Pirates (1706)
Captain Blackbeard of the *Pretender*
Captain Patrick Dalziel of the *Earl Mar*
Captain Benjamin Hornigold of the *Mari-
anne*
Captain Henry Jennings of the *Bersheba*
Captain Pierre LeMoyne of the *Nautioneer*
Captain Robert Culliford of the *Jonathan*
Captain Joseph LeMoyne of the *Loire* and
the *Griffon*.
Captain Antoine LeMoyne of the *Sala-
mandre*.

The Flying Dutchmen (1715)
Captain Louis-Armand Guerin of the
Reinforcer.
Captain Drake Murray of the *Son of the
Sea*
Captain Jimmy Duke of the *Mary Dyer*
Captain Daalman of the *Moss Maiden*
Captain Kikkert of the *Wild Hunt*

PART ONE
EXCEEDING TREASURE

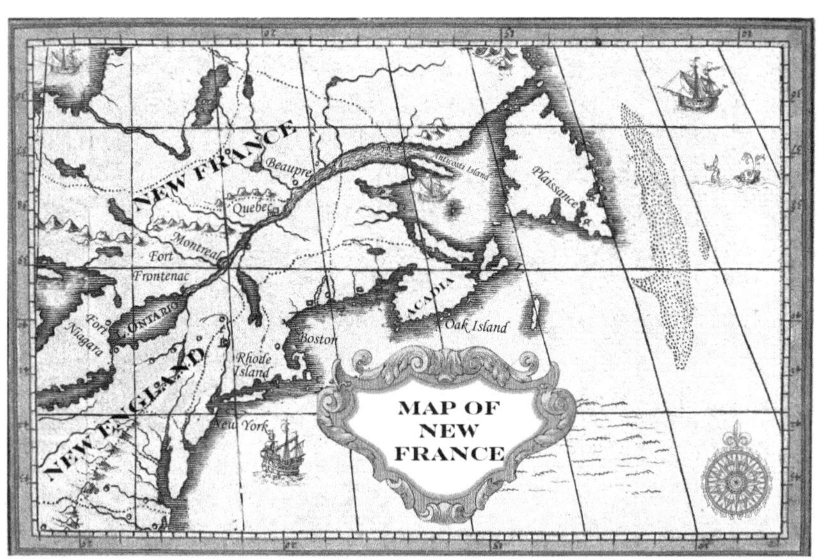

PART ONE

PROLOGUE

M O N C T O N , A C A D I A

1 6 9 3

Francois Muelles counted out the money in his head as he waited at the back of the tavern. In his pockets he only had a couple silver beavers and enough playing card money to get him back to Quebec City, yet by the morrow, he'd be the wealthiest man in Beaupre—after he killed the Baron.

I'll be able to afford a wife and as many children as I can sire, Muelles decided as his list of fantasized purchases grew so extensive he couldn't figure the arithmetic of the bounty money.

All counting—and his own heart—stopped when the assassin stepped through the tavern doors. Muelles kept his nose pointed at the ale on the table, but his eyes watched the man slither through the room like a shadow until he found a lone booth in the corner. Muelles took hold of his beverage, rose, and walked steadily across the room.

The assassin sitting across from him looked like a drowned rat. If the stories were true, the man was a French aristocrat who'd chosen a life of killing over a life of luxury. Muelles tried not to stare at the assassin's missing teeth and fingers like he'd done back in Quebec City. Any man who survived torture would have no qualms killing in a public place, so Muelles treated him as if it were a poisonous snake sitting across from him in the booth. "Is he still here?"

Muelles nodded. "The rain kept him here this morning, or else I'd still be following him down the highway. He's upstairs with a whore right now."

"And you're sure it's him and not an imposter?"

Muelles scoffed and then swallowed hard in fear of his scoff. He nodded solemnly. "The Baron is a war hero in my village. Everyone knows him. Even before the war began, I idolized the man."

"Spare me your adoration. The Baron is an agent of chaos, and his lies and schemes have brought New France to the brink of ruin. I should've put him in the ground the first night I saw him. He's taken as many lives as both the Iroquois or English, and even if the war were to end today, the wounds he has made will continue to bleed."

St. Clair—the assassin's name—was only ever whispered in the shadows. Born into poverty, Muelles killed to survive, but St. Clair chose his path of murder. To look at him, he lacked the obvious physical strength of a murderer, especially after torture claimed fingers and teeth. A weak assassin killed with poison or pistol whereas Muelles, knowing he could overpower the Baron if it came to it, armed himself with blades. When the bounty on Baron Lahontan's head whispered through alleys, Muelles assumed political motivations, but this meeting with St. Clair made him think it was personal.

"Does he know your face?" St. Clair asked.

Muelles shook his head. "No, I was just a little boy when he arrived from France a decade ago, and when he returned from the wilderness to save Quebec, I only saw him from a distance, but I'd know that peacock's strut anywhere. He slipped into Beaupre in the dark of night and departed under cover of darkness again. I've been following him ever since, and luckily, the rain slowed him down."

"Listen to me carefully," St. Clair said, leaning in to whisper. "Louis-Armand de Lom d'Arcy is more than just the Baron of Lahontan. He's more than a military hero. This man received training since childhood, and the powers that shaped him turned him into an instrument of death. If he sees my face, he'll know what's happening. You need to stay here while I gather up enough men to kill him properly."

Muelles nodded. With a pained grimace, St. Clair slipped from the booth. More men meant dividing the bounty. Dividing the bounty meant changing his dreams. Changing his dreams was like killing two of his imagined children.

The Baron is vulnerable right now, Muelles decided. The giggling whore who led the little man upstairs less than an hour ago would have him off guard.

He grabbed a bottle and made for the stairs. With each stair, he transformed himself into a loud clumsy drunk, and by the time he reached the top, he hummed and muttered one of his favorite songs.

I'm too drunk to remember which room is mine, he invented, jiggling the first doorknob before stumbling further down the hall. Surprise, not stealth, would be his strategy. If the Baron truly were the killer St. Clair described, then smashing around the hallway would be less alarming than quiet creaks of a floorboard.

When he stumbled through the Baron's door, his eyes went to the naked whore sprawled across the bed at the feet of the Baron. Baron Lahontan, despite his large title, proved to be quite small undressed. He wore only breeches, and his thin, naked chest only had a few tufts of hair upon it.

A pistol rested beside the bed.

Instead of clamoring for it, Baron Lahontan smiled. "Have you come to join us? Evangeline expected more than just conversation."

"You see…" Muelles began, feigning intoxication, stumbling and falling in a heap upon the floor. His fingers discreetly moved to locate his favorite dagger.

The Baron took the bait and his feet slipped off the bed to deal with the annoyance. "Honestly, sir. Get a hold of yourself. It's only a naked woman."

Two more steps and I'll have him.

The Baron stopped. His neatly trimmed toes curled slightly.

I'll be able to stab him in the back three or four times before he gets to his pistol, and then I'll overpower him.

Muelles gripped the hilt of the dagger and prepared to attack.

A floorboard creaked behind him, hurrying his decision to launch himself at the Baron, who didn't retreat. A strong hand gripped Muelles by the hair, and before he could even lift his dagger in a threatening manner, a dark blade passed in front of his face and dragged across his throat.

The Baron raised a hand to shield himself from the spray of blood coming from Muelles throat.

"Discretion, Gaspar!" Baron Lahontan said, rushing past Muelles to the door.

The hand released his hair and Muelles fell to the floor, clutching at the hot blood that came from his slit throat. His eyes turned to the silent killer who had appeared behind him in the open door. A gray-haired native, dressed in a heavy wool jacket, held the knife bearing his blood upon it. Instead of malice, his face displayed disgust and pity. "We need to leave immediately. He wasn't alone."

He followed me up the stairs.

For Francois Muelles, there would be no bounty, cottage in Beaupre, or even a family. Each pulse of blood between his fingers brought an end to those dreams, but he found small consolation that his dashing childhood hero was indeed the man he believed him to be.

Well played, Baron Lahontan.
Well played.

CHAPTER 1

Louis-Armand Guerin tossed his favorite hat into the fire, which dampened it for a moment before feeding the flames. The hat belonged to Baron Lahontan, who for all intents and purposes died in the Moncton Tavern.

The swell of light illuminated the face of his trusted companion, Gaspar. The stern Petun war chief held a sharpened bone in his fingertips, which he dipped into the inky mixture he'd made from ash and berries. With barely a flinch, Gaspar broke skin along the tender flesh of his forearm and the blood hid whatever pattern he created in tribute to the assassin he'd killed three nights earlier.

Ink covered Gaspar's body from the lines on his chin and cheeks to the more elaborate patterns on his chest and back. Most tattoos were made during his youth, when he was known as Kondiaronk, the Muskrat, who'd kill his enemies and vanish back into the waters. Some tattoos marked victories, others marked tragedies—like the death of his family—and because of his practice of counting coup, when Gaspar died and stood in front of his Creator, he would be able to make a full accounting of each man he killed.

Guerin had never seen Gaspar create a tattoo before. Over the past decade, Gaspar had been his trusted companion, military strategist, and moral compass on their adventures in the "New World" of "America." During the Beaver Wars, Gaspar's family and people were slaughtered by the Iroquois, and even though Gaspar was a chief of a small tribe, he spent years killing any Iroquois who would whet his blade. The Jesuit missionary Jacques Marquette, however, put out the fires of vengeance and converted Kondiaronk into the Christian known as Gaspar, named after one of the three magi.

"I suppose the debt has been paid," Guerin said to his mentor. "I saved you from certain death back at Lake Ontario, and now you saved me from certain death from that assassin. You're not obliged to follow me any further."

Gaspar tossed the stained bone into the fire. "It is my duty to the Creator."

As Baron of Lahontan, Louis-Armand had arrived in Quebec several years earlier with a company of professional soldiers. He was their leader because of his birthright. Gaspar led because of his skill. Each victory gathered more and more refugees to his camp, who joined his fight against the Iroquois. Yet the hardened warrior set aside all ego to follow Guerin for the past several years. "I'm not your chosen one," Guerin said aloud, catching Gaspar's attention. "I've heard you whisper to any holy man we've encountered between here and the Mississippi. While the comet of 1682 did announce my arrival to the continent, I'm not the Wishwee or the 'boy with a strange light in my eyes.' I'm just a sinful spy, and you can't follow me to where I'm going."

Gaspar kept his eyes on his artwork as he spoke. "I know the Serpent Star didn't send you, but still the Creator has made you his instrument. I chose to follow you because it allowed me to retrace the path. You and I visited the Seventh Stopping Place, and now I'll return to the place where the Seven Fires Prophecy was first given. I chose this path because we both serve the people in the war against the darkness. The man who tried to kill you wasn't serving Governor de Brouillan; the assassin was an agent of darkness. Eos knows what you found in the Land of the Blue Woman."

Louis-Armand Guerin unbuttoned his expensive vest and tossed it onto the fire. He'd inherited the title of Baron Lahontan from his father, and he'd earned the ranks of lieutenant and captain by serving New France in the recent global war between England and France, but he was born a bastard to Jeanne Guerin. As a boy, the brilliant bastard was sent to Rome to enter the priesthood, but instead, he caught the attention of a secret society known as the Periphery. As their agent, he first returned to France to reclaim his recognized inheritance and then traveled to New France as an investigative agent. "Eos knows what I found because you insisted that I arrest Pierre-Charles LeSueur rather than kill him. I flee the continent because of your advice. I should have killed him."

"You should have made Pierre-Charles LeSueur your ally instead of your enemy. You were wrong about him."

Guerin rolled his eyes. "He's the only witness to the death of Father Marquette. He's either an agent of the Jesuits or an agent of Eos. Either way, he is my enemy," Guerin defended his earlier actions that not only ruined a man's life but also ignited a war on the frontier. Although the Periphery headquarters were found in Rome, the organization existed "in the shadows" of the Catholic Church. If the legends were true, it predated the Catholic Church by thousands of years and served not only to keep the puppet masters in check but also to protect the oppressed. In recent years, two occult enemies—the Order of Eos and the Priory of Ormus—took an unhealthy interest in the frontiers of America. So, too, did the Society of Jesuit, known simply as the Jesuits, who seemingly allied themselves with the Anishinaabe to enter the lands west of the Mississippi, where a mighty nation known as the Oceti Sakowin, or commonly called the Sioux, protected a vast territory known as the Land of the Blue Woman.

Gaspar dabbed away at the excess blood and inspected his work. "You must decide if you are subservient to God or greater than God. Eos, the Jesuits, the Anishinaabe, and Ormus all race against each other because they believe their free will can shape the future of humanity. When I stopped being Kondiaronk and became Gaspar, I trusted the guiding hand of God to put me where He needed me to be. If you continue to fight against the will of God, your deeds will become dark rather than necessary."

"The sooner I leave for Rome, the sooner you'll be rid of me, is that it?"

Gaspar shrugged. "If I stay with you much longer, I'll be tattooing the soles of my feet."

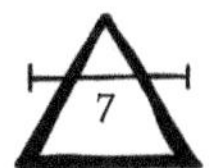

"Then go back to your people. Guard them. Protect them. You know what will happen to all the tribes around the Great Lakes if this war continues much longer. I need you to watch over the Lands of the Blue Woman—to safeguard the treasure and keep it from the hands of our enemies if necessary."

Gaspar sighed heavily.

"What is it?" Guerin asked.

"When you sail back to Rome, what will you tell the Periphery about what you've seen?"

"I'll tell them the truth and let better men than me decide what to do next," Guerin began but Gaspar's eyes demanded more. "I will let them know where to find the treasure right down to the bend of the river and how it matched the sketches made by LeSueur. I'll describe the mound of blue earth we found and how the local Sioux described the place as the Haunted Valley due to the presence of an evil spirit. I'll tell them that with some digging, they'll be able to unearth the Philosopher's Stone and perhaps much, much more."

Gaspar began to nod, paused, and then shook his head. "And what will the Periphery do with this treasure once it is unearthed."

"I can't…"

"Haven't thought this through, have you? You were so preoccupied with finding the ancient treasure that you never thought of why they needed it. What is their purpose in acquiring it?"

"For starters, it can transform lead into gold," Guerin quipped.

"And if that was its only purpose, it would make gold as worthless as sand."

"Don't belittle the power of transformation. If it can change lead into gold, what else can it change? Back in Rome, when I was still a boy, I researched King Solomon for an assignment. While there are only vague references to it in the Bible, lore suggests that Solomon turned to occult knowledge to build the Temple in Jerusalem. The maps that Eos and Ormus used to search for the Philosopher's Stone were made in the days of King Solomon, and the secret knowledge acquired by Solomon resulted in expeditions looking for a lost kingdom of a forgotten king who made a magical stone."

"But they didn't find it, did they?"

"The Stone? No, but that didn't stop Solomon. With the aid of an imprisoned demon named Asmodeus, Solomon fashioned a magical ring when he couldn't acquire the lost stone. The altar of God, it seems, could only be built of unhewn stone, so Solomon used his ring to build his masterpiece without cutting any stone. A curious story, isn't it? But here's my concern: the Order of Eos possesses a map that suggests they nevertheless found the ancient empire, the Kingdom of Marakk, they called it," Guerin said, pointing up into the heavens at the constellation commonly known as the Big Dipper. "One of the seven stars is called Marakk. That's as far as my research took me. But stay up late at night and wonder: Who is this Marakk?"

"*This* is why I follow you," Gaspar admitted. "When you're not thinking, you are quite intelligent."

"Thank you?"

"Marakk? I am researching another version of the same story. Generations ago, the Anishinaabe people lived here in Acadia and received seven prophecies, the Seven Fires, that sent them on an exodus leading west."

"To the Land of the Blue Woman."

Gaspar nodded solemnly. "You study Eos and Ormus to try to understand their motivations in acquiring the Philosopher's Stone. I study the Anishinaabe legends for the same reasons. By returning to the past, I hope to understand the future. Marakk? The seven stars? The Anishinaabe believe it represents a warrior Ojiig who battled a powerful enemy who tried to stop the seasons, time itself, from continuing, trapping the world in an endless winter. Ojiig prevailed and released the seasons, yet the battle against this Wintermaker continued into the stars."

"Are you suggesting Marakk and the Wintermaker are the same?"

"You and I stood at the place where water flows in all directions and the earth bleeds blue. An evil hand created the Philosopher's Stone. Who was its creator?

Guerin shrugged. "King Solomon had it figured out, didn't he?"

"We must understand the past to understand the future," Gaspar repeated. "The Anishinaabe have stories of a boy, Iyash, who battled an evil spirit known as the Horned Serpent. The earliest tales of the Anishinaabe speak of an island, and I mean to find this island where their prophecies began."

Guerin laughed aloud, bringing a fierce scowl from his old friend. "I should be bringing you back to Rome with me instead of my fragments and facts. I wasn't laughing at you. I was laughing at myself. I embraced my role in the Periphery because I craved adventure, but I am blind to so much. You are truly a man of faith, capable of seeing truth and lies. Before I set foot in America, the Periphery gave me instructions for my extraction. While I boldly told everyone in that tavern in Moncton that I'd be departing from the harbor of Port Royal, the Periphery chose the fishing port of Chester."

Guerin paused, knowing that the port meant nothing to Gaspar. "What's special about Chester, you ask? Aside from whisking me away to safety, the reason the Periphery has an agent in Chester is to keep an eye on a special island nearby."

"A special island," Gaspar repeated, and a slight grin appeared on his face.

"According to the tales, Eos went to Acadia centuries ago, and after their visit, they cut down every tree on the island and planted foreign trees so they'd be able to find the island again upon their return."

"Foreign trees?"

"On the morrow, you and I are heading east—to find Oak Island."

CHAPTER 2

OAK ISLAND, ACADIA

1693

Perhaps I built it up too much, Louis-Armand Guerin thought after a prolonged silence from Gaspar. He climbed up onto one of the boulders and waited for a reaction. Gaspar stood facing the open shoreline, which faced the bay and the coastline.

"You see," Guerin tried again, "These boulders form a cross. If you count the little one, there are five placed in a straight line, and then two more at a perfect side angle. Nature doesn't create straight lines. This pattern is man made."

Gaspar folded his arms. "I thought you said the men who came to this island weren't Christian. Why would they make a cross?"

"Eos adapted to a Christian culture—from their Templar days to their new masonic lodges. It's easier to hide the truth in plain sight if your enemy doesn't understand what they're looking at."

Gaspar shook his head. "We should have swam."

Still this argument? "The waters of the Atlantic are frigid, and I'm about to be stuffed in a cargo hold for my return to Rome. I wasn't about to get wet."

"You told the villagers that you were the Baron of Lahontan. It won't take the men who hunt you long to find out that you're not in either Louisbourg or Port Royal."

"I'm a petty man with petty reasons. Besides, our tour of the is-land is all but over. Even if the villagers immediately sent a rider—which they didn't—we'll be long gone before more assassins ar-rive."

Gaspar turned away from the quiet harbor and approached Guerin. He looked over the stones strewn over the woods hundreds of yards in all directions from where Guerin sat. "So what did they bury here?"

So he believes me! "That is the obvious question isn't it? But I'd like to counter your questions with 'Why did they bury it here?' and the much more practical 'How did they bury it here?'"

Gaspar leaned his back against the boulder to rest beside Guerin's dangling feet. Years earlier, their brotherly bond began with the early skirmishes with the Iroquois, and then grew even stronger when then Lieutenant d'Arcy saved Chief Gaspar's life. The trip into hostile Sioux territory, where they found proof of the buried Philosopher's Stone, transformed Gaspar into a father figure. "The Periphery is certain it was built by the Order of Eos?"

"A few centuries before the Catholic Church broke apart in the Protestant Reformation, the Order of Eos also split apart. It's most likely Eos, but there is a small possibility it could have been the Priory of Ormus. *When* Oak Island was created would help answer that question better. If I were to venture a guess, I'd say it was crafted in the 1300s by Eos."

This seemed to satisfy Gaspar. His encounters with Eos had been shaped by the French conquerors of the Great Lakes. Powerful aristocrats like Etienne Delhut, Charles LeMoyne, and LaSalle swept through countless Indigenous nations. "Last night I noticed the stars. We're almost level with the Land of the Blue Woman, and if I'd paid even closer attention, I'd say your Oak Island is almost exactly on the same line as the place where we found the blue earth."

"Of course," Guerin said with a chuckle. "The Templars had a mighty fleet, and if the old stories are true, King Solomon hired Phoenician sailors to locate the Philosopher's Stone—here on the far side of the planet." Only the midday sun was above their heads now.

"So your people use stars to determine geography?"

"Depending on the season, the stars will rise and fall upon the horizon at certain locations. Sailors know this," Gaspar answered with certainty.

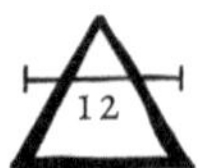

"I guess you answered one of my difficult questions," Guerin said and slid off the big center stone. "Would you like to offer your theory on *How* did they bury anything here?'"

For the better part of the morning, they'd toured the island, which was less than a mile from tip to tip at its longest. Having read about it from prior Periphery reports, Guerin noted that the oak trees had been manually planted centuries ago. He found the stone triangles used to help orient caretakers separated by years and generations. Gaspar agreed that the beach had been man made and recognized the evidence of excavated floodgates. This led to them standing upon solid stone at a depression that marked a hidden underground entrance.

"You've already given me the answer."

"No. I asked you the question," Guerin clarified. "*How'd* they make it?'"

"But you already know the answer."

Guerin could feel the solid stone under his feet. "They were masons? I suppose. The secrets of carving stone used by the Templar Knights were originally taught through the secret knowledge of King Solomon."

Gaspar nodded. "Your Templars were on the run, scattered by their enemies. If they had any treasures of value, bringing them across the Atlantic would have been shrewd, but they would have quickly discovered that the New World was already occupied, and while the inhabitants were neither ally or enemy, they would have needed to bury their treasure in a way that no human hand could easily discover it."

"If they still possess the secrets of Solomon, they'll have no problem unearthing the Philosopher's Stone from its earthly prison. If I'd had Solomon's ring in my pocket back in the Lands of the Blue Woman, I could have unearthed the Philosopher's Stone myself." The thought gave Guerin chills. *I was so close to seizing the prize.* "I should have killed LeSueur when I had the chance."

"You did what needed to be done," Gaspar said in reference to the political coup at Fort Mackinac that ousted Pierre-Charles LeSueur and replaced him with young Baron Lahontan. "If there is any blame, it falls on me. I also had the opportunity to kill LeSueur, who returned to Wisconsin as quickly as he could. I don't think he's your enemy. I believe the Serpent Star summoned both of you to the Land of the Blue Woman."

"Only he serves Eos."

"When I met Father Marquette, I killed the man who I'd once been. The waters of baptism transformed me from Kondiaronk to Gaspar—all because of Father Marquette. Pierre-Charles LeSueur spent his entire youth learning from this great man. If Eos poisoned Father Marquette, as LeSueur alleges, then I refuse to believe this man would betray his master to join his enemies."

"'Kill them all, and let God sort them out'" Guerin began. "It's a race against time now. LeSueur and I have confirmed the truth about the old maps, and when this war is over, the puppet masters will insist on returning to the Land of the Blue Woman to claim their ancient prize. I pray only that I can get back to Rome fast enough to make a difference. I need to tell them the Philosopher's Stone has been found within the foundations of the ancient kingdom."

"And I will remain here and do all I can to keep France and England from reaching the lands beyond the Mississippi River," Gaspar reviewed.

"So do you think Oak Island is the same island that Iyash visited before the Anishinaabe received the Seven Fires Prophecies?"

Gaspar paused, taking final measure of the peculiar island. "The same mystery that drove an entire nation from east to west across the continent has driven me from west to east. This mystery drives the Jesuits, Eos, Ormus, the Periphery, and even the Anishinaabe to the lands of the Sioux. Do you really think you and I can stop them from finding what they seek?"

"Probably not," Guerin said with a shrug as he began to walk back to the borrowed rowboat. Gaspar joined him at his side. "But we can delay it, and each hour we delay it, we give the old men, the women, and the children another day of life, however they choose to use it. One day, you and I will die, but we'll go to our graves knowing we fought the good fight."

"The good fight," Gaspar repeated. "I wonder if we'll ever meet again."

"I'll do my best to let God's will guide me to where I can best serve him. Who knows? Perhaps I'll live long enough to see you again."

"That would truly be a surprise," Gaspar admitted and almost cracked a smile.

CHAPTER 3

Instead of listening to Chief Gaspar's advice, Louis-Armand Guerin lingered for some sweet vengeance. He held the looking glass to his eye and focused on the small cabin on the edge of the fishing village of Chester. While the rest of the village began to glow with lanterns and fireplaces, the small cabin remained dark.

Guerin watched from a slow moving pirate ship.

The ship's floorboards creaked at the approach of the fat captain known as "The Toad" to the locals. Physically, he fit the part, with rolls of fat under his chin and belly. Yet despite his squatty nature, he dressed in extravagant clothing. Like many pirates and smugglers, Jean Crapeau's true name remained hidden; he embraced his persona given to him by the English—Captain Crappo. Before King William's War began, he was already a smuggler and knew how to hide or attack. Because of this, the Periphery hired him for a very specific smuggling job—extraction of its agent. "The men are waiting for my signal, but my boatswain heard rumors of English warships in the area."

"Just a few more minutes," Guerin insisted, reaching into his pockets for a final bribe that would leave him broke. The Periphery paid an advance several years ago with a promise of a small fortune transferred to him at the next destination. As much as pirates loved money, he also knew a ship full of criminals also enjoyed wicked behavior—which he hoped to indulge.

Dark figures moved within the village.

"Are those the men who hunt you?" Captain Crappo asked.

Eos is determined to put Baron Lahontan in the grave. A dozen men on horses swarmed the small village and immediately fanned out. After a decade in New France, his big mouth left a trail of breadcrumbs for his enemies to follow. He didn't want to just vanish or his enemies could control the narrative. Sleeping with a governor's daughter (whether true or not) shamefully ended his political and military career, but it also tested whether or not Eos knew what he'd found on the frontier. Eos assassins confirmed it, especially now that they followed the clues to his extraction site.

"Fire on my signal." Captain Crappo's order sent the crew into motion. "I don't want any villagers to get hurt." The anchor lifted. A few small sails dropped. The powder monkeys gathered at the cannons.

In addition to Oak Island, Mahone Bay held dozens of small islands, and Crappo's ship slid from its hiding place onto the dark water. Guerin handed the looking glass back to the captain and watched with his own eyes as the brute squad descended on the small cabin. He'd left a stuffed effigy of himself wearing the last of Baron Lahontan's clothing in a large chair facing a fireplace

The killers filled the cabin with light.

Let it be St. Clair.

The ship drew within a hundred yards of the shore, allowing Guerin to see the men entering the cabin on shore. Instead of the Eos killer, a bald man led the team.

Damn it all. The wrong villain found me. Guerin shrugged and nodded, summoning thunder and lightning from the cannons.

THE NEXT MORNING, when Louis-Armand Guerin woke in his cabin, he knew his role as Captain d'Arcy and Baron Lahontan had reached its end. As he dressed in the drab clothing, a smile parted his lips.

It shocked him that North America was nowhere to be seen. From horizon to horizon, white clouds and small waves amplified the elation he already felt. Captain Crappo stood with his navigator, and Guerin joined them without saying a word.

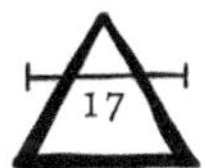

"I doubt that we killed many of those men," Captain Crappo said once he noticed Guerin. "Was it worth it?"

"If it'd been the right men, I would have insisted that you keep firing. The men who stepped in the trap were private investigators hired by King Louis, who's worried about these secret societies threatening his power. The men we fired on would have slowly tortured me to death to get my secrets. They know I'm alive and that I've fled the continent, so in that regard, yes, it was worth it."

"How can you be so cheery when you just became a fugitive without a home?"

"Oh, this lone wolf has a pack, and I'll find a comfy hole somewhere in the world to curl up and call a den. I consider it good fortune that the French authorities know I'm still alive. The bald fellow worked for the King himself. Now I'll be able to write my book under my own name."

I still wish it'd been St. Clair.

"You're going to write a book?"

"A false narrative."

"A work of fiction."

"More like a lie. My enemies know where I've been and can guess what I've seen, so I'll publish a false account of my travels, which will muddy the waters for a generation or more. I'll be dead and gone before they know my book was a lie." Guerin suddenly grew aware that the rising sun was on his left cheek. "Why are we traveling due south?"

"You insisted on speed."

"I did."

"The currents off the coast of the Massachusetts Colony will almost double our speed and let us cross the Atlantic in a matter of weeks. With your approval," Captain Crappo teased.

"We'll stay ahead of any news sent to France. By the time the warrants are written, I'll have vanished from the face of the earth." With that, Guerin disappeared back to his cabin. After a decade of strutting around New France, he was ready for silent contemplation in his cabin.

TWO HOURS LATER, he heard a bell ringing.

A few minutes later, a knock came on his cabin door.

So much for peace and quiet.

When he opened the door, the crewman delivered the tense news, "We've got company."

Guerin followed at his heels all the way to Captain Crappo, who held the looking glass to his face. "We just sailed past Nantucket Island, and that little ketch came racing after us."

"So what's the problem?"

Crappo lowered the glass to answer. "It's not part of the English or Colonial navy."

"That's good."

"No. It's foolish. We can certainly outgun that barking little dog. Well, this is your charter, so perhaps I can leave the decision to you."

"What decision?"

"If we continue, we'll pass by New York Harbor before we make our turn east. One barking dog might turn into a pack of little dogs. Or, we turn for deep waters right now and lose him."

"I certainly want to return to Rome as quickly as possible, but I'd also like to arrive in one piece. If you think that ship is following us into a blockade, by all means, head for deep water."

Captain Crappo sighed as if holding back information.

What isn't he telling me?

Instead of the looking glass scouring the coastline, Captain Crappo spent the next half hour looking ahead to the waters of the Georges Bank. His concentration suddenly doubled and he muttered "damn it all" before handing the glass to his first mate. "Please tell me that's a cod fisherman."

His first mate strained as he took measure.

A bell sounded from high above.

"What is it?"

"It's a big privateer—a pirate hunter, and we just bolted when we should have held steady to our course," Captain Crappo said with a shrug and an apologetic shake of his head. "Go back to my cabin and put on one of my feathered hats. You're going to play the part of my First Mate once we are boarded."

"They're going to board us?"

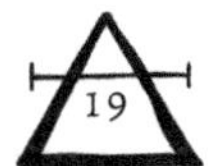

"If we had more than a promissory note, we might've been able to fight our way out of this trap, but I'm not going to allow half of my crew to be killed in the fight. If they see we have nothing of value, we might be on our way by dusk. Now go change your clothes and play the part of a pirate."

Guerin nodded, but before he took a step, the real first mate muttered, "Sir, that's Captain Kidd coming for us.

CHAPTER 4

NEWPORT, RHODE ISLAND

1 6 9 3

Patience is a virtue, Thomas Tew thought to himself as he watched the clueless French pirate ship step into the trap likely set for them. With the little ketch chasing and the big frigate waiting to intercept, Tew didn't need to wait around for the inevitable.

That's my window of opportunity, he realized with a broad smile on his face.

The commands were given and his looking glass turned from the danger to his home port.

Almost forty, Thomas Tew had spent much of his adult life away from his home of Newport, Rhode Island. His family had emigrated to America when he was a child, but Newport was where he'd grown up, gone to school, and married. His glass turned west toward Long Island. In an extravagant house, his wife and two daughters spent a fraction of his vast wealth. The girls were now almost teenagers, and as much as his heart yearned to sweep them up and take them away with him, he knew they'd live a better—and longer—life by never knowing him.

Tew didn't cross the globe to reclaim his forgotten family.

He came for his college professor.

BY SUPPER, TEW had anchored his ship near Narragansett Bay, crossed the channel in a rowboat, and escorted by a pack of five deadly killers, knocked on the front door of Professor Josiah Faero.

"Thomas? Thomas Tew! What in the world are you doing on my doorstep?" Professor Faero asked, wearing a housecoat over his flannel pants. Once, the man had been his Merlin with years of wisdom separating them. Now, Thomas saw a peer—another middle-aged man. Never an attractive man, Faero now had more hair on his jowls than atop his head. No one else stirred in the home, a sign his former teacher had remained a bachelor.

Which will make this easier, regardless of what he says.

"I happened to be in the neighborhood."

"Last I'd heard, you were supposed to be somewhere in the Indian Ocean."

"Those rumors are true, but only because I wanted my wife to know I was still alive. I wouldn't believe the details of the accounts."

"Well, come inside. Supper is still warm. Tell me all about your adventures," Faero insisted with enthusiasm, unaware of the killers scattered in the shadows.

✸

KNOWING THAT PRIVATEERS lingered in the area, Tew indulged the professor's enthusiasm for the time it took to eat, and once the meal was over, he cut to the chase. "Have you continued your fireside lectures?"

"Alas, I'm transitioning between universities. The Puritan sensibilities at my former university restricted such open forums."

"You were fired."

"Oh, no need to worry about me. Since King William's War began, I've made a living illegally shipping texts to and from the other colonies, especially Montreal. Each book in my library provides enough food for a week. It might surprise you, but there is a healthy interest in the Philosopher's Stone, and patrons are willing to spend small fortunes to acquire these books."

"You're selling your family heirlooms?"

"I've read them all and I have no children, so what is the point of hanging onto my pride?"

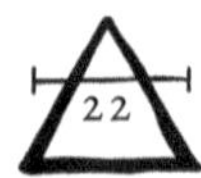

"I remember my excitement when I'd see you wink during a lecture, knowing we'd get the truth later that evening here at your fireplace. I can remember one lecture in particular about the corruption of King Solomon."

"Ah, yes, I'm surprised I managed to keep my position at the university for as long as I did. I don't suppose you've heard of the lunacy happening in the Massachusetts Colony? Witch trials! It's probably best I no longer associate the Kings of Israel with sorcery and witchcraft."

"While the local newspapers probably proclaim me as a pirate, the first trip I made with my own ship was to the Holy Lands. I sailed right up the Red Sea, into the Gulf of Aqaba, and walked in the footsteps of Moses.

"I seem to remember you challenging the Bible. Have you found faith as an older man?"

"Ah, I've found my faith, but not in the pages of your Bible, Professor Faero. I respect how you held to your own faith while trying to understand the mysteries of other cultures. Freedom for *all* religions. I've taken your lessons and applied them to my colony."

"Your colony?"

"I've done well, Professor Faero. A pirate only thinks of himself. My new colony is not only inclusive of other cultures but is the model of democracy. I'd love it if you were to visit."

"Who'd tend to my library?" Faero asked with a playful tone, but Tew knew the man had become a shut-in. Josiah Faero knew every page of his library, and while he remained conservative in deed, the man's mind explored every dark corner of humanity.

"To be honest, I could use your help," Tew began politely, knowing he had a crew of kidnappers outside if it came to that.

"Help? Of course, Thomas. What is it? It must be something for you to travel so far."

"Oh, it is. It's a bit of a treasure hunt, actually. Do you remember taking us to the Old Stone Mill in Newport."

The smile predictably left Faero's face. "A mill? You know that isn't true."

"Of course. Your theory was that it was... an observatory? Hmm, it is in exceedingly poor condition, that's for sure. I'd love to show you what it originally looked like. Back at my colony, we have an exact replica, except it is kept in pristine condition."

"Where is this colony?"

"Oh, it's on the far side of the world, I can assure you of that. It's as far from civilization as you could hope for. America was once isolated, and now look at it. It is called the Free States, which represents a dozen separate colonies—all democratically ruled—with two separate branches of government. Instead of a king or emperor, a democratically elected leader, known as the Presider, guides the affairs of the entire island."

"An island?"

"When the colony was founded, Madagascar was largely uninhabited—and few nautical charts even knew it existed. It became home to people without a flag to wave. Those who created the colony are the same men who built your stone observatory in Newport."

"Are you saying—"

Tew grinned and nodded. "You need to come see the White Temple in person. Get away from this war and witch hunts and sail the seven seas with me. You'll be safe and respected. You'll be the Pope of the Free States, able to teach whatever comes into your head. I can guarantee your protection. Along with being the democratically elected leader, the local people have also promised to make me the King of Betsimisaraka. I tried to explain that I already have a wife, but they see it as an important political marriage, which I understand."

Professor Faero drew his arms to his chest and covered his mouth with his hand.

Too much, too soon? I'll explain the rest on our voyage back. "It's time to crawl out of the pages of your musty old texts and into a real adventure. As I mentioned already, I'm chasing down an old legend that connects back to the days of King Solomon. While my visit to Jerusalem was fruitless, it led me to an obvious destination."

"The ancient Kingdom of Aksum," Faero muttered between his fingers.

"I knew you were the right man for this quest. Yes, I need your mind to help decipher the clues. I'll likely only get one chance at this, so I must do it right."

"Surely you're not chasing after the Ark of the Covenant. It's not lying in some musty vault. Revelation chapter 11 indicates that it's been taken to Heaven."

Tew shook his head. "No, I'm not after the Ark of the Covenant. What would I do with that? I need to show you something few men on the earth have seen—for several thousand years."

He reached into his bag and retrieved the etchings. Using wine glasses, he kept the newly made image flat on the corner. "The markings on this paper are from an ancient stone that we keep locked away in a secret vault. It is one of several pieces of a very complicated puzzle."

"I've seen these markings before," Faero admitted as his fingers brushed the fresh marks.

"I know. That's why I've come to see you. The original text is found upon something we call the Odin Stone."

"The discoverer of runes," Faero whispered the answer to himself.

"Yes, and while the designer of the stone may or may not have been Odin, it is nevertheless the most ancient written language known to mankind. For generations, the language upon our old relic has been lost to us. We've recently learned of another relic—a sarcophagus."

"How intriguing? Whose tomb is it?"

Thomas Tew shook his head. "The corpse matters not, but written upon the stone are three languages—Egyptian hieroglyphs, ancient Hebrew, and the language used upon the Odin Stone. Who else on this planet—aside from you—would be familiar with all three?"

"Where did you say this Odin Stone is kept? I'd like to see it myself."

"Come with me, and I can explain it all aboard my ship."

"You want me to travel to your fanciful colony? Oh, no. I'm quite happy here in Newport."

"I've always seen you as a mentor, so come with me on a grand adventure. I'll get you

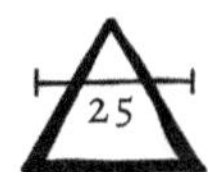

back to your books in no time. Be the best man in my marriage to this Betsimisaraka princess. Test our theories. Inspect our relics. Visit our White Temple. Help me understand this old mystery, Professor Faero. Unlock the language for us. What do you say?"

Faero's brow wrinkled in contemplation.

It didn't really matter what he said next.

Professor Faero was going to Madagascar whether he agreed or not.

CHAPTER 5

As much as Louis-Armand Guerin tried to use his imagination, he'd long ago lost track of where in the world he was. For the first few days of his imprisonment, he managed to keep track of the ship's general bearing—south. With the world at war, he knew England fought a French-Spanish alliance so he visualized the coast of Florida.

Stuck inside of the ship's brig, deep in the bottom of the ship, he had no windows to the outside world—a torture of a different kind. Following a storm, he lost all track of how many miles they'd traveled or even the general direction they sailed.

Luckily, the ship anchored the previous day, and after a few weeks of constant motion, his world grew quiet.

Papa Bones entered the cargo hold with leftover breakfast, which meant the only torture would be the slop he'd leave him.

"We've anchored," Guerin began. He was the only prisoner that Captain Kidd had taken when he intercepted Captain Crappo off the New England coast. There had been no battle or conflict, and with only promissory notes, Crappo apologized as he handled over his cargo—Guerin. "Where has Captain Kidd taken me?"

"We are a long way from Montreal," Papa Bones answered in French. Like Guerin, he'd ended up as part of the crew through conquest. Back in Haiti, he'd been forced into service by a French captain but ended up on an English ship in the early days of the war. "Are you familiar with Florida?"

Guerin nodded.

"Well, we are a long way from Florida also," Papa Bones chuckled. "Once we left the shores of Florida, we passed by the Bahamas, Turks and Caicos, my home of Haiti, Puerto Rico, and now we are in the British West Indies, at an island called Nevis."

"What are we doing in Nevis?"

"Seeking revenge," the middle-aged cook winked and passed him a plate of scraps.

Kidd paid his crew in shared booty, so taking an almost empty French pirate ship had been quite a disappointment. Yet when a thorough search of the logs indicated the cargo was a wealthy Frenchman, Captain Kidd took Guerin prisoner, hoping for ransom. Interrogation had become a game, with Kidd and his officers prying bits of information from their hostage. Guerin gave them enough so they wouldn't slit his throat and dump him overboard. "What sort of revenge?"

"These pirates—can't trust any of them. Captain Kidd led a mutiny to steal his own pirate ship. The man who helped him take the ship, Robert Culliford, did the same thing to Kidd a few months later. A few of us had gone ashore for supplies, and while we were gone, Culliford stole the whole ship from us."

"Ah, so it's personal," Guerin assessed. "Why didn't you escape during the second mutiny?"

"And do what?" Papa Bones added. "I'm a cook. It's what I do. It really doesn't matter who I'm cooking for. Life is a great adventure, isn't it?"

Papa Bones should be cooking for his grandchildren in Haiti, and I should be in Rome. "Yes, Papa Bones, it certainly has its surprises."

THE REST OF the morning, Captain Kidd's ship shook with activity as supplies came onboard. Every few minutes, spare cargo was dropped off in the belly of the ship, allowing Guerin a few moments of small talk with men he'd not yet met.

"Where are we heading next?" Guerin asked—and managed to get an answer: Hunting

Spanish merchant ships.

The anchor came up, and they soon departed Nevis.

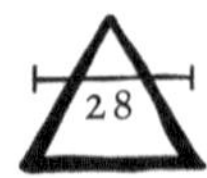

Jago Firken, the supply room manager, entered the room with keys jangling. At first, he'd been the one to torture and beat Guerin. It'd been *his* brig in *his* supply room, after all, but once Guerin made Kidd belly laugh, the torture had stopped.

"Captain Kidd wants a word with you," Firken said as he unlocked the brig and swung

the door open. When they tried to force information out of him, Firken had come with several goons. Now, he came alone.

"What's happening?"

Firken shrugged. "Bad luck for some, good luck for others. Follow me."

For the first time in weeks, Guerin walked freely through an almost empty ship. It wasn't until he stepped onto the main deck that he discovered the reason: a funeral. Firken kept walking to Captain Kidd's private quarters.

Captain Kidd looked like a baker or butcher, with a thick chest, strong arms, and a strong

Scottish jawline. Unlike the extravagant Captain Crappo, Kidd dressed drably. His office looked like an accountant's office—meticulous and tidy. Captain Kidd set a pistol on his desk and sat down. He gestured for Guerin to sit down across from him and for Firken to take the chair on the adjacent wall.

"At the end of this conversation, Beaumains, you're going to have a choice between life or death," Kidd began.

"Seems like an obvious choice." Kidd had earlier noted that Guerin didn't have a single callous on his hands, so combined with the sizable bribe given to Crappo, he rightly discerned Guerin was a man of importance. He also knew Guerin defended his true identity through the pain. Kidd made the comparison to an Arthorian tale of a knight with a secret identity—the tale of Sir Gareth. The great bully Sir Kay, like Captain Kidd, teased the delicate nature of the mystery knight's hands.

"I need a new first mate, and while I have many competent officers, educated men are difficult to find. Obviously, you were once somebody of importance, but the fact that you were fleeing New France means you forfeited your former life. But why were you traveling to Rome, I wondered. The Catholic Church protects its own, and you certainly don't talk like a priest."

"That part is true, I'm not a priest."

"I was almost rid of you. I planned to turn you over to the authorities in New York and let them sort you out. I almost let Firken take you apart to get your secrets, but an enemy of France might turn out to be an ally. Are you an ally, Beaumains?"

"Bring me to Rome and find out," Guerin answered.

"Do you know why we were in Nevis?" Kidd asked.

"Revenge."

Kidd shot Firken a cold look. "That's correct. Obviously, you're better at interrogation than my crew. It seems everyone knows of my hatred of Robert Culliford, but alas, it seems he's sailed off to the Indian Ocean to be with his friends. Mr. Firken, could you wait outside for a few minutes. I'd like to speak to Beaumains privately for a few minutes."

Jago Firken rose and stepped outside.

"Scotland has a complicated history. I'm from a whaling port of Dundee, and centuries ago, we supported the Balliol Clan over Robert the Bruce. My family is still bitter about that loss, and my father used to tell tales of the dastardly way Robert the Bruce managed to steal the Scottish throne, including an alliance with the refugee Templar Knights."

Well, is this what Gaspar meant when he told me to trust in the path God sets before me. "You're speaking of the Battle of Bannockburn in the First War of Scottish Independence."

"I knew it. You're some sort of spy, aren't you?" Captain Kidd asked.

Guerin found himself nodding in self-preservation. "And after the battle, the Templar Knights all but vanished from history. They hopped on their ships and disappeared. But what does this have to do with Robert Culliford and his friends?

"Robert Culliford and I served as officers under Captain Jean Fantin together for a few years, and one night after heavy drinking, Culliford confessed two things to me. First, he belonged to an ancient order, a secret society of seafarers that extended back to the ancient Templar fleet."

"Culliford belongs to the Order of Eos," Guerin upped the ante with another confession.

"Yes," Captain Kidd said with a bemused grin. "Oh, my instincts about you were correct. What were you doing in New France?"

"The Order of Eos had risen to positions of prominence in New France, and I was sent to investigate their motivations. Now, if your family has stood in opposition to the Templars since the days of Robert the Bruce, then by releasing me or taking me to Rome, you can—"

"No, no, no. That's not going to happen. Culliford spoke of vast treasures at their colonies in the Indian Ocean. He claimed the vaults had more wealth than I could possibly fathom."

"Secret treasure? That was his second confession?"

Kidd scoffed. "No, his second confession was that he was a ganymede and was deeply in love with me. I punched him in the face and almost killed him for saying such things. And what did the little rat do? He mutinied against me."

"I take it you're not a ganymede?"

Kidd reached for the pistol but stopped himself. "No."

"I don't know what Captain Crappo or any of the crew told you, but my investigation was out on the frontier. I don't know anything about secret Templar treasures."

"Ah, but I think you do, Beaumains. If you were sent to investigate the Order of Eos, you are likely a dangerous man with extensive training. In the days to come, I think I could use a man such as you. Obviously, you'll have no problems with my paperwork and logs, but once I deal with Robert Culliford, I plan to discover the truth about that Templar treasure vault he spoke about. When that day comes, I'll want you at my side."

"You spoke of a choice, earlier."

"Yes, I can give you a quick death today. I'll shoot you squarely in the chest, and it'll all be over within a minute."

"Or?"

"Or, Beaumains, you can swear fealty to me, become my First Mate, and continue your mission in investigating the Order of Eos."

"Do you want me to shake your hand? I gladly choose life."

"If you break your oath, I will spill your guts with my own blade, and then I'll use them to tie you to the mast as you die a slow, painful death."

Guerin extended his hand. "You've got a deal."

Captain Kidd shook the hand but did not let go. "I can't go on calling you Beaumains. What is your real name?"

"You've already discovered my identity, Captain. I am indeed Sir Gareth of Orkney."

"Gareth?"

Guerin…Gareth…it'll work for now.

CHAPTER 6

Professor Josiah Faero disliked most weddings because of the drinking, loud music, and naive optimism that hung on the air, but as a stranger in a strange land, he sat in the back corner quite happy to observe the spectacle of the wedding.

At the wedding table, Thomas Tew sat beside his young bride, Queen Rehena. Both smiled despite not being able to understand each other. Several factions filled the great hall, which was built like an old Greek amphitheater, with the wedding party down in the center and the guests filling in the ascending wings. As a guest without any importance, Faero sat high against the outer wall.

The political guests from the Kingdom of Imerina appeared to Faero to be more traditionally African in appearance, whereas the local Zana-Malata appeared to have Asian ancestry. Although Tew had insisted the marriage was entirely political, the young woman's lovely face and slender body sweetened the situation.

"Professor Faero, you are certainly far from Harvard," a voice announced as John Yarland slid into the seat beside him. A few hours earlier, Faero had seen another of his former students mingling with the guests. Tew had mentioned him amongst the other New Englanders who'd migrated to Madagascar. Yarland had never sat for the fireside lectures and had only attended Harvard as a prerequisite to inheriting his family's shipping business. The suave mathematician now served as Tew's Minister of Trade.

"We're both very far from Harvard," Faero agreed, shaking his hand. Like himself, Yarland was a mousey man compared to the wildmen that gathered at the tables below. He wore small, circular glasses, had neatly trimmed black hair, and lacked a single hair upon his face.

"Thomas certainly has created a great melting pot of cultures, hasn't he?" Yarland noted as they both took in the sights. "Don't let the smiles fool you, though. Everybody here *wants* something, so I'll hide back here with the one person who hasn't asked me for funds. What do you want, Professor?"

"I suppose I'm looking for an adventure."

"I hear tell that Thomas took you to the White Temple. What were your impressions?"

"It certainly didn't feel real. I can attest to that. I could spend the rest of the decade pouring over the relics he has stored down in the vaults."

"Yes, Thomas told me all about the insight you've brought over the last several months. Clearly, it was worth traveling across the world to acquire you. Now I hear Thomas is going to pack you up and take you with us on this raid of his."

"You're coming with?"

Yarland chuckled condescendingly. "Someone needs to be the voice of reason."

"You don't approve of piracy?"

"Well, when you serve the King of the Pirates, you do his bidding. It's a calculated risk we're taking. This convoy could provide the funds we need for our next stage, but should the Presider of the Free States be going with?"

Everything had changed for Faero once he'd been allowed to see the ancient relics. It woke something within him. Now, he had more clues to the great puzzle. He meant to solve them. "I apologize for my part in this matter. When I heard about the treasure being carried on one of the convoys, my enthusiasm got the best of me. It's like hearing it carries King Arthur's sword *Excalibur*."

"I understand why Thomas prizes his relics, but it doesn't change the fact that he shouldn't be risking his life to entertain you. As you can see, Thomas is an important man. After rising up the ranks within the Congress of Pirates, the chieftains of the Free States chose to elect an outsider rather than someone from within their own ranks. Do you see the large man sitting beside Thomas?"

"Chieftain Morrison? Yes, he's been my host these past few months."

"He's the one responsible for this wedding. If he'd wanted power, he could have taken it, but the man is a true believer, so he set aside his own desires to promote Thomas, and by uniting the Free States living here in Madagascar with the Congress of Pirates, he's made the Order of Eos even more powerful. This wedding will further strengthen our young nation. Even though the population of the Free States is in the tens of thousands, the Zana-Malata and Betsimisaraka vastly outnumber the colony. Now, thanks to this strange marriage of cultures, the Imerinese will not dare pick a fight with their rivals. Thomas will guide the nation out of the shadows and onto the political stage. Instead, he's going to go chase after relics with his old professor."

"We plan to travel together to ancient Aksum *after* the ambush. I believe that during the reign of King Lalibela that—"

"Yes, Professor, I know what you think is waiting in the Land of Sheba. Do you see that smile on his face? Convince him to stay with his young bride for a few weeks rather than a few nights. You and I can be part of the ambush, and I can keep you safe until it is time to sift through all the stolen wealth. When the ambush is concluded, you and Thomas can travel back to Abyssinia and tour the ancient lands with a heavily armed escort. Think of it as your wedding gift to the lovely Queen Rehena."

In a room filled with pirates, it was the closest Faero felt to an actual threat. John Yarland stood and nodded before walking off.

Almost four-hundred years ago, the Order of Eos flourished within the Templar Knights, but on Friday 13th, 1307, an alliance between the Catholic Church, the Kingdom of France, and the Priory of Ormus almost severed the Eos branch completely. At first, Eos fugitives found safe haven in Scotland and Portugal, but the might of its enemies grew stronger by the day. After a failed attempt to colonize America, the colony at Madagascar took root. French, Scottish, and Portuguese families sailed around Africa to one of the most remote yet fertile pieces of land not used by humanity. Under the guidance of elected Presiders, the colony cautiously expanded while maintaining its shadowy naval presence.

A stranger approached.

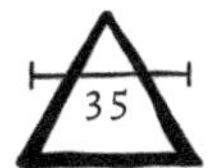

Unlike colonists, who dressed in silk and linen gowns adorned with jewelry, pirates wore modern fashion. The man who approached wore a red velvet jacket with gold embroidery and but-buttons, yet his face was tanned and weathered by the elements, and his beard was rugged and worn. "Was Yarland filling your head with doubt?"

Faero nodded and extended his hand. "He only offered wise words of counsel."

"Yarland is a rat," the stranger said, still gripping his hand. "So whatever squeaks came out of his toothy rat mouth should be immediately ignored. If Thomas Tew wanted to sail up the Thames and fire on the parliament building, I'd keep him safe, just like I'll keep you safe, Professor. Long Ben," he introduced himself before letting go of Faero's hand.

"Ben Avery, you're leading the attack," Faero assessed. "So I have nothing to worry about with these Mughals?"

"Emperor Aurangzeb is so powerful and so wealthy that he's never even dreamed of someone robbing him blind. Sure, his caravan is large, but guess what is larger? Guess?"

"Long Ben?"

"That's right. One Long Ben is worth a dozen or more Mughals. But you won't have to worry at all. I've promised Yarland I'll keep all of you safe. Our fleet is built for combat. You'll have Captain Want's *Dolphin,* Captain Wake's *Susanna,* Captain May's *Pearl,* and Captain Faro's *Portsmouth Adventure.* Our ships will run circles around those great Mughal cows."

"Don't forget Captain Tew's *Amity.*"

Avery laughed. "Oh, no. Thomas Tew might be the Presider of the Free States, but he's not going to be anywhere near this convoy. The *Amity* will linger a few miles away. Once we have our prize, then we'll bring you and Thomas up to inspect the treasure. You're not a pirate, Professor, and we mean to keep it that way. Enjoy the party because in a few days, you're going to be thinking back fondly on the sounds of merriment."

CHAPTER 7

Professor Josiah Faero vomited into the pot—not because of poor weather but due to the guilt about the bloodshed about to begin.

A slaughter I inadvertently incited.

Surrounded by his books, maps, charts, and notebooks, he tried not to think about the impending slaughter. Most of the books were about African history, particularly the ancient kingdom of Aksum. Since opening his big mouth back at Madagascar, he tried to stay ahead of the appetites of the powerful men who waged war as easily as they played cards. A fleet of five pirate ships now hunted a hippo like a pack of lions out on the African savanna.

Out on the deck, he felt the bloodlust stirring in the hearts of the men who'd taken care of him for the past few weeks—friends who would soon be dead. They roared and cheered, so when the cabin door opened, Professor Faero almost jumped from his chair.

Captain Thomas Tew immediately armed himself with pistol and sword. He turned to Faero and smiled. "Long Ben has engaged the Emperor's cargo ship."

"Are you sure? If I'm wrong about what he carries—"

"We'll be wealthy men by tomorrow either way," Tew interrupted. "Emperor Aurangzeb wouldn't waste his wealth on this convoy unless it had something precious to him. Don't worry about your reputation. My spies in Arabia told me what they carry. I'll leave it to you to tell me if they were right."

"Be safe, Thomas. Think of your wife and children back in Rhode Island."

"Oh, yes, that's right," Tew mocked. "My young queen made me forget all about them. Do you really think I plan to return to Newport?"

"Let the younger men risk their lives. We're supposed to be raiding Abyssinia after this. You're too important to be foolish to-day."

"We're the tail of the column for a reason," Tew said with a sigh. "All of the fighting will be miles ahead of us. Those men are hardened killers. I'm just making sure there is order in all of this chaos. You worry too much, Professor."

But this is all my fault.

The Arabian spies claimed Emperor Aurangzeb of the Mughal Empire negotiated the extraction and exportation of an ancient sarcophagus hidden in a secret chamber deep in the Arabian desert. Before paying the outlandish price, the Emperor requested proof, which Tew's Arabian spies briefly intercepted. According to their descriptions, the lid of the sarcophagus was covered with the cosmos and the interior lid of the sarcophagus had a map of an unknown, ancient world. For Tew—and his companions in the Order of Eos—the identity of the ancient corpse distracted from the obvious truth.

"The coffin could unlock more clues about the ancient language found on the Odin Stone," Faero had said. "It could contain some sort of cipher to unlock the symbols on the Al Marakk Map or the Abbaron Map."

A dozen ravenous eyes looked up at him from across the table back at Madagascar, and soon, the great raid was being planned.

Now, dozens of his friends—and considerably more he didn't know in the convoy—would die.

When the cannon fired on Thomas Tew's Amity, Professor Faero again jumped.

I thought the fighting was going to take place miles ahead of us.

He went to the cabin door for a peek.

He saw the billowing smoke of the main battle a few miles ahead, where the Eos ships were attacking the Emperor's convoy and fat cargo ship.

None of the crew seemed to care about it.

Instead, they all faced the distant shores that formed the Mandab Strait. Tew had chosen to ambush the Emperor's convoy at the narrowing between the Red Sea and the Indian Ocean, but it seemed as if others also saw it as a prime location for an ambush. Several smaller ships headed right for them.

A second wave of defense?

Tew raged when he saw Professor Faero, stopping his orders to deal with him. "You do not step out of this cabin under any circumstances. Understood?"

"What's happening?"

"The Mughal ship that couldn't keep up with the convoy feigned weakness. Now it is sailing right for us with a pack of smaller ships. Looks like we might've sailed into a trap," Tew said and gave him a gentle shove to close the door.

A trap?

We carry nothing of value.

The noise of the hurly burly increased as the wind and thunder intensified. Professor Josiah Faero had grown used to the flap of sails and the crash of waves against the hull—he'd even grown used to the thunderous sound of cannon fire and splintering wood—it was now the sound of abject fear that joined the cacophonous chorus of chaos.

He crossed from the starboard side of the captain's quarters to the port, where three ships angled toward the *Amity*, bringing the total to five.

Five!

In the distance, Faero could hear the other ships in the battle still engaging in their attack. *We've gone from predator to prey.* Earlier, when the attack began, the sounds of almost a thousand cannons firing upon the waters of the Red Sea made his loins quiver, but now, his nether regions tightened in terror.

Five ships!

He paced back to the window of the starboard side again where two ships loomed even larger in the window.

This is madness.

Faero stopped and looked around the captain's quarters. His cot, chest of clothing, and four crates of artifacts created a small

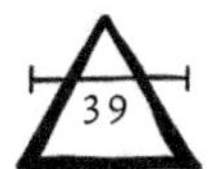

apartment. Captain Thomas Tew's bed, desk, table, and collection of oddities filled the rest of the space. Wine bottles from two nights ago rolled across the floor.

Was the mothership bait to lure us into a trap?

He looked at the crates beside his cot.

The *Amity* was a seventy-ton Bermudian sloop, fast and maneuverable. Before Faero boarded, its 46-man crew, having taken down several prizes, had already earned a fierce reputation. The attacking ship, the *Quedagh Merchant*, never would have picked a one-on-one fight with them. The four smaller vessels converging on them changed everything. Now the *Quedagh Merchant* showed why it'd lingered behind the convoy.

Beyond the door, Faero could hear Captain Tew barking out orders.

The Amity's eight cannons now fired defensively.

The cabin door opened, giving Faero a brief glimpse into the great sea battle. Past Captain Tew and the ship's rigging, the *Quedagh Merchant* loomed large, but far beyond that, the convoy of twenty-five Mughal ships stretched out for miles toward home in distant India. A bank of gunpowder rested upon the Red Sea.

John Yarland stepped into the doorway. He rushed right by and started rummaging through the captain's closet.

"What's happening?"

Yarland hauled out a four-foot miniature cannon. "The smaller ships mean to board us."

"Board us?" Faero repeated in fear. He'd come along for an intellectual adventure, not for participating in slaughter.

"We should have left you back at St. Mary's," Yarland said, glancing at the crate. "Help me drag this out."

Even though the cannon was half the size of those on the gundeck and foredeck, it still took the strength of two men to haul it out onto the stern deck. Captain Tew's telescope switched from side to side at the approaching sloops and looked forward to the big Mughal frigate they should have been chasing down.

Yarland led him to a wooden rigging being constructed by two other men.

"What is he doing out here?" Tew shouted. "Get him back inside."

"I can help fight, Thomas," Faero insisted.

"You? Your brain is the only thing of value on this ship. Get inside."

Yarland and the other two sailors went right to work, and Faero saw to his own exile. Back inside of the Great Cabin, he rushed to the rear windows. They were the end of the convoy, and he wondered if the other Eos captains in their group even knew what was happening to them.

The small sloops came swooping toward them. Gun crews opened fire, peppering the *Amity*. Faero went over to his cot and used the bookcase and crates as insulation from any stray bullets.

From the poop deck, the small cannon blasted, shaking the boards of the ceiling.

The eight cannons diminished, as only the bow chaser continued to fire.

The smaller ships are too close.

The sound of gunfire became blistering as the Mughal ships neared. Faero did the math. Even though the sloops were small and without cannons to stop the *Amity*, the gun crews appeared to be upwards of twenty men. *We're outgunned two to one.*

The pivot cannon fired, and the *Amity* sailors cheered with triumph at the sound of cracking wood from the would-be boarding party.

Tew's sinking the sloops as they pull up. Clever man.

Another roar of triumph meant another sloop had been hit, but then chaos erupted.

"Port side, bow!" Tew shouted. "Cut the lines! Cut the lines!"

After two failures, the three remaining sloops adjusted their strategies, knowing the pivot cannon could hit the belly of their ships as they pulled up alongside.

A clash of swords added to the storm of battle: the Mughals had come aboard, but the sound quickly ended with another roar from the *Amity* defenders.

The pivot cannon fired once more, and then again, and with the subsequent roar, Faero relaxed just a bit.

"They're fleeing!"

He stood and rushed to the starboard window to see the sloop peeling away to tend to the other four wrecks trailing behind the convoy.

The immediate threat ended, and prey became predator once again.

"Injury report!" Tew barked shortly afterwards as the chase resumed. Hoping to hit the big frigate's rudder, the two chase guns continued to blaze like a hyena trying to get hold of a zebra's tail. Just as Tew was about to take a bite of the big frigate, the zebra kicked hard with both legs.

First, Faero felt a strange vibration like the pluck of a bass string amplified by a hundred, then a moment later, the splintering of wood.

They hit our mast.

The ship leaned to the starboard side, and then another cannon blast hit the *Amity*.

Light flooded into the cabin as pieces of the door splintered. One of the wooden shards caught Faero in the ear, tearing an inch of ear away from where it met his head. Holding the wound with his fingers, blood ran down his face and onto his forearm and elbow.

Next, Faero turned to the aft windows, where a large hole blew glass and frame into the Red Sea. Save the aesthetic damage, it was not a crippling wound to the ship.

Dripping blood as he walked, Faero found his way toward the cabin door to let his friends know of his brush with death.

When he stepped through the doorway, the big frigate no longer appeared directly in front of them; instead, it loomed alongside them. He could see the Indian crew preparing for the assault.

He took another step and tripped.

His elbow caught the force of his fall, but his face recoiled against deck boards covered in blood. Several crew members stared up at him from the main deck, but none of the slack-jawed ingrates rushed up to offer him a hand.

Trying to keep his hand pressed to his ear wound, Faero rolled to his side, only to find his shirt soaked with blood.

There, a few feet from where he'd fallen, he saw the source of the blood—the legs and hips of half a man.

Looping around his foot, a tangled nest of intestines stretched across the deck in front of the cabin door. As if venomous, he tried to kick the slippery guts from his ankle, and as he rolled over onto his elbows, he saw the second half, the upper torso of his friend, Captain Thomas Tew.

"Prepared to be boarded!" the quartermaster shouted, but half of the crew continued to look fixedly at their disemboweled leader.

"Belay that order!" John Yarland shouted, climbing down from the poop deck, "Throw down your arms, raise the white flag, and prepare to surrender the ship. We are finished!"

John Yarland turned and jerked Faero by the arm, pulling him back into the cabin.

Once inside, Yarland rushed over to Tew's belongings and grabbed a hatchet.

At first, Faero thought he was about to be murdered by his old acquaintance, but then Yarland began chopping his way through the crate.

"Get a flame! We have to burn all of this and throw the rest out the back before they find it."

"We can't destroy it! Do you not understand how important it is? These texts contain one of the oldest known languages used by man—perhaps even the first."

"They are copies!" Yarland snarled. "And if the Grand Mughal's men find this, they will claim it and kill us all. I'm doing this to save your life, Josiah. If they find this, they won't need you. The original is locked away, far, far from here. Tew has been betrayed. We stepped into a trap. The Emperor wants to steal our research—you are our research. If we destroy these copies, you might have a chance to live."

Josiah Faero understood the logic, but as he watched the priceless scrolls burn and the ancient artifacts from King Solomon's temple tossed into the sea, it all became too much, and he staggered over to Tew's bed and wept.

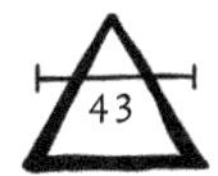

CHAPTER 8

Five days after the attack began, Captain Muhammad Ibrahim watched as the foreign wolf pack descended upon his mothership, the *Ganj-i-Sawai*. Initially, the wolf pack took the bait and paid for it with the loss of the fleet's leader, Thomas Tew. The pirate ships doubled-back when they learned of the *Amity's* capture, yet by the end of the day, they were back in pursuit. Hour after hour, they harried, harassed, sunk, and plundered the entire convoy, until only the fat mothership remained.

Who are these men?

A large pirate ship had a burthen weight of around 200 tons, but his ship was eight times that size, coming in at 1600 tons. Eighty guns were ready to send the pirates to the abyss, and behind them, four hundred soldiers stood between him and the pirates, not to mention the 600 passengers, including Emperor Aurangzeb's daughter. Hundreds of miles from port in India, he had no choice but to stand and fight while there were only three ships near them.

The Emperor was right about Eos, but can we fight out of our own trap?

"Record the names of these ships. When this is over, the Emperor will want answers."

The ship that nipped at their heels was the *Portsmouth Adventure*, whose crew had come from a port on the other side of the world. The *Pearl* had flown by them, just out of gun range, and now waited beyond the bow.

The *Fancy* turned to take them on, side-to-side. "They are only testing our resolve. Look to their rudder when they turn and flee. Save a volley for their turn."

But they didn't turn.

And they had far more cannons than a ship its size normally carried.

Sixty guns to our eighty. We'll still pound them into oblivion.

Ibrahim's confidence—along with his luck—shattered as a single cannon ball struck their mainmast and sent the rigging and sails onto the deck below.

"Sustain firing!" Ibrahim shouted, but chaos and fear already took over the ship.

A moment later, an explosion rocked the boat as one of its cannons misfired, destroying it and killing multiple nearby crew.

The *Fancy* spotted the disaster and angled for the opening in the defense.

"The Christians are not bold in the use of the sword," Ibrahim told his officers. "Prepare

the muskets and then give them the cold steel."

Unlike European Christians, the Americans could both shoot accurately and wield the sword proficiently. After just ten minutes, they had a foothold.

"Sir, the *Pearl* is attacking from the other side."

Caught in the pincers, a small mouth began to bite away at the *Ganj-i-Sawai*'s tail as the *Portsmouth Adventure* trailed with suppressing cannon fire.

"Put two hundred men on each side. Throw them back into the sea!"

"But sir, what about men in reserve?"

"I'll see to the reserve."

Captain Ibrahim rushed below deck, where hundreds of religious pilgrims waited in terror. Even if he could coerce them to fight, it would take ten of them to kill one of the American pirates. Instead, he went to the chambers of Princess Darika.

"Your highness, the mainmast is lost and we have no choice but to stand and fight."

"Then why aren't you out there with your men?"

Do I tell her the truth?

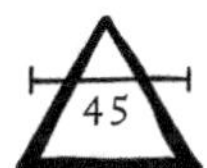

"Your father knew your presence on this ship would demand the fear and loyalty of every man and woman. Your highness, you have a hundred slave girls sworn to you. If we could arm them and flood the decks, it might give my men an opportunity to restore balance before the third ship joins."

"They are only slave girls, Captain Ibrahim."

"We will lose this battle, and then be at the mercy of the pirates. Every soul on this ship is beholden to you. We will fight and die for you, but only if you give the order."

"Is there no other way?"

You are the ship's last line of defense. Emperor Aurangzeb knew this when he sent you on a pilgrimage to Mecca. You were meant to protect his treasure. "It is the only way."

CHAPTER 9

His Majesty's Royal and Fortress of the Tower of London, more commonly known as The Tower of London, rests upon the north bank of the River Thames. Built by William the Conqueror in 1078, it has been used by British kings primarily as a prison, a tradition sustained through 1695 with King William III.

However, it served other purposes as well.

With two defensive walls, a moat, and a complex of several buildings around the White Tower, it was a stronghold for British power. The Constable of the Tower was in charge of the castle itself, but the complex also housed an armory, a public record office, the Crown Jewels of England, a treasury, and the Royal Mint, where Isaac Newton served as warden.

At fifty-two, Newton had already built a career within the scientific community with his studies on mathematics, light, mechanics, and gravity making him a known name within both Trinity College, Cambridge, and numerous universities around the world. With his professional legacy secure, Newton transitioned from scientist to government official in order to secure his personal desires.

Although Warden of the Mint sounded prestigious when secured for him by the Earl of Halifax, Newton's work amenities were...adequate. Instead of telescopes and microscopes, he had a few handheld magnifying glasses. Instead of racks filled with glass specimen jars, he had a uniform set of legal texts. Instead of rugs, tapestries, paintings, and sweet-scented candles, he had a large wooden table with a crooked chair.

An investment in the future, he reminded himself as he began arranging the coinage upon the table, picking up each piece to study and then place in its correct spot. He dutifully noted the details in one ledger and then wrote his findings in another. An hour into his tedious work, a knock came on the door.

"Enter," he called out.

The sergeant-at-arms unlocked the door from the outside, and at his side, the hunched form of Bernard Clairval appeared.

"Have I not introduced my manservant?" Newton said, removing his spectacles. "This is my shadow, a man who allows me to be in two places at once. When you see his misshapen form and grotesque features, imagine you are looking upon my avatar and treat him with all respect and authority due me. Even though I did not conjure him up in a test tube, he is one of my finest creations. If we are to work together, I need for this man to come and go as I see fit. Is that understood?"

"Of course," the sergeant-at-arms nodded, taking his chastisement meekly.

"Could you fetch the captain?" Newton asked.

"Yes, Warden," the sergeant answered.

Bernard shuffled by, sat at another chair by the fire, and stuck his hands out from under his heavy cape.

Newton, noting how Bernard focused on the warmth of the fire, walked slowly back to the table. "Apologies, Mr. Clairval, I only teased to help the sergeant understand that you still had your place."

"I am only trying to understand which of my features you feel is grotesque."

"Come now, you know I did not mean it. You must have exciting news to come all this way instead of waiting for me to get home."

Bernard grinned, his crooked teeth reflecting light from the fire. "News from abroad."

"The War in America?"

"No, but you should know that LeMoyne is regrouping for another assault, and it appears he plans to push the colonials out of

the St. Lawrence River. If he does this, New France will strengthen."

"Yes, I am aware of the talents of d'Iberville. What news do you bring me?"

"A tragic story."

"Well, let me pull the chair over to the fire and you can regale me with this tale," Newton said before joining Bernard. "Go on."

"Are you familiar with the Islamic ritual known as Hajj?"

"Yes, when religious pilgrims journey to Mecca."

"The Grand Mughal Emperor Aurangzeb allowed his daughter to travel from Bombay to Mecca in a caravan of twenty-five ships. As the convoy returned through the Straits of Mandab, they were attacked by pirates."

"Indeed? Tell me, Bernard, who would be bold enough to attempt such a vile action?"

"A bounty has been placed upon the captains and crews of the six pirate ships who attacked the convoy. Captain Richard Want and the crew of the *Dolphin,* William May and the crew of the *Pearl,* Thomas Wake and the crew of the *Susanna,* Captain Joseph Faro and the crew of the *Portsmouth Adventure,* and Captain Henry Avery and the crew of the *Fancy.*"

"Long Ben Avery? But he's—"

The hunchback nodded. "Yes, his associations with Indian Ocean pirates are noted, and are now being explored by the Crown. It's said he's gone into hiding, giving command of his ship to a Scottish rogue named Dalziel. All of them have bounties on their head, and once the first pirate is captured, it won't take long to find Avery."

"You mentioned six crews but only listed five."

"Yes, it seems Captain Thomas Tew was killed in the battle and his officers are in the possession of the Emperor already. Long Ben doubled back and freed the other half of the crew before returning his attention to the *Ganj-i-Sawai.*"

"Ganj-i-Sawai...Hindi for *Exceeding Treasure.* A poor choice for naming a ship, unless you think you've properly secured it."

"Long Ben stripped away her escort and with a lucky shot, disabled the mother ship. He boarded her with three separate crews in a battle that lasted hours. When they took the ship, the slaughter had only begun."

"Oh dear. Here comes the tragedy of which you spoke."

"When the pirates learned the Princess of the Mughal Empire was on board, they used this against the prisoners. First, they publicly tortured prisoners, and then took to raping the princess's entourage until finally they turned their vile attention to the princess herself."

"Really? Long Ben Avery let the princess be raped?"

"Raped and murdered, which is why Emperor Aurangzeb seized control of Bombay and arrested key members of the East Indian Trading Company."

"Did he?"

Bernard chuckled. "If he couldn't handle it, he never should have let his daughter risk her life for a few prayers."

"*Ganj-i-Sawai*," Newton repeated. "How did the Emperor know his daughter had been raped? Didn't Long Ben kill everyone leading up to the princess?"

"Oh, he spared Captain Ibrahim."

Newton snapped his fingers. "There it is."

"I don't follow."

"*Exceeding Treasure*. Have I not taught you about Emperor Aurangzeb, Bernard?"

"He's the Grand Mughal, what else is there to know?"

"Yes, well in his thirty years upon the throne, he's turned the Mughal Empire into the largest economic power in the world, even greater than China. And the size of his empire? Oh, he has 158 million subjects and a territory larger than England, France, and Spain combined. He's the most powerful leader in the world, but he allowed one of his daughters to be raped by pirates. Why would he even risk it?"

"Um...it was the Hajj."

"So you said earlier, but here is what you don't know. When he was fifteen, he was almost trampled to death by a war elephant. It must've been terrifying knowing that you're destined to become the most powerful man in the world yet a dumb beast does not understand who it's trying to step on."

Bernard chuckled, stamping his own foot on the floor.

"Yes, Bernard. Poor Aurangzeb was shaken to his core, which changed the course of his reign. He used the Sunni faith to galvanize his country and his aggressions to expand his territory. Before his coronation, it is told that the young princeling memorized the entire Quran. You do know what the Quran is, right Bernard?"

"It is the Muslim Bible."

"Yes, albeit a tenth of the size, but still, a remarkable feat. His piety and devotion to his faith continued once he became Emperor, but when one memorizes the Quran at such a young age, what challenges are left? Do you know what King Solomon requested of the Lord?"

"Wisdom."

"Yes, and he was granted this wisdom in his youth, and like Aurangzeb, his empire prospered; however, in his old age, King Solomon's quest for knowledge was his undoing. He began studying foreign gods and religions to satiate his spiritual and intellectual appetite." Newton took a moment to sip his drink. "Now I ask you, Bernard, would this man name the flagship after a daughter?"

"Ah," Bernard flashed his crooked grin. "The *Ganj-i-Sawai* carried a great treasure other than his daughter."

"And the most tragic part of this terrible tale is that the Emperor used her as a shield for his treasure. *That*...is the reason why Long Ben Avery tortured and raped the princess, and when Long Ben got what he wanted, he let Captain Ibrahim go free, to live with his shame, and to also shame the Emperor."

"Long Ben must indeed have quite a big bush-wacker to anger such a powerful man."

"Yes, I'm sure the emperor will rain down fire and brimstone for as long as it suits him. If he was cold enough to use his daughter to shield a treasure, he'll pressure every ambassador to deliver the heads of these pirates, and while England apologizes to him, he'll fatten his trade control in the region."

"What treasure do you suppose he had on that ship?"

"It doesn't really matter, does it? While it certainly had historical value, to a zealot, it most likely meant the world. Does that answer disappoint you?"

"For Long Ben to commit such atrocities, it must have been quite the treasure." Bernard's face flashed enthusiasm like a child at Christmas.

"Let me remind you, Bernard, that we are above all of this pettiness. As much as I despise the Catholic Church and its idolatrous pageantry, I also despise these zealots that look to the past for answers. We will help guide humanity to true freedom."

"Of course," Bernard grew solemn again. "I only wanted to understand Aurangzeb's motivations."

"Then let me speculate," Newton offered. "While most of the news concerns him expanding into the southern parts of the Indian subcontinent, he has also privately pushed through the Himalayas to a place called Mount Kailash, a holy place for four major religions and referred to as the spiritual center of the world. Alexander the Great sought to find the secrets of this place before he was forced to return to the Middle East, which is where the *Ganj-i-Sawai* just traveled."

"Ah, tit for tat. He traded treasures for treasures with the Arabs."

"This is all speculation, of course, but whatever he carried in that ship belongs to Henry Avery and the Order of Eos now."

A rap came on the door.

Newton stood quickly, "That will be the captain."

"Do you want me to leave?"

"Oh, no. Not while I have this fly caught in my web. Opportunities like this happen once in a generation. You stay right by that fire and warm yourself, for you'll be frozen to the bone by the time the day ends."

"Oh, I don't like the sound of that."

Newton opened the door. As Warden of the Mint, he had a dozen royal soldiers appointed to him although they normally spent their time patrolling the grounds of the compound. "I've examined the coins given to us by the magistrate in Surrey, and I've written my analysis. The first man should be let go. The second should be hanged for treason on the grounds of counterfeiting. The third man needs to be brought to me so I can interrogate him properly. If I am to serve King William and Queen

Mary properly, as a loyal subject, I must root out corruption wherever I see it."

"Hanged?"

"That is my recommendation, but the magistrate will have to make that determination himself, Captain. Now...go fetch this Robert Harley and we'll see what sort of tales he has to tell me."

The captain did as commanded, allowing Newton to return to the fire, where Bernard studied him for a few moments before saying, "You look at those coins with a looking glass and condemn a man to death."

"Warden of the Mint has certain privileges my predecessors did not appreciate. I will define the office before I am through."

"I'm sure you will. So...where am I going?"

"I'm going to be writing letters most of the day, so until I'm ready to have them delivered, I need you to find two men for me. First, find Captain Richard Cass down at the docks. Luckily for us, he's just arrived from America. I'd like to avoid using Captain Wiggins, so use your best charm to bring Cass here."

"And the second?"

"I need you to bring me Roger Silverthorn. He's a Norfolk man."

"Norfolk. Please don't make me go to Norfolk. I hate East Anglia."

"I didn't say he was in Norfolk. I said he's a Norfolk man. If I'm not mistaken, he's currently stationed in Nassau. Bring him to me."

"Nassau...but that's..."

"In the Bahamas, yes. We have an opportunity to strike our enemies, Bernard. When I am through, the Priory of Ormus will rid the world of these zealots. Thanks to vile Captain Avery and foolish Emperor Aurangzeb, I'll be able to collect on a bill long overdue."

CHAPTER 10

Louis-Armand Guerin stood at the ship railing and watched Captain Kidd paddle into Town Cove at the heart of Boston Harbor. For the first time in months, Guerin was surrounded by civilization. The ship anchored between the harbor barricade and the busy docks. Compared to Quebec City and Montreal, Boston Harbor dwarfed the French cities with its vast markets and grand forts filling the horizon.

If I jumped into the water, I could vanish on those busy streets before Firkin or Del Torro could muster a firing squad. Unfortunately, January snows reminded him of the hypothermia that would certainly kill him if he dared. Guerin turned back to the ship, where the crew busied themselves with supplies for the coming voyage. Guerin held a clipboard to keep track of each ship that brought supplies.

I could bribe the New Englanders. The next supply boat could ferry me away to safety.

In Boston, he'd be penniless in a foreign country. New France and New England were still at war, and he didn't know of any Periphery agents in New England. Finding passage to Europe seemed unlikely. After unloading the Spanish and French loot, the cargo holds were being filled mostly with food rather than ammunition.

An Atlantic crossing? Could I be so lucky?

A few weeks earlier, they'd been in the Bahamas when Captain Kidd scrapped all of his plans to return home. Some speculated there'd been a Robert Culliford sighting, but the insistence on speed and secrecy made Guerin doubt the theory.

Something's happened.

Typically, trips east across the Atlantic were made beginning in April instead of January, but Captain Kidd hurried like his life depended on it.

The Haitian cook, Papa Bones, appeared at Guerin's side. "Three more loads and your hold should be full," Guerin noted.

"What are we doing in this frozen hell, Gareth?" Papa Bones asked.

To the crew, he was still Gareth, the quick-witted First Mate who was better with the jokes than the sword. "This is tropical compared to New France. I suppose you and Del Torro have spent your lives sailing the Caribbean Sea. I hate to tell you where I think we're going."

"The men think we're heading to harass Acadia."

Guerin chuckled. *I certainly can't get captured in French territory.* Somewhere far to the

Northwest, his only friend and ally Gaspar served the best interests of the Petun followed by the interests of the Periphery, which meant keeping all parties out of the lands beyond the Great Lakes. *Good Lord, I've been on this ship for almost three years now. Is the Philosopher's Stone still there, waiting to be dug up?*

"Where are we going, Gareth?" Manuel Del Torro asked. Del Torro was Spanish for *Of the Bull,* which evidently was a name given to him for his thick features. With a wide face, wide shoulders, and massive arms, Del Torro was the strongest man on the ship. Even though Del Torro had a Spanish name, the portly man despised Europeans. He hailed from the original Taino chieftains who lived on the island of Puerto Rico before Columbus arrived, at least that is what his grandmother had claimed. The Taino ruled the seas around Cuba, the Bahamas, Jamaica, Hispaniola, and Puerto Rico, waging sea battles with the Carib Indians who lived on the smaller islands to the southeast. Later, his family avoided capture and slavery by taking to the sea and fishing; Del Torro's knowledge of the local reefs turned into a career upon the ocean as guide and eventually as a quartermaster. Captain Kidd won the services of Del Torro two years earlier in a poker game.

"I hate to tell you this, but I think we're about to sail across the Atlantic for jolly old England," Guerin offered. "I made the trip more than a decade ago, and I'm still a bit sea sick from the crossing. We'll need every pound of food and every drop of water. See that nothing is wasted on the fair weather days."

Both officers cursed under their breath and returned to their duties.

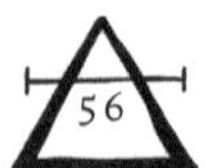

A FEW HOURS later, the ship was supplied and Captain Kidd returned from the city with five strangers. The surgeon, anchoring boatswain, and sailing master were all being retired, which Kidd didn't even bother to convey to the crew. Both the surgeon and sailing master were Englishmen looking to return home, so their stay would only be for the journey.

"I'd like you to meet Jimmy Duke, a cousin of my wife, and despite his appearance, has several years of experience on combat ships. He'll be our new anchoring boatswain. Jimmy, this French fop is called Gareth, our First Mate. Even after all this time, he still barely knows what he's doing on a ship, but he's sharp as a tack. He'll show you around."

Jimmy Duke flashed a wide toothy smile and vigorously shook Guerin's hand. With his blonde hair and blue eyes, Duke had the face of a school boy, but there was something wildly aggressive in his eyes.

I'll need this one as an ally in the days to come.

After an hour-long tour, Guerin paused for a private conversation. "We're crossing the Atlantic, aren't we?"

The grin broadened. "I suppose there's no point in the secret any more. Yes, we're lifting anchor and heading for London. We're going to hunt pirates."

"Excuse me? Why would we need to travel to London to do that? The Caribbean is—"

"Madagascar pirates," Duke said, nodding enthusiastically.

Culliford. I've jumped onto the ship of a madman.

"A group of pirates led by Thomas Tew and Henry Avery attacked a Mughal convoy and raped some emperor's daughter. The English Crown is hiring experienced captains to travel to the Indian Ocean to bring these rogues to justice. Captain Kidd heard of the opportunities through his political connections, so we're rushing to London to not only sign the big contract but to secure the new warships that are being offered. We're all going to be wealthy men."

"Madagascar Pirates," Guerin repeated. "You didn't hear anything about Robert Culliford, didn't you?"

"Culliford? Last I heard, Robert Culliford robbed the wrong ship and ended up in a Gujaratis Jail."

"A Gujaratis Jail? What is that?"

"Heck if I know, but ending up in any jail is bad. Of course, these pirates we're hunting—none of them are going into a jail cell. After raping an emperor's daughter, none of them are going to die well."

So if this isn't about Culliford, then these pirates we're going to hunt have Eos connections. Imagine the stories I'll have to share with Gaspar when I meet him at St. Peter's Pearly Gates.

"One more thing, Gareth," Jimmy Duke said, "Could you help me go through the anchoring before we leave, I don't want to look like a fool the first time I lift anchor."

Jimmy Duke, Manuel Del Torro, and Papa Bones—a few more and I'll have enough for a mutiny.

CHAPTER 11

Beginning in 1556, Akbar the Great began the conquest of several Indian provinces that resulted in the creation of the massive Mughal Empire, which would include the modern countries of Bangladesh, Nepal, Pakistan, and Afghanistan. "The Conqueror of the World" Aurangzeb prized the region of Gujarat for its historical and financial resources, and due to its proximity to the port city of Bombay, it also became the site of the imperial prisons.

Of the two dozen prisoners from the *Amity* who were subsequently taken prisoner by the *Quedagh Merchant*, only Professor Josiah Faero remained in the prison. Several months into his imprisonment, Faero's body had found its equilibrium, with several of his infected wounds now healed and the spare fat around his body gone.

Why are they trying to keep me alive?

Thousands were detained in the prison, but Faero stayed in small, individual cells high above the rest. He wasn't being punished—he was being interrogated. In the early days, he heeded John Yarland's advice to "play dumb" and despite burns, beatings, and broken fingers, the jailers simply didn't ask the right questions. The torture stopped shortly after John Yarland vanished, and in a matter of days, he remained the only one left from the *Amity*.

A week ago, however, another crew from another ship filled the cells again.

At night, in whispered exchanges, information passed between them.

"So what's your story?" the monster next to him asked.

"Wrong place at the wrong time," Faero began, and over the next few days, the details came to light.

The ogre in the cell beside him was a German immigrant named John Swan. "We were robbing some palace near Mangalore. Our boats were so full of loot that we were concerned about sinking them, but these damn local fishermen rallied together and put holes in the hull before the men on the ship even knew what was happening. We were left holding our dicks on shore. What about you?"

"I'm a former college professor," Faero began honestly. "I got mixed up with the wrong crowd. I was promised an archeological tour of ancient Aksum, and now, I'll likely die in this prison because of the actions of other men."

It took two nights to explain "archaeological" and "Aksum" to Swan. "It must've been quite a treasure to get you to leave your college."

"Are you familiar with King Solomon?"

"From the Bible?"

"Yes, *that* King Solomon."

Faero reflected on the enthusiasm his friend Thomas Tew had shown when revealing some of the treasures collected in the White Temple. The Templar Knights, Tew explained, found a hidden vault underneath the ruins of the old temple in Jerusalem. Amongst the maps and relics, the Templars had found canisters of a substance that could dissolve metal or stone along with a story about a magical ring that could control the strange liquid. Faero had little difficulty unearthing the historical legacy of Solomon's ring. Throughout art and text, the "Seal of Solomon" etched into the ring varied, but most commonly, it held the two alchemical symbols for fire and water. While in the brig of the *Quedagh Merchant*, Faero had carved the interlocked triangles within the circle along with his plea to the universe—*Josiah Faero was here*. To finish, he wrote symbols in the ancient language of the Odin Stone also.

But now, he pondered the purpose of Tew's expedition more than he had before their departure for Abyssinia.

"When all the cards are on the table," Tew had grinned. "We're going to need a key. Right now, out on the frontier of New France, rumors of one of these keys persist, but if we can acquire Solomon's ring from Abyssinia, we control the future."

"But if secrecy is important, why attack this convoy?"

"As you've seen, the White Temple holds many relics from the past, and Eos has patiently gleaned the earth for centuries for the ring and other significant acquisitions. In my dealings with a sultan from Arabia, I attempted to acquire one of the oldest known sarcophagi in the world. Emperor Aurangzeb outbid me and plans to acquire it. I'm convinced if you evaluate the ancient symbols written upon it, you can unlock other mysteries."

In the end, none of them—Josiah Faero, Thomas Tew, or Emperor Aurangzeb—laid eyes upon the ancient relic.

The big brute in the cell beside him breathed heavily during the telling of the story.

When the guards brought breakfast, keys jingled, the door swung open, and the big ogre walked down the hall. A moment later, a smaller man replaced Swan in the cell beside Faero.

That night, instead of silencing the whispers, a new voice greeted him.

"I was friends with Thomas, Professor Faero," the new voice explained. "If I hadn't been foiled by fishermen, I would have been part of the attack on the *Ganj-i-Sawai*. I might've been able to protect Thomas. I might've been able to prevent your capture. I might've been able to discover the traitor that threatens the Order of Eos."

"Who are you?" Faero asked.

"I am Robert Culliford."

"I've read your exploits," Faero admitted. "Thomas said something, right before…he…made a reference to a trap being set."

"It's no coincidence that the Emperor wanted the same sarcophagus as Tew, but I believe it might've been bait. I'm a greedy man, but Thomas Tew was a deeply spiritual man who believed wholeheartedly in his purpose for the Order of Eos. But he also had a big mouth. When the *Amity* lingered behind the wolf pack, you fell into a trap."

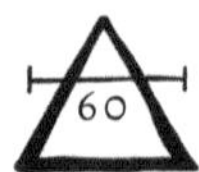

"Why would the Emperor even know about me? I'm a failed Harvard professor."

"Thomas Tew believed in you. He risked everything to put you in front of his relics. If I owed Thomas Tew my loyalty, then that loyalty extends to you. I'll let you know my secrets in trade for yours."

"I'm not sure I have any secrets," Faero admitted.

"Before my capture, I was raiding the Gujaratis coast for months, and while I did it to fill the coffers of Eos, most of it was kept hidden. I've promised one of those treasure stashes to one of the guards in exchange for my freedom. If I could bring you with me, could you still serve Eos by interpreting these ancient relics?"

"Like I told Thomas, it's all theoretical. I've spent decades of my adult life sifting through history to understand the mysteries of the past. My professional colleagues mocked my inability to focus on a specific time period or region, but I always felt that by being able to see the larger context, I could see what others didn't."

"They couldn't see the forest for the trees," Culliford teased and grew silent for a few minutes. "So your value wasn't just in identifying the location of Solomon's ring. You were meant to peel away the reasons for its creation. If you were to guess, why did Thomas risk so much to get this sarcophagus?"

"I'm not versed in the lore behind the Order of Eos, but I am well-versed in world mythology. To me, the most curious thing about King Solomon isn't the purpose behind the ring, or even the need for the Philosopher's Stone; it is the fact that Solomon believed in the existence of an ancient kingdom ruled by an ancient king. If I were to guess, this prized sarcophagus had ties to this old legend."

"Thank you, Professor Faero. I'm not sure if I can promise you your release, but I can promise you that no immediate harm will come to you. Good night."

Robert Culliford grew silent the rest of the night.

The next morning, the noise of an unlocking cell woke Professor Faero.

But his cell didn't open.

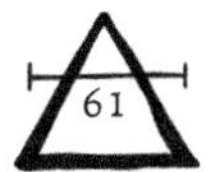

Instead, he saw both John Swan and Robert Culliford standing in the hallway together. A well-dressed Mughal diplomat stood along with a few guards.

Robert Culliford smiled. "Again, I want to thank you, Professor Faero, for your honesty. I want to emphasize that everything I've done has been to the benefit of the Order of Eos. I can't serve it while stuck in this prison, but when a gift is given to you, you have to accept it. Good luck in the days to come. I wish you well."

Culliford and Swan walked down the hall, quite obviously, as free men.

The finely dressed diplomat lingered, and the remaining guard began unlocking his cell.

"Trickery is sometimes better than torture," the diplomat added. "Your confession verified everything John Yarland told us, but we had to make sure you were the religious scholar, which you certainly are. The other men in the convoy will bear the brunt of Emperor Aurangzeb's fury, but you will provide answers to our questions. When you fail to give answers, you will join your friends."

"What is happening?" Faero asked.

"You will remain a prisoner," the diplomat added. "But your services are needed elsewhere."

CHAPTER 12

Louis-Armand Guerin stood behind the wheel so that the new crew understood his role as the First Mate who did nothing. Under Guerin's feet, the most devastating warship ever to be built waited for its maiden voyage.

The *Adventure Galley* combined oars and sails, which made it unique amongst warships. With three ship-rigged masts, she certainly looked to be fast, but in battle or on calm seas, she'd be especially deadly. She also had 32 guns—enough to go nose-to-nose with naval warships.

Jimmy Duke hadn't stopped grinning since the old crew stepped onto the new ship. "She's a beauty. Pirates won't stand a chance."

"Captain Kidd should return within the hour," Guerin called out. "Are you ready to launch?""

"I was born ready," Duke boasted, "But I ain't ever had to sail down a river before."

"It's a formality," Guerin said. "Kidd's English investors want to show-off their first "pirate hunter" to their friends. English politics is kept in balance between the Tories and Whigs, both in America and here in England. The Whigs need us to succeed to remain in power."

"They've hired the right men," Duke added and jogged off.

Kidd's crew teemed with diversity. Along with Taino Manuel Del Torro, Haitian cook Papa Bones, and American Jimmy Duke, several other officers filled the ranks. The English bulldog Drake

Murray served as the Provisions Boatswain and took an immediate dislike to the overly-friendly Duke. A few yards behind him, the new Navigator, Naro Bon, organized his nautical charts.

"Excuse me for asking, Master Bon, but how does a land-locked Tibetan end up on an English ship?"

Bon's leathery face didn't show an emotion but his eyes twinkled jovially. "By not being stupid and by following orders." After decades at sail, Bon's skin was a deep russet and his thin hair a contrast in bleached white. His mustache tapered to three-inch whisps at the corners of his mouth, and from the middle of his chin, he kept a braided tuft of hair.

"I'm a bit perplexed," Guerin coyly began. "Our majestic vessel has been put to sea in record time to allow us to hunt these Madagascar pirates, yet you've been poring over maps of France all morning. Care to explain?"

"Didn't Captain Kidd tell you?" Bon straightened his back and sighed. "We're first hunting some French diplomat."

Is this a joke? Am I the French diplomat? "How are we hunting a French diplomat?"

"Spies, apparently. We're going to stay hidden around La Rochelle until this fellow departs for America—except he's not going to make it to America."

All that time could either give the new crew time to learn the job or to go stir crazy. Time will tell, I guess. "So you just wandered down from the Himalayas one day and decided: 'I'm going to spend my life on the seas.'?"

"I'm a trained astronomer, and after learning the stars, I used this knowledge to make a map of our planet. I've spent the past thirty years gathering information, and hopefully one day it will be complete. Unlike other members of the crew, navigators are worth our weight in gold to most captains."

"Good point."

"Gareth!" a voice cried out.

Guerin returned to the wheel just in time to see the new carpenter finish climbing the stairs. Giovanni Naufragio had more black hair on his back, forearms, and ears than he did atop his head. He was born with a classic Roman nose and sweated pro-

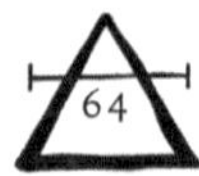

fusely. "This ship is a floating disaster waiting to happen. It's already leaking."

"Will we sink before we lift anchor?"

"No."

"Do you have a plan to deal with the leaks?"

"Of course."

"Then what's the problem?"

"It's a brand new ship! It's the principle of it. Under the fresh coat of paint is a poorly built vessel."

"I don't think they expect us to last long," Guerin admitted. "So the best way to express your frustration is to outlast the boat."

"But the leaks are already here!"

Despite his bluster, Naufragio appeared to be a good man, unlike most of the English sailors that'd joined the American crew.

Another ally in my coming mutiny.

An hour later, the men hooted and hollered as Captain Kidd returned to the vessel. Guerin stood with crossed arms as his captor soaked in the glory. A few minutes later, Jimmy Duke was lifting anchor and Captain Kidd came to the wheel.

"Gareth, I'd like to introduce you to our new surgeon, Thomas Barrow. Doctor Barrow, this rogue we just call Gareth, he's a runt but has a big brain and an even bigger mouth. You'll like him. He's also an outcast from society."

With that, the great bully walked to his cabin, leaving Doctor Barrow alone with Guerin.

"An outcast?"

"Yes, I've been disinherited and thrown out of England for illegal medical practices. This ship, it seems, is the last place on earth for me."

"Were you sleeping with corpses?" Guerin asked, straight-faced.

"Heavens, no! I just practiced my surgical arts on the recently expired. That's all."

"Then I'm happy to have you on board. Stay here for a bit, we'll be presenting our ship and crew to our financiers in just a moment. Del Torro! Assemble the officers to the top deck."

Half an hour later, the ship approached the "turn around spot" at the Tower Bridge. Captain Kidd manned the wheel, and the

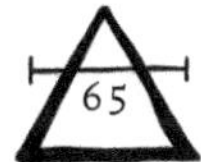

crew waited silently as they passed under the eyes of the wealthy and elite men who paid for the ship.

Doctor Barrow raised his hand for a personal salute to one of the men who stood upon the bridge.

"Who is that?"

"A friend of my father. He's the one who pulled the strings to get me on this ship. I guess I should be thankful."

Jimmy Duke waved vigorously.

"Stop it, Jimmy," Captain Kidd snarled. "These are the same men who hang pirates, especially Doc Barrow's friend."

Barrow lowered his arm and looked at his toes sheepishly.

Kidd snarled. "They've given us a ship, but if we don't follow the parameters of our mission, they'll withhold your wages or worse."

Guerin rolled his eyes and shrugged.

Captain Kidd put all his strength into the big wheel, and with the use of the oars, the *Adventure Galley* pivoted sharply and turned toward the open waters of the English Channel.

"Come with me, kid," Guerin said and turned to Doc Barrow. "You too."

On the bridge, the crowd was already dispersing as the ship sailed down the Thames. "Do you want to know what I think of these fine gentlemen?" Guerin asked and began unbuckling his pants.

"They can kiss our ass," Jimmy Duke anticipated and had his breeches down to his ankles faster than Guerin.

"These men cast you out of society, Doc," Guerin reminded him. "Show them what you really think of them."

So Doctor Barrow dropped his pants and bent over, joining Louis-Armand's mutinous plan.

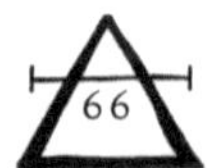

CHAPTER 13

MAHARASHTRA, INDIA

1696

After traveling for hundreds of miles, Professor Josiah Faero reached his new prison—an immaculate, empty tomb. His escort left him in shackles but gave him but a few bored glances.

Where would I run?

I don't even know where I am.

The guards didn't care if he walked around the space, so he inspected the white walls, lime green doorways, tiled floors, and latticed windows of the tomb.

In the distance, a larger and older building loomed over the smaller tomb, but Faero didn't know his Indian history well enough to know whom it belonged to.

AFTER THREE DAYS of waiting, Faero finally got some answers. A familiar corpulent man walked through the door. He wore a small white turban on his head, layers of floral print robes, and a bright red sash under his gut. He had a pencil thin mustache and no beard, which allowed his massive double chin to be seen.

"Do you remember me?" Captain Corgi Baba asked in English.

"How could I forget? You killed my friend Thomas."

"If he'd lived, you'd likely be the dead one right now. Our spies knew Presider Tew would linger behind the others, and I was tasked with pirating the pirate. Fortunately for me, you were the brains behind the operation. Just like back on the *Quedagh Merchant,* your life is in my hands, and if you want to keep on living, you'll listen to me. My future rests on your ability to provide answers. Emperor Aurangzeb is coming to personally question you on matters important to him. Do not bring shame to my name."

Thomas Tew's blood had soaked Josiah Faero's clothing the first time he'd met Captain Baba. His monstrous man-of-war had been disguised as a merchant vessel, and it towered over the much smaller *Amity* and its shaken crew. Captain Baba had all the officers gathered up and brought onto the ship, leaving the crewmen behind with the ship. By the time Long Ben Avery and the others realized the trap that'd befallen Tew, Faero was locked in the brig with the others.

The *Quedagh Merchant* arrived in Bombay ahead of the tragic news about the princess, and Faero and the others were thrown into the Gujaratis prison while the rest of the world sorted out what happened to the *Ganj-i-Sawai*.

First, John Yarland gave him up, and then John Swan and Robert Culliford betrayed him to secure their freedom. Eos shipped him from Rhode Island to Madagascar, and now Captain Baba took him from Madagascar to the heart of the Mughal Empire.

WHEN THE TIME came for his meeting with Emperor Aurangzeb, Captain Baba was nowhere to be seen. Only a handful of bodyguards accompanied the emperor inside of the tomb.

"This is where I'll be buried," Aurangzeb began the conversation. Tall and delicate with a flowing white beard, Aurangzeb reminded Faero more of an Indian version of Jolly St. Nicholas than one of the most powerful men on the planet. "Surely, you've seen my empty tomb."

"Yes, your highness," Faero answered.

"I had it built right beside one of my spiritual mentors, Sheikh Zainuddin. The Hindi call me a religious tyrant and oppressor, and yes, in my youth, I certainly was a zealot and although my religious policies continue to this day, I've changed so much since I had this first commissioned. Do you think it is possible for an older man to truly become a different person?"

"Yes. I was also a zealot when I was a young man."

"A Christian?"

"A Protestant, so I breathed fire and brimstone in my youth."

Emperor Aurangzeb nodded. "Yes, I also breathed fire and brimstone, and with a word, I had the power to lay waste to cities. Perhaps it is more power than one man should have. From what I understand, the Order of Eos has a fascination with despots and tyrants from antiquity, including Alexander the Great. What do you know about my country's history with Alexander the Great?"

Flatter him. "I know your people stopped him from reaching his destination," Professor Faero coyly stated. "I know Thomas Tew searched for the same things as Alexander."

"And what is that?"

"The Old World," Faero answered. "Or at least, proof of the Old World. My friend Thomas believed our present world and the old world were regrown from three roots that touched the world. One of these roots is found in the Holy Lands, where Judaism, Christianity, and Islam now converge. Another root is located on the far side of the world in the frozen wasteland known as North America. The third root, which Alexander searched for, is beyond India. Geography and bad weather forced his army south through the Khyber Pass rather than through the mountains of Pamir. Either way, he was doomed to defeat."

"Yet I have conquered all that Alexander failed to conquer. What a partnership we might've had together. I could have taken him to this "third root," as you put it, and showed him the Mountain of Eden."

Faero hesitated about correcting an emperor. "What is this Mountain of Eden, your highness?"

"The Book of Genesis describes the Garden of Eden as the source of four great rivers. On the edge of my kingdom, there is a sacred mountain, the source of the Indus, the Ganges, the Brahmaputra, and the Sutlej. Just as King Nebuchadnezzar was troubled by bad dreams, I am also troubled by bad dreams and visions of the future. Like Nebuchadnezzar, I have gathered the prophets from throughout my kingdom to provide answers about my dreams. I have summoned you to also provide answers."

Daniel was also thrown into the Lions' Den for displeasing the king. "What is your question?"

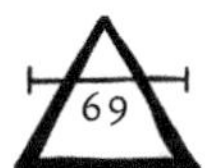

"You have answered honestly about the Order of Eos seeking evidence about the Old World, and while my bad dreams motivate my actions, what motivates the Order of Eos to search for evidence and relics instead of living in the here and now?"

I don't know. "I am not part of the Order of Eos. I am only a teacher, whose prized pupil became a powerful man."

"And now another powerful man seeks the counsel of a man without allegiances or biases. Why does Eos search?"

Josiah Faero felt light-headed as he gave the Emperor what he wanted. "Their belief in the Old World is rooted in what we call Norse Mythology, which teaches that the world is in a cycle of birth and destruction, ice and fire. Their chief god, Odin, discovered the truth about this cycle, including the endless war between the giants and the gods. Instead of continuing this conflict for all eternity, he sacrificed his own life to discover a way to break the cycle. During the last great war, which the storytellers called the *Ragnarök,* Odin died once more but found a way to break the cycle. The fruits of his labors, however, were buried in the most recent cataclysm, which in the Qur'an is told in the story of Nuh. The same flood that covered the world in water swept away two humans in the Norse tale who repopulated our present earth. Yet the Norse describe how four heirs of Odin survived yet were buried, and so too, was their archenemy, a fire giant named Surtr. Why does Eos search? They believe they are in a race against their enemies to wake a sleeping god and usher in a new era of humanity."

"Do they seek the Four or the fire giant?" Aurangzeb asked.

Faero shrugged. "Thomas studied antiquity to make an informed decision. He worried about unearthing the wrong god."

"Then we shared the same nightmare," Aurangzeb admitted. "Allah has placed you in front of me for a reason, so I will send you to this 'Mountain of Eden' to take measure. I want you to study it. I want you to discover its secrets, and when you learn them, come back to me with your answers."

How can I say no?

CHAPTER 14

The Brute spotted him. Through the smoke and din of war, Louis-Armand Guerin spotted the legendary Bear Man on the deck of the other ship. The cannons fired again, and the beast roared with fury, seemingly unharmed despite the damage to his ship.

"Kill him!" Captain Kidd barked. "Cut him down!"

One by one, the Bear Man killed Guerin's friends. Quartermaster Manuel Del Torro charged with two hatchets only to get the butt of the ax smashed into his face and a blade into his collar bone.

Giovanni Naufragio and Naro Bon tried to kill him with pistols. Both waited until they stood within ten yards of the monster before firing. Two hands reached out from the gunpowder smoke, took each man by the throat, and crushed their heads together. The two boatswains, Jimmy Duke and Drake Murray, charged with cutlasses, each kept out of range of the swinging ax by maintaining opposite distances from him. They jabbed at the Bear Man, but instead of red blood, he bled blue.

"Now, while he's engaged," Kidd ordered. "Better them than me!"

The cannons all pinpointed the place where the Bear Man stood, and this time, the French ship buckled, exploded with flame, and began to vanish into the depths. But between the two ships, a dark figure created a large wake heading right toward the *Adventure Galley*.

Guerin almost fell off his feet when the *Adventure Galley* shook from the impact.

"Impossible! Why won't he die?" Captain Kidd asked in a panic. "You knew him, Gareth, how do we stop him?"

"I have an idea," Louis-Armand said, running back to the cabin, where he found the Dakota slave huddled in the corner. He threw her to her feet and held a knife to her throat as he walked her out onto the deck.

Wenonah…her name was Wenonah.

When he reached the deck, the Bear Man was already crawling out of the hold, pierced by arrows and covered in wounds. As Doctor Barrow rushed by, the brute took hold of him, lifted above his head, and tore him in half, throwing the two pieces into the water.

"Stop, LeSueur," Guerin yelled out. "I have your woman. Take one more step toward Captain Kidd and I'll kill her."

Pierre-Charles Le Sueur's demonic eyes flashed with bloodlust and the ax cut through bone from skull to rib.

Guerin readied the knife.

LeSueur kept coming.

But a blade appeared in the middle of his chest.

He'd been stabbed in the back.

The giant staggered, falling to his knees, revealing Chief Gaspar standing behind him. "I told you not to worry."

Wenonah dissolved into smoke, and instead of holding her by the throat, Guerin stood alone.

LeSueur took hold of the blade that pierced his chest, slamming it backwards and into the face of Gaspar. The old warrior stumbled, and LeSueur took his head off in one quick swing.

Louis-Armand Guerin turned to run, only to come face to face with Wenonah. Not only had she reappeared but so too did the blade, which flashed ahead of a crimson spray.

Guerin fell.

LeSueur and Wenonah stood over him.

The Bear Man looked down and muttered, "I prayed for help. You were supposed to save me, not doom me to certain death. This is all your fault."

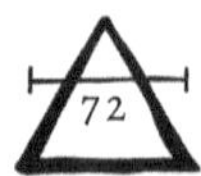

The ax began to chop into his ribs, and after turning them into a mangled mess, LeSueur knelt down and stuck his hands into the bloody bowl of eels. Instead of pulling out his heart, LeSueur ripped the Philosopher's Stone from his chest.

The object began to pulse with life.

The pain in his ribs carried from dream into reality, but when Louis-Armand Guerin reached for his heart, his ribs were still intact.

"Fevers can cause some pretty strange nightmares," Doctor Barrow said from the other side of the room. "I thought we might have to restrain you."

I'm alive.

It was only a dream.

LeSueur was just a dream.

"So who is this Wenonah you spoke of?" Doctor Barrow asked, sweeping in to inspect his patient.

"What happened?" Guerin asked.

"I thought I was going to lose you. You almost got taken out by a French cannonball. The blast left some fairly large splinters of wood in you and broke some of your ribs."

"LeSueur?"

"Successfully captured, thanks to you. Once you identified him, we negotiated with the French to give us the giant, which they did. After we had him, Kidd sank their ship so there were no witnesses. In the grand scheme of things, it was a successful mission."

"I need to speak with him," Guerin said, trying to sit up, only to see the black stains on several bandages on his legs, arms, and torso.

"You're tough, Guerin. Broken ribs are one thing, but the infection almost killed you. I think I've got all those slivers pulled from your flesh now. Give it time, we've still got a long journey ahead of us still."

"Are we bringing LeSueur to England?"

"England? My dear Gareth. You've been on death's door for the better part of three weeks. We brought the prisoner to England already and have since sailed past Spain. We're on our way to Madagascar finally."

"Can you fetch Captain Kidd?"

"Certainly, I'm sure he'll be pleased to know you live. All the officers will be pleased. Most check on you daily."

Something sinister is afoot.

Back in New France, after Louis-Armand had proven himself a competent field commander in fighting the Iroquois, he'd been sent by the governor to replace the commander stationed at Mackinac Island. The existing commander, it turned out, was a fraud. The Jesuits did most of the dirty work for Louis-Armand d'Arcy once they found out the their former servant, Pierre-Charles LeSueur, had changed his identity to Paul Bon Jean and had risen to the ranks in the fur trade industry, attaining the position of commander at the fort.

With Gaspar's help, Louis-Armand led a bloodless coup that sent Pierre-Charles LeSueur back in chains to the Jesuits in Montreal.

Guerin's Periphery orders were to observe and create chaos.

The young baron flexed his aristocratic pedigree and replaced the lying fraud. Upon inspecting his belongings, though, Guerin learned that not only did LeSueur once possess an ancient map believed to be in the possession of the Jesuits but that he'd also taken a trip deep into a land of fable and mysticism—where he'd found the resting place of the Philosopher's Stone five years earlier.

By the time Guerin discovered this, LeSueur was halfway to Montreal, so with Chief Gaspar's help, the two retraced LeSueur's route and found the mound of blue vitriol deep in Sioux territory.

"GARETH LIVES!" CAPTAIN Kidd said in the doorway. "You are no longer simply Gareth. I've dubbed thee Gareth LaGrande. My dear boy, it is good to see you well."

Guerin swam in the details of the political maneuverings. "You were paid to hunt for Pierre-Charles LeSueur. He was the aristocrat who…"

"Newton," Doctor Barrow finished.

"He was the man Newton wanted captured alive."

"Indeed he was. Had I known you knew the fellow, we might've been able to find him without the help of Newton's spies.

Alas, he's now residing in the Tower of London, and all of us are wealthier men, thanks to our benefactor."

"Did Newton say why he wanted him?"

"Who cares? The man paid a kingly ransom. Why? Are you thinking this has something to do with the Order of Eos?"

Three men on the earth knew the current location of the Philosopher's Stone. Now, Isaac Newton likely shared that information.

Captain Kidd was a tool—a blade.

The sculptor was Isaac Newton.

But what does Newton want?

By the time they reached their destination, Guerin needed to know as much as he could about Isaac Newton and their mission to Madagascar.

CHAPTER 15

Born to Puritan parents in Massachusetts, Josiah Faero still felt he was a Calvinist at heart even though his ever-expanding world views led to his removal at Harvard, which brought him into the service of another former pupil, Thomas Tew. His private research into old conspiracies swept him up.

Now, he needed these conspiracies to stay alive.

Back on the *Quedagh Merchant*, he'd carved his name and theories into the wooden beams of the brig so that the world would know what became of him. Now, he walked out in the open of the Alamgiri Library beholden to none and known by none.

Yes, he still had his guards that had traveled with him into the north, as well as his translators—prisoners who could translate texts into English—but he now lived only to serve Emperor Aurangzeb's curiosity.

At the end of the year, he needed to provide Emperor Aurangzeb his theory on the history of the Order of Eos or lose his position, a euphemistic way of saying he'd lose his life.

So Faero decided he needed to take a break before returning to his outline. The emerald green pleasure gardens dazzled the eyes, ears, and nostrils with its samples of perfection from the empire. The wealthy and elite from Lahore often gathered here, outside of the library, but he couldn't speak with them and they couldn't speak with him.

Back in Newport, he was a lonely bachelor.

Now, in Lahore, he was a lonely bachelor with a vast library of texts and relics.

The longer it takes Aurangzeb to read my theories about Eos, the longer I'll stay alive. So where to begin? I must begin at the beginning.

Back in Massachusetts, his Puritanical views of the Earth came from Genesis 10, which listed out the known nations that spread out from Mount Ararat approximately two millennia before Christ. But in the Alamgiri Library, he had oriental texts going back hundreds and thousands of years before the dates of Genesis. While the timeline challenged his world age views, the shelves reinforced another unique aspect of humanity—the world flood. Neither the dates nor details aligned, but from country to country and continent to continent, the song remained the same about the flood.

And so too did stories about an alchemist.

The name of the ancient sorcerer king changed in the telling, but Faero saw pieces of him wherever he looked.

King Solomon studied him when trying to create a temple of unhewn stone.

A thousand years before that, King Nimrod unearthed a broken sculpture dedicated to him.

Must I begin in the garden? Faero wondered as he ended his stroll through the manmade paradise.

It didn't matter what was true or not—the thesis just needed to fit the broken clues Aurangzeb collected.

Returning to his lonely writing desk, Josiah Faero dipped quill into the ink and began:

Once there was a mighty warrior king, who stole the secrets of the gods. He had a purpose in his thievery. While gods lived on and on, men perished.

So the warrior king decided that he would attain immortality while also bringing about the death of the gods.

To do this, he needed a great weapon—an Elixir of Life.

Since the gods helped shape our world, they knew the secrets of our world, so the warrior king befriended them, and little by little, learned their secrets.

What harm could there be in telling a mortal man, the gods wondered, so each took turns telling the warrior king their part in creation.

Finally, the warrior king had the knowledge to create his Great Work.

Imbued with the secrets of creation, his magical stone could transform matter, for the gods taught him the song they sang at the dawn of the world. The elements obeyed the commands given to them.

Just as the gods determined the limited span of a man's life, they also established the lifespan of the world, determining great catastrophes to begin the world anew lest humans discover and collect too many of these secrets.

Knowing his time was limited—and the time of his world was limited—the Alchemist King willingly gave up his life to ensnare the gods.

But instead of his soul descending into the depths, the soul of the Alchemist King lingered, held in place by the magic of his Great Work.

The gods took his life and destroyed his world, but he left behind his secrets—the song. He used the Great Work to imprint the song into the hardest stone known to man, knowing another great catastrophe would soon come.

And it did come.

Death claimed the Alchemist King.

Catastrophe claimed the world.

But his Great Work remained.

So too did the Black Stone, upon which he wrote the song.

And the soul of the Alchemist remained caught between worlds.

Following the Great Flood, the men who began the story anew understood their duty. The Men of the Dawn, which are now called the Order of Eos, held onto their Black Stone and the deeds of the Alchemist King passed from one world to the other.

Now they search for the Alchemist's Tomb, and if they are able to sing the song within the presence of his Great Work, they will not only be able to transform elements but will be able to restore the Alchemist back to life, ending the cycle of destruction.

Josiah Faero set his quill down, almost believing his own tale.

But was it a story fit for an Emperor?

Would his tall thesis save his life?

CHAPTER 16

At long last, Louis-Armand Guerin commanded his own ship—the *November*—and he didn't even need to stage his mutiny. He stood at the wheel as his small sloop approached the coast.

Captain Kidd had given him a skeleton crew and a mission—to acquire supplies. So he headed to an unknown port in an unknown country to bargain with an unknown queen.

"Benjamin, come here for a moment," Guerin called out as his little sloop approached the city.

His only officer approached. Benjamin Horne, a rail thin Abyssinian slave they'd acquired a few weeks earlier, towered over him, "Yes, Captain."

"I'm a prisoner of circumstance, just like you. You don't have to call me Captain."

"Aye, but you are the captain, and you deserve the honor of your rank."

"Well, Master Gunner, are the four cannons ready?"

"Three of the four, Captain. I wouldn't fire the fourth unless my life depended upon it."

Louis-Armand Guerin turned to see the captured *Quedagh Merchant* anchored in the distance. Captain Kidd and *Adventure Galley* were nowhere to be seen. He turned to his newest acquaintance. "Can I trust you?"

"You are now my captain, and I will obey your orders."

"Well, as an African man about to step foot upon an African island, you might be tempted to abandon me at first chance."

"I gave you my word, Captain LaGrande, and I can only hope you are also a man of honor."

There had been little to no honor aboard Captain Kidd's ship during the past year.

At first, Kidd took to his mission earnestly. He discreetly mapped the east coast of Africa, especially Madagascar, without ever engaging other ships. At port, he'd collect tales and allow Guerin to piece the intelligence together. Slowly and steadily, he served Newton by gathering information on the Order of Eos pirates.

All the while, Louis-Armand Guerin acquired the same information about Eos and also about the new enemy, Newton. While being Kidd's only confidant, Guerin secretly stoked mutiny, knowing that he'd one day need to return to the Periphery with his knowledge.

Kidd made it easy.

The cracks began to appear back in November when Captain Kidd murdered the previous Master Gunner William Moore after being pressed about engaging ships rather than skirting around ports. After crushing Moore's skull, Kidd forsook his mission and preyed upon a French ship, the *Rouparelle*, which he renamed the *November*. Now with two ships, he could easily prey upon any ship that crossed his path.

Back in January, Captain Kidd buckled to the pressures of the mutinous crew when a larger merchant ship appeared. Although Kidd's directives were only to scout out the pirate strongholds, the crew began to realize their wages had only been a promise that would be paid upon a return to England. Knowing they were at war with France, the sight of a French flag upon the *Quedagh Merchant* sent the men into a frenzy, and Kidd agreed to rob her cargo and claim the ship. Instead, Kidd stepped knee deep into shit.

The *Quedagh Merchant* deployed layers of subterfuge, which puzzled both Guerin and Kidd. An English Captain, a French First Mate, Armenian officers, an Indian crew, and Abyssinian prisoners. She'd surrendered without firing a shot, and when it became clear that Kidd meant to claim her as a prize, the *real* captain appeared with legal papers from the Mughal Empire.

"I'm not worried," Kidd had boasted. "The crew needs this."

"Captain, the only thing of value is a load of cotton, yet they have ransom papers worth more than the actual cargo."

"My boys need spending money. Figure it out later, but let them know we're taking this ship and its cargo."

In the brig, Guerin had found Benjamin Horne and a carved message from a man named Josiah Faero in a language Guerin knew well.

Before reaching port to offload the prisoners and cotton, Guerin interrogated Corgi Baba, the insulted former captain of the *Quedagh Merchant* about the history of the ship, only to discover that Professor Josiah Faero had been captured aboard Thomas Tew's *Amity* and delivered to Emperor Aurangzeb as a prize.

At this, Guerin insisted on keeping all the Abyssians rather than selling them to the slavers.

Now, like Benjamin Horne, Guerin had an opportunity to be a free man simply by keeping the ship and sailing to a friendly port. He needed Horne, so finally away from Kidd and the others, he pressed further.

"Yes," Guerin agreed, thinking of the sound of William Moore's skull breaking, "we certainly did need a gunner, but unlike the other men on this ship, I'm not a heathen. I've seen you praying with your countrymen. Abyssinia is a Christian nation, isn't it?"

"One of the Magi came from my country."

"Yes, it was Balthazar. Melchior came from the Black Forest of Germany, and Gaspar came from the Orient."

Horne looked at him with silent incredulity.

"I'll put my life in your hands," Guerin agreed. "I'm a spy. I was sent to spy on the Order of Eos, which brings us to Madagascar, but Kidd serves a different master than I, and I fear it might be a darker master than anyone understands. The symbol carved into the brig—"

"The Seal of Solomon," Benjamin finished. "yes, I saw it also, along with the message. Who is this Faero?"

"Like us, a man in the wrong place at the wrong time. You're familiar with Solomon?"

"Of course I am, my people are descended from King Solomon."

"You have Hebrew blood?"

"A bit," Benjamin raised his eyebrows and grinned. "After the fall of Jerusalem during the reign of King Nebuchadnezzar, the Ark of the Covenant was brought to Sheba, as it was called then. For almost two thousand years, we were the caretakers of the Ark, until enemies came."

"Let me guess…The Knights of the Temple of Solomon."

"Captain Kidd was right about the *Quedagh Merchant*—it isn't a merchant vessel at all. The Emperor Aurangzeb uses it to acquire his prizes. How do I explain this? My crew and I hunted a great fat water buffalo, and while we waited in ambush, a lion attacked us.

"The *Quedagh Merchant* was the lion," Guerin gathered, "So tell me about this great fat water buffalo."

Benjamin took a moment to gather his thoughts. "Abyssinia is a landlocked African nation, yet I was made a captain of a vessel with a specific purpose—to find and secure stolen valuables. When the whole world learned of the Nation of Pirates living on Madagascar, all sorts of predators took an interest in the great, fat, wounded water buffalo. I knew that time was of the essence, so I kept my ship near Antongil Bay hoping to learn about our stolen treasure."

"And what treasure is that?"

"The Ark of the Covenant. After the real Ark of the Covenant was brought from Jerusalem to Sheba, eleven exact replicas were made, so that there were twelve churches that held the sacred treasure. When the Templars came, they managed to steal one of the twelve Arks, and only the High Priest knew if it was the right one. To us they all represent the same promise from God. For generations, the Templars hid from the world, and with the bright lights now upon them, I hoped they would leave their hole with our treasure."

"An honorable purpose," Guerin added. "So instead of finding it, a Mughal ship captured you instead. The lion attacked the hyena instead of the fat buffalo."

"They used my crew to man the cannons of the *Quedagh Merchant*, and when they discovered my purpose, they locked me in the

brig with plans to bring me back to India. Of course, Captain Kidd kept that from happening."

"Yes, he did," Guerin added. "What would you be willing to pay for the return of the Ark?"

"I don't know how to answer that."

"Would you be willing to trade a lesser relic for such a sacred relic?"

"Likely."

"I'm beginning to form a convoluted plan, one that the Lord has placed before me. First, we have a queen to meet, and then, we'll talk more about my plan."

WITH HORNE AT his side, Louis-Armand Guerin knelt before Queen Rehena. It had taken a week and countless bribes, and just when it seemed like the whole idea was going nowhere, an envoy from the Queen invited the diplomats to court.

"Ambassador LaGrande," her vizier repeated in French to her.

"Why have you come to my country?" Queen Rehena asked in French. In addition to her ability to speak his language, her youth and beauty also surprised him. One look at the palace at Foulpointe, and it became obvious that the secret island had been trading on the global market for centuries.

"My lady, I serve upon an English ship charged with hunting down the pirates who attacked Emperor Aurangzeb's daughter."

"The world has been fed a lie," Queen Rehena boldly stated. "The Emperor has four daughters and none of them were killed in the attack of the *Ganj-i-Sawai*. Do not believe the lies of Aurangzeb."

What lies is she talking about? "Nevertheless, England is an important trade partner, and the pirates who attacked the *Ganj-i-Sawai* were English."

"Those men might've spoken English, but I can assure you, none of them acted on behalf of England."

She knew them. "How do you know the pirates that attacked the Emperor's caravan?"

"One of them was my husband and king, Thomas Tew. He made promises also, but now I am a widow, ignored by the men who hold my country hostage."

And what did Tew promise her? "I come here only asking for supplies so that we might hunt down these criminals. That is all that I want. What does your highness want?"

"Honesty, Ambassador LaGrande. How is that for a beginning?"

"The world is dangerous, and an honest man is always at risk in a world filled with dishonest men." Guerin turned to reference the international crowd.

"Ah, I see. Then walk with me. I've had enough of promises made in public. Perhaps you can find your honesty in private. Your man can watch from a distance, just like my brother will be watching from a distance, so that no harm will come to either of us in my garden.

A FEW MINUTES later, Louis-Armand Guerin walked with the beautiful young queen.

"Where are you from?" She asked.

So he told her some truth, including being born a bastard and his time in New France. She deserved the truth of his birth name—Louis-Armand Guerin. "And I will offer you a coin worth much more than the story of my birth. I am also known to the world as Louis-Armand de Lom d'Arcy, the Baron of Lahontan. For seducing a governor's daughter, I am a wanted man with a great bounty placed upon my head. So if you'd give my head to the King of France, along with my name, you could make yourself a small fortune and a temporary ally."

"Seducing a governor's daughter," Rehena repeated.

"There are many fathers and husbands that had reason to take my life, but when the fate of humanity is on the line, a little seduction is the least of crimes."

"And how is it that an explorer from the far side of the world ends up at Foulpointe?"

"Your highness, it is my turn to ask a few questions."

"And what would you like to know?"

"What did Aurangzeb promise you to betray your husband?" Guerin asked in turn.

This took the smile from her face. Instead of an immediate denial, she took several moments to process what he said. "I'm trying to save my people from extermination. For generations, we've been an invisible nation hidden away from the rest of the world, but we are not isolated. I know all about the wars that are waged around the world. Here on Madagascar, I rule as Queen. My own people, the Betsimisaraka, despise the Zana-Malata for being mixed race. In the highlands, the Imerina plot our downfall and try to rally other tribes to their cause. Emperor Aurangzeb promised to give the country back to my people. He promised to free us from our overlords, including my own master, my husband Thomas Tew. Now Thomas is dead and the chieftains remain."

"The emperor will now sit back and let his enemies fight amongst themselves," Guerin explained. "England is preparing to do his dirty work for him. You were right to fear, but Aurangzeb was a poor choice to save you."

"What would you have done?"

"Would you believe it if I said that I had the power to help you?"

She laughed. "You are only a handsome face meant to garner kindness."

"I am serious," Guerin added. "I did not get a choice in matters, and I serve Captain Kidd under threat of death. If I had my freedom and means to travel, I'd return to my powerful allies, but alas, they have no idea where I've gone."

"Are you asking for me to save you?"

"Not at this time. As I said, I'm a spy, and fate has brought me to the other side of the world, with all of its secrets. You know my secret, and I know your secret. I sincerely would like to help you and your people before the dark days come. But for now, I play the part of Gareth LaGrande, and if you can manage to help us with our supplies, I would be in your debt if I ever return in a position of strength rather than weakness."

"I don't believe a word you are saying," Rehena admitted, "but you've put a smile on my face. I'll send you back with as many

supplies as your ship can carry. And then what will happen to you?"

"We'll have three ships to properly hunt for these pirates. I'll likely die in battle or of some foul tropical disease. This will likely be the only time we meet."

"That's a pity," Rehena said and smiled. "Before you leave, tell me the story of the governor's daughter."

CHAPTER 17

Who am I, you ask? I am Louis-Armand Guerin, my mother's only child—bastard son of Isaac de Lom d'Arcy, the Baron of Lahontan. I am King Louis' trusted officer—the savior of Quebec and the defender of Placentia. The Huron are my friends, and the Iroquois are my enemies. More recently, I am the pirate Gareth LaGrande, the first mate on Captain Kidd's Adventure Prize.

I have stood at the doors of the secret city, walked over the treasure vault at Oak Island, and discovered the resting place of the Philosopher's Stone beyond the River of Death in the dreaded Haunted Valley.

I am the Sword of the Spirit.

Oh yes, and by blind luck, I stumbled across the lost Templar fleet and discovered clues to one of the world's great mysteries. Is that enough to make you put the knife away? Will all this useless knowledge in my head save me from the flames?

Just ask the right question and I'll give you the answers.

Louis-Armand looked up to see John Swan holding a heavy chain, which he swung in a circular motion at his side as he advanced on the next victim. Including himself, there were fifteen crewmembers of the *Adventure Prize* still alive. The others were savagely slaughtered by the great beast, Swan.

They're looking to me to save them, but I've sworn a holy oath.

I'll die rather than betray the secrets of the Periphery.

Kill me next so I don't have to see my friends die.

John Swan towered over the average man, but with Nuno Caverelli already on his knees, the savage executioner looked like a giant. Swan wore a leather pocket vest over his blood-splattered torso. All manners of torture protruded from those pockets. If not for the certainty of the gun crew behind him, Louis-Armand would have thrown himself overboard to drown.

Still swinging the heavy chain, Swan looked to his master, Captain Robert Culliford.

The bait for this trap.

Few crewmembers remained from 1689 when Captain Kidd's history with Captain Robert Culliford began. Nine years ago, on the other side of the planet in the West Indies, Culliford and Swan stole Kidd's ship while it was anchored offshore of Antigua. The crime was not forgotten, leading Kidd right into the trap.

Now, one by one, we'll die because of the great fool.

Unlike the beast Swan, Culliford was a small, dainty man, dressed in a yellow and black checkered cloak and matching yellow pants. With a nod from Culliford, Swan began to remove chunks of flesh from poor Nuno's head. The screams kept coming even after the heavy chain shattered the left side of the man's jaw—but terror was the point. For several hours, the executioner worked his way up the captured crew's hierarchy until now only the officers remained, disgusted and terrified.

Finally, with a downward swing of the chains, the screaming stopped and the death spasms began. Men from Culliford's crew dragged the body away.

"That one," Culliford said, pointing right at Louis-Armand. "He's the smallest one of the bunch. Surely a man lacking physical value must have intellectual value. Put away your chains. This one will need the slow blade."

Louis-Armand felt himself go limp, and Culliford's henchmen pulled him by his armpits to where the brains, bone, and blood of Nuno Caverelli pooled.

For dust you are, and to dust you shall return.

Dear Lord, why did you give me the pieces of the puzzle if I am not meant to live long enough to solve it? How do I protect my oath and still find a way to survive this ordeal?

How, Lord?

More than a dozen men had died in the spot where Louis-Armand now sat, and the gaze of Captain Culliford burned its light upon him. "And what is your name?"

"Who do you want me to be?" Louis-Armand teased playfully, bringing chuckles from the surviving crew of the *Adventure Prize*.

Louis-Armand winked in their direction. They were mostly ruthless brigands doomed to the fires of Hell, but he'd developed the bond of kinship over the past several years.

Several Ethiopian boys also sat amongst his friends. Swan had mercilessly killed a few of the "powder monkeys," the young boys who manned the guns during battle, but aside from bawling like terrified lambs, the boys knew nothing about Captain Kidd's mission.

The knuckles of John Swan backhanded his cheek.

"Then call me Georgetta," Louis-Armand said, remembering the governor's daughter that sent him from North America to the Indian Ocean, and blew Culliford a kiss.

At this, Culliford walked over to Swan and took one of the blades from his vest. "Hold him! Open up his mouth. Fetch the pincers."

"Hold!" one of the guards shouted, although Louis-Armand couldn't see which of his friends risked everything.

The pincers appeared, ready to take hold of his tongue.

"Wait, wait, wait, wait," Captain Culliford said, turning to his own crewmen. "Are you sure this man is Captain Kidd's first mate?"

"Aye, he's the one who took charge once he sensed our trap. We even found a notebook on him."

"An educated man pretending to be obstinate," Culliford assessed. "No, no, no, we'll save him for the end. But, I want him to think things over while he waits, so…hold open his eye!"

The rough hands that held him by the jaw suddenly shifted to his forehead and two hands spread open his eyelids.

The tip of the blade loomed.

And then a crimson sheet blinded him just before the flashes of pain blinded his brain.

With his good eye, Louis-Armand saw Culliford leaning in, inspecting his macabre work as he shifted from blade to spoon and back to blade.

When they threw Louis-Armand back with the crew, the screaming stopped—his own screaming this time. Culliford set the eyeball on the deck in front of him and walked back to torture the next victim.

How did I get here?

It had been an impressive trap. A few weeks earlier, the *Adventure Prize* hunted down the pirate ship *Fidelia*, whose captain denied knowing Henry Avery or any other pirates associated with the *Ganj-i-Sawai* massacre, but he did know the pirate Culliford was hiding at an island north of Foulpointe. Sure enough, Culliford's ship was anchored and Kidd went rushing in to blast his old rival out of the water, only to have several other pirate ships seal the bay behind them.

Captain Kidd had immediately surrendered, hoping to hide the fact that they were hired by the British government to hunt down pirates. After negotiations failed, Kidd was kept aboard Culliford's *Mocha Frigate* and Swan methodically began torturing the crew.

Am I going to die beside these pirates?

Louis-Armand wallowed in agony for the next several minutes, but when Jago Firken's screams ended and his body was tossed overboard, Louis-Armand sobered up.

Think, damn it, think.

Or all this will have been in vain.

Captain Culliford pointed to Benjamin Horne, the Ethiopian Gunner.

Son of a bitch. Of all the crewmen, I need Benjamin the most.

I have to give him something of value.

Louis-Armand shouted out, "Spare him, the remaining crew, and the ship—and I will make you a wealthy man. Do we have a deal?"

Swan held a blade under the chin of Horne. Robert Culliford threatened to destroy all of their plans. "A deal? Who do you think you are?"

"You're all going to die if you don't listen to me," Guerin added.

Culliford mocked him, looked out over the horizon for help that wasn't there. He even looked up to the blue skies of the heavens. "I don't…believe you."

The two men chuckled.

The nerves in his severed eyeball echoed and rattled at speaking, but Louis-Armand found the resolve to bargain for his life. "Captain Kidd was hired by the English government to hunt down and kill the pirates responsible for the *Ganj-i-Sawai* massacre."

"We knew all of this a dozen men ago. How is this worth saving your lives?"

"But we're not hunting pirates. I tried to warn Captain Kidd about seeking revenge against you, but he ignored my advice and chose his own selfish agenda above the mission he'd been hired to perform."

Culliford raised his eyebrow as if curious and then muttered, "Cut off his ear."

Swan sliced Benjamin Horne's ear from his head, leaving a bloody inner-ear hole behind.

"Is this where you threaten me?" Culliford said.

"You're only a hired gun, or else you'd be interrogating Captain Kidd rather than turning him over to your masters," Louis-Armand taunted. "I can give you a spot at the table. I can give you a treasure greater than trade goods and coins if you're smart enough to understand."

"Smart enough? Perhaps you're the fool. How many more body parts must we hack off before you just give me what I want?"

Show him you're serious.

Even though his arms were bound behind his back, keeping him from attacking the men taunting him, Louis-Armand still had a way of striking. He bent down, face to the deck planks, and when he straightened his back, he spit his own severed eyeball into the chest of Captain Culliford, who stepped back in shock and disgust.

"We are hunting the lost Templar fleet," Louis-Armand confessed. "Even if you spare our lives today and set us free, Captain Kidd is a dead man. The man who hired us used the *Ganj-i-Sawai* massacre as a pretense to wage war. Your enemy is mobilizing a great fleet that will wipe your secret pirate colony from the face of the earth. For centuries, the Order of Eos has hidden from the eyes and ears of Europe on the far side of the world. Instead of hunting pirates, Captain Kidd was tasked with scouting Madagascar and all the known pirate hideouts so that when the hammer falls, the next massacre will be complete."

Culliford looked down at the blood spot on his chest. "Who hired you?"

Louis-Armand let himself become the scholar again and muttered the old Sanskrit proverb, "'The king who is situated anywhere immediately on the circumference of the conqueror's territory is termed the enemy. The king who is likewise situated close to the enemy, but separated from the conqueror only by the enemy is termed the friend (of the conqueror).' The enemy of my enemy is my friend. We should not have to pay for the blunder of our foolish captain. Promise me you'll abide by my terms and I'll give you the name of your true enemy."

"I'm content skinning every last one of these men alive, including you, to get the truth from your lips because tonight it won't really change anything, will it? You'll be dead, and I'll be stuck in Madagascar."

"You and I are both soldiers in this war, but I don't think you know what's at stake."

"The Templars? Yeah, I know about it. How is that going to change my lot in life?"

"The world is controlled by puppet masters, not by kings and queens. You have a master. I have a master, Captain Kidd has a master, and Kidd's master will soon destroy each and every last one of you unless you heed my warning."

"A name for your life? You give me the name of the Boogeyman and I let you and your friends free? That's not fun. You could say John Swan is the puppet master."

John Swan, the monstrous butcher, chuckled at the comment.

"I agree, which is why you must let Captain Kidd live."

Culliford chuckled. "Where are those pincers?"

"If I give you the name, the value in that knowledge lies in identifying your enemy. Right now, he is a phantom, hiding behind a mask. The man who hired Captain Kidd will not allow him to live after betraying his purpose. Kidd ruined the element of surprise. If you send Kidd back to civilization like a spanked child, the ally that gives him up is none other than the Great Shepherd for the Priory of Ormus."

The smile left Culliford's face and he turned to Swan. "Dalziel told me stories about the Priory of Ormus. He said the Priory joined with its enemies to wipe out the Templars and hunt down the Order of Eos. How do you know about the Priory?"

"I've been spying on Kidd and the Priory of Ormus for the better part of five years now, which is why my name may as well be Georgetta. The Priory of Ormus and the Order of Eos have been battling each other for control for centuries now. I was sent to the New World to discover what they were chasing after."

"And what are they chasing after?"

"On the surface, they are hunting for something called the Philosopher's Stone, a

legendary object rumored to be able to transform matter from lead into gold."

"I've heard of it? So what?"

"On its maiden voyage, the *Adventure Galley,* Captain Kidd's previous ship before he took this one as his *Prize,* we attacked a French warship carrying a crew of miners and a man who discovered the location of the Philosopher's Stone. The same puppet master who ordered us to capture this man then sent us to the Indian Ocean to scout Madagascar. Unfortunately, ego got in the way. If I give you the name of this man, your puppet master will simply watch to see what happens, and when the truth is confirmed, he will know his enemy and will save his people from another Friday the 13th massacre."

Captain Culliford motioned to John Swan for a private conversation, and the two stepped away.

Despite wincing in pain, Benjamin Horne nodded in affirmation.

Louis-Armand turned to his wide-eyed friends, who like Captain Kidd, had no clue about Eos, Ormus, or even the Periphery. He didn't need to tell lies to them or Culliford—he only had to give them a peek at the truth.

This might work.

Back on the frontier, the truth had turned Chief Gaspar into a blood brother and ally. He didn't mind spreading chaos into the world, and he certainly had something to trade if it came to more torture. When the conversation took ten minutes, Guerin winked at the captured crew with his good eye.

"We accept your proposal," Culliford gleefully announced. "Shit, what do we have to lose? Before we release the thirteen of you and return your foolish captain, we're going to strip your ship of anything not fastened down just to make this seizure slightly profitable and…to give us a head start. If what you say is true, I need time to get ahead of this global catastrophe about to erupt. I need to warn my allies, and then find a spot to hide. Swan and I want to live long enough to spend our wealth."

Swan nodded and cut Benjamin Horne free of his bonds. A moment later, he walked over to stand behind Louis-Armand and cut his bonds free. His hand immediately went to his empty eye socket.

At least the Lord gave me two. "The Grand Shepherd of the Priory of Ormus began as a scientist with an obsession with the Philosopher's Stone and alchemy, but now, he is the Master of the Mint for the British Empire. With other people's money, he's building a fleet that will destroy his enemies. A few years ago, when I brought him Pierre-Charles LeSueur as a prisoner, he was using the Tower of London as his base of operations. Your enemy is Isaac Newton."

THE END OF PART ONE

PART TWO

THE RESURRECTION OF THE WHITE ZOMBIE

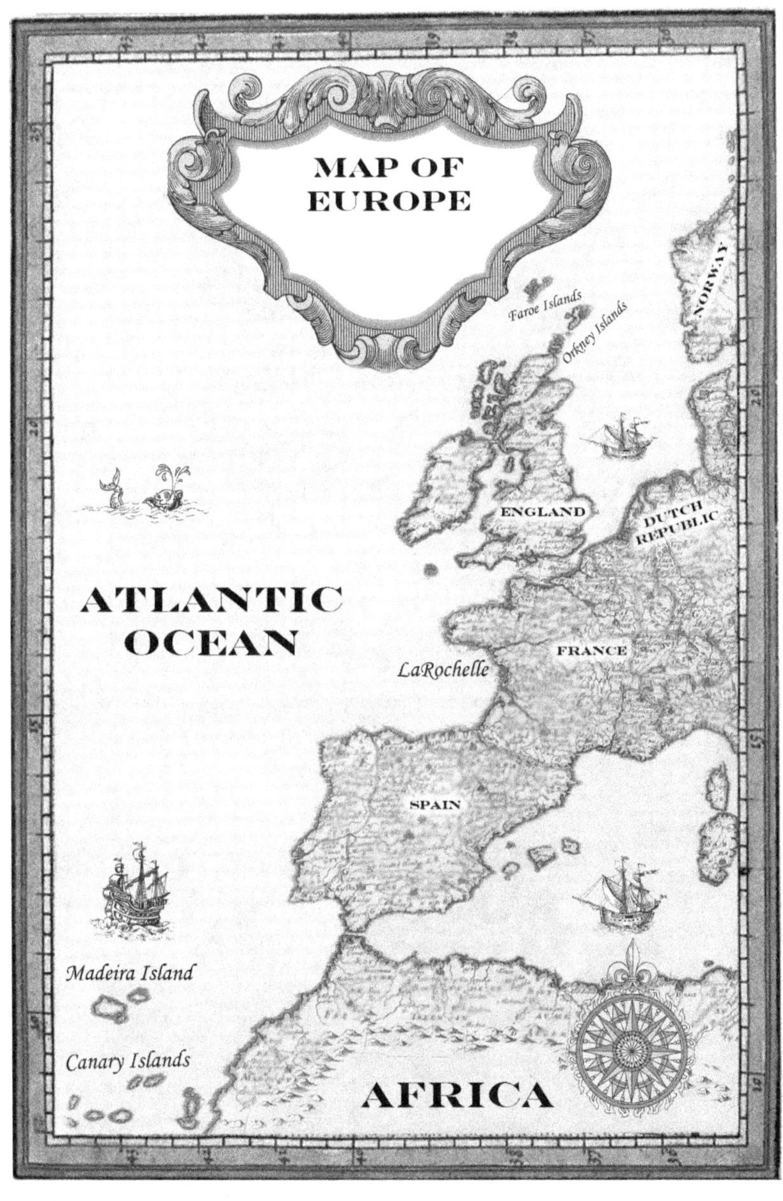

PART TWO

CHAPTER 18

T I L B U R Y ,   E N G L A N D

M A Y   2 3 ,   1 7 0 1

Jimmy Duke slipped his feet back into his boots as he sat on the edge of the bed, which still held the whore he'd found at the tavern. Unlike whores found in brothels, a whore found in a tavern needed a place to sleep for the night, which is why she drank all of his wine and ate the last of his food. Even after he'd spent his last bit of lust, Duke still needed her for one last thing, so he took his time getting dressed.

After a few minutes of gathering his belongings, she woke. "What time is it?"

"It's quickly approaching noon, which means I have to vacate the room soon. Do you want to come with me to the hanging? I could buy you lunch before I have to leave."

Lunch perked her right up. "Of course I'd like to see the hanging. Especially after what happened to you."

"Well, then start getting dressed and we'll watch the hanging together."

Duke didn't bother to learn her name, for in a few more hours, he'd be on the

English Channel enroute to the Caribbean.

"I think I understand why you're called a bosom's mate," she raised an eyebrow. "When will you be back to England again?"

Jimmy rolled his eyes, annoyed. "First of all, it's bosun, not bosom. One is tits and the other is anchors. I'm in charge of the anchors and hull repair."

Jimmy Duke was twenty-six but felt as if he were already an old man. His arms were a series of cuts, gauges, and bruises from a decade on the ocean, and his boyish looks were now rubbed raw by wind and spray. The sun had turned his golden locks a bleached shade of white, but he still had his rugged physique and his dimples. "When will I be back? I can't honestly tell you. For the first time in a decade, I'm a passenger. I'll need to find a new crew when I return."

"Where will you go?"

"I have friends waiting back in the Caribbean. Perhaps they will have it all sorted out by the time I return." *I hope they're all waiting still.*

"You came all this way just to see a man hanged?"

It's our mission. "After what he did to me, absolutely. Fuck him and all pirates like him," Jimmy partially bluffed.

Another pirate entered his mind—Captain LaGrande. LaGrande taught him a trick about lying. The previous night, he told the whore a story about betrayals and mutinies and how he and a dozen other men ended up marooned on an island, left for dead on the far side of the world. Instead of using the name of the real enemy, Robert Culliford, he used another pirate name that justified his presence in London—Captain Kidd.

"They say he is the last of them," the whore interrupted.

"The last of what?" Duke asked.

"The pirates who killed the Indian princess."

"The *Ganj-i-Sawai?*" Duke began to question the lies about Kidd but let them go. "It wouldn't surprise me if the bastard was involved in that bit of devilry. He isn't the last of them. Dalziel and Long Ben Avery are still out there."

"I heard Avery died in a shipwreck, which is why no one was able to find him."

"Faking your death is one way to become anonymous," Duke said, thinking again of LaGrande, and then of the other dozen men who'd survived torture at the hands of Robert Culliford. "Let's get this over with."

He double checked his belongings, making sure his personal items were secure, and then led the whore out of the room and tavern.

Oh, Good God, Duke despaired as he saw a large crowd already gathered at Execution Dock. Unlike greater London, whose crowds plugged the roads leading into Wapping, the little village of Tilbury was tucked in behind the docks, allowing him a good view of the execution as well as a quick escape if necessary.

LaGrande warned us of spies, Duke thought as he walked arm-in-arm with the whore, and for that reason, he did his best to look like a curious local. Standing on a deck overlooking Execution Dock, Duke scanned the crowd for familiar faces to no avail. *I feel like I am the last one.*

When they brought out the doomed man, Duke almost gasped. "He looks so small."

The whore scoffed. "I've found small men can be the most cruel and big men like yourself can be the kindest."

The crowd recoiled with boos and hisses, but the doomed man in the white tunic no longer appeared capable of killing a man with his bare hands. He looked frightened...and already dead.

Gareth LaGrande staged a bloodless mutiny three years earlier, and for all intents and purposes, Captain Kidd never even learned of it. Before Culliford returned their disgraced Captain to them, LaGrande explained his great scheme. If Kidd hadn't done what LaGrande predicted, they would have mutinied. Instead, Kidd walked right into the trap set for him by Newton.

Joining the prisoner upon the stage were a series of magistrates and officials. A year after being arrested in Boston, and a lengthy court-battle in American and London, the legend only grew, and the public execution of Captain William Kidd had become a spectacle.

"I can't hear what they are saying," Duke muttered as the announcements were made and the rope was prepared.

LaGrande had been specific, though. Duke was to linger in reserve, near the water, ready to ferry the others away as quickly as possible. Even though he couldn't see them, they were there—waiting.

"I thought you would be happy," the whore said.

"Captain Kidd killed many of my friends," Duke lied, thinking of the snake Culliford. "I'm glad he's been brought to justice, but it is still a bitter day for me, thinking of what he took."

In truth, Captain Kidd *had* killed one of his close friends, a gunner named William Moore. The two had quarreled over attacking a Dutch ship, and in frustration, Kidd threw a bucket at Moore, who shockingly fell dead from the head wound. For this crime, Kidd was arrested in Boston, but now, upon the docks of London, he stood accused of piracy, which meant Gareth LaGrande was right about the puppet masters.

With the noose around his neck, Captain Kidd spoke his last words, which were too soft to be heard from the distant deck overlooking the execution.

The lever was pulled, but instead of Kidd's neck breaking, the rope unexpectedly snapped, and the captain of the *Adventure Prize* fell to the decking like a newborn calf. Chaos ensued on the platform.

He deserves death but not humiliation.

"It's a sign from God," someone shouted from the crowd.

"He paid his price. Release him!"

Was that Murray?

A soft roar came up from the crowd, but the officials on the deck quickly procured a new rope, looped it around his neck, and hauled him up to be slowly strangled.

Kidd jerked and convulsed for several minutes instead of succumbing to a quick death from the force of the noose.

"I think God broke the rope just to make him suffer," the whore said.

As an American, he'd hoped she'd help him blend in with the crowd. "Get away from me," Jimmy Duke muttered and flashed his killer's eyes at the woman. She left without another word.

He stayed at the railing after much of the crowd began to disperse, watching as they transferred Captain Kidd's body into the metal gibbet, which would hang over where the Thames opened up to the Atlantic.

None of these sons of bitches even understood why he was hanged.

The answer came walking across the open square in the form of Drake Murray. Murray was another Boatswain, a smaller, portly man with a quick mind and even quicker fists. Duke learned the meaning of the word pugilist along with how quick those fists truly were shortly after the American crew took possession of the new

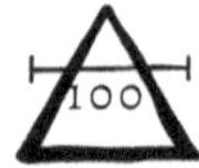

warship, *Adventure Galley*. While the original sailors were Kidd's New York men, the operations of the ship now fell to Murray, and the English bulldog quickly put him in his place.

That was six years ago, ironically at the same place Captain Kidd now hung.

"LaGrande was right," Murray said as he joined Duke at the rail. "Kidd was betrayed by the men who hired him." Then he added, "You do know we could walk away right now. No one knows who we are. We could jump on a new ship and leave all of this LaGrande business behind. Fuck that foppy Frenchman."

What about the treasure? And the adventure? How could I walk away from that? "Yet here you stand. Is it greed or vengeance that keeps you here?"

"Kidd didn't deserve this. He never would have turned himself in if he knew his powerful friends actually wanted him dead."

On this, we agree. "Kidd was a miserable bastard, and this is justice for what he did to Moore and the others, but this is also proof that this conspiracy goes as deep as LaGrande claimed. If he's right about all of this, then I'm standing here because we'll soon be wealthy men."

The two crewmen waited as the large crowd dispersed.

"Do you see that fellow in yellow with a red cap?" Duke asked. "Is that Naro?"

Murray shook his head. "It's some Mughal diplomat. Apparently they show up whenever there's a pirate to be hung, just to report back to their Emperor."

"No, look. That's Bon," he said with relief. "He moves like him."

"Why would he be wearing those ridiculous clothes?"

Both men watched from fifty yards away as the yellow-garbed diplomat walked along the boardwalk but then deftly slipped in an alley between two small shops. Less than a minute passed and a much more familiar man emerged.

Instead of the ornate yellow jama and red turban, the familiar red shirt, black vest, and brown pants of the old sailing master affirmed Duke's sharp eyes. With the cap gone, Bon's white hair and wiry mustache could be seen from a distance. Decades older than any other shipmate, the lean Bon moved with the light steps of a

young man. As he neared the two sailors, he leaned in to say, "We're not safe staying here."

Duke turned to see Bon already ten paces ahead of them and heading toward the English Channel.

He doesn't even know how to get back to the ship, Duke had to laugh, jogging with Murray to catch up.

"What happened to those fine yellow threads?" Murray asked once they caught up to him.

Naro Bon spit in disdain.

"Do you even know where you're going?"

"It doesn't matter. We need to leave before they find him."

"Find who?"

"The Mughal diplomat. I could not kill him, so I left him tied up. When all of those fine English gentlemen return, they will realize I'm only a dark skinned imposter."

"Wait, you pretended to be a Mughal? You hate Indians."

"To an Englishman, we are all the same," Bon stated. Then he turned to confirm their mission, "LaGrande was right about Kidd."

"So we assumed."

"I've met our enemy," Bon added. "I shook his hand."

"You shook his hand?" Murray asked, raising an eyebrow.

Naro Bon swallowed hard before explaining. "The Tory Ministers were behind Kidd's trial and conviction, but it was a Whig minister named Newton that allowed it to happen. He's the same man who hired Kidd six years ago."

Murray shot Duke a concerned look. "You met this man?"

Bon nodded. "The man is a sorcerer, which is why we must leave before I tell you more about him."

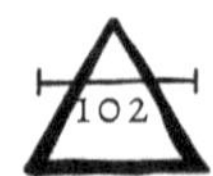

CHAPTER 19

The cold waters of the Atlantic soothed Drake Murray's nerves as he stood on deck in the early morning hours. For the first time in six years, he'd returned home, yet the deck of a ship was his true home now. Murray watched the alien crew adjust the rigging and course for the conditions of the new day. The return to the Caribbean would be a warmer path than had been their departure, following the Canary Current south to the Cape Verde Islands and then riding the Equatorial Current west to the Caribbean.

Even though he'd only recently boarded the *Daphne*, he knew it was a Caribbean pirate crew looking for French shipping vessels to hunt. In the coming days, as they passed by the coast of France, they were in the most danger from attack, but Captain Archibald Vero knew when to attack and when to hide, especially when protecting precious cargo—three fugitive members of the *Adventure Prize*.

A sailor made a direct approach from the stern. "Captain Vero wants to speak with you."

Murray found himself in the shadow of Captain Vero's monstrous hag. The sailor's eyes tightened as the sight of her broad shoulders, lack of discernible breasts, and arms the size of small tree trunks, and her eyes tightened in awareness of Murray's judgment.

Two years ago, LaGrande had put his plan and fate in a collection of bizarre outlaws—the Flying Sylphs. While all four captains were effective pirates, their reputation for carnal depravity isolated them even in the ranks of Nassau criminals. The *Daphne*, unlike most other crews, specialized in sunken treasure extraction, which meant any sailor who could swim and dive found a bit more money working for Captain Vero.

Broad shoulders, thick arms—she is a champion swimmer, I'm sure.

Murray was led from the prow all the way to the captain's quarters, where the scent of freshly made breakfast greeted him even before the door was opened.

Inside, Jimmy Duke and Naro Bon sat at the table with Captain Vero. "Have a seat, Mr. Murray. Will, you too."

The thick woman obliged the order. *Of course, Will Thomas, first mate. Short for*

Wilhelmina? Wilma?

Captain Vero took a moment for them to join the table. "As the ranking officer from the *Adventure Prize*, and out of respect for Captain LaGrande, I wanted you to be present as Mr. Bon and I talked about the conspiracy surrounding the death of the late Captain Kidd."

He wants verification that the story is true. Very smart to learn this as we sail through French waters. If we are taken, Vero will have something worthy of trade.

"I want him to tell me about this sorcerer who betrayed Captain Kidd."

Jimmy Duke snickered.

"Bon misspoke. The man is a scientist."

Bon recoiled, the wrinkles in this dark brown conveying his agitated mood. "I know the difference between a scientist and sorcerer. While you two were bedding whores and drinking London dry, I performed the duty tasked to me. The man is a sorcerer."

"Perhaps you misunderstand the word sorcerer," Murray offered. "Why do you say sorcerer?"

Naro Bon sighed in frustration. "The man of whom I speak, Minister Newton, is indeed a renowned scientist at one of England's finest colleges, but privately, he traffics in the occult and secret knowledge of the world. The items he pays the most for are ancient religious texts, especially those related to *Magnum Opus*."

"The Great Work?" Murray translated the Latin.

"A sorcerer," Bon repeated.

"I don't know what Magnum Opus refers to," Captain Vero said

"It's known as the Philosopher's Stone by some, and the Elixir of Life by others. By reputation, it can grant immortality, and in other tales, it can transform ordinary objects into gold."

"Please tell me this isn't a ruse from Captain LaGrande to pay with items dipped in golden paint. If he tries to pay me with a bag of magical beans, the last thing any of you will see is Willow Thomas about to pluck out your eyes with a red hot pincer."

Willow! A woman built like a tree.

"Captain Kidd's treasure is real, and the second half of your payment will be of the same value as you received to take us on as passengers," Bon insisted.

LaGrande let Naro Bon lead the covert mission, sending Murray and Duke in support of the elderly navigator. Murray enjoyed a trip home to England, but his real home was on the sea, and despite his advancing age, he enjoyed the thrill of adventure as much as Duke.

And surprisingly, Murray trusted LaGrande more than he trusted other pirates, including Vero.

The Flying Sylphs were enemies of the French government, despite their French ancestry, so alliances with English pirates suited them when needed. "So this Newton fellow dabbles in dark magic—so what? What does that have to do with Captain Kidd's death?" Vero asked.

"Governor Bellomont hired Kidd to hunt down Long Ben Avery's pirate fleet—to bring them to justice and to also restore the name of the American colonies in the eyes of the Grand Mughal," Duke began. "And while our crew was at it, we were to sink and plunder any French ships. We expected to lie in wait for Avery's allies to return to the Caribbean, but instead, we were first sent to England."

Murray continued, "It was there we received a brand new, top-of-the-line ship, the *Adventure Galley*, and we were fitted with an English crew, all hired by Bellomont's investors."

"Newton's men," Captain Vero surmised.

"From the very beginning, Kidd made a series of mistakes. Instead of saluting a Naval yacht anchored at Greenwich, Kidd allowed his American crewmen to insult the royal vessel, resulting in us being fired upon and ten random men detained. Even though the newspapers write that Kidd committed piracy when he took the *Quedagh Merchant* as a prize—"

"Another Mughal ship?"

Murray nodded. "Yes, enflaming repaired relationships between England and India. The only crime Kidd truly committed was breaking the orders he'd been given by our phantom puppet-master."

"This Newton fellow."

"Kidd's orders were clear—scout the Red Sea, the Horn of Africa, and the Island of

Madagascar, and in a year's time, report the comings and goings of pirate activity. For a while, he followed orders, but when he engaged Robert Culliford outside of Madagascar, he sealed his fate."

Hearing the name Culliford twisted Murray's guts. As much as he wanted treasure, he wished also for revenge against the man who killed so many of his friends.

"So it wasn't the pirating of the *Quedagh Merchant*?" Captain Vero asked. "Or the murder of a crewmember? You're saying he lost his life because he attacked an actual pirate? Culliford? That doesn't make any sense."

Murray nodded in agreement. "Newton wanted the element of surprise."

"So he executed the man he'd hired?" Vero asked.

This time, all eyes went to Naro Bon, who explained. "From halfway across the world, Isaac Newton ordered the captain's death because Kidd broke his trust. Kidd also knew too much. You see, despite Britain's bold talk against piracy, Newton has been holding back in dealing with his true enemies, which is why he issued a warrant for the disrespectful and disobedient Kidd. LaGrande was right about this puppet-master, and not only was Newton the one who betrayed Kidd, but he also is planning a major offensive in the days to come."

"A major offensive? England is too preoccupied with its war against France to allocate any naval resources."

"Which is why Newton is creating the Black Fleet."

"The Black Fleet?" Vero scoffed at Bon.

"Newton is seeking pirate crews to do his dirty work. Before we received our commission, Captain Kidd attacked a French ship destined for Montreal. We killed every last man on that ship except for the giant we brought back to Newton. He's the Warden of the Mint, and English gold can buy a lot of secrets."

Captain Vero put his head in his hand for a few minutes and scratched under his extravagant wig. He looked to Willow Thomas and rolled his eyes. Thomas only shrugged. "Explain to me what LaGrande is doing in Canada if his quarrel is with this Newton fellow.

"Before LaGrande goes to war with a sorcerer, he has to prepare himself for battle."

CHAPTER 20

The War of the Grand Alliance was fought between the years 1688 and 1697 and was considered the first global war. It began in England, where control of the British Empire fractionated between two claimants to the vacant throne. When King William emerged as the heir, war broke out throughout Europe as alliances with the Holy Roman Empire, the Dutch Republic, Spain, Savoy, Portugal, and France witnessed mighty empires seeking to establish dominance in Europe and abroad.

America was not spared by the conflict.

Colonists in New France and New England immediately went to war with each other since control of the continent's vast resources was on the line. While the colonial war threatened the French presence in the Great Lakes region, especially Montreal, an international war erupted between Native American tribes.

With the American colonists aligned with the Iroquois Confederacy (Haudenosaunee), France turned to the tribes of the Great Lakes region for alliances, the Huron (Wyandot), the Chippewa (Anishinaabe), and Illinois to defend their interests. These nations, along with other smaller tribes, found themselves crushed in a vice between the mighty Iroquois in the east and the powerful Sioux (Oceti Sakowin) west of the Mississippi. For a decade, it was a war of survival.

Yet in the summer of 1701, peace finally returned to the continent, and commerce again flourished, allowing a man like Dr. Thomas Barrow to visit without notice.

THE ALCHEMIST'S RING

Captain LaGrande was right. The St. Lawrence Riverway is so busy, no one will have time to take notice of us, Thomas Barrow decided as the small sloop neared Montreal. He looked once more at the map, wishing he had Naro Bon to properly read it for him. After leaving LaGrande at Anticosti Island, at the mouth of the St. Lawrence, Barrow traveled several hundred miles as the banks of the river grew tighter by the hour.

Ahead, he saw a wall of green, as if the river somehow ended, but upon closer inspection of the map, he realized his part in the great game would soon begin.

"We're approaching Orlean's Island, Doctor Barrow," Captain Athena McCormack said.

Her smile unnerved him. Thomas Barrow was thirty-five, handsome apart from his required spectacles, well-dressed, and totally terrified in the presence of the hired captain. Since his release from prison six years earlier, he'd seen all manners of horror that stiffened his backbone, and he'd also served diabolical captains, but Captain Athena McCormack of the Flying Sylphs terrified him because she was a woman.

"This is as far as I'll be taking you," she said. "You'll have to get to Montreal all on your own. There are plenty of ships heading upriver. You could go into Quebec City and get a ride the rest of the way."

"Passage has been arranged," Thomas said. "On the northern side of the island, there is a small river along the shore—that is our destination."

"You'll have to get there yourself. I'm not bringing the *Eurydice* into the narrows. Even with our new rigging, there are ships coming and going that might recognize us. If I am discovered, I need room to blast my way out of this channel. Understood? No amount of promises from your sweet talking Captain LaGrande will let me endanger my crew. Agreed?"

It flustered him that a woman gave commands. "We'll be back in less than a week. You have my word. Remember, LaGrande will only pay if you bring us back unharmed."

"My loyalty to LaGrande goes beyond money," McCormack insisted. "Now go fetch your Voodoo priest and be ready to disembark. The sooner he's off my ship, the better."

The Eurydice was the smallest ship amongst the Flying Sylphs, which was why LaGrande had chosen Captain McCormack to take Barrow and Papa Bones back to New France. There were rumors that LaGrande and McCormack were former lovers, but no one dared speak those rumors around McCormack, or especially around her current lover, Captain Wart Jacobs, who stayed with LaGrande back at Anticosti Island.

Could she ever be interested in a man like me after loving LaGrande?

TWO HOURS LATER, Dr. Barrow found himself in a small rowboat as Papa Bones struggled against the current of the St. Lawrence.

Even though Naro Bon was the oldest member of LaGrande's crew, Papa Bones had the longest tenure. The glares from the cook chilled Barrow, who kept his mouth shut as the rowboat angled toward the shore. The crew knew that along with being a culinary master Papa Bones practiced a strange religion that would summon spirits to do his bidding. A man who'd complain about the food would die in his sleep or have a horrible accident— usually attributed to the glare of Papa Bones.

Papa Bones steered the rowboat into the mouth of the Jean LaRose River and slumped forward, exhausted. Barrow allowed him a few moments to rest before suggesting anything.

"According to the map, the plantation should be less than an hour's walk from here,"

"Shall I fetch your bags, sir?" the question followed a diabolical glint in his eyes.

"I'm sorry for making you do this," Thomas said. "It wasn't my idea to involve you."

"LaGrande hatched a good plan, and I will play the part of your servant. Do you really believe he was a French nobleman before he became a pirate?"

Thomas nodded. "I've always been able to tell he was an educated man, but I assumed he was just a skilled liar. He always gave Captain Kidd shrewd council, but a spy? For a secret society? It sounds far-fetched."

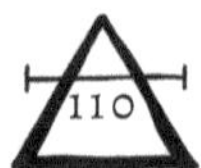

"Yes, but he's been right about everything so far. We kept our mouths shut, and they arrested Captain Kidd—just like he said they would. They brought Kidd to trial in London, and his own Whig supporters turned on him—just like LaGrande said they would. If LaGrande really was a French lord, then why would he risk his life for stories about a treasure unless the stories about the treasure were true?"

I'm more worried about risking my own life. This plan will never work. "If he really was a French lord, and the treasures he told us about are true, what are we doing here in Quebec? It seems…unnecessary."

Despite being a foul man who hated most men, especially doctors, Papa Bones nevertheless worshiped LaGrande and defended him as vigorously as the rest of the crew. "Perhaps we don't don't need this fellow at all. Perhaps LaGrande is testing us. If we manage to abduct this fellow, we'll prove that we are worthy of a share of the treasure."

Thomas pondered the thought. "I never thought of it like that, but if this man we're after used to be friends with LaGrande, then why can't we just ask him nicely to come with us?"

"Quit trying to outthink LaGrande and just follow orders, Doctor."

AN HOUR LATER, the two stood at the stone gate to a large plantation. After failed attempts to get the attention of anyone within, the men lingered outside for a few moments.

"This is the place, isn't it?" Papa Bones asked.

"Right down to the arrangement of farm buildings. Maybe we'll have to take McCormack's idea and secure a ride in town aboard a ship."

"Maybe the real owner is away."

"We're pressed for time the way it is," Barrow said. "Let's find a low place and hop the fence. Your letter will explain the loss of a few horses."

So they walked the perimeter, until the stone fence dipped below the height of a man's head. Papa Bones set the bags on top of the wall, and the two found footholds and climbed up and over

the fence. They walked over an untended field, which had once been set up to grow food to feed a small village. Even the farm buildings held the capacity to grow livestock to feed a small army, yet only a few dozen chickens roamed the yards.

"Hello!" Barrow shouted. "Is anyone home?"

A disheveled man came bursting from the front door, with a musket and a white shirt in his hands. "Not another step!"

"We have letters of introduction," Barrow shouted, "We are friends of the owner."

"I'm the owner of this plantation."

"According to these letters, your name is Abraham Lairet, a farm manager from Mont-de-Marsan. Are you indeed Lairet? "Who are you?"

"I am Doctor Thomas Barrow, a friend of Louis-Armand," Barrow said, waving the letter.

"The Baron is living in Holland. I only manage the farm while he's away. How do I know you are his friends?"

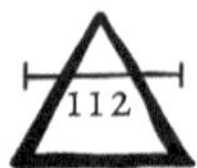

THOMAS HAD BEEN given enough evidence to convince Lairet, and for the next two hours, the men took turns investigating the double-lives of Louis-Armand Guerin as Baron and Captain. Everything Captain LaGrande said about his time in New France was validated by the servant, and in turn, they gave his former servant enough details about the man that both sides were convinced they knew the same man.

"So Baron Lahontan is alive?" Lairet summarized at the conclusion of the tale. "And living in London?"

The letter was a lie, meant to spread disinformation in New France. "Yes, with the War of the Grand Alliance ending, and local aggressions ending here in New France, your Baron thought it best to reveal himself to you. When he learned we were traveling to Montreal, he insisted on sending us with this letter."

"We heard he was killed by English pirates off the coast of Maine," Lairet said. "After nine years, I feared he was dead. I assumed if the government ever arrested him, someone would come to claim the farm. Until then, I kept things running just to keep myself alive."

"Well, we are not here to claim the farm. After a brief rest, we'll continue to Montreal and be on our way with haste."

"Of course, it is an honor to host friends of the Baron. The estate is yours while you are visiting. What do you need?"

A fresh corpse would be helpful, Barrow mused. "I'll need to borrow a team of horses and a carriage," Barrow said.

"And some ink," Papa Bones added, winking mischievously at Barrow.

CHAPTER 21

For the first time in his life, Papa Bones did not feel as if the color of his skin mattered. He found a place upon the hill and watched the inspiring site unfolding in the valley below. Even without Dr. Barrow, he understood well enough what was happening.

The French government presented themselves first, with delegations from King Louis's court, the local governor of New France, and local leaders from Montreal.

Next, a strange silence came over the valley as the enemies presented themselves alongside their French hosts. A delegation from London and from the American colonies represented the English interests in North America. For that matter, Papa Bones also recognized foreigners from the Netherlands, Hessia, Spain, and Portugal watching the ceremony as well, dreaming of ways to make more money.

With the Americans came a coalition of their Indian allies—the Iroquois. The fiercest of the Native American tribes in the east, the Iroquois had fought side-by-side with the British and American leaders to attempt to seize the wealth of the Great Lakes. Prior to the War of the Grand Alliance, the Iroquois had defeated and uprooted countless tribes for their English-speaking partners, bringing chaos and bloodshed to the frontier.

The reason for the peace treaty became clear, for while the delegation of Iroquois stood tall and fearless, they were dwarfed by the rest of the delegation that stood with France.

Even if he hadn't heard the number, Papa Bones's eyes could have counted the remaining delegations in the valleys below, with each nation clustered together in the massive field. Thirty-nine Indian nations stood together in opposition to the Iroquois, forcing the bully to the table four years after England and France ceased hostilities. From what Papa Bones heard, over 1,300 delegates descended upon Montreal to deal with the Iroquois threat.

Following the Iroquois, a coalition of Indians approached, wearing black jackets with red cuffs and bright red pants with colorful blue turquoise both up the sides of their legs and upon their arms and shoulders. A strange mixture of European metals as well as feathers, beads, and ornate necklaces covered the most regal of delegations as they approached the other three players in the drama.

A few feet from where Papa Bones sat, a group of Jesuits were commenting on the arrival. From what LaGrande told them, the Jesuits were rivals but not enemies. They knew about one of the treasures—the one out on the Frontier—and for this reason, LaGrande could come no closer to New France than Anticosti Island or risk being recognized and arrested. Instead of recoiling at his presence, the Jesuits hardly took note of him as he moved closer to join their conversation.

"Who are those fellows?" He softly asked the priests.

"They are the Petun, the People Among the Hills," one of the priests said, as if he understood.

Another priest caught his eyes and explained further, "They are the leaders of the Huron Confederacy. If you were to meet one up close, you'd notice how they tattoo their bodies. While the Petun are a small tribe, they rallied the disjointed nations fleeing west to stop and make a stand against the Iroquois nation. If not for them, we'd be sitting in the newest English colony right now."

"You don't say," Papa Bones raised his eyebrow and shrugged. *See, Dr. Barrow, LaGrande has thought of everything, including the need for ink.*

Even a few hundred yards away, Papa Bones could see the ink upon the cheeks and chins of the ornate men, and all across the valley, their allies whispered upon their approach.

"So the fellow with a felt hat stuffed with feathers, the one holding the big peace pipe—is he the big chief then?"

LaGrande's old friend.

The priest shook his head in disbelief, "Big Chief? The man of whom you speak is the greatest tactician upon the continent and perhaps its greatest man. No Indian has ever possessed greater merit, a finer mind, more valor, prudence or discernment in understanding those with whom he had to deal."

Another priest quickly added, "He's a devout Christian, also. Took the Holy Sacraments when he was a young man and has been a champion of the faith ever since. Upon his lands, the French will build Fort Detroit. He is the rat, Kondiaronk."

They worship him, Papa Bones thought to himself, keeping his reaction private. He felt the hairs on his neck stand on end and looked desperately for a sign of Dr. Barrow. *What have we agreed to do? LaGrande should've sent me to watch Captain Kidd die.*

For a few moments, it felt as if a great spotlight had been aimed upon his spot on the hill, and the great mob sharpened their knives to descend upon him. Papa Bones took a few controlled breaths as he watched the Huron Confederacy join the negotiation table. "Is he the same man known as Gaspar?"

Three of the priests shot him a dirty look, but the fourth grinned. "I would not use that name. Despite his age, Kondiaronk is still a powerful warrior, and that name is reserved only for those who he considers his friends."

"A great warrior, huh?"

"He stood side-by-side with former Governor Frontenac during the war. New France was outmanned by New England 10 to 1, but again and again Kondiaronk stole victory from the aggressors. His Confederacy has brought the Iroquois to their knees. This is a great day for New France."

And the worst day of my life.

I am about to be torn to pieces by an angry mob.

Governor Calliere opened the ceremony with a long oration in French while an English translator echoed his words for those gathered at the stage. Papa Bones only caught bits and phrases, and like many on this high hill, took in only the visual spectacle of it.

"So all of these other tribes have just come to watch the Iroquois lay down their arms?" Papa Bones asked as he saw leaders of the Haudensousaunee perform a condolence ceremony by exchanging gifts with the Huron Confederacy.

"At first," a priest said, "But when they heard both England and France had come to Montreal to sign treaties, and that Kondiaronk represented the Huron, they flooded Montreal to join. If there is to be war in the New World again, England will face a united coalition of Indian tribes west of the Alleghenies. The Illinois, Kickapoo, Menominee, Ho-Chunk, Abenaki, Miami, and even the vile Fox have come to be part of Kondiaronk's treaty. When the Iroquois learned the mighty Anishinaabe nations decided to pledge to France, they had no choice."

"One man's efforts brought this global war to a sudden conclusion," another priest added.

Governor Calliere finished, and Kondiaronk stepped into the vacated place.

To Papa Bones's surprise, the gray-haired statesman opened in English, then spoke to the Iroquois, and then continued his speech in French. During the oration, Kondiaronk shook his fists, and his bright red cuffs brought another level of intensity.

Sensing the inspiration felt in the lower parts of the valley, and watching the pockets of native tribes collapse to get a better spot to hear the man speak, Papa Bones almost rose to join them, but one figure moved opposite of the crowd—the Doctor.

As he passed, he glanced from time to time back to the stage, but for the most part, he watched his toes until he stood beside Papa Bones. *He even walks like a snake.* "What took you so long?"

Doctor Barrow noticed the nearby Jesuit priests and lowered his voice. "After I introduced myself to Gaspar, he pressed me for quite a while, but finally, I was able to have a few moments alone with him to offer him LaGrande's gift."

"Did he accept it?"

"Yes, but he insisted we drink it together, to the health of our shared friend," Barrow said. "So after I left him, I forced myself to retch it all up and I took a tincture of calabar bean to offset the effects, so I think I'd like to just sit here with you for a few hours. Don't let me fall asleep, whatever you do."

"Then you delivered the gift?"

"Delivering a speech to a crowd this size will certainly accelerate a person's heart rate. My guess is that he'll be dead by nightfall."

We should run while we have the chance, Papa Bones thought, but as he watched Kondiaronk unite a continent, he knew why LaGrande sent them.

CHAPTER 22

The mad dog has been let off his leash, Dr. Thomas Barrow thought as he rested on his elbows in the hot sun.

Is it hot or am I dying?

He took careful measure of his own heart rate and rinsed his throat with water three more times as the internal clock inside of his head ticked forward. While Papa Bones was fetching him some water, he had even struck up a conversation with the Jesuit priests, which caused him to fester in the still moments until the Haitian returned.

If the conspiracy is discovered, at least I will not be thrown into a prison. I'll be torn to pieces by the mob surrounding me.

He'd once faced another mob, back at Cambridge, when the entire medical department turned on him, condemning him for his private anatomical studies and illegal procurement of corpses. While Barrow believed he'd committed only clerical mistakes in the registration, the ambitious men in his department rallied against him, resulting in a five year prison sentence. After Barrow served two years, a friend of his uncle, a professor at Cambridge, helped secure his early release. His penance and freedom meant he'd be surgeon on a new warship, the *Adventure Galley*, which would be departing London to hunt pirates in the Caribbean Sea and Indian Ocean.

After the arrest of Captain Kidd, Barrow told the crew that it'd been Isaac Newton who arranged for his position of surgeon to be restored—on a ship he'd built for a specific purpose. The crew of the *Adventure Galley* openly despised Kidd, but they loved their first mate LaGrande, and after helping them to survive Culliford, they left William Kidd to his fate.

"If we can slow down the French along the Mississippi River," LaGrande told the crew two years ago, "then we'll rob King Louis of his most precious gem. To do this, however, I'll need some help. One ship can't do it alone. I need Gaspar."

Still feeling the effects of the Atropa Belladonna mixed with laudanum, Thomas had to steady his heart as he saw a Petun warrior running up the hill toward him.

A single runner means this plan might actually work.

Thomas remained still under the umbrella until the man stopped.

"We need a doctor. Chief Kondiaronk has fallen ill," the young man said loudly and desperately. A wave of concern came over those listening within range, and Barrow mirrored concern.

"Ill?" Thomas said and looked to Papa Bones to help sell the lie. "I just saw him speaking a few hours ago."

"He began coughing and his throat constricted, and then suddenly, he collapsed. Are you a doctor?"

For two days, Barrow had loudly declared his title to everyone he met, including men from the Huron Confederacy. "Yes, yes, of course," Thomas jumped up, grabbing his travel bag and medical satchel. After a few steps, he stopped, "One moment. Pierre, go bring the wagon down to Chief Kondiaronk's tent in case I need certain supplies."

"Of course, Doctor Barrow," Papa Bones said, blinking incredulously at the unfolding and imminent abduction.

I've known brilliant men in my life, but LaGrande is the only genius I've met, Barrow thought as he jogged through the curious crowd. At the stage, lesser chiefs continued to sign the document as raised voices began to sound through the crowd.

I feel like Daniel entering the lion's den, he thought as he passed through a mass of a hundred concerned Huron warriors.

Earlier that morning, he'd met many of them, but he'd met privately with Gaspar, so no one saw the men share the special vintage of wine gifted by Baron Lahontan.

When the effects of the nightshade took hold, the constricted throat made most men mute to any tales. Approaching the tent, the door flap was being held open by one of the black and red leaders of the Huron Confederacy, allowing Barrow to see men, including another doctor, gathered around a bed.

Damn it all. Where did he come from?

"He has a high fever," the other doctor said with panic in his eyes.

"Thomas Barrow," he said, extending his hand for a quick handshake.

"Andreas Alarie," he said. "These men shouted for a doctor, but I'm only a surgeon's assistant. I don't know how to treat him."

I can't have him here. He can't see what we're planning on doing. So Thomas pulled rank. "Don't worry. I was trained at Cambridge in pharmaceutical arts and anatomy. I'll take responsibility for this patient. Before you go, could you go find my slave; he's bringing around my medical wagon, but I'm afraid he might get lost in all of the confusion."

"Of course, Doctor Barrow, of course," Alarie said, withdrawing from the tent.

Okay, I got rid of him. Now I need to get rid of the others.

Thomas earnestly checked Gaspar's vitals, measuring the effects of the poison he'd administered a few hours earlier. He fed the onlookers a healthy dose of negative nonverbals and even bursts of frustrations, barking out requests until both Papa Bones and Alarie returned. At that point, it became easy to remove onlookers from the tent and to close it for privacy.

Lagrande had given them the pretense for privacy.

"I worry he has Dutch Influenza," Barrow said loudly to Alarie. "His fever is aggravating the lining of his lungs, which is why he lost consciousness so quickly. He is drowning on his own fluids."

"The Dutch Influenza?" Alarie asked, losing interest in helping.

"Before I left England, we'd just heard of its sudden and terrible effects. With so many folks attending the signing of the peace treaty, I'm afraid to tell his friends what he has contracted. I will do my best."

"Can he be saved? Kondiaronk is an important man?"

Thomas shook his head. "First, we need to lower the fever. Fetch ice and thick blankets. We'll wrap him to slow the progression."

Alarie nodded and burst into the crowd, barking out the requests. While the Huron men scrambled, Barrow could hear concerned voices. News of an influenza outbreak spread fear through the crowd. He looked over at Papa Bones and nodded confidently. "Is the wagon ready?"

"I pulled it right up to the back of the tent, as you wanted."

"Good, now start hauling in the ice. That will get their attention. Have them clear away from the door, too, for their own good." For effect, Thomas wore the long black gloves, the heavy black apron, and even a face shield to do battle with the Dutch Influenza.

When Alarie returned, Thomas heightened the tension by saying softly. "If this is Dutch Influenza, the whole crowd assembled here is in danger. I can tend to Kondiaronk, but I need your help getting these people to a safe distance."

"I understand." By early evening, all of Barrow's requests had been met, and the tent was lit by lamplight. This added to the tensions in the waiting men, and the sound of weeping began to be heard.

It was then his time upon the stage began. As a boy, Thomas had starred in a production of *Romeo and Juliet,* so he found a bit of perverse pleasure in the quality of his performance. As he'd done every few minutes for the past few hours, he took measurements of Gaspar's vitals.

A cold and drowsy humour…

He took Gaspar's temperature.

No pulse shall keep his native progress…

He took the chief by the wrist, and after shaking his head in frustration, he repositioned to put his finger to the jugular vein.

No warmth, no breath, shall testify thou livest.

He tore away the cold blankets and placed his ear upon Gaspar's chest.

The roses in thy lips and cheeks shall fade
To pale ashes, thy eyes' windows fall.

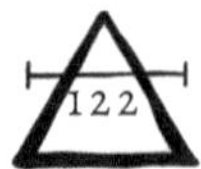

"Oh, no," Barrow said and collapsed upon Gaspar's chest. "No, no, no."

Papa Bones jumped up. "What's wrong?"

A Petun relative rushed over to the bed. The man gasped and draped himself over the body of the fallen chief, cold to the touch and without breath or pulse.

"We must tell the others," Papa Bones said to the teary-eyed warrior beside him. "Together, we must tell them that he is dead."

Holding the Petun man by the shoulders, they rose, and upon emerging from the tent, he altered the plan. For weeks, he'd thought of what he'd say, but now, all he could do is say, "Kondiaronk has died. May flights of angels wing him to his rest."

A groan filled the crowd, and it doubled once the Petun man shared the news in his language. With night upon them, the crowd drifted away in tears.

FINALLY, ONLY THE Petun delegation remained. Two went bursting into the tent to confirm it, causing him to call out, "His body is still infected. It isn't safe for you to touch him."

Papa Bones immediately began to wipe the arms and hands of the men, leading them outside.

"I will have my man clean and prepare his body, but make sure none of the men touch him. It isn't safe." For the better part of an hour, Barrow stood with the men as they grieved. "I am sorry I could not have done more," he insisted to them.

And now for the final act.

As the grieving subsided, Barrow committed to the most dangerous part of the plan. "I must collect my belongings and go."

He stood there, waiting at the door flap for a few minutes, offering one more condolence.

With a dismissive nod, he entered the tent, only to discover both Papa Bones and the body of Kondiaronk already absent.

A moment later, the rear of the tent lifted, and Papa Bones crawled through backwards, dragging the body of a dead man. The skin was pale and the ink fresh, but the doppelganger would likely work, especially after placing the corpse upon the bed and hastily replacing the linen and clothing.

"I'm shaking with fear," Papa Bones admitted softly.

"Stand outside as I wrap the body in linen. Tell them I do it for their own safety, is that understood?"

Thomas quickly wrapped the doppelganger. Once wrapped, the hoax would be complete. Even if a relative demanded to see the body, the poor lighting and tattoos would sell the trick.

Carrying the lantern from the tent left it in complete darkness, and already many of the Petun who'd lingered for hours outside of the tent had gone.

Thomas removed his plague mask and began tossing his large gloves into the fire. "I've wrapped his body for protection from the Dutch Influenza, but you must take all precaution when handling the body that you do not touch his flesh." He and Papa Bones walked around the tent, climbed up in their wagons, and quietly pulled away.

Papa Bones found the path through the valley that led to the main road leading back to Montreal, even though they had no intention of returning to their hotel.

At dawn, the Petun would likely begin preparing a funeral for the legendary chief. If any of them inspected the corpse closely, they'd discover a fifty-nine-year old Mi'kmaq man marked with Petun tattoos. Even so, Barrow wanted to be hours from Montreal and on his way to Beaupre.

Who would risk their life to do such a thing?

Obey my orders. Leave him wrapped.

"Did you bind him well?" Barrow asked. "The antidote should begin working within an hour or two."

"Yes, and I wrapped him in warm blankets to take away his chill," Papa Bones said. "LaGrande had better be right about this treasure of his. I'm beginning to think we should have negotiated better."

Barrow glanced back at the still but living body.

Gaspar...a great and noble friend.

I hope this ruse is worth it in the end.

CHAPTER 23

Louis-Armand Guerin watched the deep pool for several minutes, confirming the location of his prey. Three beautiful trout emerged from the depths. He ignored the discomfort in his cold, wet legs, silenced the sounds of the wilderness surrounding the isolated lake, and dismissed the birds reflecting on the still surface.

He prayed earnestly, even if he didn't know what to ask the Lord.

"Be strong in the Lord, and in the power of his might."
Which one do I choose?

Just like with the three trout, Louis-Armand had three personas he could claim.

The shallow trout? As Baron Lahontan, he'd both saved and destroyed New France. In 1688, he personally unleashed chaos and began a war on the frontier. After maneuvering into a position of command as Captain d'Arcy of the Lahontan marines, he burned French outposts, ignored military orders, and abandoned his post to go with his friend and ally deep into hostile Sioux territory to verify the location of the Philosopher's Stone at a place called the Haunted Valley.

Unable to acquire the treasure, he had antagonized the mighty Seven Council Fires, known to the French as the Sioux, who then went to war and pushed back every fur trader and tribe all the way to the forts of Montreal. He returned to Montreal just in time to save it from the English—becoming a hero and celebrity during the War of the Grand Alliance—but he barely fled the continent before his deeds were discovered by his enemies: the Order of Eos and the Jesuits.

"Put on the whole armour of God, that ye may be able to stand against the wiles of the devil."

The wild trout? Hadn't he earned a wicked life after giving a decade of his life to the role of Baron Lahontan? Living his days as the pirate Gareth LaGrande could be fun and profitable. The Periphery (and the world) all but assumed Baron Lahontan was dead, so it'd be easy to let it remain that way. With Captain Kidd killed by his own master, Gareth LaGrande could take the ship to any of the seven seas and live a free life.

"For we wrestle not against flesh and blood…but against the darkness of this world, against spiritual wickedness in high places."

The large trout? Lurking in the depths, Louis-Armand Guerin waited to fulfill his purpose. He'd joined the Periphery as a young man, and they'd sent him to America to thwart the plans of the Priory of Ormus, the Order of Eos, and even the Society of Jesuits—at his discretion. So at the first opportunity, he went to see if the ancient tales of the *Elixir of Life,* the legendary Philosopher's Stone, were true. Keys to unlocking the larger puzzle, however, appeared during his encounter with Benjamin Horne and the *Quedagh Merchant.* He and Chief Gaspar stood upon the soil of an ancient kingdom ruled by an ancient king but lacked a full understanding of what to do with that knowledge. Now, the answer to his prayers were in reach—if he had the courage to chase after them.

AN HOUR LATER, he emerged from the pool with three trout tied to his belt, and crossed through the rocky stream until he stood at the shore of the Atlantic. He packed up his borrowed gear and threw the three trout over his shoulder as he walked back to the village at Port Menier. He had enjoyed his stay at the island, and the solitude gave him time to think.

"Take unto you the whole armour of God."

He thought of Jimmy Duke, Naro Bon, and Drake Murray returning from England—*the Helmet of Salvation.*

He thought of his sailing master and carpenter waiting on Tortuga Island—*the Shield of Faith*.

He thought of Barrow and Papa Bones's audacious mission to Montreal—*the Breastplate of Righteousness*.

Fate had blown his friends to the four winds, and soon, he'd find out how the leaves settled. *But am I a madman driven by ego? Or am I indeed the Sword of the Spirit?*

His ears caught a foreign sound in the forests of Anticosti Island—the flap of sails. Situated in the middle of the gulf of the St. Lawrence River, Anticosti Island stretched 135 miles from tip to tip and was filled with thick forests, dozens of rivers, and a dangerous population of bears. Yet the rocky shores and submerged bars caused enough shipwrecks to keep the island free of settlements, except for the four homes built by the Joliet family. The Joliet family were allies of the Periphery and victims in the game, with their father vanishing from the face of the earth a short time earlier. With a treasure chest of loot and a weak explanation, Louis-Armand had been their guest for most of the summer.

Will it be doom or good news?

Knowing the approach into the narrow channel of the bay would take a skilled captain, he did not rush returning back to the bay.

When the sails came into view, his heart sank, but just for a moment until he remembered the ship had re-rigged to hide its identity.

Captain Vincent Galloway's thirty-two-gun sloop, *the Meliae*, quietly drifted into the bay, transitioning from sail to oar to navigate the tricky shoals. Behind it, he saw the *Eurydice* following.

They did it. Those two madmen did it.

Now Guerin hastened his pace, if only to keep the Joliet family from becoming alarmed. Jacques Joliet, the eldest son, stood with his three young sons; all four were armed and ready. Deeper in the bay, Nicholas Joliet stood with his rifle also. At the center of the bay, Therese Galiote stood with her mother and husband at the main house.

When they saw Guerin approaching from the woods, they remained steadfast.

"It's okay. They are friends."

While he waited for his own pawns to complete their moves, he wrote a fictitious narrative of a baron and his noble Indian guide and their travels deep into the frontier. *A bluff, a lie, a distraction…for my enemies.*

Why choose Lahontan, LaGrande, or Guerin when I can continue to play the game as all three roles.

Now, as he returned to the Joliet compound where he'd written the tale, boats were being lowered from the two ships.

"Is this a good sign?" Jacques Joliet asked him. "Or is it trouble?"

"Those are the two ships I sent to Montreal, which is a very good sign, but until Captain Jacobs arrives, the future is unsettled."

"The one anchored on the southern end of the island?"

"Yes, we'll need all three ships for this endeavor to succeed. Mrs. Joliet, could I trouble you for a final meal before I depart?" The ship from Montreal meant the acquisition of an important ally. "Unless I'm mistaken, we have a funeral and birth to celebrate today."

When the two rowboats came ashore, Guerin recognized each person. Captain Vincent Galloway and his navigator came on the first boat. Athena McCormack, Dr. Barrow, and Papa Bones came from the *Eurydice* with a familiar fourth figure—Gaspar. *Ah, my old friend lives, which means the real man has died and the fictional man is about to be born.*

With the Joliet men greeting the two rowboats, Guerin took a moment to jog up onto a rocky bluff. In the distance, he saw sails cutting through the thin trees of the southern horizon.

Captain Jacobs has proven his friendship.

The *Phoebe* joined the small fleet in the bay, and Guerin watched it all from the stony peak. Jacobs came ashore with his navigator after having spent the summer hunting and fishing the southern parts of the island. If spooked by warships, Jacobs would have bolted back to the Caribbean.

But he stayed.

My suit of armour is almost complete.

With all three captains assembled in Claire Joliet's home, and no foul play visible, Louis-Armand Guerin descended from his perch to deal with his first crime against humanity. Knowing

members of his crew, as well as three captains from the Flying Sylphs would be present in the main house, he donned the gear befitting his new captaincy.

To distinguish himself from English and British captains, he wore green and gold, from his wide-brimmed hat to his bone-buttoned jacket. For the flash and fashion, his cravat and waist sash were also gold. Knowing he was a short man, his hat held plumes that would have been the envy of a Sioux chieftain. The folds of his jacket concealed a cutlass, rapier, and a leather baldric that held holsters for four flint-lock pistols. His black boots hid two daggers. His favorite accessory was his eye patch with a ruby eye sewn into the fabric where the eyeball should have been.

Although he lost the eyeball to Culliford's blade, he gained the loyalty of the *Adventure Prize*. The other officers, the men he now saw as friends, hid the truth from Kidd when Culliford released him.

Now, pausing at the backdoor, Guerin listened to the dinner happening at the Joliet table, and threw the door open, letting his boots silence the room. Losing his eye gave him a new sense of being a true pirate. *One day I'll get revenge for my eye, and also give the Baron a proper ending—but now I serve more important matters.*

Chief Gaspar sat at the table between Dr. Barrow and Papa Bones, with captains Galloway, MacCormack, and Jacobs on the other bench. The Joliet men sat at the ends of the table.

Guerin walked up to the head of the table and stood beside his host and stared at his old friend. "Behold, Gentlemen, our Belt of Truth. This old native sitting in front of you has spent his life standing in the way of mighty nations to protect his people. The old muskrat, as his enemies called him, was a legend upon the frontier and perhaps the smartest man I've ever known. I once helped him get vengeance upon his enemies, and now, he will return the favor."

"Baron Lahontan?"

"In the flesh and bone, but I've not been Lahontan for many years now. As far as the world knows, the fugitive Louis-Armand de Lom d'Arce, Baron of Lahontan, is hiding somewhere in Holland or England. Since we've parted, I've become Captain Gareth LaGrande, scourge of the seven seas. Now you will repay your promise to me, but not as Kondiaronk, or even Gaspar, who is buried in Montreal. I was born Louis-Armand Guerin, then became Baron Lahontan, and to survive, I became the pirate Gareth LaGrande. So I've written you a new story, a new identity, and a new name. In this new life, you will be Adario."

A living figment of my imagination.

And do I have plans for you!

CHAPTER 24

Gaspar listened as Louis-Armand Guerin tried to convince him of the convoluted logic of the plan. He let the Frenchman go on and on for hours as they sat in front of the Joliet fireplace.

The truth: Baron Lahontan's biographical account would be published shortly in *New Voyages to North America* and chronicle his early days in New France, from his youthful days of hunting and trapping, then to the later years of fighting the Iroquois, and finally, to an account of how fate led him to his position at Mackinac Island.

The opportunity: The role of Adario, the fictionalized sidekick of Baron Lahontan, would serve as a juxtaposition of cultures. Playing the part of the Noble Savage, Adario's philosophical nature would question institutional Christianity, especially the Jesuit Order and their dealings with the Indigenous tribes. "Call it theological revenge," Guerin mused.

The lie: A completely false account of their journey to the Haunted Valley in the heart of Sioux territory was purported. Instead of describing the real Seven Council Fires or the Land of the Blue Woman, a false narrative with false tribes and false rivers would be included in the soon-to-be-published book. "It'll take them decades to figure out where the blue earth is located."

Gaspar added a log to the fire. "I am not angry at you. After all, I no longer have any family or loved ones to watch over. But why did you need to lie about my death? If you'd sent for me, I would have come. Instead, you killed me."

"For the next stage of my plan, I needed a military tactician and also a diplomat. I didn't have time to wait for you to agree, and if anyone saw you leaving in anything other than a coffin, there'd be too many questions asked. Since I've been away, I've learned much more about the legend of the Philosopher's Stone. In fact, I've encountered two men with knowledge about Marakk and Solomon's ring. Do you remember talking about this ring during our visit to Oak Island."

Gaspar nodded.

"When you spoke to me about trusting in the Creator, I didn't understand, but now I do. He put these two men in my path. He connected my right hand and my left hand. At the same time my manuscript is confusing our enemies, we will be stealing the Philosopher's Stone out from under their noses."

Lahontan smiled proudly.

"I honestly never expected to see you again," Gaspar admitted. "But the Lord did see fit to place answers in front of you. Did you discover what your masters will do if you indeed recover the lost stone?"

"I've been back and forth across the globe, yet I haven't had an opportunity to return to Rome yet. I suppose, I must inform them of what I've found in case something goes afoul. Another reason for your abduction is that you know the location of the Haunted Valley. You are an ally and a safeguard in case things go awry. This gives us an advantage over our enemies."

He doesn't know.

"Why do you think Eos searches for these relics?"

"Does it matter? I just need to keep them from acquiring the Philosopher's Stone. The rest, as you like to put it, I'll leave in God's hands."

"So you acquired a ship and a crew, and you plan to obtain the Philosopher's Stone by stealth?"

"A bit convoluted, yes."

He needs to know.

How do I tell him?

"What is it, Gaspar? What do you need to tell me?"

"While you were gone, Montreal heard rumors about the fate of Pierre-Charles LeSueur."

"Oh, yes, of course they did. I know all about LeSueur."

"You do?"

"Yes, the Lord put him on my path. When I still served Captain Kidd, and he still served Isaac Newton, we were given a mission to acquire a French nobleman sailing to the New World. Of course, I had no idea that it was my old nemesis. I only managed to witness him from a distance before a cannon blast almost claimed my life. Captain Kidd delivered him to Isaac Newton, and I can only imagine that poor LeSueur lived out the rest of his life in great discomfort in the Tower of London."

Gaspar shook his head. "When the War of the Grand Alliance ended, LeSueur was released."

"He was? So time will be of the essence. It's unlikely the Sioux will let any Frenchmen anywhere near their lands for years to come, especially now that your Treaty of Montreal has ended Iroquois hostility."

"I did not defeat the Iroquois or the English. I only managed to find a way for my people to survive. The English pressured the proud Iroquois to sign, all the while knowing…"

"Knowing what?"

"LeSueur has beaten you at your own game."

"The Bear Man? That big hairy ogre? How's he beaten me at my own game?"

"After he was released from the English prison, he returned to France, received a new ship, a new crew, and a fully funded mining expedition, and he joined his LeMoyne kin at the mouth of the Mississippi."

"The Mouth of the Mississippi," Lahontan repeated, suddenly realizing where the story was about to lead.

"The news only reached Montreal a short while ago. Apparently, LeSueur traveled up the Mississippi with his team of soldiers and miners, snuck behind the Sioux, who were guarding the edges of their territory far to the east, and in the span of several months, not only built a fort but also managed to mine several tons of copper in the process."

"Copper…that means LeSueur has the Philosopher's Stone?"

Gaspar nodded solemnly. "I know the fort has been destroyed, but the Sioux have not lashed out like they did when you and I journeyed to Mahkato. If LeSueur had stolen something from them, they showed no indication of following him either south into Illinois Territory or east toward the Great Lakes. Their silence is most curious, but the news of LeSueur traveling with the barges certainly means he found *something*, doesn't it?"

"I've waited too long. If I'd known he'd been released from his imprisonment, I wouldn't have...no...you're right. Something smells funny. The man who held him prisoner, my nemesis—Newton—would not have trusted an Eos ally to return the frontier with the ability to betray. Why would he release him?"

"Newton supplied the miners," Gaspar answered. "All he needed was the location, which only you, LeSueur, and I knew. Releasing LeSueur meant a chance at finding the treasure. Killing LeSueur meant the search needed to begin anew—in hostile Sioux territory," Gaspar explained.

"So he either bought LeSueur—which is doubtful—or our old friend assumed he would be able to obtain the prize once it was found. You say LeSueur himself returned with the barges?"

"He would not have returned unless he'd found it," Gaspar surmised.

"If he did find it, what would happen next?"

"Duty would force him to transfer his prize back to his benefactor."

"He couldn't sail a French ship into London. He'd have to return to La Rochelle with it. That is where I'll find my answers, one way or another."

"So your plans for me on the Mississippi River have turned to ash?" Gaspar asked.

Guerin ignored him, pondering the new facts for several moments. "Even though my plans have changed, my uses for you have not. If our enemies learn that the Philosopher's Stone rested at Mahkato, then they certainly will not stop chasing the legend down the dark hole. Since we've parted, I've learned they are after much more than just the stone. Finding the stone was only the first step. You know LeSueur better than I...would he give the Philosopher's Stone to either of our enemies?"

"No."

"Why not?"

"Love. He is a man of honor, who will do everything in his power to protect those he loves."

"His pretty little wife in Montreal?" Guerin scoffed. "She's a LeMoyne."

"No, his true love is the Sioux slave, Wenonah."

"Oh yes," LaGrande muttered. "Then he'll hold me responsible for what happened between them?"

"If he indeed found Wenonah's White Egg at Mahkato, his choice will be to protect her."

"A romantic? I would not have guessed. Well, even if all is lost—which you do not believe is the case—our enemies will discover the Philosopher's Stone is only a single key. Since we've parted, my friend, I've learned that there is more than one way to pick a lock."

CHAPTER 25

With his day finished at the Royal Mint, Isaac Newton prepared for his ride home. He gathered up his belongings, collected a few of his notebooks, and inspected the room a final time before turning to depart.

As Master of the Mint, he was given a carriage to bring him home, which allowed him to transition to his private affairs. The route could be distracting. Much of it followed the northern bank of the Thames, with glimpses of history along the way, such as the London Bridge. After several years of the same three mile journey, it had all become mental wallpaper though, and only the most subtle changes would catch his eye.

Today, he anxiously anticipated a briefing three days in the making. His personal companion, Bernard Clairval, had been gone for two days on errands, and with his pending return home, the next stage of the game would be revealed.

Despite the influx of wealth after his appointment as Warden of the Mint, and two years ago, as Master of the Mint, Newton used his money to buy influence instead of luxury. He rented a three-story apartment with no grand views other than the other side of the street. It was a far cry from his childhood home in Woolsthorpe or his regal residences in Cambridge—but it was situated in the heart of the city.

Almost hidden by a tailor's shop, the front door to his residence was a nine-foot wooden door with a greeting area. He had a small garage behind the greeting area, which he filled with crates from Cambridge since the Royal Mint took care of his transportation. Upon closing the big door, his two servants quickly descend-descended the stairs.

"Mr. Clairval has returned," his housekeeper began. "I've set up his room and given him freshly laundered clothes. Do you have any requests."

"We might be traveling after supper concludes. Find my winter coat and have it ready. Make sure I have a coach ready at eight o'clock that can take me to Westminster."

His cook spoke next, "Supper is almost ready. Do you have any special requests to celebrate the return of Mr. Clairval?"

"Just give him what he asks for; I'm sure he's earned it."

Newton took a few minutes to freshen up and change clothes before he joined Bernard at the large dining room table on the second floor. "How are the arrangements?"

Bernard raised an eyebrow. "Everyone has been briefed, and all their needs have been met. It's strange how the most savage have the simplest needs yet the simple ones are so needy."

"I'm sure you did all that was needed. What about the ships?"

Clairval took a deep breath as if he was about to dive. "All eight ships are ready for their captains. We're not going to be able to launch them all at the same time and have them sail by in formation, but they'll all be ready within the month for departure." He paused as if he needed to answer more but waited to be prompted.

"All of this good news, and yet you seem a tad dour. What have you learned, Bernard?"

"Unsettling news."

"Do tell."

"It was an unsolicited account from our youngest captain, the one out of Nassau."

"Edward Drummond," Newton commented, knowing the names of the eight captains as well as the twenty who had been rejected.

"While meeting with him, I pressed him for tales of the Caribbean just to make small talk. I asked him about the slave trade, the various islands, and the end of hostilities between nations. He wondered if the end of the war meant anything to the Caribbean

pirates, and upon further questioning, he told me about the sinking of a French merchant vessel off the shores of Bermuda. While the crew was rescued, the ship was lost. The ship came from a fort in the newly established territory of Louisiana, and the cargo was well guarded—until it sank to the bottom of the ocean."

"Just say it…"

"It was bearing Pierre-Charles LeSueur."

Newton had to force himself to swallow the bile building in his throat. "Did LeSueur survive?"

"He did, and despite losing the ship and its cargo, he brought several chained prisoners back to France with him."

Back to L'Huillier and the Order of Eos. "So were we betrayed? What about our embedded spies?"

"Mr. Drummond did not witness the sinking of the ship, but he did say the crew claimed there was an explosion, and that the ship sank suddenly."

A bluff? Or is the Philosopher's Stone on the bottom of the Atlantic? "Do you think our prize is at the bottom of the Atlantic?"

"If the tale is true, it is a most unfortunate turn of events."

"However…"

"The prisoners. Why would LeSueur save his prisoners? Knowing what we know, LeSueur would have some explaining to do, especially if he found something. He must have fought his way through the trap we set, and if he did secure the Philosopher's Stone, he would have uncovered the plot against his mission. Bringing prisoners back with him instead of executing them or letting them drown would mean he needed to justify a return. The only reason to return to the frontier is if he didn't find it."

Thank you for trying. "Or…he found something else." *Ponder that for a moment, Bernard.* "Securing the prisoners—the men we sent to steal the treasure—allows the Order of Eos to know of our involvement. It gave LeSueur a bargaining chip to save his life."

Clairval pondered the idea. "What about the possibility that the Philosopher's Stone sank to the depths of the ocean?"

A lock without a key? Could it forestall the End of the World? Would the ticking clock stop ticking? Would God change his mind about his failed creation? "Several years ago, I would have jumped into the Atlantic to search for it. Possessing it meant power over my enemies.

Now…I honestly would like to study it—to understand—but ultimately, it would have met the same fate if I'd managed to acquire it. Destroying it, or in this case, losing it—it frees humanity from a prophesied doom. We are the Defenders of the Elm, the Priory of Ormus, not a bunch of religious zealots like Eos trying to bring about the end of the world."

"How shall we deal with LeSueur?"

"If any of his prisoners were our spies, and he allows them to live, then we will know the truth of what happened and the location." Newton scoffed. "Could he be that foolish? If the Philosopher's Stone is still buried, we no longer need LeSueur to lead us back, do we? The needle in the haystack has been clearly identified. If we can acquire him, we'll get the truth from his lips before we kill him. If not…let our enemies know why he's returning to France, empty handed. They can kill LeSueur for us."

"When you say enemies…do you mean Eos or—

"All of them, Bernard. The Jesuits, Eos, the Periphery…all of them. Let the world know that LeSueur dug a copper mine where there was no copper and returned empty handed."

"And what about the Philosopher's Stone?"

Perhaps it's best that it's at the bottom of the ocean. Now, the location of where it was found is the only thing that matters. "It took the Order of Eos a hundred and thirty years to send Christopher Columbus back to the New World to support their failed colonies. This will distract them, and in the chaos, we will strike. Let them worry about LeSueur and his stone. We have bigger fish to fry, don't we?"

"We certainly do."

These clumsy fools have made their move yet have no plans for what comes next. "First, let's have dinner, and then we will plot the destruction of our old enemies."

CHAPTER 26

Edward Drummond sat alone in the booth. Focused on getting to the bottom of the glass of beer, he'd sat in a booth beside the black-framed windows out of nervousness and paranoia. Having grown up on the sea, the strange motion of the London crowd made him nervous. Out on the ocean, spotting a ship ten miles away caused alarm. Here, folks could sneak up on you in a blink.

"Will that be all, sir?" the waitress asked, clearly enamored by him.

"One more beer and then I'm off." The winter sun had already set, creating a reflection of himself in the window.

At 21, he was still considered a young man, even if the sun and the wind had turned his skin to bronzed leather. It made him laugh to see the tan marks on his cheeks and the pale skin of his jowls and chin, but he didn't want to look like a barbarian, so off the beard went. He wore a simple black suit, nothing outlandish or extravagant to draw attention to himself.

The hunchback had visited him in the morning, reminding him of the meeting with Newton in the evening, but that had left much of the day to nervously consider the meeting. Even though his hotel was in Kensington, he decided to visit friendly streets. If things went sour, he knew where to seek shelter.

When the last beer was finished, Drummond stood and then felt the effects of the alcohol upon his six-foot frame. He wasn't drunk, but his sea legs gave him pause. He paid the bill and walked out into the cold London night.

Even though he didn't fear any soft city folks, he still looked both ways, knowing traps in alleyways had taken down even the mightiest of men.

Once outside, he walked past the Royal Courts of Justice and onto Strand Street, which paralleled the Thames. With gardens and the river on one side and the seat of the British government on the other, Drummond could not help but notice the irony of stone and flora. Like the other governmental building, the new Warr Office was straight-stacked stone.

Drummond could see the upstairs windows emitting light.

What do I have to lose?

He knocked firmly on the door, and a small man answered the doorway. Drummond handed him the invitation, and was quickly let inside.

"I'll take your coat. The others are assembling upstairs."

Oh, I want that on my ship, Drummond thought as soon as he walked into the crowded room. A golden wall with the entire planet painted upon it stood as the interior backdrop for the whole room. *Keep your land; I want to rule all that water.* On the table, a monstrously large twenty-by-eighty foot structure, a mirror of the image allowed those seated around it to visualize the space and size of the empires in their sights.

"It took me a few moments to wrap my brain around it also," one of the men said as he smoked a pipe. The man had a mustache that flipped up into three-inch horns and a goat's beard of equal depth. "George Farrington."

Does he know me? "Edward Drummond," Drummond reciprocated.

"So do you know what's about to happen here?"

"I've got a general idea. It's all been a bit clandestine from the start, but from what the hunchback told me, we all have a common experience and purpose."

"And what is that?"

"Hunting pirates. I know your reputation, Captain Farrington. You were a scourge to the Spanish merchant vessels along the Bay of Honduras."

"Strange that I've never heard of Captain Drummond."

"I'm probably the only man in this room who has yet to be selected as captain."

"Then why are you here?"

"I can provide what none of you other men can provide."

"And what is that?"

"I've served under one of the most wanted men in the world, and I'll never forget his face."

Drummond walked past Captain Farrington and the other captains who looked up at him, and soon he stood at the great golden wall. The continent of Africa loomed large upon the wall, with Europe, especially England, small up near the ceiling. His eyes studied the large island below the horn of Africa.

"So you must be the Scot," another man approached. "Clairval told me there was a wildcard in the mix, and since I know many of these other men, it must be you."

Drummond suddenly wished he had his beard, if only to feel like a seasoned sailor and not some pup. "I've never set foot in Scotland, yet I am the Scotsman. Edward Drummond."

"I'm Roger Silverthorn, and from the looks of it, I've been on the sea as long as you've been alive. As senior captain, I'll be the admiral of this assembled fleet. Don't be a hero, don't get in our way, and all will be made right."

Drummond knew of Silverthorn, too. After meeting with the hunchback, he'd done his own investigation into the other men. "Last I heard, you were raiding Portuguese merchant ships off the coast of Brazil. Our benefactor certainly has patience for his plan to develop."

"I know the name Drummond, yet you've never been to Scotland. How do you reconcile that, young Edward?"

"Second sons. My father was a second son who came to Barbados to oversee sugar cane production. My older brother took to managing the plantation, and I took to the sea. I know what I am doing on a ship."

"We will soon find out," Captain Silverthorn added.

The last man to go out of his way for an introduction had little of the pomposity of the others. Dressed to dazzle, he had a white complexion and a double chin, a sign of wealth and luxury. "Don't let these pompous fools intimidate you, young man. Most of them inherited their wealth and position, but when the cannons fire, we'll see if any of them can command men."

"Will you be commanding men?"

"Me? No. I'm only a cog in the wheel. I helped assemble all of this, though. By trade, I'm a fisherman, although for the past few decades, I've managed my expanding fleets. Woods Rogers."

"Edward Drummond."

"If this goes well, we'll both be governors of Caribbean Islands. Follow orders, and we'll rise past all of this pettiness to take our place in the New World."

A few minutes later, both the hunchback, Clairval, and his master, Newton, walked through the doors and sat at the head of the table. Clairval began with brief introductions for the men gathered together.

Along with Roger Silverthorn and George Farrington, Drummond was introduced to Captain Ned Ireland, Captain Thomas Bennett, Captain Robert Walsh, Black Robin Bellomont, and Captain Richard Cass. All were pirates, in some fashion or another, looking for restoration. With all the money and allure thrown at them, Drummond understood perfectly well why they were there.

When Newton rose from his place to speak, the purpose of the mission became clear. "Gentlemen, six years ago, the *Ganj-i-Sawai* was attacked while on a religious pilgrimage between Bombay and its destination at Mecca. The graphic accounts of the incident notwithstanding, the sovereignty of England was challenged by a fleet of pirates, and the relationship between two powerful empires was threatened. While many of those responsible were brought to justice and hanged, justice has still been withheld, and men like Long Ben Avery still live. Both the Royal Navy and privateers were enlisted, to no avail, to find these men, which I anticipated shortly after the incident.

"Six years ago, I sat down with Mr. Woods Rogers and Captain Roger Silverthorn to discuss what needed to happen to bring these men to justice, and that is why each of you has been brought here today. While we did not know which captains would be sitting here tonight, we did know what would be necessary for victory. All across England, our shipyards began producing state of the line

warships, faster and more powerful. These ships have now been fitted, supplied, and given crews; and now they only wait for their captains to set sail.

"You may be wondering by what authority a college professor commands such a force, but as Mr. Clairval certainly explained, I received my authority a decade ago, long before I associated myself with the British Government. My sovereign title has given me wealth and influence that goes beyond royal houses, but as Master of the Mint and representative of His Majesty, I can assure you, King William is as motivated as I am."

He's talking about the Priory of Ormus. The roots of the Old Elm still produce new growth. Do the others know this?

"For your majesty, the insult is still fresh. For my office, this is a wound that has festered for hundreds of years now. It is a wound fashioned by betrayal, theft, and bloodshed, and if civilization is to continue, we must cut away the rot for healing to begin.

"You are my Black Fleet, and in darkness, without a political flag, you will also be the swift hand of justice. I have chosen two of you for leadership. For Admiral of the Black Fleet, I have selected Roger Silverthorn. For commander of our marine forces, Edward Drummond has been chosen. First, I will have Admiral Silverthorn explain our naval strategy."

Drummond felt a smirk, knowing Newton had given him power the others wanted.

Even while Silverthorn spoke, Drummond could feel the eyes of the other captains upon him, judging him. One-by-one, he stared down each pirate, until they looked away. Finally, his eyes joined the others as Silverthorn positioned each of the eight ships around the island of Madagascar.

Eight warships, with a hundred marines on each, gave him command of 800 men.

And I mean to put them to good use—just not for the purpose Newton imagines.

CHAPTER 27

THE WARR OFFICE, LONDON

1701

Once all the other men were on their way, Newton turned to Edward Drummond, who once again, stood at the golden wall.

Such an imposing figure.

Lesser men will follow him to their deaths.

He's perfect.

"Your briefing was all I could have hoped for," Newton said honestly. "Your service in India with Pitt has made you the perfect man for coastal invasion and siege tactics, but I asked you to stay to discuss other matters, older matters."

The towering Scot did not move from the map. *He's almost as big as Pierre-Charles LeSueur. I should have hired him to kill the traitor. Alas, LeSueur is probably dead already.*

"Come, sit down, Clairval will bring the fine wines," Newton said, turning a chair so the two of them sat together at the end of the table, each near a corner. "Clairval has told me the story, but could you tell me, in your own words, what happened with the mutiny of Captain Gibson?"

Still, no emotion emitted from the young man's face. *Alas, a soldier but not a general. With such perfect physical traits, I must forgive his simplicity.*

Drummond glanced down at the wine glass and began telling his story without a sip. "It seems like a lifetime ago. I was a young junior boatswain, and because of my education and size for my youth, I found myself at the side of Admiral O'Byrne."

"Yes, you joined the crew out of Bermuda in the spring of 1694. I've read the official records of his mutiny. I want to hear it from your perspective."

"There were two ships, the *Charles II* and the *James*. While Captain Humphreys was a decent bloke, Captain Gibson was a buffoon, and Admiral O'Byrne was a coward. We knew if we were to engage the Spanish, these men would bring about our ruin. Long Ben Avery was First Mate on the *Charles*, but he championed the crew in the unfair wages and treatment while we were still in Spain. When we anchored prior to our first battle, Captain Gibson took to drinking, further disgusting the men who knew their lives were on the line. Admiral O'Byrne, however, decided to sleep ashore."

Old slights fester within him. My slights go back centuries. "Prior to the engagement?"

"We were still a few miles from our destination, and when O'Byrne learned there were exotic women in the village, he insisted on disembarking to enjoy himself on shore. When Avery heard of this, he knew it was time to act. He took twenty-five men from the *James*, paddled across at night, and rushed the crew of the *Charles*. The two ships were in constant communication, even though not all men knew of the mutiny."

"So you were aboard the *Charles II*?" Newton asked, enjoying the first-hand account much more than the one he'd already read.

"I was, but the mutiny was bloodless with Admiral O'Byrne on shore. By the time Captain Humphreys discovered the situation, Avery had taken possession of the ship, and when the *James* fired on us, we fled for open sea, as did Humphreys, once he collected the admiral. The Avery I knew was not a bloodthirsty villain, and after bringing us from America to Africa, he left us at the British Fort James in Gambia, where I again found myself resuming service in his Majesty's Navy."

"It is time for us to speak plainly," Newton said. "Officially, I have selected you to lead this expedition because you personally know Long Ben Avery. Both King William and the Grand Mughal want Avery's head on a spike, and I do believe you are the right man to deliver it, but you will have another purpose, in addition to exterminating pirates. Once, the Drummond Clan controlled Scotland, and if you achieve the goal of your mission, I will restore your family to prominence, both in Scotland and here in England."

"What do I need to do?"

"I need you to return something that has been stolen from me," Newton finished.

The world will soon learn the strength of the old Elm remains as strong as ever.

CHAPTER 28

Even though Newton had scheduled himself a day of rest following the meeting with the Black Fleet captains, he found himself at the Royal Mint shortly after lunch. Knowing all of his tasks had been completed for the rest of the week, he listlessly walked through his offices, tidying for the better part of two hours.

When done, he still had no purpose.

The solitude left Newton feeling morose. Catherine tended to the political side of his ploys, and Woods Rogers left ahead of the fleet to prepare the net that would crush any survivors from the coming slaughter. He already missed his collection of captains leading his Black Fleet. All of them had departed for their various ports, and with them, Bernard had also left on new errands.

Now, he just had to wait.

It crossed his mind to drive up to Cambridge, but matters of science no longer filled his thoughts. Cold revenge filled his heart.

I never should have given myself an unscheduled day.

I know better than to waste the time I've been given.

He put his jacket on and stepped out of his office.

The Tower of London was a misshapen hexagram with a private walk inside the outer wall that allowed him to take strolls from time to time. After four years as Warden of the Mint and another year as Master of the Mint, he knew the complex well. Today, after three laps around the grounds, he paused at St.

Thomas's Tower and walked inside, ignoring the guards and soldiers until he stood upon the ramparts overlooking the Thames.

Standing in the open air, he took in the view from atop the wall, scanning the river below, the city along the opposite bank, and the Tower Bridge spanning the Thames. He stood there only a few minutes before a guard stopped beside him.

"I don't see any French ships sailing up the river," he smugly told the guard, who earnestly looked downstream for a moment.

"No, I suppose they wouldn't try it seeing us on duty."

Newton chuckled. "When it is time to serve, all you can do is your duty."

"I would drink to that sentiment, but perhaps not on duty."

"Ah yes, duty." Duty dropped onto his lap a decade earlier. He did not ask for it, nor did he inherit it, although he did inherit Bernard Clairval, who was given to him without condition. Years earlier, a faceless conclave within the Priory of Ormus voted, and he was given the strings of the marionette. He'd almost suffered a nervous breakdown trying to take in all of the knowledge at once, but when he came out of it, he knew what needed to be done.

"Were you here during Thomas More's imprisonment?" Newton asked.

The guard smirked at one of the Tower's most infamous prisoners. "Sir Thomas More was lodged here a few years before I began working here."

"Thomas More believed it was possible to create a Utopia here on earth. Then again, he was a bloody Catholic. Do you believe it is possible to create a paradise on earth?"

"I'm not one to speak on politics or religion."

"I agree, but the concept of a Utopia is that mankind can create a civilization that attains perfection. Why else does God let us linger for so long if not to strive for this? Mankind has already sunken to the depths of depravity, but what if we can build something close to the Garden of Eden once again. Do you believe mankind is capable of such a thing?" Upon becoming the Grand Shepherd of the Priory of Ormus, he'd been given the troves of secret knowledge that all but drove him to madness. In his insanity, he'd even calculated the end of the world. Now, he could only hear the ticking of his Doomsday Clock.

The guard shrugged. "Garden of Eden? It depends upon the management, I suppose."

"The management...yes, I suppose it does." *The Catholic Church wants to subjugate the world with tyranny. The Order of Eos wants to destroy the world and give it back to fallen gods and demons.* "How can we create a *New Atlantis* when we fight with our cousins in France? Do you know why France is our enemy?"

The guard shook his head.

"It all began with a fight over a tree."

"A tree?"

"A great elm tree, a sacred tree to some. It's strange how so many of the world's religions revere the tree as sacred. Genesis tells of two trees, while Norse mythology has Yggdrasil, upon which Odin sacrificed himself for knowledge. While those trees were symbolic, the tree that began our great conflict was quite literal—planted in a field near Gisors."

"In France."

"Yes, but this was long before France existed. This was a time when the Roman Empire still stood and we were still savages upon this island. A tree was planted as a promise."

"What kind of promise?" the guard asked, even though he acted as if he'd rather be any other place than with Newton.

I'm doing this for you and your dull children. "That we could make the world a better place, that we could create a New Atlantis. For eight hundred years this tree grew, and those that planted it became the Normans, populating both England and France. Even though the progress was slow, it was steady progress, and the plan, like the tree, grew strong and bore fruit."

"So what happened?"

"Common cause brought nations together for a Great Crusade. Are you familiar?"

"Of course, we took back the Holy Lands from the Muslims."

"Yes, a purpose like 'taking something back' gave these men clarity. They took back Jerusalem and more, but then the path of destiny reached a fork. Two branches of the same Norman family began to develop different plans for the future. King Henry II of England and King Phillip Augustus of France met at the 800-year-old Elm to discuss their differences. Each had claimed part of a

great prize in the taking of Jerusalem, but just like the Catholic Church broke apart because of differing opinions, so too did this union.

"In giving his answer, the French king sent men, not to assassinate his cousin, but to cut down the tree. The English king had his men defend the Elm."

The guard looked disinterested yet formed a simple question. "So what happened to the tree?"

"That was five hundred years ago, so the tree was always destined to collapse, but the Defenders of Ormus, or the Elm as we call it now, remain," Newton said, patting the man on the shoulder and walking away.

And I am the Grand Shepherd for the Priory of Ormus.

A new tree had been planted, and when Newton was given care of the tree, he became the nineteenth Defender of the Elm. He could only imagine the reason he'd been chosen, but he knew his role would be different. While the others had diligently cared for the new tree in hopes of creating a new paradise around it, he knew the garden could not grow unless he ripped out all the weeds and old growth.

CHAPTER 29

TORTUGA ISLAND

1702

The island of Tortuga was first colonized in 1625 as an establishment for buccaneers in the Caribbean. Located a few miles off the coast of Hispaniola Island, it became a stronghold for buccaneers attacking Spanish colonies.

Originally named Tortuga, or The Turtle, by Christopher Columbus, possession of the island switched from Spanish, to French, and then to English control during the 1600s. In 1640, Fort de Rocher was built by the French to defend the ships in the natural harbor between Tortuga and Haiti from Spanish attacks, resulting in it becoming a pirate haven.

Famed Buccaneers such as Henry Morgan and Francois L'Ollanais used Tortuga as a base for their raids, but after the Spanish destroyed the fort, it became more valuable for its lumber than as a port. By 1697, Spain surrendered ownership of the island to France.

By the spring of 1702, marooned ship carpenter Giovanni Naufragio had seen enough of the island to last a lifetime.

As usual, none of the other men were awake when Naufragio woke, and the small hamlet of half-a-dozen simple homes was silent. He'd built each house himself. The largest building, now the canteen, had been the first structure the crew of the *Adventure Prize* built of unhewn timbers and thatch three years earlier. It stood the first night and lasted through two hurricanes. The other buildings came in order of rank. Quartermaster Manuel Del Torro received the first cut wood structure, replete with an elevated floor, two windows with shutters, a shingled roof, and steps down to the sand. For the next five months, each of the sailors received a home, and finally, the three powder monkeys, who were now men rather than boys, received their homes also. Wooden sidewalks connected the homes, and a dock was built into the lagoon, followed by two fishing boats.

That was the first year—the year Captain Kidd was arrested in Boston.

While Kidd was being taken to England, the summer of 1700, Naufragio busied himself by harnessing the power of the mountain streams to build a small mill that allowed them to cut enough lumber to trade at Port de Paix across the channel. Once a month, one of the sailors and a powder monkey would be chosen to row the goods over to Haiti and sell the lumber, bringing back enough goods and entertainment to last the month. They even had enough lumber on hand to directly sell to pirates or privateers that came looking for the old fort or the port of Captain Morgan.

By the summer of 1701, they were well-to-do businessmen in the small village of a hundred.

Now, Naufragio only had to decide if was would he walk the beach or the mountain path.

Every other day, he would leave his house in the small village of Basse-Terra and walk along the beach trail for ten miles until he reached the hidden alcove. Today was one of those days. Up the slope from where he stood, the wooded mountain allowed a more direct path in the shade of the trees. It had solid footing—but no visibility.

Three years after self-marooning on the island, Naufragio still liked his walks on the beach, which allowed him to view the wildlife, Haiti across the channel, and the sleeping green giant looming to the north. Walking the beach in the morning meant he'd have the shelter of the mountain path in late afternoon.

Midway through his patterned journey, Naufragio reached Mare Rouge, where Huguenot refugees found shelter after France took possession of Haiti. First Mate Gareth LaGrande had purchased their patience, and the religious exiles greeted Naufragio with breakfast each day he passed. The refugees were happy to know a small militia of armed men protected them.

Just before noon, he reached his familiar destination—Trou Basseux. Captain LaGrande had named the place—when the crew was still together—after he told them about his plan.

"Hike up those *farmer pants* and get to it!" LaGrande barked with his devilish grin.

Every other day, Naufragio dropped his trousers at Farmer Pants Pool, wrapped them around his shoulders, and walked out into the pool.

LaGrande had speculated that either a landslide or massive hurricane had created the pool, which was protected from view by the fifty yards of jungle growing upon the fertile soil. A narrow underwater sandbar separated the main pool from a smaller pocket. It was the underwater sandbar that served as a loading dock for the past three years.

Sitting in the pool, waiting for its daily inspection, the 350-ton Mughal ship, the *Quedagh Merchant* rested.

The bane of my existence.

For the past three years, he'd maintained it. Stripped of its three masts and rigging, and camouflaged by jungle brush tied to its side, the ship Captain Kidd renamed *The Adventure Prize* had been all but neutered. Naufragio climbed up the side of the ship to inspect it for rot or damage. Every few weeks, when warranted, the rest of the remaining crew would join him and give the ship a good once over before returning to the lumber mill and village.

Naufragio hated the ship as much now as he did four years ago.

Kidd was wrong about Culliford, and the fool was wrong about the Quedagh Merchant. No wonder he was arrested and sent to London.

LaGrande, however, saw the ship as a miraculous omen, and after filling men with tales of glorious wealth and the supernatural, the crew chose to listen to him and delay their mutiny of Kidd. Patience, LaGrande argued, would allow him to gain information about an enemy and possibly reveal an even greater treasure. First, LaGrande's instincts were proven correct when Kidd was arrested. Then, he explained his plan. Some would go to London to verify what happened to Kidd. Others would accompany LaGrande back to the edges of New France. Naufragio and the rest simply had to wait, just like the treasure would wait. They voted to enact his plan—to the man.

Now, Naufragio did his part to keep the ship seaworthy.

After inspecting the entire ship, he waded back across the sandbar and found the place in the trees where the ship masts were stored. The ship had not shown rot, thanks to his proper maintenance. He leaned against the stumps supporting the masts and caught his breath for a few moments.

Although Naufragio had been born in Naples, he'd spent his whole life upon the sea, so three years on the island of Tortuga left him yearning for a good storm—just to fix something. As the ship's carpenter, he'd experienced the thrills of battle, sinkings, storms, and fires, and in all cases, his ability to improvise and create solutions from thin air made this work so rewarding.

Reassembling the ship was the next challenge that awaited him.

Naufragio began the arduous hike up the mountain slope, knowing the walk back to the village would be more efficient. His only companion for his walk home were the birds that filled the jungle forests.

In one of the forest clearings, his heart suddenly stopped.

Then his feet propelled his body running down the trail as fast as he could.

A large ship had not only entered the canal but had anchored off shore from the village.

CHAPTER 30

TORTUGA ISLAND

1702

Quartermaster Manuel Del Torro set his loaded rifle aside but tucked his pistol in his holster along with his cutlass.

"This could be a trap to lure us out," Del Torro said to the men. "I'll meet them down at the docks, and if they are friendly, I will bend down and tie my shoelaces. If I keep my shoe untied, it's a trap, and you need to run to the hills or these men will flay you alive to get the secrets in your head. Is that understood?"

Even though a single boat rowed to the docks, the ship readied other boats—for either resupply or attack. He looked up and down the shore and even turned around to see if a war party was coming from the north side of the island up and over the mountain.

Where are you, Giovanni?

Giovanni Naufragio was still not back from his trip to the ship, and if the others had been taken prisoner, then the interlopers might strike at the ship first. *Giovanni could be dead, for all I know.*

In curiosity, the villagers had already rushed to the docks. In the days of Captain Morgan, the village hosted hundreds of people who provided services to the pirate ships. Now, few ships bothered to pull into shore without a purpose.

Del Torro recognized the ship—and hoped.

The Flying Sylphs were a fleet of pirate ships based out of Port-au-Prince on the western side of the island. Organized by Captain Vincent Galloway, it behaved like Robin Hood and his merry men—outcasts who robbed from the rich and gave to the poor.

Perverts, more than pirates, he'd once observed of the lot. Gareth LaGrande had once had a swordfight with Galloway, and instead of killing each other, they became close friends. Del Torro had hoped to see the *Meliae,* or even Wart Jacobs' *Phoebe,* or the bitch pirate, Athena McCormack's *Eurydice,* but that was not what he saw. The ship in the bay, *the Daphne,* once belonged to Captain Archibald Vero.

It could all be a ruse, Del Torro told himself as he walked down the path to the docks. Even though Del Torro had a Spanish name, he despised Europeans. He hailed from the original Taino chieftains who lived on the island of Puerto Rico before Columbus, his grandmother had claimed. The Taino ruled the seas around Cuba, the Bahamas, Jamaica, Hispaniola, and Puerto Rico, waging sea battles with the Carib Indians who lived on the smaller islands to the southeast. Although his family gained independence from slavery through fishing, Del Torro's knowledge of the local reefs turned into a career upon the ocean as guide and eventually as a quartermaster. Now, the descendant of Taino chieftains prepared to defend the last island of a once mighty empire.

Using the crowd as a shield, the squatty man wove through the local villagers until he saw the boat tying up to the dock. His grip on the pistol eased when he saw his friend Naro Bon amongst the group of white men.

Bon stuck his finger in his ear and began scratching, and Del Torro knelt down and began to tighten his laces, but just as he tightened his laces, he saw another ship entering the channel.

CHAPTER 31

That night, the officers of the *Adventure Prize* sat around a fire to exchange information. For Master Gunner Benjamin Horne, it was the first time in two years he'd seen the rest of the crew sent off on separate quests. He sat at the little wooden village built by Naufragio, the ship's Italian carpenter, in a primitive structure referred to as the cantina.

"Captain Kidd is dead," Jimmy Duke, the boatswain from Boston, began, explaining how the charges and trial had all been a set-up, culminating in the hanging of their former captain in London.

"But our true enemy has been revealed," Naro Bon added, and the navigator from the Himalayas explained the story about how a Whig minister named Isaac Newton, who first commissioned the *Adventure Galley*, had turned on its American captain when he broke faith.

"LaGrande's theory about a stolen treasure checked out," English boatswain Drake Murray confirmed. "Not only were these secret societies real, but they were also quite active. This Newton fellow has been building a private fleet, and if we're not ready, he's going to steal the Templar treasure before we do."

For agreeing to the plan, the surviving crew all shared Captain Kidd's existing loot, but LaGrande had promised much more. They then spent a few minutes debating the value of the original plan involving the Mississippi River quest against the merits of returning to Madagascar. Horne had no interest in the Philosopher's

Stone, but LaGrande promised him to help find the missing Ark stolen by the Templars centuries earlier.

"So where is LaGrande?" Del Torro asked.

The men returning from Canada explained their part of the story next. LaGrande insisted that his most valuable men stay with the ship—including Benjamin. Now that the plan slowly came back together, Horne dreamed of leaving Tortuga soon.

"We abducted an Indian Chief in Montreal," Papa Bones said bitterly.

"Kondiaronk had information about the treasure," Doctor Barrow explained.

"Hold on," Duke interrupted. "Are we talking about a fellow from India or a Native?"

"A Huron Chieftain from the Great Lakes region," Barrow clarified.

"Are you kidding me?" Duke continued his exasperation. "What the hell information would a Huron Chief have about our treasure? He's a bloody savage."

"Actually," Dr. Barrow defended. "He is one of the most brilliant men I've ever met. He united dozens of tribes against your colonies and knew several languages."

"I don't care how many languages he knows," Duke pressed. "Why did we spend all that time and energy getting a man from Montreal when Newton is preparing to beat us to the punch."

Dr. Barrow had no answers and looked down.

"Where is LaGrande? Why didn't he come back with you, Doctor?"

"He departed on the *Eurydice* for France," Barrow carelessly explained.

"He's after the Philosopher's Stone, stolen by our enemies," Bon added.

A small uproar erupted in the men.

"He left us here so he could chase after the treasure for himself!" Del Torro shouted.

"This wasn't the original pact," Naufragio added.

A good first mate would not allow the men to question a captain, Horne thought in the silence. *While LaGrande was brilliant as Kidd's First*

Mate, he should have found a First Mate before we flew to the winds. All of the other roles are filled except for the man who watches his back.

I must watch his back.

Horne cleared his throat, preparing to do his part to keep the crew together. Horne was the newest of the officers but he'd spent his life upon the sea. Now he needed LaGrande to return or risk being lost on the far side of the world. "I was here when we elected to make Gareth LaGrande our new captain, and I listened as he convinced all of you of a treasure even larger than the one previously offered. While I cannot claim to know what's inside of his mind, I do understand what he seeks."

"Go ahead, Horne, explain it to us," Drake Murray said with a mocking tone.

"Are you familiar with King Solomon?" Horne asked.

"From the Bible?" Del Torro asked. "King Solomon of Israel."

"Yes, the King Solomon from the Bible," Horne placated. "This might surprise some of you, but my native country of Abyssinia is a Christian nation. One of the magi traveled from Aksum to visit the Christ child, and after our Lord and Savior was crucified, we welcomed the Gospels long before the Romans did. Before Christ, we were as devoted, if not more, to the God of Abraham as were the ancient Hebrews. In the time of King Solomon, our great Queen Makeda traveled to ancient Jerusalem to behold the wisdom of the legendary king."

"The Queen of Sheba?" Jimmy Duke asked. "I call bullshit."

"Yes, Abyssinia was once known as Sheba, and when our queen returned, she returned with more than just an heir of Solomon— she returned with secret knowledge."

Drake Murray scoffed, "You're starting to sound like LaGrande."

"Did you ever wonder *why* he spared my life?" Horne asked.

"Because we needed a gunner."

"No, I was spared *before* the Culliford incident. He spared my life because I knew his secret, but before he could act on this knowledge, he had to confirm his friends and enemies. We've all come back to this place because we are friends, but I hope it will be for something greater."

"Money is money," Jimmy Duke said. "More money is more...better."

The rankled crew suddenly enjoyed a laugh. All their greedy eyes looked for more inspiration to wait even longer to become rich.

"When King Solomon first became ruler, he was tasked with building the temple in Jerusalem. When he finished, it was the greatest wonder in the world, rivaled only by the pyramids in Egypt. The cost of building it was high, but not in financial terms. It cost Solomon his soul. To build a Temple worthy of God, and as grand as his father King David dreamed, Solomon was faced with a paradox."

"A pair of what?" Duke chuckled.

"A Gordian Knot, you fool," Murray chided. "A no-win possibility."

Horne had been highly educated in his youth before committing to a life at sea. The men he needed were mostly simpletons, including his own countrymen. "Solomon knew that according to Mosaic Law, the altar of God could only be built of unhewn stone. Solomon's plans were far more elaborate than a great pile of rocks, so he began walking down a path that would eventually lead him to setting aside God for the dark gods of his concubines."

"Is that where the Queen of Sheba comes in?" Del Torro asked.

"No, Solomon first came to Aksum in order to learn secrets from antiquity. My people still knew the stories of the Old World, and she offered him a strategy for building his Temple without breaking the code. She told him of an ancient, foreign Sorcerer King who first learned the dark arts and of how he'd crafted an entire city out of a mountain face with a mystical stone. She had ancient maps of the lands where the Sorcerer King lived, but none of it matched the known world. Solomon quickly became convinced of the veracity of the map and created a great expedition to find the lands.

"Queen Makeda gave him her most trusted adviser, Kokebi, as part of this great expedition. With Phoenician sailors and a coalition of the known-world's greatest minds, Solomon sent a fleet to scour the world looking for the Sorcerer King's magical rock that

could transform any known material. For all the world knew, these men walked off the edge of the earth and vanished. Years later, news came that Solomon had somehow managed to build the temple without the Sorcerer King's magical rock, so Queen Makeda went to Jerusalem—to see for herself what Solomon had done.

"History forgot all about the failed expedition. Twenty years ago in Canada, a young fur-trader found what King Solomon's expedition could not."

"LaGrande's treasure is a magical rock?" Jimmy Duke asked.

The men chuckled. Despite being hard men, they all wanted to believe in the supernatural.

"Solomon did not seek treasure. He sought a tool capable of breaking the paradox. When his men did not return, Solomon began turning to the dark arts himself, and according to the legend, he became as powerful as the original Sorcerer King, but with imperfect knowledge. He crafted a new device to shape matter without human toil."

"How did he accomplish this?" Naro Bon asked.

"He consulted the dark spirits, who witnessed the laying of the foundations of the earth. With his new knowledge, he harnessed a demon, and with stolen knowledge, he created a strange green substance known as the shamir. This is how he learned to command stone."

"LaGrande's treasure is green goo?" Duke restated, seeking smiles.

"Command stone?" Naufragio asked. "Could he also command wood?"

"How did he command stone?" Del Torro asked.

Horne took a deep breath, knowing that he needed to reveal to the crew the big picture. "Solomon created a ring, and the inscriptions upon it contained magical phrases once used to help form our world. With his ring, he built the Temple of Solomon without breaking Mosaic Law. The Temple was made without seam or fissure, making it the world's greatest wonder. When Queen Makeda heard, she traveled to Jerusalem to see for herself, which is where you've heard of her in the Bible. For Solomon's idolatry, God brought ruin and destruction to the Kingdom of Israel, but the secrets of Solomon, and his treasure, remained hidden for almost

two thousand years, until a new religious order from Europe arrived to steal both away."

"The Knights of the Temple of Solomon," Naro Bon said, nodding his head. "The legendary Templar Knights."

"We're going back for the Templar Treasure?" Naufragio asked.

"LaGrande saved my life because I knew the story that sent men like himself into the frontier after the Philosopher's Stone. Together we had several pieces to the old puzzle, but he needed to clarify much of the rest. Even if the Philosopher's Stone is lost to us, we still have two other great treasures to pursue."

Naro Bon nodded in appreciation as the crew relaxed. "LaGrande has been true to his word so far. Yes, he had to alter the first plan, but he promised he'd return soon with answers."

Benjamin Horne stood with the navigator and gave the men a new dream. "LaGrande left me here because I know about these other two treasures. He needs me and I need him. LaGrande will return to us as soon as he can."

"A lowly thief can know where a treasure is locked away," Bon added, "but if it is guarded, or locked in a vault, what good does this knowledge do for a thief? The Huron Chief we met...he took Captain LaGrande to the place where the Sorcerer-King's kingdom once stood—that is why LaGrande had to risk abducting him."

How much does Naro Bon know about these treasures? For now, he seemed like an ally. *I'll give them the same promise LaGrande made to me.* "The treasure I seek is locked in a vault none of you could fathom, and there are two known keys that can unlock it. You wanted to know where Captain LaGrande went? He went to find the man who possesses one of the keys."

CHAPTER 32

L A   R O C H E L L E ,   F R A N C E

D E C E M B E R   1 7 0 3

The port city of La Rochelle had a complicated history, switching hands between English and French control. When tensions rose between the two nations allied for the Great Crusades, it became part of a dowry in 1152 when Henry Plantagenet, later Henry II of England, married Eleanor of Aquitaine, bringing the sea port temporarily under House Plantagenet control. After the Splitting of the Elm at Gisors in 1188, the Knights Templar expanded control of the port, making it their primary port during three centuries of influence.

Legend asserts that Knights Templar Grandmaster Jacques de Molay brought his fleet of 18 ships from Cyprus to La Rochelle as a show of force—but it was too late. When the edict of Friday the 13th, 1307 was executed, and Knights Templar all across Europe were killed or arrested, Grand Master Jacques de Molay found himself arrested by his united Papal and Norman enemies. Although de Molay did not personally escape, rumors grew that the 18 ships vanished, laden with secret treasures and a small army of Templar fugitives.

For the next two centuries, the port saw frequent conflict as the empires of France, Spain, and England filled the strategic bay with blood. From 1568-1572, French Protestants, the Huguenots, declared themselves an independent Reformed Republic. This "state within a state" eroded over the next century until the Wars of Religion in France left them persecuted, exiled, or killed for their beliefs.

THE ALCHEMIST'S RING

At the time of the attack of the *Ganj-i-Sawai* in the Red Sea in 1695, the rejuvenated port of La Rochelle had recently witnessed the departure of Canadian Explorer Robert de La Salle with the commission to establish a French fort at the mouth of the Mississippi River. Although LaSalle had managed to explore the Great Lakes and the newly discovered upper Mississippi River, his 1684 expedition ended in failure and his own death.

Knowing all of this, Louis-Armand Guerin sat on an old rug between two barrels and simply watched. With his head shaved to the scalp, a bandana wrapped around his face to hide his eye, and clothing of a beggar, he sat in anonymity just as he'd done for the better part of a month. Beside him, hidden in a barrel, a dead Englishman with a fresh knife wound kept him company. They'd discovered the assassin also waiting to find and kill LeSueur. In the dead man's pocket, a letter from Master of the English Mint, Isaac Newton. Guerin had fabricated it himself, but Farmer-General Alexander L'Huillier—and a leader of the Order of Eos—would blame Newton.

Regardless of how this ends, our enemies will tear each other apart.

Nearby, the *Loire* waited at the dock, its heavy cargo loaded and its crew of soldiers now accepted. Once its commander—Pierre-Charles LeSueur—arrived, it'd set sail. The thirty-gun warship was destined for the Caribbean, specifically to reinforce the newly established Fort Mobile near the mouth of the Alabama River. Its most important item had yet to be loaded.

Then Guerin saw the monster walking through the crowd.

Even at 46, the bear of a man seemed the most formidable person on the docks, especially with his tall, muscular frame that held almost three hundred pounds. Guerin had met him three separate times over the past two decades: when he took control of Fort Mackinac, at the Battle of Quebec, and a few years earlier when Captain Kidd took him to Newton. Now, servants and low ranking soldiers began to unpack LeSueur's belongings from the carriage.

LeSueur—the world's most wanted man.

Their search for the French explorer had been relatively easy. Instead of hiding, Pierre-Charles LeSueur embraced the spotlight as he visited noblemen and the royal court after his recent "min-

ing" expedition to America. Strangely, despite returning without copper, the royal court and financier Alexander L'Huillier funded a return trip to the Louisiana Colony.

LeSueur must be stopped from returning to America, Guerin decided as he hid. *Kidnapping him will be our secondary concern.*

At a hiding place near the gangway leading to the *Loire*, another beggar emerged from hiding, weaving discreetly through the flow of traffic, stopping twenty yards from where the carriage parked.

Even if Newton or L'Huillier still have spies nearby, they would not see my trap for what it is. None of the crowd understood what was happening, for the busy port saw thousands of passengers loading hundreds of ships, both merchant and warship.

Guerin looked for Captain Galloway's small vanguard of killers who dispersed across the docks. Each wore orange, but he could only spot two of the ten. *Four of us against an ax-wielding maniac. Those are terrible odds.* Although it had taken several years to catch up to the quest for the Philosopher's Stone, Guerin had finally gotten ahead of the Jesuits, Order of Eos, and even Newton's Priory of Ormus. *Now we'll see if my gambit works.*

Gaspar had the honor to spring the trap. The squatty beggar wore gray, simple clothing, and as instructed, found a place just adjacent to the path to the *Loire* so an embedded spy would not be watching.

Finally, the trap was sprung.

"Hey Beanpole!" Gaspar's call went out. "Beanpole, it's me!"

Guerin had made Gaspar practice it a dozen times to get the inflection and tone just right. The giant's head swiveled, sensing danger.

He's weighing the coincidence of it all.

Father Marquette called him that name.

No one in La Rochelle would know to call him by the name.

Guerin grinned at the cruelty of his trap and counted time in his head. Thirty seconds passed, and the well-dressed ogre continued unpacking his belongings for another trip across the Atlantic.

Neither the men helping with the carriage or the crew passing by took any note when the beggar called out and waved in the wrong direction from the intended prey. Nor did they give it much

note when he called out again, a minute later, "BonJean? Paul Bonjean? It's me, your old friend Jacques!"

This time, the new Magistrate of the Alabama colony stepped away from his belongings to follow the voice.

Gaspar turned around to face Pierre-Charles LeSueur.

It took a few moments for LeSueur to recognize his political rival from his days at Fort Mackinac, for he no longer looked like Kondiaronk, the Chieftain of the Huron Confederacy or Gaspar, the village leader of the Petun. The two titans of the fur-trade industry stood fifty-yards from each other for the better part of a minute, and then Gaspar slowly began to walk toward the monolith of confusion.

As Gaspar passed, he whispered the words he'd practiced upon the *Phoebe,* and as soon as they were spoken, LeSueur clutched his pistol and his head spun around, knowing the trap had clamped down around his foot. He looked for only a few seconds, and then followed, lest he lose Gaspar. As he passed the wagon, he spoke something to his men, but none of them followed.

Guerin locked eyes with Gaspar as he neared the hiding place.

He's as terrified as I am.

Still unseen by LeSueur, Guerin looked to his men in orange, who stayed where they were until the signal was given.

Guerin rose from his spot, turned his back to the approaching men, and tipped the barrel over, making sure the lid came loose. *Blame must fall on Newton.* He took the canteen of blood from his side, uncapped it, and opened it at the opening of the barrel. *They must learn LeSueur was taken by force.*

As Gaspar reached him, he joined him, step-for-step, with the canteen trailing blood as they walked.

As LeSueur neared the blood trail, Guerin glanced back, winking at the man who'd almost killed him at Fort Mackinac.

This time I don't have a company of marines to save me, he thought, *and if LeSueur doesn't take the bait, I doubt a shipful of pirates could save me from his wrath.*

CHAPTER 33

Gaspar rose almost as tired as when he'd entered his bed. The sounds of torture filled the night as they anchored off the French coast. Shortly before dawn, Pierre-Charles LeSueur stopped screaming.

Did they kill him?

Gaspar donned his foreign clothing and walked out onto the deck of the ship. Several of the crewmembers had been part of the abduction, and their esteem for him and his successful plan grew in their eyes. *I've gained their respect and lost respect for myself.*

Wart Jacobs, Athena McCormack, and Louis-Armand Guerin stood on deck, their conversation stopped when they saw Gaspar.

"Tough brute," Jacobs admitted. "I see why you held him in such high regard."

"Is LeSueur dead?" Gaspar asked.

"He's alive," Guerin said. "But Athena had a difficult time getting a consistent story out of him. We were just debating what to do."

Gaspar noticed the blood splatter on the white she-devil's forearms and cheek.

"I told you," she said to Guerin. "Another hour or two, I'll get the full story from him."

"Oh, I don't doubt you, darling. You are Hecate incarnate in a torture chamber, but I think it is time we try another tactic. It's time we let Gaspar have a turn with him. On the morrow, we must return home to Tortuga."

"What did he claim?" Gaspar asked.

"Come," Guerin said, putting a hand on Gaspar's shoulder. "Let's catch you up on the details."

Perhaps I should have returned LeSueur to Keoxa's pyre and saved him from all this pain. He doesn't deserve any of this.

At the prow of the anchored ship, Guerin stopped to speak privately with Gaspar. "Do you remember the fellow I introduced you to a few weeks ago? Before LeSueur? The man who collected my fictitious manuscript? The Dutchman?"

The false narrative about our trip to the blue earth.

New Voyages to North America by Louis Armand de Lom d'Arce de Lahontan, in which Adario played the role of the noble savage. During the past year, while they hunted for LeSueur, Gaspar had reviewed the manuscript. He nodded.

"The Dutchman was an agent of the Periphery. He briefed me, and I briefed him. Most of what you learned on the frontier is true. LeSueur was released by Newton, sailed directly to the gulf, and with the help from his brothers-in-law, went up the Mississippi River with a crew of miners. Beyond that, the details are…murky. Before you feel pity for our friend, know this: Pierre-Charles LeSueur is a dead man. Regardless of the status of the Philosopher's Stone, he's been marked for death by Newton and the Priory of Ormus. Understand?"

"No," Gaspar held firm. "I do understand why we need to torture him to get information, but we do not need to kill him. Years ago, when you explained how the Periphery was different from the kings and popes of Europe, I thought we were servants of the same God. I believe you are torturing a righteous man."

"LeSueur? Righteous? Please. He murdered prisoners with his ax!"

"We are at war with forces of darkness. Do you remember when you said that to me? The man you tortured last night was sent by a star to find a sacred object to use in the war against this darkness. What sense is there in killing him?"

"If he gave the Philosopher's Stone to our enemies, then he *is* our enemy. It's that simple."

"Life is never simple," Gaspar added, frustrated. *Am I wrong about LeSueur?* "What else did you learn?"

"At first, much of what he said matches what your spies heard coming out of the frontier about a French ship traveling up the Mississippi," Guerin said. "The Periphery's spies in Europe confirm that he returned earlier in the year, and that he went directly to Farmer-General L'Huillier—an alchemist. The ship he was about to board was an Eos ship, bound for the gulf."

"If he brought them the Philosopher's Stone, why would Eos send him back?" Gaspar asked.

"You're missing my point. If not for us, the Priory's assassin would've killed him. We forestalled the inevitable."

Gaspar shook his head. Yes, Guerin ran the show, but he'd also purposely abducted Gaspar for his counsel. *I must hold firm on this. I must not let him kill LeSueur.* "It doesn't have to be us," Gaspar insisted. "We are supposed to be Godly men."

"I suppose that's why I let Athena do the torturing," Guerin chuckled and then grew solemn in remorse. "I can't honestly release him."

"What did he confess?" Gaspar asked again.

"At first, he told Athena the same story the rest of the world is learning. He reached the fabled land of the Undine, the Land of the Blue Woman that the Sioux call Mahkato, where he spent the better part of a year building Fort L'Huillier and mining the copper. He told tales of buffalo, bitter cold, curious bands of local Sioux, and how they crated tons of blue vitriol."

"The Sioux let him?"

"Apparently, most of them were fighting Etienne Delhut and the Chippewa in the far north, leaving only old men and women behind in their Haunted Valley. When spring came, he left the fort in the hands of some Canadians sent by Delhut and traveled back down the Mississippi River with his cargo, which he loaded into a LeMoyne ship and crossed the Atlantic to La Rochelle, where we found him ready to return. That's the story we've heard from other sources, as well."

"If he is being honest with us, why are you still torturing him?"

Life with pirates had hardened Guerin over the past decade, who laughed beneath a smirking grin. "When Athena McCormack has your balls in one hand and a needle in the other, it's surprising

what comes out of your mouth. LeSueur told another tale last night. Would you like to hear that tale?"

What did you do, LeSueur? Gaspar nodded.

"The Periphery had an agent on the expedition, a carpenter named Penicaut, and when we told LeSueur this detail, the story came apart quickly."

"Have you spoken to this Penicaut?" Gaspar asked.

"No, but it rattled LeSueur. It takes a great deal of concentration with a dozen of Athena's needles in you. LeSueur began making mistakes. He talked about surviving Indian attacks, which changed from Sioux to Fox, and how there had been spies, how there had been a great slaughter after the Philosopher's Stone was discovered, until finally one detail came into clarity. Not only had he found the Philosopher's Stone but he brought it with him."

"He wouldn't do that," Gaspar muttered. *The Wishwee must wield it against the darkness.* "If he gave Eos the Philosopher's Stone, all is lost."

"Don't be so dramatic," Guerin mocked.

"Do you have any proof LeSueur gave the Stone to Eos?" Gaspar asked.

"I don't need proof. I have Athena, and if I give her a few more hours, I'm sure I'll be convinced of his betrayal. Either way, my new plans will spring into action. We'll either be in a race against Eos or in a race against Ormus. I can't afford to wait any longer."

"Then I will get your answers," Gaspar said and walked to the ship's brig.

Pierre-Charles LeSueur was stripped naked, tied to a long, wooden table, and covered with a bloody blanket. Gaspar noticed the scars on his legs from Keoxa's pyre. He walked around to the front of the table and stood in front of him so he could speak to him. He pushed aside the instruments of torture, causing Guerin to step to the doorway. "Don't worry about me, Guerin. I'll get your answers."

Guerin rolled his eyes and stepped away.

Gaspar moved closer to LeSueur's ear. "Do you remember the day the Peacemakers came to speak to you? This ancient group of tribeless prophets came to me first, asking if the stars had sent a warrior to fight the evil spirit No Soul. At first, I couldn't believe a vile man such as yourself was sent by God, but then I saw the truth about your destiny. I hoped you were the Wishwee."

LeSueur's weary eyelids opened, one swollen with a red prick mark upon it. Behind Gaspar, a table with a hundred needles and several knives of various fashions waited to be used. He picked up a simple knife.

"I'm the only one who can save your life," Gaspar said. "And I don't even know if you deserve to live. The she-devil will return soon to get the truth from your lips. You will not survive this confession. I know the secrets of the Peacemakers. I know the story of the White Egg and Wishwee. I've been to the Haunted Valley and have seen the blue earth. I know about the evil spirit known as No Soul and the Wintermaker. What happened to the Philosopher's Stone?"

LeSueur closed his eyes. "I had to protect Wenonah. I made a promise."

"Where is the stone?"

"It was alive. We found it at the bottom of the excavation. When Orell touched it, it burned the flesh from his hands. A spirit lived inside of the stone. It moved inside the white rock like pulsing blood. The unholy heat it gave off filled the space." LeSueur groaned. "It was evil. Gaspar, how could I leave it there with Wenonah?"

"What did you do with it?"

"I was surrounded by enemies, and even well-intentioned allies, and it became obvious what I had to do. You made me promise. I did what you wanted."

Fight for the future rather than living for the moment. I nursed his wounds and then sent him back to our enemies. "And?"

"I waited until we were off the coast of Bermuda, in open water, and then I sank the ship. I made sure the damned thing rests at the bottom of the ocean."

With the knife in hand, Gaspar stood inches from LeSueur's face, tapping his nose with the flat of the blade. "Does Eos know it rests in the sea?"

"Yes, I told Alexander L'Huillier the same truth I just told you."

Why did he hold back? Why did he let himself be tortured? "Then why did they send you back?"

LeSueur hesitated. "The Sioux still control the region, and they needed me to return to help secure it."

A half-hearted lie. "But the stone is lost."

LeSueur moaned and sobbed lightly. "Just kill me. My wife has already slit my throat."

"Why do you say that?"

"Marguerite's undone everything, and I have nowhere else to turn. It's only a matter of time before my wife's cousins learn of my betrayal."

"Undone what? The location of the Stone is no longer a secret."

"She gave Eos the *Al Marakk Map* while I was away. The Stone is not the only thing Eos is searching for."

Marakk…

The Wintermaker.

He knows. He's telling the truth. We need him. Gaspar cut the bonds from LeSueur's feet. Then walked back up front to cut his hands free. As soon as the final bond was cut, LeSueur's hand clamped onto Gaspar's arm like a vise.

The giant had him.

CHAPTER 34

After being dead for three days, Pierre-Charles LeSueur returned to the land of the living, beaten and bruised, especially his battered hands and knuckles. Stripped down to his underclothes and bloodied, he walked back to the docks as locals along the coast gasped and gaped.

This is my chance.

I could run to the hills and never look back.

In his gut, Pierre-Charles LeSueur knew his days were numbered. Gaspar gave him another life, even if he served as bait for a larger trap. The plot also gave him a final chance at revenge.

I've lost everything—at least I'll get my revenge.

Glancing at the docks to confirm Joseph LeMoyne and the *Loire* had left port, LeSueur walked right up to the port authorities. "My name is Pierre-Charles LeSueur, and I just killed three of my abductors."

The lie worked.

The port sergeant on duty immediately brought him in from the streets and set him down in a chair at his office. For the next hour, the office buzzed with orders and excitement about what had happened to him. The apologetic port sergeant explained, "We suspected foul play when you vanished prior to departing. We found a dead Englishman with incriminating evidence."

Yes, Lahontan effectively put the blame on Newton. I'll sell it further. "Yes, when those Englishmen grabbed me, I stuck one of them with a knife, but then they threw a bag over my head and got me off my feet. They brought me to a building down by the point where they kept me tied and tortured me for the past few days. I finally broke free of my bonds and strangled one of them before the others showed up. I beat one of them to death with my bare hands, and turned the knife on the other. I could take you to them, if you want."

In truth, he had pulled Gaspar in for an embrace—his only ally left in the world. After Gaspar informed the others about the new details about the Philosopher's Stone being at the bottom of the sea, and the Al Marakk map being in the possession of Eos, LeSueur thought Baron Lahontan might kill him on the spot. The pirates seemed willing. Instead of being impulsive, Lahontan listened as wise old Gaspar came up with a plan to test LeSueur's truthfulness.

Lies built upon lies built upon lies.

Even now, the port sergeant had to confirm another of Gaspar's lies. "You'll stay here with me, for now, and I'll let my men confirm the details. Your servants came to me when you didn't board the *Loire*, and I let them know about the dead Englishman."

Good. Lahontan's plan worked … Now we'll see if Gaspar's plan will work. LeSueur looked down. "Could I get a towel to wipe off some of the blood?"

The port sergeant quickly obliged.

While he waited, he sorted through what Lahontan told him about the Priory assassin. *It was only a matter of time before Newton came for me. Gaspar saved my life again. I owe him this.* "I don't suppose my belongings are nearby?"

"We didn't know what to think, so everyone agreed to load them up and send them to Fort Maurepas, where your family could sort out the details."

"Do they think I'm dead?"

"I informed the captain of the *Loire* about your sudden disappearance, but we had no details other than you missed the launch. The servants lingered for the next two days, and we notified the authorities about our suspicions.

Good, then LeMoyne will believe I was attacked by Newton's men. This might just work. "I don't suppose you know when another ship sets sail for the Gulf?"

"I do, in fact," the port sergeant said with a mischievous grin. "I was just talking to a friend of mine about the *Pelican* girls."

"I don't know what that means," LeSueur admitted.

"The *Pelican* is a ship docked across the harbor at Rochefort. The chancellor is sending twenty virtuous young women to the new Louisiana colony. I'm sure a nobleman such as yourself could do worse. But first, let's sort out this mess. Sit down, and we'll see to matters."

Yes, let's sort out this mess. All of LeSueur's plans had come undone in the past two years. Newton knew about his betrayal, and Eos sent him back to certain death. Marguerite and the LeMoynes would learn once they arrived in the Louisiana Colony. *I likely would have been executed in front of my own children while Marguerite and her cousins watched.*

"How soon until the *Pelican* sets sail?"

"It was supposed to follow the *Loire,* but I've heard there is an issue with the hull, so the chancellor is trying to keep the women chaste until the ship is ready. If you want quicker passage, I could—"

"No," LeSueur interrupted. *More time will allow Lahontan time to properly set the trap.* "If the *Pelican* is sailing to the Louisiana Colony, I'll book passage on it. Is there any way I can send news ahead so my relatives know my plans?"

"Of course," the port sergeant answered.

I must do this for Wenonah, even if I am killed in the process.

CHAPTER 35

For the better part of two centuries, the territory of New Spain expanded since Christopher Columbus first arrived in the Caribbean. Possessing Florida, the lands west of the Mississippi River, Mexico, and Central America, Spain shared control of South America with Portugal. The heart of its financial empire was control of the largest island in the Caribbean, Cuba.

With wealth pouring out of the Americas and back to Europe, colonial Cuba found itself a target of other nations fighting for control of the new world. Throughout the 1600s, the French, Dutch, and English invaded the island, resulting in the building of the fortress of Castillo de los Tres Reyes Magos del Morro, which allowed Havana to grow into one of the largest cities in the western hemisphere. With the War of Grand Alliance over, ships from all nations, including the French *Pelican,* used Havana as a key port.

From the port in Havana, Louis-Armand Guerin watched as the tall masts of the *Pelican* drifted into the channel to the ringing of bells. Two small escort ships accompanied it. Suddenly, the city went from preparing for defense to preparing for trade as the French flag announced the nature of the visit.

Guerin prickled with anxiety as the big frigate passed by the protective walls that guarded the port built along the western shore. Men, women, and children ran down to the docks to await the travelers from the ship. Months earlier, it had been decided Pierre-Charles LeSueur would die in Havana, with or without an assassin.

So Guerin sat in the shade of the little tavern deck as the kitchen staff prepared for the rush of travelers. He'd been waiting in Havana knowing the true predator waited in the Cuban shadows. The rest of Guerin's wolves followed the big freighter since it reached Cape Haitien in Hispaniola.

The *Pelican* was unlike any other ship that had visited the port of Havana in recent weeks. Four priests, followed by four nuns, led a colorful procession of twenty young women dressed formally from toe to wide-brimmed hat. In the heat of summer, the scene was almost ridiculous, leaving the Cubans as stunned as he was.

"Bienville's brothel," someone near him referenced the rumor that the LeMoyne brothers requested maidens for the Canadians that were building the new colony. The Catholic escort given to the young women indicated that they were far from being prostitutes or orphaned peasants.

Guerin kept his good eye on the docks. If LeSueur walked off the ship on his own accord, Guerin's wolves would kill him. If LeSueur was carried off the ship, Gaspar's trap continued as planned.

Next came a parade of seventy-five soldiers, laborers, and even a few families of women and children. A new conflict, the War of Spanish Succession, or Queen Anne's War as it was being called in the colonies, had delayed supplies and reinforcements to the French colonies of Louisiana and Alabama, making the arrival of the *Pelican* a welcome sight. *Where is Magistrate LeSueur?*

The two escort ships were just tying up when four men carried out a passenger on a stretcher. Two men could handle a normal stretcher. Four men meant they carried a passenger of some size.

Guerin remained motionless as he watched those watching the *Pelican.*

LeSueur's going through with this.

Is he actually telling the truth?

No sooner did the body get brought past the dock than a stranger emerged to take command. *The Eos assassin?* The large body was quickly transported to a nearby inn, with a small entourage staying with the body. When it was brought inside, Guerin smiled and waited.

Conveniently, an English doctor happened to be nearby, slipping into the inn moments after LeSueur was brought inside. While the *Pelican* girls became the talk of the town, another rumor quickly spread about the new magistrate of Alabama falling sick with yellow fever. Guerin heard the news himself, albeit from half a room away, as Dr. Thomas Barrow arrived in the tavern to tell another man, quite loudly, about Magistrate LeSueur's declining health.

The arrival of Barrow meant the bait had been taken.

Guerin sipped his coconut beverage and prayed for restraint.

AN HOUR LATER, Naro Bon entered the inn and confirmed the story that the *Pelican* would be remaining in port as they waited for the health of the colony's new magistrate to improve.

A few minutes later, Jimmy Duke rushed over to Guerin's favorite spot in the tavern to view the harbor and said loudly, "Magistrate LeSueur has taken a turn for the worse."

Let's see what we've caught in our net.

Outside of the hotel, more of Guerin's men waited, but he walked right past them, with Jimmy Duke peeling off to provide security. He marched up the stairs to find Dr. Barrow pacing outside of a closed door. "The fool might have killed him," Duke grumbled.

Stepping inside the room, the scent of LeSueur's disease filled the air, in this case, a mixture of urine and lemon. The source of the odor could be seen upon LeSueur's body, tainting his skin yellow, although, only a superficial coating and not the jaundice caused by a failed liver. LeSueur turned to the doorway, a red circle upon his forehead with a trickle of blood coming down the side of his nose.

"Don't worry, he's alive. I just knocked him unconscious." LeSueur, dressed in a white linen tunic, sat upon the chest of the Eos assassin, Bartolome St. Clair, whose nose had been smashed, bending to one side, still oozing blood that covered his battered face. "Help me tie him up."

Guerin rushed over to the side of the ogre, and together, they turned over the unconscious assassin and tied his hands and feet.

It was then that Guerin again noticed how St. Clair's fingernails had been removed in prior torture. *He's not going to spill secrets.*

"Barrow," Guerin called out, prompting the doctor to quickly step inside of the room. "I want the coffin brought up in plain sight and for you to prepare a final will and testament for LeSueur to sign. He's only got a few hours to live."

Barrow smiled as he helped prepare for his second abduction. As he ran off, Gaspar came up the steps to join them inside of the room. "Your ridiculous plan seems to have worked." Gaspar had discreetly traveled aboard the *Pelican* for the final stage of the plan—a feigned bout of Yellow Fever contracted back on Cap-Haitien. He also made sure LeSueur didn't try to escape his fate.

"Charlie Johnson," Guerin said, nodding to LeSueur. "We can't call a dead man by his given name. We need a new identity for him, one that makes people think of an English commoner rather than a French Aristocrat, so in the name of the Father, the Son, and the Holy Ghost, I baptize you Charlie Johnson." Guerin made the shape of the cross upon LeSueur's forehead. "Do you bear witness to this baptism of blood, Adario?"

"I do," Gaspar said and shook his head.

Then the three men all turned to face Bartolome St. Clair.

CHAPTER 36

Well, the gang's all back together again," Louis-Armand Guerin declared to the other three. "I had hoped it would be you waiting here in Cuba, but I can hardly believe our good fortune. What's the saying? If you want a job done right, do it yourself."

LeSueur finished tying up St. Clair and slid away from their prisoner. He glared at Guerin for a moment before rummaging through St. Clair's apartment for fresh clothing and water to wash the yellow film from his body.

"Ironically," Louis-Armand Guerin continued. "By showing up to kill LeSueur yourself, you've granted him a new life. Funny, funny."

Guerin made himself comfortable on a chair beside the bound prisoner. "I couldn't be certain if LeSueur's preposterous story could be believed, so we snatched Charlie at the Port of La Rochelle. Granted, we thought we were going to torture him to death to find out what happened to the Philosopher's Stone, but the more we learned about his encounters with Isaac Newton's Priory, the *Al Marakk* map, and his most recent meeting with Alexander L'Huillier, the truth slowly began to emerge from all the lies. Do you remember Chief Gaspar of the Petun?"

St. Clair winced through his pain and predicament, the only sign of recognition.

"Of course you know him," Guerin teased. "You made it your business to know everyone that came and went from Montreal, especially your enemies, but being an agent of Eos, perhaps you overlooked him because he was a native. Without Gaspar's help, I might never have figured out your personal interest in killing LeSueur. Remind me of your connection, Gaspar."

"Father Marquette," Gaspar said with hate in his eyes.

"Oh, yes, the man who washed away the sins of Kondiaronk and baptized a new Christian named Gaspar. The Order of Eos sent you to kill Father Marquette and steal back the *Al Marakk* map, which they'd obviously been using to locate the legendary lost kingdom where the Philosopher's Stone could be found. Poisoned wine?"

LeSueur hesitated . He'd been a boy when his mentor died. "His torment lasted for days."

"Unfortunately, Bartolome, your torment won't last for days. We can't afford to bring you onto our ship for more fun. The plan is to put you inside of the coffin for Magistrate LeSueur. You've wronged all three of us at one point or another," Guerin leaned down closer to his face. "When did you learn that I was an agent of the Periphery?"

"Slit my throat and be done with it," St. Clair responded.

Guerin laughed. "You're fierce, but I once spit out my own eyeball at my torturer. Alas, I don't have time for games. I remember a dinner party—a May Day party—when I first arrived in New France, and I bet you had your suspicions then. My treachery on the frontier was likely learned when I sabotaged forts and all but handed the Great Lakes back to the Sioux. I shouldn't have lingered as long as I did. I'd not only located the lost kingdom but I'd also thwarted French efforts to return for years."

Behind them, LeSueur redressed in St. Clair's own clothes, tearing off sleeves and stretching pants over his tree trunk legs.

"I visited the Joliet family to offer my condolences and financial support from the Periphery. In the end, you were determined to kill anyone associated with Father Marquette. When did you finally learn that Pierre-Charles LeSueur was the young donnes assisting Father Marquette?"

St. Clair sighed, his eyes closed, resigned to his fate.

"Charlie? Do you want to answer this one? This little tidbit likely saved your life."

"Just let me kill him and be done with it," LeSueur grumbled.

Guerin gestured back and forth between the two. "I just need a minute for all of this to sink in." He snapped his fingers. "Yes, that's right. Marguerite. Everyone in Montreal knew of her beauty, but it turns out she was a Delilah. Sorry, Charlie. That's a bit harsh, isn't it? She likely didn't mean anything. After all, her cousins were all powerful members in the Order of Eos. Etienne Delhut was a friend, a colleague of her husband. When the map surfaced, you knew that LeSueur was the lost donnes who'd kept and hidden the map all those years, and if he hid that truth from the Order of Eos, that likely made him a Jesuit spy. While everyone else in Eos made plans for LeSueur to return to the frontier to continue his fine work, you needed to finish the mission given to you years earlier. Tell St. Clair the truth, Charlie."

"I'm not a spy for anyone," LeSueur shrugged. "Father Marquette was a decent man, and I swore to get revenge against the man who killed him." LeSueur's eyes softened for a moment as he looked to both Gaspar and Guerin, who not only spared his life but had given him his chance at vengeance.

A knock came on the door.

Gaspar armed himself and answered. "It's LeSueur's coffin."

"*Your* coffin, Monsieur St. Clair," Guerin said, standing up and walking to the far side of the room to clear space. Dr. Barrow, Jimmy Duke, Papa Bones, and Benjamin Horne wrestled the wooden box through the doorway. "It's time."

Gaspar stepped forward. "Before we let LeSueur kill you, do you have any last words?"

Guerin rolled his eyes, but to his surprise, St. Clair cleared his throat to speak.

CHAPTER 37

Captain Patrick Dalziel pondered his options as he studied the burning island. *What has happened here?* "Prepare for battle," he shouted as he continued to check the horizon for any ships coming or going.

The crew of the *Salome* immediately stopped gazing at the pillar of smoke and went to their duty stations.

Once he satisfied himself that they were alone on the sea, he put his looking glass down and spun the navigational wheel. "Get the canons ready. We're going to swing around the point and surprise them."

Did a volcano erupt?

Why are there no ships in the area?

The sailing routes to the New World were defined by trade winds and oceanic currents. To reach the Caribbean Sea and the Americas, the fastest route was not the most direct route. Ships from England, France, or Spain sailed south, past the Straits of Gibraltar until they reached the Canary Islands, where the prevailing winds pushed storms and ships to the west. The Portuguese island of Madeira was the first island off the coast of Africa to serve as a landmark for sailors. The little island, whose export products included sugar and wine, was normally passed by in favor of the Canary Islands, but Captain Dalziel chose a route less traveled.

Even though his ship had seen plenty of battle, his new crew had no clue that their captain was one of the most wanted men on earth after the attack on the *Ganj-i-Sawai*. Dalziel's former crew had taken the Emperor's frigate.

Bloody hell. The port of Funchal has been destroyed.

The small settlement of several dozen homes and buildings burned up and down the slope, including the beautiful plantation nestled in the hills. The harbor itself looked like the back of a porcupine, with only masts sticking up out of the water from the sunken ships.

Not a natural disaster—an attack.

At the approach of the harbor, small boats waved brightly colored flags, indicating submerged wrecks.

As the *Salome* approached the harbor, Dalziel's first mate stood at his shoulder. Since the rape of the *Ganj-i-Sawai*, Dalziel had taken a new ship, found a new first mate, and murdered any eyewitnesses to the incident. Two empires wanted him dead, so Dalziel cut ties and vanished for a decade before returning back to the Atlantic. *My new crew has no idea what this is about.*

Fifteen years earlier, when Dalziel had first sailed from Scotland to the remote island headquarters of the Order of Eos, his heart swelled with pride at the beauty of the port. Madeira existed between the two Eos colonies, America and Madagascar, and served as a hub for information and transportation between two oceans.

"Sir, a survivor," his first mate called out.

Dalziel barked out orders to his crew to slow the ship's approach. He gave the wheel to his navigator and rushed down to the deck as they approached a local boat.

"What happened?" Dalziel asked.

A young man, stained with soot and blood, looked up from his rowboat. "Three days ago, a fleet of eight warships fell upon us, bearing no flag of origin except for a black flag with a cross of bones upon it."

Veritas Caput…the truth about the Head. As a soldier for the Order of Eos, Dalziel had served Thomas Tew from their secret kingdom on Madagascar. If not for an impulsive, violent nature, Dalziel might've been an Eos priest rather than a pirate. He knew what Thomas Tew searched for in Africa, just as he knew what the LeMoyne family searched for on the American continent.

"A cross of bones," Dalziel repeated.

The young man nodded. "First, they fired on each ship in the harbor, targeting them one by one, as if practicing. Then they turned their guns to the docks, blasting it to oblivion. Not once did they make any demands. Then a force of about a hundred men from each ship disembarked, but instead of butchering the population and taking slaves, they circled the Lady of the Mountain," he said, pointing to the steep mountain overlooking the entire bay.

They targeted Alvorez. His looking glass went to the beautiful estate built atop the hill, which now burned, dark and lifeless. Years ago, he'd been a guest. Here at Madeira, the Grandmaster for the Order of Eos, Marco Alvorez, orchestrated the ancient purpose for the Men of the Dawn. Instead of showing patience, Alvorez sought personal glory by finishing the quest in a single generation. His arrogance brought far too much attention to Eos and ultimately, cost him his life. Their new enemy taunted them with their new flag. "Crossbones, but no skull?"

"I've never seen it before."

Dalziel knew his symbolism. A black flag means surrender. A red flag means no quarter. In Templar history, the skull and crossbones had existed for centuries. For enemies caught upon the sea, it was a barbarian's way of bellowing "DEATH!" at the top of his lungs. But to those versed in Eos lore, it represented Mimir's Skull, which whispered the secrets of the universe to Odin, which he recorded upon a black stone. For generations, Eos had scoured the world for these ancient treasures and locations.

When the Catholic Church tried to exterminate the Templars on Friday 13th, 1307, they did so because they'd discovered the truth behind the Templar Knights. Misinformation led the Church to the conclusion that the head belonged to a god called Baphomet, and the imprisoned Templars being tortured spun lies and truth into their confessions. Ultimately, the Catholic Church tried to kill them to the last man. *If it had been the Catholics, the symbolism would be a red flag.*

This flag is black.

Surrender what?

"What happened to Governor Alvorez?"

"They killed him. They killed everyone. At first, they rushed forward like madmen, with no one in their path, and all but van-

ished for three hours, but then we saw platoons advancing up the mountain. They killed Governor Alvorez and his entire family, removing their heads and taking them to adorn their ships."

Alvorez kept no treasure on the island because of its vulnerability. During the Splitting of the Elm at Gisors, the Templars kept all the stolen treasures, which they safeguarded until they could be placed in secure vaults out of reach from the Catholic Church and its allies. The Priory of Ormus knew all the legends and lore but came away from the schism without the treasures.

Ormus did this?

After all these years?

"The hundred men you spoke of…they…circled the mountain? Explain," Dalziel insisted.

"While the seven warships blasted away at the town, the single ship put its men ashore but they didn't engage in the obvious fight. Instead, they practiced maneuvers against an invisible enemy. Hours went by before they engaged Governor Alvorez's estate."

"Practiced," Dalziel muttered. "How long did they stay?"

"After killing Alvorez and his family, they came down to the port and killed anyone they could find. They didn't even steal provisions, and a day after they arrived, they left."

"Which direction did they sail?"

"South."

To Africa. Ormus cut off the head of the snake and now they are coming for the old treasures. One pirate ship could not stop a fleet of eight warships.

And this man has seen my face.

"Kill him," Captain Dalziel said, pointing to the survivor.

His men dispassionately killed the man, then shot holes into the rowboat to sink it. *None of my men know I serve the Order of Eos, so I will play the part of the rogue pirate.*

Dalziel narrowed his eyes. "Obviously, this Black Fleet left plunder behind. The fat ox is bleeding, and we will feast like a pack of hyenas on her flesh. We'll enter Funchal with guns blazing. Take as much pillage and plunder as we can carry, but by nightfall, we will set sail for the Caribbean."

His first mate barked out the orders but a few minutes later, he hung at Dalziel's elbow. "Explain to me what has happened."

The less you know, the longer you'll live. "A great war has begun, and this is not a war between nations. A great lion has feasted here, and soon, it will be feasting on its favorite prey."

"And what is that, sir?"

"Hyenas," Dalziel explained metaphorically. "Pirates like us."

Fortunately, the great lion was heading east to Madagascar. *And I must head west to warn Eos about what is coming for us all.*

CHAPTER 38

ere I go again…ready to jump from the cliff and float upon the breeze without knowing where I'll land. Louis-Armand Guerin hadn't seen Tortuga for almost five years, but a hope still remained. Soon, his crew and ship would assemble again. Just a few miles off the northern shore of Hispaniola, the small island put a smile on his face.

Beside him, Pierre-Charles LeSueur gripped the railing. "Should we be concerned about those ships?"

Three Sylph ships anchored off shore from Port de Paix.

"Don't worry, Charlie. Those ships are allies that can't so easily be bought," he stomped his boot on the deck of the *Meliae*. "The Periphery has nurtured alliances with the oppressed, and in turn, they willingly give their support. With the addition of this ship and my ship, I command a fleet of five ships. For that reason, they will remain here, protecting people without a nation."

"What people?"

"My Huguenot friends. They are refugees from Catholic France with nowhere else to turn. Even though the Periphery has no official denomination, its current allies are mostly Protestant. Against Eos, I would like to believe the Jesuits are my friends also, despite our recent differences. Just like you are now my friend, now that you are no longer LeSueur."

Along the shore of Tortuga, the sails of another ship came into view.

Mon Cherie.

As instructed, the *Adventure Prize* had undergone a radical transformation in recent months, just as Louis-Armand Lahontan became a new man, Gaspar had become Adario, and Pierre-Charles LeSueur became Charlie Johnson, his trusted First Mate. He didn't care about keeping LeSueur's identity hidden from the crew, but at any port, Captain LaGrande and First Mate Charlie Johnson were the only names to be used.

LeSueur's thick black beard had been shaved, leaving his chin whiskers braided into short ropes. The big lumberjack also shaved his head, wrapping it in a bandana. Instead of the garish clothing of his captain, LeSueur wore only a leather vest, leaving his hairy chest and arms to be bronzed by the sun. For his introduction to the men, the new First Mate dressed for battle, with two small swords strapped to his tree-trunk thighs, a pistol strapped to his baldric, and mostly for effect, an ax strapped to his back.

"I still can't believe a little runt like you is leading a fleet of pirates," LeSueur said with a bit of disdain.

"By the grace of God, I like to believe," Guerin admitted, "and with quite a bit of luck."

During their passage from Cuba to Tortuga, Guerin tried to explain the past decade's events to his former rival turned ally. He explained his bad luck with Captain Kidd and his chance encounter with LeSueur back in 1697. LeSueur already understood the truth about Newton and the Priory of Ormus. He next explained his good luck when they took the *Quedagh Merchant*, giving him clues about the next stage of the adventure.

Guerin turned back to his ship, looming larger and larger. "The ship you see is the *Adventure Prize,* formerly known as the *Quedagh Merchant.*"

"The one with carvings in the brig. The old language found on the *Al Marakk* map?"

"You see, this is why you'll be my new First Mate. First, men will fear you because of your size, and second of all, you're well versed in the lore we're about to chase."

"A lost kingdom," LeSueur repeated the story. "A buried kingdom."

"It explains why the Philosopher's Stone was found so far from obvious civilization. Alas, losing the Stone did not end their efforts, which is why we'll need to sail back to the Indian Ocean."

"Killing St. Clair didn't quench the fire in my heart. I look forward to killing more Eos men."

Guerin chuckled at LeSueur's sentiment. "I mean to return the *Quedagh Merchant* to Emperor Aurangzeb and her owner, Captain Corgi, in exchange for Josiah Faero."

"Why wouldn't the Mughals just blow us out of the water for piracy?"

"Because we'll have something they want, something very personal—I know where to find Long Ben Avery."

He smiled thinking of his night with Queen Rehena.

Hopefully, our deal still stands.

"We're going to trade Avery for Faero?" LeSueur asked.

"His life mocks the mighty empires. Avery is a pure villain. I will bring him to justice, and in turn, unlock the secrets of the Dawn."

"The secrets of the Dawn?"

"Haven't you thought this through? You dug up the key. Solomon understood the nature of the key, Aurangzeb seems to suspect, and I know Faero understands the truth. A key is used to unlock a vault. While the rest of the world chases after a lost key, I chase after the vault."

"I have no life to go back to," LeSueur added. "I'll be your right hand man in this quest."

CHAPTER 39

T O R T U G A   I S L A N D

1 7 0 4

Under instruction, "Charlie" said little and acted as Guerin's shadow once they reached the little village on Tortuga. Now, Pierre-Charles LeSueur sat beside him in the sand, a First Mate. The other officers sat with him also. The celebrations and revelry ended hours ago when Guerin offered each of them a final chance to leave when the Sylphs finished loading at dusk.

Would he have let me leave, I wonder? LeSueur felt the stubble upon his head. *No, Guerin needs me as a bodyguard and sounding board when times get tough.*

That night, Louis-Armand Guerin's full crew gathered around the large bonfire upon the beach. The light reflected off the still waters of the channel and illuminated the 350-burthen-ton vessel anchored and ready for their long journey.

Earlier, he'd been introduced to the new crew of almost a hundred men, including the thirteen veterans who'd survived Robert Culliford's blade. In the past two years, Guerin's officers gathered up enough for the great crossing. Unlike most other ships, these men chose to serve.

"So on the morrow, gentlemen," Guerin began, "we become the right hand of God. Three great enemies—the Order of Eos, the Priory of Ormus, and the Mughal Empire of Aurangzeb—are about to tear each other apart limb from limb, and in the chaos, we will strike to keep these mighty titans from crushing the weak and oppressed."

Guerin turned to his left hand where wise Gaspar sat in the sand. "Gaspar will be our shield. He will go ahead of us to the Mississippi River and organize a resistance to the French, keeping them from uniting the continent along the Mississippi River corridor. Like I have, he's looked death in the eyes and is now willing to give his life to keep our enemies from achieving their goals. Even though the details of our plans have changed, our enemy has not. Somewhere out there, Robert Culliford still serves the Order of Eos, and where we find the Order of Eos, we will also find the hidden Templar vault."

Guerin looked across the fire to Benjamin Horne. "Master Gunner Horne and I share knowledge of these ancient treasures, and in my absence, I'm sure he's told you only a fraction of what is out there. Those of you with only greed in your hearts will be the first to fall, and those with righteousness will be rewarded—that's what the priests would say."

The friendliest officer serving on the ship was Master Gunner Benjamin Horne. The Ethiopian did not look like other Africans LeSueur had met. Tall and angular, with a lean face, Horne's complexion was lighter, and instead of short ebony hair, he wore it in swept back braids, leaving linear rows that flowed back from a thin silver band that circled his head, creating a curtain of flowing braids. A slight tinge of red could be seen both in the tips of his hair and the whiskers of his thin beard. Even though he flashed a bright smile and happy eyes, he displayed a mangled right ear and a brow that seemed wrinkled as if deep in thought.

This man also has secrets.

Quartermaster Manuel Del Torro immediately seemed to hate him the most, so whenever matters of importance were discussed regarding the ship, LeSueur took a step back and never, ever, offered his opinion or even a grunt.

Navigator Naro Bon, the eldest member of the crew, gave sideways glances as if dissecting a strange monster they'd pulled up from the deep. Throughout the previous day, he grumbled about the shortcomings of the men and did his best to keep them on course.

The chubby English Boatswain, Drake Murray, remembered him from the attack on the *Cuivre Sirene* when LeSueur killed a dozen men before he was beaten to submission. This created more whispers amongst the curious crew.

The blonde-haired American from Boston, Jimmy Duke, confronted him shortly before the bonfire. "I know who you are," he said with a wry, dimpled smile. "I've heard the tales from New France."

"Does my name matter?" LeSueur asked.

"Oh, sure, you're Charlie now, but I know who you *were*. Murray hasn't put it together, but I think I have it all figured out. You're educated, which allows you to know more than French, but when I was a boy, I read all the tales coming out of the frontier. Many of the tales spoke of a giant, whose feet shook the ground as he walked, creating lakes. Instead of a horse, he rode upon a massive bull buffalo, and when he fought the savages, he went into battle with two axes. You are Paul Bonjean, aren't you?"

LeSueur laughed at the alias he'd used after burying Father Marquette. *I have become a myth.* "You're right, of course," he mocked. "With my giant buffalo, I carved out the Great Lakes, and during the winter of the blue snow, I single-handedly cleared the lands of the Sioux of all trees, and when I take a shit, islands are formed large enough to plug mighty rivers. Oh yes, I am Bonjean."

The mocking did the trick to silence Duke, but hero worship did not flee from his eyes. *Let him fear me.*

Dr. Barrow also took interest in him, wanting to inspect his scars. "You are certainly a brute of a man, and I'm sure your scars could tell a thousand tales."

Without a defined purpose except to keep Guerin safe, LeSueur spent most of the day working with the ship's carpenter, Giovanni Naufragio. Whether sawing or chopping, LeSueur knew it was an opportunity to secure his place with the crew. Seeing him hack down twelve inch logs into kindling reminded men of what he could do to their soft flesh.

But now, it was the Voodoo cook, Papa Bones, who stared at him strangely while Guerin finished discussing the route to Madagascar. LeSueur avoided the cook's glare by listening to Guerin talk about the history behind Eos.

Then Papa Bones stood, taking a moment to glare once more at LeSueur.

Few noticed Papa Bones walk away, for dozens of crewmen sat in rows behind the ring of officers, but when he returned, he caused a stir.

Is that a chicken?

Papa Bones stepped into the light of the bonfire, bringing Guerin's speech to a sudden end. "What are you doing, Papa Bones?"

Papa Bones all but ignored LaGrande, and he took off the head of a chicken. Chanting foreign words, he began to circle LeSueur, sprinkling blood on the sand and his legs. By the time he finished, a hush fell over the men, and when he finished his strange chant, he loudly said, "Ayibobo."

When the men didn't respond, he snapped at them "Ayibobo!" and they repeated it back.

"This one…" Papa Bones said with wide eyes as he studied LeSueur, "this one has *cho djab*. His destiny has been written in the stars. I've never seen such *cho* in a man, except for our brave captain." Then Papa Bones fell down, bowing in submission.

"And you worried the officers wouldn't respect you," Guerin said softly with a smirk. Then he raised his voice to ask, "What are you doing, Papa Bones? Explain yourself."

For a moment, LeSueur thought of the appearance of the comet, the serpent star, as Wenonah called it, and her insistence that he was a prophesied warrior called Wishwee. Then he looked at the wry smile on Guerin's face. *Is this all a show?*

"A *djab* was a powerful but wild spirit," Papa Bones preached to the congregation, "capable of both good or evil. When I see him through the fire, I saw both of these spirits fighting each other for control, so I fed these spirits the gift of blood. Now, he shall be given new life."

Paul BonJean, the fur trader on the frontier.

Pierre-Charles LeSueur, the explorer.

Now, Charlie Johnson, the First Mate.

Gaspar leaned forward, nodding in affirmation.

Papa Bones wasn't finished. "There is the legend of a creature called zombie in my culture, of a man who dies but is not allowed

to die until he fulfills his destiny, and in the state of life and death, he wanders the earth. Many of us live borrowed lives, just as our ship has lived borrowed lives, and is once again, brought back from death."

Papa Bones sat back down on the opposite side of the fire, but then Gaspar shared tales of the frontier with the crew, including all the near death experiences and a retelling of what had happened with the Philosopher's Stone.

When morning came, Louis-Armand declared a new name for a ship that had first been called the *Quedagh Merchant* and later the *Adventure Prize*.

The dinghies came and went, bringing first the crew, and then the officers, before finally returning for Louis-Armand Guerin and Pierre-Charles LeSueur, who stepped aboard the newly Christened *White Zombie* in honor of LeSueur.

CHAPTER 40

Upon returning to England, Michael Sikkar gave no thought to keys or vaults. The War of Spanish Succession grew by the day. Newton had unleashed his Black Fleet upon the Order of Eos in Madagascar. And Pierre-Charles LeSueur died of Yellow Fever in Cuba.

So now Sikkar turned his attention to other enemies of the Priory. His assignment was simple—find an author. His hunt took him to Fleet Street.

He sat against the wall in a corner of Ye Old Cheshire Cheese tavern in London, with a half empty glass of beer and a leather bound book in front of him. He had no poisons or weapons tucked away—only questions and a pocketful of bribe money.

The fat man he'd fantasized about strangling for most of the day followed a tavern wench into the backroom, and with a ges ture from her, he gave an arrogant nod on his way to the table.

"Sorry to keep you waiting," the fat man said. "My assistant said you have questions about a recent publication of ours."

Sikkar shoved *New Voyages to North America by Louis Armand de Lom d'Arce de Lahontan* across the table.

"Ah, one of our best-sellers. Who would have guessed?"

"Yes, I am a great admirer of this Baron Lahontan, even though my friends tell me he is a fictional character."

"Oh, he's certainly real," the fat man insisted.

"After trying to find him, I'm beginning to believe he's a fig ment of someone's imagination. Now, I understand your publishing company only translated the manuscript from French into English, but I assume the profits from any sale should—"

"You need to speak with Nicolas Gueudeville. He's the French journalist who contacted me about the manuscript. He lives in Rotterdam now."

"Holland?" Sikkar asked. *The rumors might be true. Baron Lahontan hides in Holland.* "I know you are a busy man, but do you have a few minutes to talk about the details of the book? You have read it, haven't you?"

"Of course, and yes, you can have my attention for the duration of a glass of beer."

"If you've read it, then you must have theories." He opened the book and turned to the page where it described Lahontan's journey deep into the frontier. His finger traced the route along the dramatically named River of Death and to the watershed of two great rivers. "This image here. What is it supposed to be?"

The publisher leaned forward. "Ah, it was much easier to see on the original drawing, but it's so small it's hard to see. What was it called? The Death Head?"

Caput Mortuum, Sikkar answered to himself. A breadcrumb Lahontan left for the alchemists. *But what is the truth about the head?* Sikkar closed the book. "Do you think the anecdote about visiting the Long River is true? Did he really travel deep into the American continent?"

"Of course it's true."

Baron Lahontan is certainly real, but his story is a fraud. The only question is why did he write such lies? Sikkar hoped to find the answers, because when he found Lahontan, he wouldn't give the Baron an opportunity to speak before he killed him.

THE END OF PART TWO

PART THREE
THE WITENAGEMOT
AT LIBERTALIA

PART THREE

CHAPTER 41

FOULPOINTE, MADAGASCAR

1705

Queen Rehena tried to keep her composure. While her officials went about routine business, she found herself staring past the courtiers, past the small crowd of onlookers, and through the pillars that allowed a view of the Indian Ocean. The sea called to her, but she could not answer.

Am I a fool to hope?

How many days do I have left?

As Queen of the Betsimisaraka people, she sat upon a throne like the monarchs of Europe and held court, knowing her kingdom was crumbling around her. She'd seen the cracks a decade ago, and now that the fissures had grown, total collapse was certain. Yet she held her head high, providing stable, regal beauty that would keep her people calm—until the maelstrom arrived.

For seven years, she held onto a wild card given to her by a scoundrel with one eye. Somewhere, hidden in a small cove, the means to her escape waited to be used. Only her noble brother knew the details.

She looked over to Prince Andriana, the man who should have been king. He'd only been a teenage boy when he was passed over for the throne, and now he'd grown into a chiseled warrior. *He has every reason to kill me or seize the throne for himself, but he is the only man I can trust.*

Two snakes waited in the grass of her court. One she saw on a regular basis: Vizier Falcoa, the right-hand-man of her dead husband's replacement, Presider James Morrison. After Tew's death,

Falcoa often traveled from the capital of the Free States to keep its allies informed in political matters. The other snake was a man returned from the dead.

Thankfully, Vizier Falcoa presented himself first. "Queen Rehena, I come on behalf of Presider James Morrison to request the presence of King Ratsimilaho."

"And why do you request the presence of my little Laho?" Rehena asked without obvious panic. *A hostage, perhaps?*

"Presider Morrison is calling a great meeting, a witenagemot. Since King Laho represents both the Betsimisaraka and Zana-Malata of the Free States, Presider Morrison wanted his presence at the meeting since many of the decisions will be made on behalf of the next generation."

"Shouldn't Presider Morrison also request the Queen of the Betsimisaraka?" Rehena asked. "If important decisions were to be made." She knew her marriage to Thomas Tew had only been ceremonial, but after his death, she still represented one of the largest groups on the island—the racially pure. Her son, with mixed blood, represented a new ethnic group formed from marriages of the locals and the colonists.

"In due time," Vizier Falcoa answered. "Yet you are only the Dowager Queen since you placed the crown upon your son's head five years ago."

It was a desperate act in a desperate hour. She'd managed to keep the pregnancy hidden, but now even a premature birth could not explain why the boy looked to be seven instead of ten. Only fools believed him to be the son of Thomas Tew, but the Free Clans needed the Betsimisaraka, and she needed the Free Clans. "Laho is extremely bright, but he does not understand matters of statehood yet. Can I send my brother to accompany him on this trip north?"

Vizier Falcoa quickly whispered to the entourage surrounding him and answered, "That is an acceptable proposition."

"I'll have Laho ready to travel within the week. Is there anything else, Vizier Falcoa?"

"Yes, your Highness. Can you explain to us the presence of John Yarland in your court."

Those who didn't recognize him now murmured and turned.

"Mr. Yarland, step forward and explain your sudden return to our port."

John Yarland was a shell of the man he'd once been, with signs of torture and torment visible upon his body. With the eyes of the court upon him, he shrunk even further. "Like Clever Odysseus and Brave Aeneus, the seas have thrown me to the corners of the earth since I left Foulpointe ten years ago. First, I was a witness to the death of your husband and my friend, Thomas Tew. In the attack, I was taken as a prisoner of Emperor Aurangzeb, tortured and tormented for my part in the attack on the *Ganj-i-Sawai*. When the War of Spanish Succession broke out, I was put on an English ship for more torment and torture, but it was intercepted by a French warship and I was taken to Pondichéry, where I've spent the past four years. With the help of trade ships, I have finally made my way back to your court."

How many lies did he just feed us? "Vizier Falcoa, inform Presider Morrison that after a short stay here at Foulpointe, John Yarland will be returning to his home in time for the Witenagemot."

The end has come sooner than I expected.

That night, away from public court, she met with John Yarland and her brother Prince Andriana in a private alcove of her palace gardens.

"Now tell it true," Queen Rehena said. "Why has Emperor Aurangzeb allowed the Men of the Dawn to stay here on my island?"

"He still views Queen Rehena as a faithful friend," Yarland began.

"But he got what he wanted," Rehena snapped. "He killed my husband and took Professor Faero in the process. Surely he must know Henry Avery is kept on this island. Why does he not liberate us as he promised?"

"Complications have only delayed his promises."

"What complications?"

"In truth, I believe he fears the new English puppet master. Once I gave him the *Amity,* he released me as promised but gave me over to England. I was taken to the Tower of London, and under threat of death, I revealed the truth about Madagascar. For most of the past ten years, I've been locked away in England, but now, I return as a harbinger of doom."

Queen Rehena looked to her brother for fortification before turning back to Yarland. "Explain this doom."

"Instead of Emperor Aurangzeb liberating your country, it will be a private army funded by England. For your part, you only need to keep this secret and you'll be seen as an ally."

"I don't understand."

"The English have made a pact with King Ramano of the Kingdom of Imerina, your neighbors on the western coast of Madagascar. Two forces will attack the Free States simultaneously. The Imerinese will attack by land while the private English fleet will attack by sea, crushing the Free States in one fell stroke. All you need to do is withdraw the Betsimisaraka from the battlefield and let the Imerinese do the dirty work."

Do I tell him?

No, I'll let him find out for himself.

But how can I use this to my advantage?

"She is to let our enemies cross into our lands?" Prince Andriana disdainfully asked.

"What is your goal, your highness?" Yarland asked. "Your greatest enemy is the Free States. This deal would allow you to maintain your strength without lifting a finger against your enemy. When it is over, you can unleash your brother upon King Ramano and go take the wealth given to him in bribes. All you need to do is pay a small price."

"And what is that?"

"Your son, Laho, needs a proper education, especially if Madagascar is to emerge from the shadows to join the international community. Upon the destruction of the Free States, he will be returned and allowed to rule as King of Madagascar."

"An international community?"

"For securing this plot, I will be named co-regent, for a while, until your son is old enough. We will have secured allies with both England and India, and I will help your son take his country into the future."

Now, I definitely will not tell him. Does he think he is worthy to sit in my throne when this is done? "Laho is about to be sent to this witenagemot in the north. You heard me promise it."

"And so am I. The ship that brought me here will linger for a month in order to send him back. If your son is not received, your answer will be known."

"You are a tireless servant, Mr. Yarland, and you've still managed to give me what I wanted, albeit in a surprising manner. For now, rest and relax, for you're about to enter a den of lions."

Yarland nodded and walked away, leaving Rehena with her brother. "So what do you think?"

"This explains what we've been hearing from the Imerinese," he said.

"Do the Free States know about King Ramano?"

Andriana shook his head. "Morrison will know Yarland is a traitor."

Thanks to Culliford and Swan's warnings. "We lose nothing if we accept this deal. How is it to our disadvantage?"

"If you take this deal, you'd trade one master for another."

Yet a third option remained. "What about the two ships given to us by Laho's father."

"What about them?"

"Never mind. I wouldn't want to risk Laho's life with foolishness."

"Are you still holding onto the promises given to you?" Andriana scolded.

"Much of what he said has come true," Queen Rehena confessed, thinking of the vultures that descended upon her home. "Allow me to hold out hope for his return. Then I'll decide the fate of my people."

CHAPTER 42

MARSH ISLAND, LOUISIANA

1705

As night set on the Indian Ocean, dawn arrived at the Gulf of Mexico, where Gaspar stirred the gray coals of his fire. He tried to imagine Lahontan and LeSueur chasing after ancient relics on the far side of the world. Though the waters of Marsh Island directly connected to the distant island of Madagascar, Gaspar had never felt so alone—or so alive.

The first phase of his covert mission was now complete. While upon the four ships of the Flying Sylphs, he gathered information from the Caribbean on the comings and goings of Eos. The LeMoyne family, including LeSueur's ex-wife Marguerite, had settled in the new colony, leaving Etienne Delhut to supervise Eos plans in the Great Lakes and Pierre LeMoyne leading Eos in the Gulf. Just as Louis-Armand Guerin anticipated, Eos invested in the plan to unite the Great Lakes to the Gulf via the Mississippi River. Fortunately, the new "War of Spanish Succession" or "Queen Anne's War" created turmoil in the Caribbean.

With Pierre and Joseph LeMoyne called to service, Gaspar took the opportunity to implement the next phase of his mission: blocking France from conquering the Mississippi River.

Gaspar's little tent had done its part to keep the swarms of Louisiana mosquitos at bay during the night. His only other possession was the fat canoe gifted to him by Captain Jacobs when they dropped him off at the selected rendezvous island. Unlike the lean canoes of the Great Lakes, his new vessel was of European fashion, designed to be captained while sitting backwards, and motored by oars instead of paddles. The "row boat" held enough supplies to last a year.

Captain Jacobs' *Phoebe* came to life in the distance, ready to return to its home in Tortuga. With war between Protestant and Catholic superpowers, the little colony on Tortuga could easily be attacked by either French or Catholic warships, which is why Jacobs dropped off Gaspar under the cover of darkness.

Somewhere up river, an agent of the Periphery named Penicaut hunted and trapped in the land of the Natchez Indians, which is where Gaspar would soon be heading.

In a year, I'll either be dead…or preparing the way like the Baptist did for the Christ.

CHAPTER 43

THE GOLD COAST OF AFRICA

1705

The Kingdom in Prussia came into existence in 1701, when Frederick II, Elector of Brandenburg, elevated his status to King in Prussia. The union was approved by the Habsburg emperor of the Holy Roman Empire, making it a new global power. Although the new region was called Prussia, King Frederick kept the capital in Berlin.

For hundreds of years, the Margraviate of Brandenburg was a major principality of the Holy Roman Empire. Its powerful naval presence in the Baltic Sea gave it prestige and security within the empire. Its global presence most recently expanded to the western Gold Coast of Africa in 1682.

The Brandenburger Gold Coast, located in present day Ghana, also changed its name in 1701 to the Prussian Gold Coast Settlements. Cape Three Points held the capital Friedrichsburg and also Fort Dorothea, a popular hub along the western shore of Africa.

And now Fort Dorthea's gone, Louis-Armand Guerin realized as they approached. Master Gunner Benjamin Horne and Quartermaster Del Torro readied their men. Beside him, LeSueur studied the coast in silence.

"Is it the Black Fleet?" LeSueur asked grimly. Unlike the chaos they'd discovered weeks ago in Madeira, Fort Dorthea's condition improved the closer the *White Zombie* came.

"Who can tell in war? Prussia is an ally of England, but the Priory of Ormus might not care about alliances," Guerin added.

Dr. Barrow came out from his cabin. "Will we give them aid?"

Guerin nodded solemnly. "This was supposed to be a safe port on our journey. Hopefully it's not as bad as it looks."

Benjamin Horne climbed the steps to the deck and asked, "Will they fire on us?"

For the Priory of Ormus, England had been its chess piece. For the Order of Eos, it naturally claimed France, New France, and Madagascar. The Catholic Church fought the old war through the Jesuit Order, but it lost influence in the Protestant countries. So for the past two centuries, Periphery agents infiltrated the courts of Protestant countries like Holland and Prussia to act as a counter-balance to the chaos.

"Raise the Dutch flag and prepare to anchor," Guerin answered. "We are allies—if any of them survived."

LATER THAT EVENING, Louis-Armand Guerin sat at the private table of Governor Johann Munz. LeSueur and a squad of men waited outside the residence in case of trouble. The first time he'd stopped at Cape Three Points, Captain Kidd dined with the governor. On the return, disgraced Captain Kidd remained in his quarters while First mate Gareth LaGrande negotiated for enough supplies to let them limp back to America. Now, Guerin and Munz shared pleasantries and information before getting to the heart of the matter.

Governor Munz began. "Three times in three months a fleet of warships appeared and blew our port to pieces."

Three months? Perhaps we'll catch them after all. "Did they fly black flags with a white X?"

"Yes, you've seen them?" Munz asked.

"Seen them? No, but we've heard of them. They targeted the city of Funchal in Madeira, leveling the settlement and killing its governor. You should consider yourself lucky." *Marco Alvorez wasn't so lucky.*

"They even came ashore, abducted men, and dropped them off down the coast without harm. It's the strangest thing I've seen. I've heard of pirate bloodlust, but this…this has no logic at all."

You're not Eos. "They are practicing," Guerin explained. "A green crew needs to rehearse before its hour upon the stage. Patience might not be a virtue after all."

"So what good news do you bring?"

My empty promises might come too late.

If the Black Fleet reached Madagascar first, his plans would turn to ash. He prepared to give Governor Munz the same promise he'd given to Queen Rehena. Ormus acted, and it would take a few more years for the Periphery to react in an equal manner. "Both of us are servants of powerful men. My master chooses to let others get the glory while he remains in the shadows."

"And for others to take the blame?"

Guerin laughed. "In a way. You've heard of the metaphor for a bitter pill and how it must first be sweetened. My reports are often the other way around. I like to give my boss bitterness wrapped in a sweet center. I explained the condition of the Savage in Canada, the slave in the Caribbean, and even worse, the French Huguenots in the west. I have heard it on good authority that my master is investing a sizable fortune into the new Prussian Navy. Even though he won't officially take sides in the conflict of Catholicism and Protestantism, he can bring balance and a new fleet."

A navy I'd also promised to Queen Rehena.

Guerin finished, "Rebuild, and I can promise you in the days to come, a new Prussian Navy will protect these shores. This port will be a hub of activity, and you'll become a wealthy man."

"Why haven't I heard any of these rumors?" Governor Munz asked suspiciously.

"My master can keep secrets, and when he learned about the creation of the Black Fleet, he knew he had to bring balance."

"So you're hunting for these maniacs?"

No, I'm no longer a privateer. "Hunting them? Oh, heavens no. Very soon, they will be hunting us."

But only if I can get there before it's too late.

CHAPTER 44

At 593,000 square miles, the island of Madagascar is the fourth-largest island in the world. Although just 250 miles off the eastern coast of Africa, it was one of the last places on earth to be settled by humans, somewhere between 350 BC and 550 AD, and aside from this initial settlement, it remained ignored by the world until 1500 when the Portuguese visited.

Because of its isolation, Madagascar has some of the most unique flora and fauna in the world: wild highlands and rivers along the western side of the island and lush rainforests along the eastern side. While friendly and fertile for plant and animal populations, powerful trade winds, annual monsoons, and destructive cyclones suppressed human civilization.

For the first time in his seven years, Laho finally saw the rest of his empire.

He traveled with his uncle Andriana and a small military force to Bannockburn Palace to pay tribute to the Presider of the Free Clans.

Bannockburn Palace was built upon a solitary bluff that emerged from the flat lowlands north of Antongil Bay. He'd been to the stone castle twice before. The trip as an infant held no memory for him, except in the imagined telling from his mother; five years ago, he visited the castle with his mother when Presider Morrison placed a crown upon his head.

At the foot of the bluff, troops flying the white flag of the Free Clans waited for him. His own escorts outnumbered them four to one, a tribute to the boy king.

A familiar face, Laho thought, sighing a bit.

"Your Highness," John Yarland greeted him with a grin and a bow.

My father's friend, Laho remembered. *The man who saw him die.*

"Presider Morrison asked that I meet you here. Chieftain Valencourt and his men arrived just a few hours before you, and when they learned you were coming, they insisted on letting you lead the way."

With a bright blue jacket and flowing white beard and hair, Chieftain Valencourt also bowed before him. Unlike the pale Yarland, Valencourt had the tan skin of the Zana-Malata. "I knew your father, and I am here to support the alliance of our peoples."

"Then ride with us, Chieftain Valencourt. King Laho would be honored," Prince Andriana said carefully in English, without emotion or inflection. English was the language of the future, he'd been told, and he did his part to master it, along with French and Portuguese.

Yarland hobbled to his horse, which his pirates helped him mount. Valencourt, despite being older than Yarland, deftly mounted his own steed.

Every so often, a stone threshold manned by a small squad of soldiers appeared along the road—defenses for the Presidential Palace. By late afternoon, the column of visitors reached the top of the bluff where a three-story military fort, a large barracks, a circular temple, and the presidential estate, Bannockburn Palace, stood as capital of the Free Clans.

Presider James Morrison, with banners and assembled guards, greeted him in the open yard. A thick man with a protruding chest and belly, he bore a strange mixture of Scottish and Madagascar culture, befitting his heritage. "Welcome to the people's palace. This will be your home long after my term of office ends, and I am your host."

For the rest of the evening and into the next morning, Laho found himself pampered, an attempt to ease the awful tension of the summons. John Yarland shared anecdotes of his father's cun-

ning and bravery, and Chieftain Valencourt told tales from the Dawn Era. Growing up at Foulpointe, Laho knew the ways of Europeans and Americans, but the men with Presider Morrison were men from an older era.

THE NEXT AFTERNOON, his uncle Andriana brought him to the highest part of the palace where Presider Morrison waited alone for him on a carved stone balcony overlooking the jungle valley below.

"Go ahead, Laho," his uncle said. "Morrison is a faithful friend. He's already told me the important news. I'll be right here when you're done talking to him."

"Come, your highness, sit with me and talk of the future and the past," Morrison said, patting the stone bench a few feet behind the short stone wall. "How is your mother?"

"She is well. She's pleased with my lessons. My teachers all give me good marks, which makes her smile."

"That is good. I was the best man at your parents' wedding; did you know that?"

"I knew you were my father's friend."

"The legend of your father has grown in recent years, but I want you to know he was a scholar long before he became a pirate."

"Is it true he was an American?"

"He was. He was born to English parents in a colony called Rhode Island. Are you familiar with your American colonies?"

"Yes, I finished a unit on them a few weeks ago."

"So do you know the namesake for the Rhode Island colony?"

"Is it named after the Island of Rhodes in Greece?"

"Hah! Thomas would be proud of you. You might be small for your age, but you have a quick mind. Your mother has done a fine job with your education. Do you know what made the Island of Rhodes unique in the world?"

Laho knew this one. "The Colossus of Rhodes. It was a statue of the sun-god Helios standing over a hundred feet tall with a spiked crown upon its head to resemble the rays of the sun."

"Very good, your Highness. Your father certainly might have explored Greek legends and myths, but instead, he studied an oddity right in his own backyard. Do you see the temple behind us?"

Turning, Laho studied the three-story white structure. With a conical black roof that sat upon a circular tower, it had small, narrow windows around it, with a short skirt built around the stone nave. "What of it?"

"Ours is in much better shape even though it was built hundreds of years ago. Our priests tend to it annually. Rhode Island, your father's home, also had a similar temple built upon it, by men who also belonged to the Order of Eos. Did your mother explain the history of the Order of Eos?"

Laho nodded. It's what made the white men different than the Zana-Malata or the Betsimisaraka.

"While our colony here thrived," Morrison continued, "the colony in America failed. When the explorer Giovanni da Verrazano sailed the coasts of America, he dubbed it Isola di Rhode. Any ideas on why he did so?"

"Because the temple was big like the colossus?"

Morrison chuckled. "Yes, it does seem obvious. Your father's curiosity led him to discover its purpose. The Knights Templar built the tower as both a place of worship and also an astronomical measurement tool. His unorthodox beliefs were discovered, and he was kicked out of school. To support his family, he had to take to the life of a privateer."

"My father had another family?"

Laho only knew his father from stories, and this rewrote the entire story.

"Yes, you have two half-sisters living in New York. Do you know what the world says about your father?"

"My father was a pirate who was killed by a cannon ball while attacking a Mughal convoy of religious pilgrims," Laho coldly repeated the truth found in the global news.

"The world knows how Thomas Tew died, but it had no idea how he lived—or what he lived for. Your father was so much more than a pirate, and he sent more than money back to his family in Rhode Island. Even after his death, the concepts and beliefs he learned here were brought back to America, and one day soon, you will have the same opportunity to make this place into the democracy that your father envisioned for the land of your sisters. You must be the guardian of your people's rights and liberties. You must be a barrier against the rich and powerful, not only from the tribes in the south, but from the tyrants in Europe."

"I hope I can be a fair ruler."

"The Free States elect leaders based on talent and merit, not blood, which is why we elected your father. You must prove yourself worthy before anyone will vote you as their leader, their presider. Have you read the stories of King Arthur?"

Laho nodded enthusiastically. "Wart."

"Yes, baby Arthur became Wart before he could become King Arthur. Do you know why?"

"He had to learn humility."

"Yes, and so must you. Think of me as Merlin. I served your father, and now I serve you, so I must do something that is difficult but necessary."

"Are you going to kill me?"

Morrison laughed loudly. "Oh, my dear boy, you might be the only one to survive the days to come."

"Are you ill?"

"No I am not ill, but I am more likely than not the last Presider of the Free Clans here in Madagascar. Our Eos priests teach us that time is a cycle of death and rebirth. We have been betrayed by a man your father trusted, John Yarland. He has brought an ancient enemy to our doors."

"Why?"

"Cycles. It is time for a rebirth, and you, little Laho, will rebuild this country from the ashes. Your father was brave. Are you brave?"

"I think so."

"I need you to be brave. Many men are afraid of death. Even I have struggled with my fears now that I am old. Now I know that like Odin, I must face my enemy without fear so that the youth, like yourself, can begin the new cycle of rebirth. Can you promise me that you will be a wise, fair king like King Arthur."

"I think so."

"Then I need you to become Wart."

"I don't know what that means."

"Have you ever pretended to be asleep when you weren't?"

"Yes."

"That's what I'm going to do. In order to make my enemy think I'm sleeping, I'm going to have to send you far, far away, but it's for your own good. Your mother also agrees to this. You can ask your uncle when we are done."

"I don't want to leave."

"You will be brave like your father and Wart. You will travel under the name Thomas White in remembrance of your father and the white flag of the Free Clans. I doubt any of this will remain when you return, but I want you to remember sitting here with me. Can you promise me that?"

"Yes, I promise," Laho said and looked out over the jungle valley that led to distant Antongil Bay and the vast Indian Ocean.

CHAPTER 45

Located forty miles south of Madagascar's Antongil Bay, St. Mary's Island regularly harbored pirates, who used the thin island to store their loot and as a camp to resupply for decades. While most Templar refugees from the Friday the 13th purge settled on Madagascar, many continued a life upon the seas. For years a Congress of Pirates presided over the smaller settlement, yet it remained beholden to the Free States, who, in turn, were beholden to the Grand Master of the Order of Eos.

This must be decided democratically, James Morrison decided as he purposefully avoided the men assembling. Eos had purposefully spread out power. Twelve chieftains ruled over one branch of government and four admirals ruled over the Congress of Pirates, the other branch. Serving in his role as Presider simply meant he would ensure fairness and equality, so while the men ate, laughed, and lobbied, Morrison stayed in a small alcove, watching the scene.

As a student of history, Morrison knew the pitfalls of monarchs, despots, and tyrants. Within the past decade, he had the opportunity to crown himself like the rulers of old did. After his son died out in the wilderness of the American frontier, grief and rage filled his heart for the American colonists in New France who put his son in jeopardy. More recently, when the Grand Master of the Order of Eos was killed in an attack on Madeira, he certainly could have seized power for himself.

But he didn't—although he was tempted.

Marco Alvorez ruled two balanced colonies in New France and Madagascar. While a decade of war recently ended, leaving the superpowers England, France, and Spain exhausted, the Madagascar Colony grew wealthy and strong, untouched by the global war. Now, as war was coming again, this time Madagascar would not remain unscathed. Luckily, Captain Robert Culliford warned them about the intentions of the Priory of Ormus, allowing Morrison time to develop a coda for a song four centuries in the making.

Knowledge is power, after all.

He knew the Priory of Ormus had taken root in the English government and meant to finish what the Purge of 1307 failed to accomplish. For four centuries, the Order of Eos had been carefully cultivated, and now, when it was about to bear fruit, a great threat sailed to their island sanctuary. As a dictator, Morrison could muster the ground defenses with the power of the Free Clans and weaponize the Congress of Pirates to crush the Black Fleet when it arrived.

But I must trust the plan.

The war between the colonists of New France and New England certainly muddied the waters, and the bold LeMoyne family drew the attention of Eos's enemies while the seeds of the next plan took root in New England.

Our days in Madagascar have come to an end—regardless of the outcome of the coming battle.

"Presider Morrison, the Congress is ready," an aid declared.

But am I ready?

After the Splitting of the Elm in 1188 and the Great Purge of 1307, the surviving Templars were exiles for the first few decades. While some survivors found shelter in Scotland and Portugal, it was decided to create a colony on the far side of the world from France. While the colony in America failed within a few decades, the colony in Madagascar grew slowly and steadily under meticulous planning and leadership.

And I will not get drawn into a battle of egos with this Sir Isaac Newton.

Presider James Morrison took the empty spot at the table for a meeting of the Congress of Pirates even though many of the faces were unfamiliar. On his right hand was Vizier Falcoa; on his left, John Yarland, the traitor. "Thank you for answering the call.

THE ALCHEMIST'S RING

Through the years, we've tasked the Congress of Pirates to be our eyes and ears, and for the past few years, you have borne an undue burden on our behalf. Most recently, after an encounter with the East Indian Trading Company, a threat has been levied against the Free States: Surrender Captain Avery or incur the wrath of England. Today we vote upon the resolution to surrender one of our own, Captain Henry Avery, to English authorities. What say you?"

Admiral John Pro spoke first. "On behalf of the pirates here at St. Mary's Island, I reject this proposal, just as our predecessors rejected it when it was first proposed. If we bow to the pressures of tyranny now, all that we've built here is already lost."

Morrison turned to Admiral Abraham Samuel, who led another pirate settlement at Port Dauphin. Located on the extreme southeastern corner of the island seven hundred miles away from Antongil Bay, it was led by the mulatto. "Many of those involved in the attack on the *Ganj-i-Sawai* ran and were hunted down. Many innocent men were also hanged for the crimes. For generations, an alliance has existed between the Free Clans and the people of Madagascar, so when Captain Avery came to us seeking sanctuary, we gave him the protection of this promise. I reject this proposal."

James Plantain, another young captain not present at the earlier congresses, hesitated when it came his turn. "As King of Ranter Bay, I continued this alliance because of the network of information it provides, but I remember when England threatened all of us for the sake of a few. Yes, Avery has been given sanctuary by this congress, and for that reason, I reject this proposal, but I ask you all—if we took matters into our own hands, if we policed our own, would this not allow us to exist beyond this matter?"

"Is that a proposal?" Morrison asked. *If we give them Avery, would the world look from our colony? Most likely not.*

"No, it is only something to ponder."

"Then shut your mouth," Pedro Dias said from the opposite side of the table. "We didn't come here to have a young whelp offer his opinion. We have an alliance that is stronger than nationalities, so I wholeheartedly reject this proposal."

Morrison turned to John Yarland, the discovered traitor who'd been sent ahead of the Black Fleet as a paroled prisoner of Newton. *Play along. He must be blind to our plans.* "It appears as if the

Congress has rejected the latest proposal given to us; however, I do not wish to burden you with a return trip to London. As a known associate of Captain Thomas Tew, our enemies might hang you in the place of Captain Avery. I propose that you stay here with us."

Yarland offered no reaction.

"I accept that proposal," Dias added, and soon the other three admirals followed suit.

"Whom shall we send in his stead?" Morrison asked.

"Could we risk Culliford?" Dias questioned. "He's just a Cornwall man. He's not one of the old families."

No, we have other plans for Culliford and Swan. Their loyalty to Eos will be rewarded.

"No, send the Mouth," Plantain suggested. "I'm sick of that young braggart."

"Lavasseur?" Morrison clarified. "What do you say?"

The proposal was quickly accepted.

Morrison knew it was all a game. Since Robert Culliford and John Swan brought them news about the plans of the Priory of Ormus, he prepared for the inevitable attack and the plans for the future of the colony. The Congress of Pirates knew about Newton, but he'd managed to keep the traitor Yarland in Madagascar for the coming storm, be it days, weeks, or months away. "It will take Lavasseur several months to return our answer, and when England learns of our final rejection, we can be sure that the East Indian Trading Company will come en force," Morrison said. "For this reason, I want each captain to return to his port and begin patrolling. We must anticipate a coming attack, and I do not want any raids on the Red Sea or the coasts of India. At any sign of retribution, our congress will reconvene. Is that clear?"

It was clear.

Now all Morrison needed to do was to let the traitor Yarland do his part.

And then we will show Newton the willpower of the Men of the Dawn.

CHAPTER 46

Upon returning from the Congress of Pirates, Presider James Morrison purposely walked the grounds of Fort Wallace, knowing it might be his last time to see it. Forty Portuguese guns on each side of the harbor looked down on the fishing village and port. Although most pirates stuck to St. Mary's Island or Ranter Bay, the heart of the Free States was found at Antongil Bay and the docks below Fort Wallace.

Although the guns were new, the fort itself blended in with the surrounding jungle. Its exterior walls were covered by lichen and vine, hiding it from any warships firing from the exposed bay. Inside the stone walls, the walkways, windows, and storage chambers were meticulously clean.

And soon put to good use.

Beside him, John Yarland along with Denis Falcoa, his young Portuguese vizier, walked silently as they inspected the troops.

The Free States soldiers were represented by the twelve clans, each bearing different colors and symbols upon their uniforms and exhibiting a slightly different ethnic appearance. All of them had European blood, which made the Zana-Malata people unique in the world.

A melting pot of nationalities.

The twelve clans settled in four regions along the eastern coast, with patriarchal clans from French, Scottish, and Portuguese families in each region—to prevent feuding or cultural pride. Despite the best intentions of the founding fathers, however, the women in each region came from specific local tribes. The clans in the south married mostly Imerina women, producing soldiers who were lean and athletic. The clans in the western highlands married the Vazimba women, producing children of darker complexion who were smaller but sturdy. In the north, freed African slaves, marooned Indians, and pirate blood created the largest soldiers, with the most diverse pigmentation and hair color. Retiring sailors from the Congress of Pirates would often leave St. Mary's Island and settle within the Free States, adding fresh Caucasian stock into the local population.

Our children are strong, healthy, and diverse.

Turning to the traitor John Yarland, he used flattery to keep the man in the dark. "We should have listened to you instead of Tew." Yarland had been planning for integration into the global community, ignorant of what Eos had planned for the future.

"Thomas believed in the mission to Abyssinia," Yarland said. "But how could he know our enemies were about to discover our utopia?"

"He was not a soul of caution," Morrison continued. "When he heard about the Philosopher's Stone and discoveries beyond the Great Lakes, his ambition made him reckless. What do you think would have happened if he'd survived the ambush?"

"Thomas Tew would have ransomed the Emperor's daughter in exchange for some ancient artifact," Yarland scoffed. "And I'd probably be traipsing around Africa right now and carrying Professor Faero's notebooks."

"You've always been loyal to Tew," Morrison lied, knowing that loyalty ended long before the cannonball took Tew's life and legs. "Do you think Faero would have broken the code written on the Odin Stone?"

"Emperor Aurangzeb's spies believed he could, and if the rumors are true, he's tucked Faero away to help him translate his own ancient texts. Faero and Tew had too many theories to keep track of. I don't think the secrets of the Odin Stone will be revealed until it is time."

If only Tew hadn't taken the bait. Morrison now broke the poorly kept secret. "I know you have endured much for the Free Clans, and your recent imprisonment and torture deserve a reward. Your

sage advice in recent months has led me to realize how important you are to us, and as a result, I want you to be the new commander here at Fort Wallace. In the days to come, I will need you to be our shield, and your experience in combat and in leadership makes you the perfect candidate. What do you say, Mr. Yarland? Will you be our shield against enemies?"

Yarland needed to take the bait.

"Is that why you sent Lavasseur back to Europe? You know what his answer will bring upon us?"

The request was a ruse. As Culliford and Swan ascertained, Yarland was freed by their enemies in order to destroy them all. "By the time Captain Lavasseur returns with our answer, the war in Europe will have grown, distracting them from their perceived insults. The Grand Mughal is not a young man either, and here, hidden away from civilization, we might soon be forgotten again."

"I will serve here with honor," Yarland accepted the proverbial poisoned cup offered.

How could you say no? You want to rule. "I'm pleased." Morrison turned his attention to Vizier Falcoa. "Tell me again about the Englishman who tried to steal Yarland back to England." Despite the lies Yarland told about being kidnapped by the French, this had indeed happened. "Tell me about the man who blows idle threats from the other side of the world."

Morrison held the letter delivered via the East Indian Trading Company instead of from Yarland. It'd been signed by *Sir* Isaac Newton. In a cruel jibe, Morrison had asked Vizier Falcoa to research Newton while standing beside Yarland. Now, he wanted his answers.

"Sir Isaac Newton?" Falcoa repeated. "The whole world knows his name. He's one of the most celebrated scientists alive."

"What do we know of his family?"

"He was born in Lincolnshire, but little is known about his birth father. His mother married when he was young, a reverend named Barnabas Smith."

"Is Newton religious?"

"He's a scientist."

"But is he religious?" Morrison pressed.

Falcoa vacillated. "Again, his fame came from his various study of sciences, but from what I've heard, yes, he became quite passionate about religion for a time, yet his views are considered to be a bit unorthodox."

"How so?"

"He's done studies in alchemy, the Philosopher's Stone, the apostasy of trinitarianism, the Arians, the prophecies of Daniel and Revelation, and there are even rumors he has calculated the date of the Apocalypse."

"Tell me it isn't 1706," Morrison said with a smile, prompting a smile from Yarland also.

Falcoa shook his head. "No, it is a far off date sometime after the turn of the millennium."

Falcoa continued showing off. "Although quite eccentric, Newton's a politician at heart, and the disruption of trade between England and India has threatened him politically, so he hoped to gain favor with the Grand Mughal with a final offer."

"The head of Henry Avery. What made him think Henry Avery was still on the island of Madagascar?" Morrison opened the question to both of his advisers.

Yarland answered. "The *Ganj-i-Sawai* was loaded with so much treasure that had Avery gone to a civilized nation, he could not have gone unnoticed. Hundreds of men who sailed with Avery have been brought to justice and interrogated. Newton must assume he's found sanctuary here where his financial bribes amount to nothing."

Newton doesn't give a fig about Avery. He knows what I have here and means to take it. Well…we'll have a surprise for him. "How will Newton react when he learns I won't surrender Avery?" Morrison had prepared for the attack for years. In 1307, the Priory of Ormus almost exterminated the Order of Eos and the Templars. Morrison knew the attack would come long before the ship reached England. Lavasseur headed to the Caribbean.

Falcoa answered. "Sending Lavasseur will be seen as an insult, which I can only assume you knew. Newton's risen to his stations quickly. A man like Newton won't allow his reputation to be insulted."

"So what should we expect?"

"I assume he'll use his influence at the East India Trading Company. An armada of armed merchant ships could be devastating," Falcoa finished.

"Unless we can outlast them," Morrison boasted in front of Yarland. "They will flash like lightning and roar like thunder, but if we weather the storm, it should end their threats, allowing us to continue with a bit more discretion. Wouldn't you agree?"

Yarland said, "I'll make them pay for entering this bay, and the cost will not be worth their efforts."

"That's the spirit, Yarland. That's the spirit. I'll send Falcoa back to help you with setting up your position here at the fort, but for now, I need him to accompany me back to Bannockburn Palace. I leave the fort in your care."

If only I could spill this traitor's slimy guts upon my hands.

No sooner did Yarland leave than a messenger came for Presider Morrison, taking him away from Fort Wallace.

Beyond Fort Wallace and the village, the road ran straight to the solitary bluff of Bannockburn Palace, but two miles from the ocean, an intersection of trade roads held an armed squad of his Zana-Malata troops, but not the ones who would accompany him back to the palace.

Chieftain Teixeira, from the southern region, waited with the Zana-Malata troops.

"My good friend," Presider Morrison said. "What news?"

"A coalition of envoys from King Ramano follows me. It seems he is ready to negotiate peace terms with the Free Clans."

Another lie, and thanks to the warning from Queen Rehena, I know it is anything but peace being offered.

"The Kingdom of Imerina wants peace?" Morrison scoffed. *Newton's spies have indeed made contact with them already. They offer peace and then will slip the knife into me while smiling.* "This will certainly help solidify King Laho's kingdom for years. I will accept the Imerinese diplomats, but first, I will hold the Witenagemot. Ride with me, Chieftain Teixeira, and tell me what other news you've heard from our borders."

CHAPTER 47

Presider James Morrison found his place at the northern pillar, and for just a few moments, the office of Presider no longer belonged to him. To his right, Jonah Drummond, the eldest of the chieftains, stood in front of the other northern pillar.

As a young man, the ritual had thrilled him, knowing that it dated back centuries; now, the ritual terrified him with the weight of responsibility looming over him.

In total, the eight pillars of the White Temple had eight chieftains standing in front of them, representing the ancient Scottish clans of Drummond, Halyburton, Pennycook, and Morrison and the French families L'Blanc, deVilliers, Valencourt, and Derry. Serving as priests, the lot fell upon the ancient Portuguese families of Moniz, Lordelo, Teixeira, and Perestrello to perform the rituals.

Unlike the hall in Bannockburn Palace, the interior of the White Temple remained silent and reverent. Instead of debate, the chieftains simply prayed for wisdom. Even the bare feet of the element bearers could be heard as they approached. Bourne by the four men, the elements of earth, air, fire, and water were carried to the center of the chamber and placed evenly to bisect the eight pillars. Morrison found himself closest to the empty chalice of air.

Sylph, the air spirit.

After a few moments passed, upon a copper platter, a severed head was carried in and placed between the elements. Morrison knew the three-faced idol was a fabrication, but even with his years of living, he still gazed upon it the same way he first had done as a young man.

The craftsman had taken three human skulls, and in both a process of destruction and creation, seamlessly merged all three skulls, allowing their faces to peer into the past, present, and future simultaneously. Morrison gazed into the hollow eyes of the future.

LATER THAT EVENING, he found himself staring down into his empty wine glass.

Delhut is lost on the frontier.

L'Huillier and LeMoyne have died of old age.

Alvorez died during a pirate raid.

It seems the cycle of death will soon come for me, but I will be ready for it.

Eos is not doomed—it is ready to be reborn.

Wonderful mirth, merry music, and fine Madeira wine brought joy to the palace for the first time in months, but Morrison knew he could wait no longer to give the chieftains their final instructions. Unlike the stark emptiness of the White Temple, the hall was filled with noise and color. Behind each chieftain, the family flag and each wooden totem, or Fylgia, stood at the grand table.

"My fellow chieftains, a final drink, to your good health and good hamr, may we all be strong in the days to come."

The smiles left their faces as their President spoke of mortality. They drank and then listened.

"A trap has been set, and with it will come the fight of our lives. Each of you has served your clan's Fylgia well, and now, your totem joins the rest of our totems to create a powerful nation. The spirits of our ancestors have walked this path before us, and their hamingja was passed down to you and to your family. The Dawn Era ended with violence and death, but as you know, we still celebrate the deaths of our great heroes, and even after the terrible day passed into the darkness of night, a new dawn came, bringing rebirth, for the spirits of the slain, the hamingja, did not descend into the depths to be locked away. No! It passed on to the next generation, for it was found to be worthy," Morrison said.

He felt so weary but flashed anger and bluster to the chieftains. "Earlier today, when we prayed together, I asked for the oppor-

tunity to be proven worthy so that my spirit might live once my hamr loses all of its blood or is hacked to pieces. While my enemies rejoice over my slain corpse, my hamingja will remain in this world, growing stronger until I avenge myself upon my killer."

He looked at the chieftains, confirming their commitment.

"A day of reckoning has come," Morrison concluded and gathered himself for a moment. "For some time, we have known of the plot against us here, and I have taken measures to ensure our survival. We are once again reaching a Twilight, and instead of an army of giants, a fleet of English pirates bearing a black flag with crossed thigh bones approaches."

No one spoke, but they all stirred at the reminder.

"I have been making preparations for this day for some time now, but our idyllic world will soon come to an end, and there is nothing any of us can do to stop it."

"What do you want from us?" Jonah Drummond asked.

"We will meet them as our ancestors who stood upon the walls of Asgard. For a new world to begin, the old one must die. We've planted seeds that will rise up and grow, both here and in America, and like the Asir, we will sanctify the fertile ground with our blood sacrifice. Our Pirate Brethren will give us time when the day comes, but each of you must see to your houses. Vizier Falcoa has prepared instructions for each clan."

His young adviser distributed the instructions, which each chieftain read gravely.

"When the Ragnarök began, wise King Odin led the vanguard, just as I will lead the way for you. But know this: If Odin hadn't stepped out from the walls, the mighty wolf Fenris would not have been slain. If Thor hadn't stepped out onto the battlefield, the Midgard Serpent would have stayed hidden in the depths of the sea. By the time Ragnarök finished, all of the enemies of the gods had been destroyed, and when this is over, I mean to see all of our enemies destroyed as well. Our foe has revealed himself, and now we must do our part to make him pay."

CHAPTER 48

1 7 0 5

Following the meeting with the tribal diplomats, Presider Morrison sat alone on the stone bench overlooking the valley. *All of the pieces have been moved into place. Now I just wait for the first pawn to be taken.*

He could see the diplomatic convoy heading down the narrow road back to the major road that led far off to the southwest where the Kingdom of Imerina waited for the chaos.

Vizier Falcoa returned to act as his shadow. "The Dowager Queen would like to visit the tomb."

"Rehena is here?" She'd been an unexpected ally with her disclosure of Yarland's treacherous plans. *Although I would like to think I would've smelled the foul plot.*

Falcoa nodded. "All of Madagascar has prepared for the coming conflict. With her son being sent away, and then the Witen, and now the Imerinese diplomats—she is no fool."

"I suppose I owe it to her."

"Do you? She might not understand the old ways," Falcoa added.

I don't know if I understand the old ways myself. "How are the preparations with the chieftains?"

"Dutifully following orders, as only we could have dreamed."

"They are true believers. They understand the sacrifices made by our ancestors and how they will be remembered long after this."

"The tributes have been selected from each village and are now being moved to the secure location."

Tributes? That has a harsh tone. "And the Congress of Pirates?"

"They are all staying where they were told, offering patrols."

That's surprising. Many of them are young Americans, clueless in the old way. "And Fort Wallace? How is our new commander doing?"

"Yarland has his men ready, and with each merchant ship that arrives in Antongil Bay, he keeps abreast of all threats, foreign and domestic."

Newton's spies? "I'm sure he does," Morrison muttered. "I will receive Queen Rehena alone."

He'd known her for less than a decade—when she was chosen as Thomas Tew's bride. Despite the title of Dowager Queen, Rehena did not look the part of an aging matriarch. At thirty, she held her head high and kept her back straight as she parted from her entourage of servants. Her royal bloodline came from a history of Betsimisarakan merchants who traded with foreigners from their home at Foulpointe, and as a result, generations of civilization and sophistication produced a woman at home with both African and Caucasian leaders. Under a green dress, she wore the corset and low bodice to remind everyone, including Presider Morrison, that she was still a woman in her prime. The white lace around her exposed shoulders matched the white gloves that reached from fingertip to elbow, and at the curve of her cleavage, a red seam descended all the way down to her hidden feet.

"Presider Morrison, I thank you for taking the time away from your preparations to indulge my sentimentalities."

"Of course, your highness. I serve all the free peoples."

The two walked side-by-side across the great yard.

"Yes, and I thank you for the guidance you have given my son. When he returns from his studies, I am sure he will be a wise ruler. I wonder, though, what will remain?"

"His people will remain, even if every stone here is pulled from its place and rolled down the hill into the jungle. You will remain, waiting for his return to Foulpointe."

"What of the rumors coming out of Imerina?"

"They will certainly take some territory, but when Laho returns, it will be restored."

"What kind of enemy could destroy all of this?"

The Priory of Ormus. "It is a shadow of ourselves, not an enemy from the unknown, but an enemy from within. We are two branches from the same tree, and only one branch can continue, while the other must wither and die. The split has festered and rotted for centuries, and in the coming storm, there will be a permanent break."

Unlike many of the other leaders and chieftains, Queen Rehena seemed to accept the dire warnings. *And then she will be rid of us.*

They walked around the White Temple, which seemed especially brilliant in the clear blue sky. Just past the white tower, between the distant castle and the temple, a small garden with a series of paths and a short stone railing at its center welcomed the two representatives.

Queen Rehena, having been granted entrance at the burial of Thomas Tew, already stared at the small gate of the stone wall, for she knew it was not really a decorative wall but a railing.

The two stopped at the top of the well and looked down.

"I remember thinking this place was made by the gods," Rehena admitted.

Morrison chuckled. "Carved with skill by determined men. Before becoming pirates, we were global bankers, before banking, we were soldiers, but before that, we were simple stone masons. The skill of working stone is the common thread through all of these years and generations."

As Morrison spoke the words, he was nevertheless chilled as he looked down upon the wonder carved into a bluff hundreds of years before his birth. Near the surface, the lichen grew over the exposed stone, making the hole in the ground seem like a natural fissure, but a level beneath, the spiraling stairs and pillars began, leading all the way to the bottom of the empty well, where a mosaic stone floor caught a bit of light.

As a boy, Morrison had asked his father about the depth of the well and learned it descended almost two hundred feet through solid stone. Entering the small gate, he and Rehena began their descent. With one side exposed to the open air of the well and the other to the foundation of stone, the dank, moist air near the surface quickly lost humidity and grew cool after just two spirals, by the time they reached the third spiral, armed guards appeared from alcoves in the wall.

"Who comes here?"

"Brother James."

"Brother James, is it of your own free will and accord?"

"It is."

"Has the person with you been found worthy?"

"I vouch for her."

"By what further right or benefit do you expect to gain admission?"

"By the benefit of the password."

"And what is the password?"

Morrison leaned forward and whispered, "Tubal Cain."

"The password is right. I will allow you to pass on to the Senior Warden's station for his examination."

The guard withdrew from the narrow passage that led to a small underground barracks that could flood the well with enough guards to plug the passage with their bodies. The guard who questioned him knew him well, and even knew about the Queen, but the ritual was observed nonetheless.

The Senior Warden's station was at the bottom of the spiral staircase, and he too asked his questions and performed his part, allowing the two guests to step onto the stone mosaic floor and gaze up at the tower of light above them.

As Morrison and Rehena reached the bottom, the walls of the crypt expanded in all directions, a great catacomb and vault built in the heart of the bluff. *If she is fortunate enough to survive the coming fires, she must help her son make wise choices.* "Before I take you to your husband's tomb, there is something else I must show you, so that one day your son can understand why his father gave his life."

Presider Morrison led her to the door that could only be opened with the keys to his office.

CHAPTER 49

Queen Dowager Rehena knew the truth about her slain husband, as well as Presider Morrison's plans to have Laho follow in his footsteps, so she coyly kept her mouth shut as Morrison tried to educate her about the Order of Eos.

Centuries earlier, the Order of Eos had carved the chasm into the mountain with a combination of sorcery and technology. It intimidated her to think of the intellect of such men, but Morrison wasn't one of his forefathers.

Will he see through my schemes? Just as Morrison and Yarland put their schemes into motion, she'd begun weaving her own web. Now, she played the honest role of doting mother. Having her son so far away from home allowed her to scheme with reckless impunity. She followed at his side as he brought her deep into the recesses of the mountain vault.

I know war is coming, but I must anticipate how he will react in the days to come.

Morrison lit the torches to illuminate a room carved out of solid stone. Many of the relics were transferred from the old Templar vaults to Madagascar following the Friday the 13th purge. In the past four hundred years, new rooms had been carved out to add to the Order of Eos collection. Most recently, her husband's corpse came back with one of those relics—an ornate sarcophagus. "Was it worth it?" she asked Morrison, who stood beside her husband's stone coffin.

This seemed to rattle Morrison, who blinked quickly as he turned from her and back to the treasures. "Perhaps I haven't explained the significance of what Tew died trying to obtain."

"I wish I'd known Thomas better."

Morrison's arrogance led him to say, "The treasures we keep locked in our vault are relics from the Dawn Era. Modern civilizations have records that date back only a few thousand years, yet we believe the world to be far older. The explanation is that great catastrophes frequently cause mankind to restart a cycle of growth, much like the seasons. While most civilizations blindly work their way through these dark hours, the Order of Eos carries secret knowledge with them to pass on from generation to generation."

There it is: a cycle. "What role will my son play when he returns from England?"

"I hope he will represent both of his parents as he rebuilds his homeland."

"You speak as if you will not be here when he returns."

"Regardless of what happens in the coming storm, Eos must now prepare for a new cycle, and I will serve the old cycle to the bitter end, regardless of my fate. Eos does not only exist here on Madagascar. Years ago, I sent my son to America to oversee our plans, and had he lived, I would likely be preparing him for the mantle of leadership, but alas, I'll prepare Laho as if he is my own son."

Does Morrison believe Laho is the son of Thomas Tew?
Surely, he must have his suspicions.
Or is he really that gullible?

Morrison put his hand upon the lid of the sarcophagus. "With each passing generation, we come closer and closer to restoring what was lost. Your husband believed in this commission, and together with Josiah Faero, set off to obtain the treasure you see before you."

Queen Rehena looked at the foreign words and the strange map carved into the lid of a stone sarcophagus, which now held the corpse of her husband. Beside it, in a freshly cut stone coffin, the dust of the original inhabitant gathered, displaced.

Does he suspect I betrayed Thomas? Then I shall be brazen. "Who was he?" she asked in reference to the former resident of the sarcophagus.

"We don't know. The sarcophagus was found in an obscure oasis and claimed by an Arabian emir. Its value is not the person it held but that it used an ancient language long forgotten. Eos has other artifacts which use this language, and Thomas wanted to be the one who unlocked the meaning of it."

He's blaming Thomas. "Why did the Emperor want it?"

Morrison shrugged. "Emperor Aurangzeb collects ancient relics also, and the Arabians not only sold it but also helped the Indians lure out your husband."

"And the Emperor lost a daughter and I lost a husband," Rehena repeated the lie told to the world. "Did this sarcophagus help your cause?"

Morrison looked at the map, an uneven X made by flowing rivers. "The information carved upon its lid was priceless."

"What is it?" she had asked, and then quickly rephrased it. "Where is it?"

"Apparently, my son stood near this place before his death," Morrison said, almost in tears. He gathered himself to add, "Whether you ascribe to a great flood, a volcanic explosion, a meteor from the sky, or disease and pestilence, modern history quickly leads to a bottleneck of dead ends. Civilization, it seems, is like the leaves of a tree blown away by the changing seasons. While the stars remain the same, to have them properly guide us, we still need landmarks."

America? "Are the mountains the landmarks?" Rehena asked, noting the seven mountains carved upon the lid.

"The mountains hold the secret for what we search for," he answered coyly. "The landmarks are the stars. Mountains and rivers can change with time, but the stars remain the same. If Thomas had lived, and if Faero had not been taken from us, they would have compared this ancient artifact with others we've gathered."

Morrison walked over to another treasure. "This map, for example, shows the same stars found upon the sarcophagus, a puzzle waiting to be solved."

Rehena turned away from the sarcophagus to reference the other artifacts and other rooms full of artifacts that surrounded her. "What is all of this? Where did it come from?"

"Once, long before Emperor Aurangzeb, there was another powerful ruler who tried to gather up all secret knowledge. His name was Solomon, and the treasures you see gathered around you once belonged to him, and now belong to the Order of Eos. Upon gathering these treasures and texts, King Solomon turned away from the god of his childhood when he learned the truth. Even great men die, but we must pass on our knowledge to the next generation."

Morrison sounds like a man who expects to die soon. "What will become of all of this in the days to come?"

"The Well of Initiation is built to defend itself from sudden attack, but the enemy that approaches is predictable...inevitable. I've made preparations to pass on most of this knowledge, letting it take root in fertile lands in the west. When your son returns to take his throne, what remains of this place will be locked away from our enemies, and only he will have the key. I give this to you freely."

Morrison picked up one of a dozen containers wrapped in sheep's wool. Even though the canister was slightly larger than a cup and smaller than a vase, he strained to pick it up. When he handed it to her, she strained to hold the unnatural weight.

It feels evil.

"The container is made of lead," Morrison added. "and within is an unholy substance created by the blackest of magic: shamir, it was once called. If your son or his descendants ever want to access the treasures left in this great vault, the substance you hold in your hands could open the vault, but he does so at his own peril and only as a last resort. Have I made myself clear?"

Rehena nodded.

I now know what he is going to do.

CHAPTER 50

Located five-hundred miles off the coast of Madagascar, deep in the vast Indian Ocean, the Island of Bourbon was originally discovered by the Portuguese around 1507 but was ignored for most of the next century. In 1649, the island was claimed by the Kingdom of France and named after the royal House of Bourbon. Aside from its grandiose name, the island had no other purpose than to serve as a penal colony.

When a fleet of warships bearing the black flag arrived, surrender came immediately.

Admiral Roger Silverthorn demanded only two things from the islanders—the use of the port and for all slaves and prisoners to be handed over.

Now, after a year of careful preparation, Admiral Silverthorn was ready to secure a place in England for generations to come.

The name Silverthorn will be spoken in Buckingham Palace, he fancied. *And one day I may replace Newton as the Grand Shepherd for the Priory of Ormus.* Unlike Newton, he held no animosity or vengeance for the Order of Eos. Nothing had been stolen from him, nor had anyone from Eos wronged his family. Destroying Eos, however, would allow him to rise.

With the return of Black Robin Bellomont to port, the final piece of the plan had fallen into place.

Just as the Black Fleet captains had done in the Warr Room back in England, they once again gathered, albeit in a smaller room and a smaller table. Instead of a map of the world, a twenty-foot map of Madagascar had been created for them to study.

Now, each captain sat around it for the final time. After they all finished greeting Bellomont, Admiral Silverthorn quieted the men and began.

"Give us a report on Antongil Bay," Silverthorn began.

"It is ripe for the taking," Bellomont responded quickly, but then gave a more detailed account. "We arrived under the British flag and were met by a simple harbor patrol. My navigator has created a map of the docks, the key defensive structures in the town, as well as the fortifications protecting it."

"And Yarland?" Silverthorn asked.

"Our Trojan Horse will open the Gates of Troy to us," Bellomont promised. "I did not want to draw personal attention, so I had one of my crewmen pick a fight with one of the locals, which spilled over into involving one of his soldiers stationed at Fort Morrison. My first mate was sent to deal with the issue while I stayed a healthy distance. Information was exchanged; Yarland remains Newton's man, and when the day of the attack comes, the guns will be silent."

Black Robin Bellomont then distributed a letter to each captain.

As Silverthorn read it, a smile crept onto his face. "This certainly explains what our other patrols have observed. Presider Morrison believes too much in honor and diplomacy. He's sent his boldest captain, Lavasseur, back to England, thinking Newton actually expects a reply. He's worried about Newton killing the messenger, unaware he's already stepped into the jaws of our trap."

While they had waited for Black Robin to arrive, the other captains had already exchanged information with him. Silverthorn looked over at Ned Ireland, "Tell them."

Captain Ireland glanced back down at Yarland's traitorous intelligence report. "The Free Clans have spread their fleet thin in a defensive maneuver." He stood by the southern tip of Madagascar. "There are two strategic ports: An old Portuguese port where Pedro Dias lurks, and Port Dauphin, protected by Captain Abraham Samuel. They have two warships and a dozen small sloops and cutters. Again, just a spider web looking for trouble."

"And we're already on the other side of the web," Silverthorn said. *We'll be an arrow that pierces the heart of the web without detection.* "Cass?"

The old bulldog rose. "I've patrolled the Mozambique Channel," Richard Cass began, "and aside from a few unaffiliated pirate ships, it remains international waters with a steady flow of traffic passing north and south. As instructed, I sailed that damned western shore, but aside from all the rocks and reefs, there were no surprises hidden in any of the coves. Only small ships could exist, which is why the Free Clans originally took hold of the lush eastern coast."

Newton is five moves ahead of these poor fools.

"Captain Bennett, could you share the report from your trip to the Seychelles?"

Thomas Bennett answered, "The Seychelles mark the open ocean route between Mombasa and Mogadishu with India. Normally, it is just a place to refit, or for pirates, a place to evade patrols. There were rumors of John Swan stopping, but—"

"John Swan is reportedly in Barbados," Edward Drummond interrupted.

"But…" Bennett continued with a roll of his eyes, "the reports were unfounded. We heard rumors of Robert Culliford as well. Only rumors. As we were leaving, a squad of six British warships arrived."

"Which is where they will remain," Silverthorn reminded them. "Woods Rogers commands those ships. They will act as a net should anyone manage to flee Madagascar alive. Newton fed the courts enough misinformation for England to worry about another catastrophe like the *Ganj-i-Sawai* incident. All we need to do is our part, gentlemen. Drummond…update the men on your reconnaissance."

Silverthorn barely recognized his co-commander. While the others had grown haggard since leaving the Warr Room, Drummond thrived. Drummond had transformed from a clean shaven lordling into the most intimidating captain at the table. His six-foot-two frame had filled in with chest and shoulder muscle, and his hair and beard had turned into an ebony mane befitting the king of the jungle, but his eyes had changed the most. As instruct-

ed, his vanguard practiced the raid on Bannockburn Palace nearly two dozen times on unsuspecting settlements. Since Madeira, where Drummond personally beheaded Marco Alvorez and kept the severed head as an ornament in his cabin, fear of the burly psychopath spread through the Black Fleet.

Will he stand in my way for leadership of the Priory?

He is much younger.

Drummond finished his briefing, "We've selected a landing place called the Ant Hill."

"Ant Hill?" Captain Walsh jeered.

"All the names of those villages and rivers along the coast sound the same. It has a small river whose headwaters begin at the base of Bannockburn Hill. As the crow flies, it is a twenty mile hike across relatively flat terrain. A short distance from the coastal village, a much larger river creates a border of sorts. This river is wide enough to prevent transportation of loot, so we will have patrol boats up and down this river—for anyone who manages to escape our ambush."

Silverthorn locked eyes with Drummond and nodded in affirmation. "We've decided that seven ships will attack Antongil Bay in force. When the guns of Fort Wallace remain silent, Bannockburn Palace will know they are betrayed. It is our belief that the palace is safeguarded with booby-traps, so even if we were to sneak the vanguard right up to the base of the hill, the treasures could be lost with a show of force."

Drummond continued, "For this reason, we will lie in wait. Right after the last monsoon, we spotted workers clearing away mudslides from the base of the bluff, a clear indication that the palace has escape tunnels to smuggle the treasures out of the palace and country."

"What the Free States and the Betsimisaraka don't know is that the Kingdom of Imerina has been enlisted to join our efforts to wipe our shared enemies from the island. After our initial strike on Antongil Bay, we will immediately withdraw our ships. Three will travel to St. Mary's Island to eliminate John Pro while four others will travel south to wipe out Pedro Dias and Abraham Samuel. Our coordinated attack will be met with a pincer move from the Imerinese."

"Between the destruction of Ranter Bay and Fort Wallace," Drummond continued, "the isolation of Bannockburn Palace will lead them to the inevitable conclusion that all is lost."

"A withdrawal will get them out of their hive," Silverthorn said, "and out into the open. Our immediate purpose is not murder and mayhem. We will retrieve what has been stolen, and thus steal the heart from our enemy. Without a heart, the body will die."

CHAPTER 51

Captain Henry Avery could see men coming for him long before they saw him. It was this reason that he'd invested his fortune into his small farm upon the rocky crag in the Andapa valley.

Is today the day I die?

I deserve death for unleashing Dalziel upon the Ganj-i-Sawai.

For a decade, he'd lived upon the crag, building up his temporary home, outbuildings, and barns. Together with a hundred freed slaves and their families, he worked the hundred square miles of fields tucked away in the mountains and flanked on all sides by rugged wilderness. Rory Halyburton, the nearest Eos chieftain, provided security to the east, and the rugged terrain and open fields provided security from the west.

Who will betray me?

The men who traveled across the farm fields appeared to be a mixture of Halyburton's Zana-Malata and Betsimisaraka men, who would have intercepted and interrogated anyone who did not belong.

With the right price, anyone would betray me.

Luckily, contentment brought loyalty from his surviving crew. Several of them still stayed with him, and in the course of a decade, they'd also made homes and families upon the crag. The children understood the tension in their fathers, and everyone was armed, including Avery.

Presider Morrison had sent occasional updates on not only the global manhunt but also the political maneuvering of their enemies. Avery's service to the Order of Eos had purchased him a decade of sanctuary.

Has my value run out?

Prince Andriana rode upon a speckled Highland warhorse, unique in its short legs and thick torso. Avery first met the prince at the union of Presider Thomas Tew and Princess Rehena, a pact meant to strengthen the Free Clans and the Betsimisaraka. To accomplish this, Prince Andriana had to step aside for his nephew. *Has he come to claim what should be his? Will his rebellion start here?*

Chieftain Halyburton rode on an Arabian. Of the twelve chieftains, Halyburton most-often sought contact with the outside world. *If any of the chiefs would turn Judas, it would be him.*

Behind them, the two columns of men, altogether numbering thirty, followed down the long road. If they meant to kill him—or take him alive—it would be enough.

"Should we hide until we are certain?" Bridgeman, his ship's carpenter, asked. When he'd gone into hiding, Bridgeman joined him, leaving the ship and crew to the villainous Dalziel.

Can I fight my way out of this? Or will I just get the women and children slaughtered? "No, something is happening, and we must remain to see where it will take us. Get the women and children out of here and have the men arm themselves."

The crag allowed him time for fight or flight, but Henry Avery chose to sit at a table on a porch that overlooked the valley below, where he could see and be seen by his two allies. Bridgeman returned, his face pale. "The men are ready."

Half an hour later, he listened as Chieftain Halyburton and Prince Andriana explained the coming doom posed by the armada carrying the black flag and crossbones. As a former member of the Congress of Pirates, Avery knew much of the lore surrounding the Order of Eos, so he patiently waited to hear about the plan.

"So Morrison wants the Free Clans to unite against Imerina?" he asked once the initial explanations were given.

"No," Halyburton said, but his eyes withheld something. "Prince Andriana will be leading the Betsimisaraka in a defensive maneuver, intercepting the Imerinese forces before they flank us."

"Leaving the Free Clans to defend Antongil Bay."

"The chieftains have special orders. We are to maintain a reserve position while the Congress of Pirates intercept the Black Fleet. Since we do not know where the assault will come, we will be able to redeploy at whatever port is attacked."

Bullshit. He is lying. What has Morrison done?

Electing Thomas Tew as Presider had allowed the Congress of Pirates to gain a place at the table. Instead of being the hired help, Tew became the united leader of the Betsimisaraka, the Free Clans, and the Congress of Pirates. Yet with Tew's death, the traditionalists put one of their men into place—Morrison. Too many of the clans either married between clans or brought in freed European slaves to their communities, which divided themselves ethnically from the natives. *Morrison thinks he is better than pirates and the natives.*

Prince Andriana also held a strange look in his eyes when he said, "Dowager Queen Rehena understands the logic in Presider Morrison's plan, which is why she allowed King Ratsimilaho to depart for training."

Understands the logic? What is that supposed to mean?

"And you've just now returned from the Witenagemot?" he asked Halyburton.

"Yes, like Prince Andriana, we both had orders. He's rallying the northern tribes, so we shared the road. From here our paths depart."

Fie! One of these men is about to make his move against me. Which is it? Pick wisely or die.

Halyburton elaborated. "Queen Rehena understood the sacrifice she was making when she married your friend, Thomas Tew. His sacrifice was part of an alliance made centuries ago, and the blood of the Zana-Malata sanctified the ground then, and for the sake of the future, it will join the sacrifice made by our brothers."

Oh, no. Sacrifice? That's it, isn't it? Morrison is calling for Endura. "I am forever in the debt of both the Free Clans and the Betsimisaraka. Just tell me what needs to be done, and I'm willing to do it. Say the word, and I'll do the deed."

Prince Andriana understood, looked over at Chief Halyburton, and then said,. "Queen Rehena thanks you for all that you've done, and we hope you will endure in the days to come."

Endura! What is Morrison thinking? That's the answer I needed. Andriana is my ally and Halyburton my enemy. "Chief Halyburton and his men must be thirsty," he said to Bridgeman.

His old carpenter understood the coded message.

Bridgeman fired the first shot at Halyburton's officer, and then chaos ensued. Like a trapped predator, Avery's middle-aged men snarled and growled as they attacked only the Clansmen.

A moment later, Prince Andriana thrust a dagger into Halyburton's side and another into the base of his throat.

The Clansmen were quickly outnumbered in the alliance of blood. Knives flashed as the Betsimisaraka produced small daggers, which they turned on the Clansmen.

Avery stepped away from the table, stunned by the sudden and violent bloodshed. *Oh, how I missed the life.*

The carnage continued for several minutes, with Avery's men creating a protective shield and the Betsimisaraka routing the unsuspecting Clansmen. He looked down to one of his old friends, Halyburton. As much as Avery respected Halyburton and the others, he loved living more. *Sorry, old chap, I just spared you the inevitable.*

Endura! "I always knew the clansmen were fucking madmen. Do you have any idea what Endura means? Obviously, you must have a bit of an idea or else you wouldn't have stopped Halyburton," Avery added, his heart racing and his breathing heavy. "Thank your sister for her protection."

Prince Andriana nodded and put his hand to the chest. "Queen Rehena sent me out to protect the Zana-Malata children from the rite of Endura. Her alliance with Eos is at an end, which means she no longer needs your services either."

Bridgeman turned in a panic. All of his men had gathered into one place to defend Avery. The Betsimisaraka daggers flashed in the sun while Avery's men frantically tried to reload their discharged pistols.

Son of a bitch... a trap within a trap.

It was over in seconds.

CHAPTER 52

FOULPOINTE, MADAGASCAR

1705

As the name would imply, Foulpointe was one of the worst ports in the Betsimisarakan Empire, but because of its defensive advantages, its proximity to a major river, and access to the Indian Ocean in two directions, the royal family took up abode.

A few generations earlier, Queen Rehena's family gained prominence amongst the eastern tribes because of the ability to produce vast amounts of freshwater and saltwater fish. One hundred miles south of St. Mary's Island and Antongil Bay, Foulpointe kept its independence through its distance.

Prior attempts to attack the small city by sea earned it the name Foulpointe. With a combination of river floods, tsunamis, and landslides, the small rise of land along the shore had become surrounded, almost entirely, with mudflats that extended up to two miles from the false shore witnessed from sea, snagging and marooning countless vessels since the Portuguese arrived two centuries earlier. Only with knowledge of the secret channels could a ship sneak through the quagmire to the fishing port.

For this reason, Louis-Armand Guerin anchored the *White Zombie* far away from the mudflats.

"We should send an envoy," LeSueur repeated as both of them watched the tender being prepared to launch. "This Queen of yours could take off your head and offer it to Eos."

But she won't. "I wouldn't be here today if not for her mercy," Guerin insisted. "Culliford and Swan stripped the ship and killed most of the previous crew. If she hadn't proven herself to be an ally, we would've been marooned." Guerin had first met Queen Rehena as First Mate to Captain Kidd, when he'd been sent to beg, borrow, or steal supplies. Weeks later, he returned to her in an even weaker position after Robert Culliford left Kidd with only a dozen men and a stripped ship.

"And we're just going to abandon you here?" LeSueur pressed.

If Foulpointe still stands, so does the rest of the Templar empire. "The Priory is coming, and the Congress of Pirates will be on patrol looking for the Black Fleet. We can't afford to keep the ship here while I meet with her. It's just not safe. Plus, there's work that needs to be done."

"What work?"

Guerin summoned his officers.

Once they gathered, he reviewed the plan. Del Torro would assume command of the *White Zombie* while Guerin was away, and with Naro Bon's navigational chart, they would travel to a cove where Captain Kidd had abandoned the *Adventure Galley* in his pursuit of Robert Culliford. "Once Naufragio gets it seaworthy, LeSueur will take command, giving us two warships. Then we'll set our trap."

"I'll captain a ghost ship?" LeSueur asked.

"You're right," Guerin added impatiently. *None of this will matter if Rehena changes her mind.* He'd kept the next stage of the plan close to the vest in case it was foiled by a fickle mind. "For any of this to work, I'll need more men for a second crew. That's why I need Rehena."

"What makes you think she'll give you any men?" LeSueur asked.

AN HOUR LATER, as the tender angled toward the narrow pass that blocked larger ships, he thought of the promises the two had made to each other. While he'd loved many women as the brash baron, Rehena had been the only woman he'd loved as Louis-Armand Guerin.

Will she risk helping me a third time?

The men around him were largely strangers. Some were refugee Huguenots with nothing left to live for; others were local Tortugan teens looking for adventure. None of them had been part of the crew who last visited Foulpointe.

A swarm of smaller boats came buzzing out from the corners of the harbor—the net protecting Foulpointe from any enemies.

"We are friends of the Queen," he said in the Betsimisarakan language he'd learned seven years earlier. The tension was terrifying, even for him, but he'd not allowed any weapons of any kind to be carried. The men were snatched up and taken to the docks for further questioning.

Luckily, the port patrol quickly handed them over to the royal guards, and by the end of the harrowing afternoon, Guerin was being led to the Queen's Tower.

Built by the Free Clans centuries earlier, the five-story observation tower gave her majesty a view of the jungle and mountains beyond, the Palace of Pillars, a ten mile panorama of Foulpointe and the shore.

Did she see me coming?

Is she even still alive?

He waited in a prison cell that night, but in the morning, they took him, alone, out into the Palace of Pillars, where he saw the queen waiting.

"I'm sorry it took so long," he shouted out and then bowed dramatically, which brought a smile to her face.

"I see you still wear the patch I gave you," Rehena said.

"It makes me think of you every time I look at it," he teased, closing the distance.

They stopped ten yards apart from each other. In the distance, he saw armed guards.

"Your predictions came true," Rehena said. "The Order of Eos and the Priory of Ormus plotted against each other; both sought my help."

"And did you give it to them?"

Rehena looked down, a bad sign. "You were supposed to arrive much sooner than this."

"I told you my priority rested on the American frontier. I had to contend with other matters before I could return. In that regard, I did not lie."

"I pondered what you told me about Eos, and your wise counsel helped me navigate these confusing times, but because of your delay, I had to make choices."

She's chosen a side.

I left her too vulnerable.

Her face withheld any clues about her decisions. "I also pondered what you told me about the American frontier. How did you describe it?"

"An ugly copy of Europe," he said with a grin.

"No, the part about its beauty."

To convince her to be an ally, he'd withheld nothing from her during his 1698 visit. "'The European nations gnaw away at the flesh of a creature once beautiful and free. Even a thousand miles away, the beauty is spoiled by forts and trading centers, where Europeans bring alcohol, money, and war to each tribe they meet.' I tried to capture those sentiments in a book I penned."

"And the free people you met on the edge of the frontier? What were they called again?"

"The Oceti Sakowin. The French called them the Sioux, and in my false narrative, I named them the Mozeemleks—just to confuse the matter."

"I couldn't remember the exact words you used, but I remembered the translation of the name—the Seven Council Fires. Did you ever return to the frontier?"

"My plans were foiled," Guerin said and shrugged.

"So what became of the mighty Mozeemleks?" She teased.

"For now, they hold strong, but the men who secretly rule these European countries believe it is their destiny to conquer all the lands of the world. Had the tribes of North America united their strength, they could have easily cast them off of the continent, but now...now it is too late. As I wrote, 'Rot has taken hold, and the maggots will reproduce and swarms of flies will return to bite away' at the mighty Oceti Sakowin until only bones remain."

"Exactly," she answered, suddenly relieved. "That is what almost happened here."

"Almost?"

"They came for my son," Rehena began, "thinking he belonged to Thomas Tew. Had I denied them, I would have made my people an enemy of either of the victors."

"A son?"

"Ratsimilaho, little Laho, your son."

Guerin's heart stopped for two reasons. "What did you agree to?"

"I almost sent him away on one of the ships you left for me," she began. "But I had to be mother to all my people, and your stories about what is happening in America shook me. They also wanted to pit tribe against tribe, so instead, I sent my brother out to unite the tribes. We'll do what the tribes of America didn't do…rise up against our masters."

"When do you plan to rise up?" Guerin asked, feeling hair stand on the back of his neck.

"It has already begun, unbeknownst to Presider Morrison. When Eos and Ormus begin fighting each other, we'll take back our country."

"And sacrifice your son?"

"Our son," she insisted. "It took considerable effort to keep the fact hidden from others."

"So where is *our* son?"

"Sent to England, apparently, for his education. If I can take this country back from Eos, on my terms, then I might be in a position to negotiate for the release of my son. The other ways all meant serving one master or another."

A political prisoner of Sir Isaac Newton, Guerin assessed. It'd take months or years for news in Madagascar to travel back across the globe. *A reckless plan but not a foolish one.*

"What of the promises you made?" Rehena asked. "My spies claim to have only seen a single warship as opposed to an armada. Where is the promised fleet?"

"I couldn't wait for it to be built," Guerin said. "I did not lie—it is being built under false pretenses—but it will not rescue your country from this harrowing threat, which is why I came back."

"A single ship to save my people?"

"No, but there is a reason why the Priory of Ormus has been cautious. The Grand Shepherd wants to eliminate his enemy root and branch, but he also searches for items that have been stolen from him centuries ago."

"Yes, I've seen some of the relics and treasures," Rehena boasted.

"The Order of Eos believes in cycles—"

"I've heard about the cycles also. It's what let me know the stories about Endura are true. The Chieftains were given orders that a mass suicide would happen as a sacrifice to the old gods and to bless the rebirth of Eos. Instead of fighting, Morrison is commanding most of his people to take their lives."

"So you understand the enemy I face," Guerin concluded. "In the past, they have moved their relics from vault to vault. It is my plan to ambush their attempts to extract these treasures, and in doing so, I'll have leverage."

"Leverage to have Laho returned?"

"I don't know if I want these treasures falling back into the hands of the Priory any more than I want Eos to have them. But if it comes to that, yes, I would leverage anything I acquire for the return of your son."

"Then I will give you what I promised," Rehena said, turning to her men. "Bring in Captain Avery."

CHAPTER 53

Admiral Silverthorn's Black Fleet entered Antongil Bay from the northeast, cutting close enough to the shore that he could see the blue reef nearby. Ahead of him, Farrington's ship increased the distance between it and the other six ships. With Farrington's fast ship as leader of the vanguard, Silverthorn kept the others in tight formation.

Closest to his ship, Ireland's ship remained the center of the formation, with Bennett and Walsh to the starboard side of the formation and Farrington and Cass to his port. The wings of the formation slowed in order to be directed once the battle began.

A relatively empty bay. Let's see how Yarland behaves.

As directed, Farrington entered the inner part of the bay with guns blazing. At the center of the bay, a small river emerged, with its mouth facing two small islands, essentially dividing the bay in half. While Farrington went right into the teeth of the defenses, Bennett veered toward the islands, just in case a ship was hidden.

A mile ahead, Farrington began to blister the fishing port with cannon fire. No return fire answered from the two cannon platforms of Fort Wallace.

The bribe worked. Yarland has handed us victory. "Give the signal," Silverthorn said, and the flags were raised and the cannon fired to give Farrington permission to press the attack. The vanguard ship blasted a path right up into the docks, and as it did, the starboard wing began to blast away at the right shore, which included Fort Wallace.

From the port side, Bennett appeared between the river's mouth and the island. His ship stopped, its bow chaser blasting away at Fort Wallace's western gun batteries, and its starboard cannons blasting the village on the western bank of the river.

Just like we practiced, Silverthorn observed, amazed at how the cautious, calculated plan finally came to fruition.

The signal was given, and Cass veered to the eastern shore to blast away at any soldiers rushing to get to Fort Wallace's guns.

How did Yarland do it? Silverthorn knew the Yarland ploy had been the least important part of the plan. Even if the traitor had been discovered, Eos had no clue the day or hour the Black Fleet would arrive. Yet the fact that they arrived at their destination with little opposition exhilarated him. After Cass unloaded all of his starboard cannon, smoke and dust obscured the fort, preventing him from seeing the damage.

Did they surrender? A white flag climbed a pole, which normally meant surrender, but Silverthorn recalled the Free Clans flew a white flag. A few feet below it, a black flag bearing only crossed thighbones unfurled—*Yarland's doing.*

Seeing their own flag, the Black Fleet erupted in cheers from all seven ships in the bay.

The warships coasted to the docks, which seemingly were empty. With his looking glass, Silverthorn focused on the black flag. But next to the flagpole, another pole was elevated, and upon it, a distinct sight—a severed head.

Yarland's head. The men in Fort Wallace were not turn-coats, but they somehow knew who had come to attack them.

Silverthorn rushed to the aft deck, looked back at the wide mouth of the bay, and although just specks in the distance, knew what he saw: the Congress of Pirates.

So there will be a fight after all, Silverthorn thought. A moment later, the cannons of Fort Wallace unleashed hell upon the Black Fleet.

"No Quarter!" he bellowed as the cannons of the Black Fleet joined in the symphony of destruction.

CHAPTER 54

FORT ROLLO, MADAGASCAR

1705

After days of hard riding, Prince Andriana and his cavalry squad reached the southernmost outpost of the Free Clans. Tucked away near the border of the Imerina Kingdom, the fort stood as a stronghold for potential invasion. Capable of holding several hundred soldiers in its barracks, Fort Rollo had served as the ancestral house of Clan deVilliers. For almost three centuries, the Free Clans lived in settlements just like Fort Rollo, where the chieftains came with a few hundred settlers, and then multiplied until each region had extended families all over the eastern coast.

Although Chieftain deVilliers commanded a small force, he also had hundreds of Zana-Malata men, women, and children living in the adjacent village. While Rehena and Andriana certainly wanted to defeat their oppressors, they also wanted to rescue as many of their countrymen as possible. After discovering the Rite of Endura plot that Presider Morrison planned for the twelve settlements, Andriana rushed from Henry Avery's Edinburgh Castle to the French settlement of Fort Rollo.

Imerina flags flew in the mountains behind the stronghold, yet none of the deVilliers forces had organized to defend themselves.

Am I too late?

Prince Andriana lashed his horse, and his men followed, even though they knew it might be a trap. The road to the settlement remained unguarded and silent.

Upon reaching the top of the bluff, the bodies of men, women and children were placed in front of each home in methodical order. The orderly scene was horrific. Most received a single sword thrust at the base of the neck.

"The Imerinese will pay for this atrocity," one of his lieutenants indignantly declared.

"They didn't do this," Prince Andriana said grimly.

"Then who did this?"

Queen Rehena had sent him to secure the southern border, blocking the Imerinese from double-crossing them. However, the Imerinese had beaten him to the location, yet didn't take the prize. Obviously, their scouts found the same atrocities. "Clan deVilliers did this to their own people."

His lieutenant showed no ability to fathom the concept even though they'd intercepted Chief Halyburton with the same grim orders for the residents of Edinburgh Castle. "Why would they kill their own people?"

"It is a sacrifice to their gods," Prince Andriana muttered. Seven years earlier, when Louis-Armand Guerin visited the palace at Foulpointe, the foreigner explained the history and nature of the Order of Eos. He'd spoken of Odin, hanging trees, and Cathars, but now, looking upon the silent slain, Andriana understood his enemy. "Those without the willpower were helped by their own soldiers; those with the willpower took their own lives. Before they came to our lands, they made a similar sacrifice with hundreds taking their own lives rather than surrendering to their enemies."

The theory became fact a short time later when Prince Andriana's men found a woman and daughter hiding in the well. Earlier, when Chieftain deVilliers had returned from the Witenagemot, twenty children, ten boys and ten girls, were chosen to depart with Vizier Falcoa's men, but the rest of the village gathered to hear the grim news from their chieftain. Lots were drawn, and healthy warriors were selected to dispatch the weak.

Chieftain deVilliers was found dead, along with his family.

The scene shook Andriana's men. "Had we not gotten to Avery in time—"

"Chief Halyburton would have forced Avery and all of his men to kill themselves or be killed," Andriana explained the lesson he was also fully comprehending.

"So where are the adult men?"

Only old men, women, and children decorated the silent landscape. "They believe their immortality rests in dying in battle. They've undoubtedly marched off to face their death at Antongil Bay."

"Send messengers to the Imerinese," Prince Andriana ordered. His men now held a ghost town. "While we wait, tell our men to begin tending to the dead. If the Imerinese need motivation to join Queen Rehena's purge of foreigners, they now have a reason."

CHAPTER 55

B A N N O C K B U R N   P A L A C E

1 7 0 5

The harbor burned, and Presider James Morrison smiled. He sat on the same bench where he'd sat with the boy king, Ratsimilaho.

Thanatosis—the art of playing dead.

The animal world perfected it long before Morrison attempted it. The pselaphid beetle would feign death, allowing ants to carry it back to the nest, where the beetle would spring back to life and gorge on the ant larvae. Fire ants when surprised by a predator would curl up like a motionless husk. A type of African cichlid learned to lie down on the lakebed, motionless, until smaller fish investigated—only to get swallowed. The unique American opossum, however, went beyond just stillness, excreting liquids from their anal glands meant to mimic the stench of death.

Adaptation.

Evolution.

Endurance.

In 1404, twelve families representing the Free Clans settled in Madagascar. After a century of persecution from the Catholic Church, the French Bourbon dynasty, and the Plantagenet Dynasty in England, the Order of Eos first tried flight and later camouflage to no avail. Three hundred years had passed and its enemies still found their private Utopia on the far side of the world.

Knowing what had happened to their Cathar and Templar kin, James Morrison did not underestimate his enemy, so he left tracks that could be followed, led the predator to the lair, and when the enemy finally came sniffing around the nest, played dead.

Another messenger came up the road to the bluff, and while the entrenched forces of the Free Clans watched from the palace fortifications, he looked out to the ocean.

Somewhere on the Indian Ocean, two vessels, *Lif* and *Lifthrasir,* carried an invaluable treasure: 240 children and his prized vizier, Falcoa. A third vessel, an armed escort provided by Captain Robert Culliford and John Swan, made sure the children made it safely to America.

A reward for warning us of the doom.

In the old tales, Lif and Lifthrasir were the two humans who survived the global catastrophe described in the *Ragnarök.* While the giants and gods tore the world apart, these two humans hid in a tree while fire and ice reshaped the world. When they emerged from their hiding place, they found a fertile new world, and the cycle continued again.

Now, a different type of wooden shelter, two frigates, carried the children of the Free Clans to a new world.

We sacrifice ourselves for a better tomorrow.

The messenger jogged across the yard but couldn't catch his breath to share the news.

"Take your time," Morrison said. "Take a few deep breaths."

"Their flagship has been destroyed," the messenger let out.

I wish he'd concluded with that bit of information. It makes me wonder what he holds back. "And our losses?"

"Their flagship turned and directly took on the Congress of Pirates. It took down Abraham Samuel's ship and John Pro's ship before Pedro Dias managed to subdue her."

The Priory of Ormus meant to exterminate them, but Morrison knew he had to take out as many of them as possible. With the Rite of Endura sanctifying the rebirth of Eos in America, the gathering chieftains and the Congress of Pirates would render Ormus toothless. *Thor and the Midgard Serpent perished in mutual slaughter. I'll take out as many enemies as possible.* "What of the rest of the Black Fleet?"

"They destroyed the docks and flooded the port. They took out one of the gun ramparts, and when I left, they were trying to besiege Fort Morrison."

Of course, they still believe their marines are swarming in from the north. Thanks to Culliford's advanced warnings about the Priory of Ormus, countermeasures were taken to make sure the Templar relics were also transferred off the island. "What else?"

"We've received strange news: a warship was spotted off the coast of Foulpointe."

"Bearing the Black Flag?"

"No, we could not identify it."

Is Queen Rehena fleeing?

"But there is something else that is troublesome—Henry Avery has vanished."

Morrison rose from his bench. "I hope you are being coy with me. What do you mean vanished?"

"Chieftain Halyburton was found murdered at Edinburgh Castle, along with a platoon of his soldiers. The Rite of Endura was not performed. The local Zana-Malata said Prince Andriana killed them and took Avery away."

Morrison laughed aloud. *The air is thick with treachery.* With Odin, every enemy he'd ever faced showed up simultaneously at the Walls of Asgard for the Ragnarök. Morrison had been ready for Newton and Ormus and even Imerina.

But Rehena?

I was prepared to hand Laho the kingdom and his mother threatens everything.

"Tell me more about this ship seen at Foulpointe."

"After the Black Fleet withdrew to the Island of Bourbon and after the Congress of Pirates assembled at St. Mary's Island, a solo warship arrived and anchored several miles off the coast. Fishermen confirmed it to be a rogue ship, but then an armed party of ten men arrived, just before the battle began and took away a prisoner."

"Any sign these were Mughal men?" *I'd wager she gave up Henry Avery to Emperor Aurangzeb.*

"They were led by a white man with a red eye patch, and the men on the dinghy were mixed race but definitely not Indian."

Who is this new player in the game? "Where is Prince Andriana now?"

"He's led his cavalry toward Fort Rollo, but the Betsimisarakan army is gathering at Foulpointe."

I never expected Rehena to be the one to send me to Valhalla. She feigned weakness by sending off her son, and then let her enemies tear themselves apart. "All seven ships that entered the harbor have been destroyed?"

"Yes."

Then Lif and Lifthrasir will be safe from pursuit. "And Captain Dias remains?" Unlike the Free States, the Congress of Pirates had not be counted on to fight to the death, yet Dias surprised him.

"Yes, along with a few of the smaller vessels."

During the Ragnarök, one monster after another presented itself until nothing remained of Asgard. Morrison expected more than the Black Fleet, Imerina, and Rehena to descend on them. "I don't care about Fort Wallace. Blast those ships into splinters. I don't want those Ormus men to have any recourse but to swim back to England. If we don't kill them, Rehena will. Is that clear?"

"Yes, sir."

"Bring me the fort commander. You are dismissed."

Have I waited too long on Madagascar? We should have fled the day Thomas Tew died.

Morrison nevertheless still followed old orders, and he trusted that Marco Alvorez's wild card would still prove itself helpful in the end.

With *Lif and Lifthrasir* departing days earlier from Antongil Bay, the mysterious warship didn't threaten the children, but it did threaten the extraction of the treasure. *Newton can't know about the children, but he certainly knows about our relics. Did Rehena tell him about the Alvorez wildcard? How could she know?* Morrison tried to calm himself as he saw the palace commander approaching.

Shortly, the commander appeared. "Yes, Presider Morrison?"

"I want you to put the bulk of our forces along the southern wall. After the Priory forces take Fort Wallace, they will abandon the beach and send every man they have up here to us. Your men need to buy us as much time as possible. Protect the southern wall."

"Yes sir," the commander said. "What of the northern wall?"

"The northern wall is already fortified, so all you need to do is hold the southern wall as long as possible. Can you do that?"

"It will be my honor."

Morrison left the stone bench and walked to the northern wall, where he stood alone. Even undefended, scaling the slope would be challenging and conspicuous. He looked down the slope. Nary a man was in sight.

Now, it's your turn for vengeance, Alvorez. May your plan be fruitful.

Under the protection of the jungle, near the base of the bluff, Morrison knew a small force waiting for Alvorez's contingency plan already camped.

May I live long enough for the plan to work.

CHAPTER 56

As sun set upon the bloody day, Edward Drummond watched the Black Fleet burning in the distance, and a smile crept onto his face as the plans of Isaac Newton and the Priory of Ormus turned to ash. His hand scratched his long black beard, and he subconsciously realized he'd never have to shave for another English gentleman again.

I've become a true pirate now.

Flames and the setting sun created a red blanket to contrast with the black mountain fortress. Cannon fire continued as two hated enemies, unaware of the single ship drifting into a remote harbor twenty miles east of the battle, tore each other apart. Newton's plan had been for him to intercept any treasure being smuggled out of the complex. Instead, he'd betray Newton.

Unlike Newton, who'd risen suddenly to a position of global power, Clan Drummond had long served Eos for countless centuries—but often on the losing side. While most believed Drummonds were an ancient highlander clan, they came from mountains far more remote—Transylvania. When Danish Vikings invaded Wessex in 1016. Edward's Hungarian-Saxon family took in the Anglo-Saxon royal refugees and brought them to their ancient mountain stronghold. After all, the Dromainns were an old house with ties to Eos going as far back as the ancient Goths. As a result of this alliance, the Dromainn Family not only took in their distant Saxon cousins but also stood by the side of Edgar Aetheling as the Saxons joined King Harold in 1066 at the Battle of Hastings to retake their homeland.

The Dromainn family picked the wrong side.

Stranded after William and the Normans defeated the alliance of Saxons, the Dromainn family became the Drummonds after receiving sanctuary from the Scottish Highlanders. Over the next centuries, the Drummonds witnessed Eos break apart at the Splitting of the Elm in 1188, followed by the eradication of the Templars in 1307. With Eos in ruin, and the Priory of Ormus on the rise, Malcolm Drummond swore fealty to Edward I of England when the Wars of Scottish Independence broke out.

The Drummond family picked the wrong side.

Rebel William Wallace quickly rallied the Scots against the more dominant English in a series of shocking defeats, and by the Battle of Bannockburn, the Drummonds joined refugee Templar Knights to help Robert the Bruce win Scottish independence. For a few decades, the family grew stronger as it made alliances with the Scottish Stewarts and Orkney Sinclairs, whose ancient relics included a Black Stone and a map of an ancient land to the west. After all, Prince Henry Sinclair had ambitious plans for creating secret colonies across the Atlantic.

Again, the Drummond family chose poorly.

First, the Black Plague devastated its wealth and resources. The Sinclair family fractured, and after losing the Battle of Knockmary against Clan Murray, David Drummond was executed for burning a group of Murrays alive in a church. After picking a fight with the MacGregor Clan, Edward Drummond's ancestors found themselves as cast outs in Scottish society. Alliances with the seafaring Sinclairs took them to the island of Madeira for a while before Edward's father settled at the English colony of Barbados, which is where Isaac Newton first learned of Edward Drummond. As the second son of a struggling shipping merchant from Barbados, Edward Drummond became a sailor just to survive. After a few years at sea, Henry Avery crossed his path. During Avery's 1694 mutiny, an opportunity finally presented itself.

Instead of running off with Avery and the other mutineers, Drummond, like many of his forebears, picked the losing side in

the matter, choosing loyalty with the foolish Captain Gibson and Admiral O'Byrne.

Yet when Avery became the most wanted man on the planet a year later, Drummond finally had a chip to play in the great game. Instead of letting the entire world know he could identify the arch-fiend Avery, he kept the knowledge secret until he could meet with the Grandmaster of the Order of Eos, Marco Alvorez. To a man like Newton, the Drummonds were a poor family who could easily be bribed.

They were poor—and easily bribed.

But this time, the Drummonds were on the winning side.

Newton's desire to find Henry Avery alive let Edward Drummond play the part of Judas. Before Newton's spies even interviewed him about the possibility of identifying the criminal Henry Avery, Drummond served Eos. By the time Drummond reached Eos headquarters at Madeira, Marco Alvorez already knew the doom of Madagascar was at hand, thanks to information from Robert Culliford. Yet after ten years of global war, Alvorez knew Eos couldn't outlast Ormus in Madagascar, so he concocted a plan that would appear as if Eos lost. First, he let every trading vessel that stopped at his port know that Edward Drummond of Barbados knew the face of Henry Avery, which brought Drummond into the service of Newton. When the Black Fleet arrived at Madeira, Drummond secretly evacuated all of the documents important to Eos, and after helping Marco Alvorez and his family flee to safety, he put the heads of anonymous peasants upon his ship for the Black Fleet to see his feigned loyalty.

Now, Edward Drummond prepared to give Alvorez a complete victory over Newton and the Priory of Ormus by absconding with all of the sacred relics kept on Madagascar.

"Drop anchor," Drummond ordered. Instead of killing Eos, the crew would help quickly load all of the relics. "Prepare the dinghies to launch."

At the break of day, Drummond would slip away into oblivion with all of the old Templar treasure.

CHAPTER 57

Am I a coward with a soul destined for the frosty torments of Helheim? Have I shamed myself for such dishonor? Burkhard Wachter returned to the vault where others like him carried on their secretive mission.

Atop the mountain, his brothers fought to the death like Asgardians fighting giants while he moved wealth from vault to wagon. Elsewhere, in the twelve strongholds, the elders spilled their blood as a sacrifice to the Allfather so that the next generation might begin with fertility.

There is honor in both deaths.

Yet Wachter would not partake in either death, despite the enemy being at the door. His sworn duty was to the Well of Initiation and to the relics held within. Most specifically, he along with several of his lifelong companions was a Keeper of the Elixir. Having spent his whole life guarding the vault, it now shook him to see it all departing from the secret back door.

A collection thousands of years old.

His lifelong companion, Torc Campbell, stood beside him, trying to catch his breath.

Wachter patted him on the shoulder. "The worst is behind us, and the future is secure. Bring one of the vats up to Presider Morrison and let him know we are ready to die at a moment's notice."

Campbell took a deep breath and pursed his lips. He wrapped his hands around the side of the vat, but when he tried to lift the lead container, it slipped and dropped back down to the floor.

"Careful, you fool," Wachter snapped. "You'll kill us all and fail your ancestors."

"My hands perspired," Campbell said, wide-eyed and terrified.

"I know you're ready to make the sacrifice," Wachter said, "but not until you get your vat into place."

Like himself, Campbell was a Keeper of the Elixir and had served Eos much of his adult life. For a decade, doom had hung over their heads, but now, in the final moments, the reality of their sacrifice became all too real.

Instead of attempting to lift the container again, Campbell walked back over, threw his arms around Wachter for a hug, stepped back, and firmly shook his hand. "Good luck in the New World."

"May the Valkyries guide you on your way to Valhalla," Wachter added, knowing that Campbell was going off to his death.

"I wonder what it'll feel like," Campbell said.

"Better than dying of old age," Watcher said. "All the warriors in Valhalla that have died from arrow, knife, sword, and spear— none of them will be able to claim they died like Torc Campbell."

"I will stay with Presider Morrison until the very end, you can count on that. Get as much out of the vault as you can. I Mak Sikkar."

"I Mak Sikkar," Wachter repeated.

The other Keepers of the Elixir shook hands with Campbell, who lifted the lead vat to his chest and carried it away.

Wachter's family had been part of the Keepers of the Elixir since 1128, when the secret trove was discovered under the foundations of Solomon's Temple in Jerusalem. Although he'd only stared upon the lead cases, he knew what rested within. According to legend, King Solomon's quest to find the Philosopher's Stone had failed, and in desperation, he turned to the dark arts to create his own version—the shamir. The demonic, living liquid could dissolve any material except for its lead container imbued with spells. Solomon had used the shamir to craft the Temple out of unhewn stone, but he'd been unable to subdue the evil spirit within the liquid. Poor Torc Campbell went to the Well of Initiation to open a vat and unleash hell on earth.

As soon as he did open the vat high above, a second vat would be opened at the base of the mountain, sealing any remaining treasures behind.

"Leave one of the vats at the entrance," Wachter said to his men. ."I want the rest of the elixir loaded onto these two separate wagons."

All around him, other men continued to evacuate the relics that Grandmaster Alvorez had chosen for relocation to the various Eos vaults around the world. Wachter would accompany the surplus to the far side of the world, where he'd train new Keepers of the Elixir to watch over the remaining stockpile. Along with the cannon fire from the other side of the mountain, the thunder brought a small army of foreign men.

Wachter turned to face Alvorez's secret agent—the man from Barbados. "Shouldn't you be waiting on the ship?"

Edward Drummond shrugged. "The more efficiently we remove these relics, the sooner we can be on our way. The first of the wagons has been unloaded onto my ship," Drummond explained. "Is that the Elixir?"

Wachter nodded. "How much more can your ship hold?"

"Whatever we can load by dawn," Drummond said. "I have orders to follow."

He turned to other Keepers of the Elixir. "Accompany Captain Drummond back to his ship and secure this first load. I'll inspect your work when I arrive with the final load," Wachter said and then turned to Drummond. "I only hope that the Elixir doesn't devour the remaining treasure."

Drummond returned to his ship with half of the known elixir upon the earth.

Wachter returned into the tunnel for the newest addition to the vault.

Tew's treasure.

Five other men stood with him, and they flanked, three to a side, the stone sarcophagus with the ornate carvings upon its lid. The simple coffin, holding the original inhabitant, would stay where it was—for now.

Wachter took a moment to catch his breath and then nodded to the others.

The six of them lifted the stone sarcophagus from its base, Wachter's fingers straining against the wooden poles inserted into the loops along the length of the coffin. Across from him, Daerg Dobie took hold of the other pole and with careful steps, the six of them walked down the gentle slope.

Like Torc Campbell, Daerg Dobie had been chosen to close the bottom of the vault, but knowing his death was only hours away, he continued to help move some of the relics to safety.

If not for the lit candles, Wachter would not have been able to find his way to the exit, for the treasure vault was a maze of tunnels and chambers. Generations earlier, the Well of Initiation had been carved out by releasing some of Solomon's shamir, which cut through stone from the high peak to the base where they stood. The rest had been carved by men, with turns and twists to create pockets of air to safeguard the treasure.

Having made five trips already, Wachter's fingers and legs knew to withstand the pain as he transferred the relics from the viewing room to a deeper location. With the last of the remaining relics tucked away, Wachter returned to the elixir outside of the tunnels.

Standing outside of the tunnel, the towering Drummond already stood with the second wagon, ready to receive the last load.

Only...there were two Drummonds.

In a flash of swords, Wachter realized there were several men lying dead on the ground around the wagon.

Past the wagon, other men fought in the jungle.

The real Drummond roared, doubling the speed and ferocity of his attack, but the hulking man he faced was his formidable match—taller, thicker, and stronger.

But Drummond was quicker.

He dodged the mighty blows from the attacker, but in the midst of the attack, he reached back and sliced desperately, producing a grunt from the bigger man.

Now hobbled like a great lion surrounded by hyenas, the towering beast stood his ground.

Wachter picked up a weapon from a fallen soldier and rushed to aid Drummond in the slaying of the monster.

Bodies, both enemies and allies, littered the ground around the empty wagon,. Whatever advantage the ambush had upon Drummond's men had been lost.

"I want him hobbled," Drummond shouted. "I want the brute alive."

Drummond and the six men surrounded the mighty man, who glanced down at the bloody wound on his leg.

"Pas de probleme," the giant said in French, flinging his cutlass at the closest man, catching him in the base of the neck. The left-handed throw was deflected by Dobie's own blade, but no sooner had the giant thrown his weapons in a suicidal surrender than a long-handled ax appeared from behind his back.

Gripping the ax with two hands, the man pivoted left and right, ready to demolish the first man to try. A strange growl rumbled through his grit teeth.

Wachter felt his bowels quiver in fear.

Drummond gave the nod.

In the swing of an ax, four blows were struck. The first two came from the giant, whose heavy steel cleanly cut through the bone of the closest attacker and continued until it sunk into the side of the second man. The next two blows came as Drummond and Wachter jabbed at the giant's exposed back.

Instead of falling, the giant used the force of his swing to counterbalance, and the embedded axhead served as leverage for him to deftly spin around to face the remaining men. He willed his wounded leg to follow a short retreat to the wagon, where he positioned himself for defense.

"Let me die with the Philistines," the giant next spoke in English.

"Get to your ship," Wachter said to Drummond. "Safeguard the treasures we do have. Get them out of here before it is too late. Hurry! I will wait until you've reached a safe distance."

I will die a Keeper of the Elixir.

Drummond hesitated, gave a simple nod, and then ran into the darkness, leaving Wachter and the others to wait in a standoff with the ogre.

"We shall meet in Valhalla," one of them said, and the others echoed the sentiment, except for Wachter, who knew what needed to be done.

"We rush him on the count of three," he said, knowing he had no intention on charging ahead. "One, two, three…"

They charged and he retreated, but not as a coward.

While groans and screams came from the wagon, he ran back to the opening of the tunnel, and at full sprint, he dove at the solitary lead container, knocking it over, creating the sound of water being poured onto hot coals.

And then the strange mist enveloped him.

CHAPTER 58

Is this my Ninth Life? Pierre-Charles LeSueur wondered as he felt hot blood oozing out of the numerous wounds he'd just endured. He stepped backwards to balance himself against a wagon, which had sealed lead canisters.

As a boy, he almost died in the belly of a ship that took him from France to Montreal—*my first death.*

Flatulence saved him from a second death, when Father Marquette sent him back to camp along Lake Michigan. If he'd stayed with the missionary, he would have certainly drunk some of the poisoned wine offered by Bartolome St. Clair.

The Fox Indians—a third death narrowly avoided.

The Mdewakanton warrior Keoxa caught him and tied him to a post with the intention of burning him alive as a sacrifice to the Dakota creator god Inyan. The frozen ground aided him in a dramatic escape and leap to freedom—a fourth death.

Was that before or after the Battle of Quebec? The loss of blood left him lightheaded and unable to remember the exact timeline. Either way, Jacques LeMoyne caught the bullet intended for him—*a fifth death.*

Surviving the English pirate attack had been good luck, even if Captain Kidd had orders to take him alive. *My sixth death.*

After that, he certainly had a series of hardships during the mining expedition into the Land of the Blue Woman, and when the discovery was made at the bottom of the pit, everyone at Fort

L'Huillier tried to kill him. Had it not been for Keoxa and Weno-nah, he would have been tortured to death—*my seventh death.*

Gaspar saved him from his eighth and most ironic death at the hands of friend and enemy Louis-Armand Guerin.

So this is it.

Today I certainly die on the far side of the world.

"Let me die with the Philistines," LeSueur shouted out, intending to die like Samson—surrounded by enemies. He pointed his axhead to the black-bearded devil who'd poked him with holes.

"Get to your ship," one of the enemies said to Blackbeard. "Safeguard the treasures we have. Get them out of here before it is too late. Hurry! I will wait until you've reached a safe distance."

Blackbeard nodded and ran off into the darkness.

Oh God, the boys.

Just days earlier, Louis-Armand Guerin returned from his meeting with Queen Rehena grinning ear-to-ear. Eos hadn't attacked yet, he'd secured Henry Avery as a prisoner, and he had dozens of young men to serve upon the *Adventure Galley.*

Guerin had then explained the final stage of the Madagascar Plan. "We don't need you to navigate around the world," Guerin said in reference to LeSueur's new captaincy. "Once Eos begins to move their relics, you'll unleash hell with the cannons. The *Adventure Galley* might not be seaworthy, but she's got thirty-four canons and oars. You'll dispatch any transportation vessel, and then the *White Zombie* will swoop in to secure the treasure."

Dozens of boys waited back on the *Adventure Galley* with loaded cannons. LeSueur had taken some of the seasoned Caribbean adults to scout the area only to run right into the Eos evacuation efforts.

Now LeSueur was all alone.

"We shall meet in Valhalla," one of them asserted.

"We rush him on the count of three."

I'm not ready to die quite yet. LeSueur lifted the ax defensively, and as he began to defend himself, his thoughts turned to Wenonah on the far side of the planet. *Sorry to disappoint you.*

The red haired attacker stayed wide of the ax, waiting for it to sink into the ribs of another. In that moment, he lunged forward,

sinking four inches of cutlass into LeSueur's side just below the armpit.

The ax fell to the ground.

LeSueur fell to his knees.

He glanced up at the red haired man who looked like a Viking of old about to kill him. The killer's blade paused. Despite holding wary eye contact with his prey, the man's ear turned toward a strange sizzling sound.

With life draining from his body, LeSueur puzzled at the strange glow emanating from behind them along the base of the mountain. *It's beautiful.*

Then it became horrifying.

A mist rose up like a fog cloud, and whatever it touched was devoured. The redhead swatted at his skin as if it were covered by ants only to see his skin, hair, and clothing wisp away, leaving a bloody statue writhing in agony. Soon the muscles stopped quivering and bones fell to the ground.

Nearly slain a few minutes earlier, LeSueur bowed his head in submission.

"This one has been marked," a crystalline voice whispered within the whirlwind.

Curiously, LeSueur found enough strength to lift his head. In the space where the red haired man once was, a dark silhouette stood in the current of mist, which flowed around both of them and into the jungle.

My guardian angel? LeSueur wondered. *Or the Grim Reaper?* Despite sitting on his haunches, LeSueur grew dizzy as he fought to stay conscious.

He put a hand down in front of himself to keep from toppling over and felt something wrap around his finger—a child's hand.

A surge of energy electrified his whole being, giving him strength to lift his head. In the shadow of the silhouette, he saw not only the child but also its mother and father. His first thought—*Wenonah.* The woman did have dark hair and a dark complexion but her clothing and age were all wrong. The man beside her—obviously a doting husband—also was not a Lakota warrior.

LeSueur commanded his thumb to touch the top of the infant's hand—to hold on for all eternity—but the image disappeared to the depths of memory.

Yet the dark silhouette remained within the flowing death that came out of the mountain. Once again, it raised its voice to the din. "Foul spirit, you are commanded to heal him. Restore this Child of Wutach and then descend into the Abyss."

Suddenly, he was alone.

Defenseless.

The vapor took him.

CHAPTER 59

The night sky filled with an unholy flame. From both the peak and base of the mountain, strange blue-green flames burned like a great furnace. Each minute, the demonic glow grew.

So as Edward Drummond hopped onto the dinghy, he shouted, "Drop whatever you're doing and get back to the ship."

Drummond took inventory of his wounds. The butt of the ax handle had smashed into his forehead, leaving a bloody crater that ripped flesh almost to the bone. He took a bandana and wrapped it tightly over the wound. The monster had also taken a chunk of forearm flesh when the blade of the ax grazed him. His left fingers were numb while the slice raged with pain, reminders of how lucky he'd been to leap back and not lose the entire arm.

Shit, my foot.

Looking down at his foot, he realized a small dagger had been sunk through the top of the boot and into the flat of his foot between the toes and ankle joint. *I don't even remember when the monster did that.* He pulled it out and let it clatter to the bottom of the dinghy

Two wolf packs had met in the jungle, and fur flew in a frenzy of teeth.

Who was he?

Where did he come from?

Had Isaac Newton or the Priory of Ormus suspected treachery, Drummond never would have been allowed so close to Madagascar.

Marco Alvorez and the Order of Eos trusted him with the most sacred relics of the Order, and any traitor within would not have waited until the last moment for thievery. Other enemies like the Mughal Empire also didn't seem to fit the facts.

"Drop sails and lift anchor," Drummond shouted out.

"Sir, what about the other loads of treasure? It's still three hours before daylight."

"Now!" he bellowed and turned back to the growing glow of the jungle. "We don't have much time."

Despite his wounds, Drummond climbed up the netting on his own strength. "Where are the lead vats?"

The boatswain pointed to a pile of plunder still on the deck. The lead containers sat in a pile like munitions.

"Do you see what's happening to the mountain?" Drummond asked. "Two vats are responsible. Secure these as if your life depended upon it—which it does!"

King Solomon's evil experiment was hastily brought down to the hold as the sailors got them ready to depart.

Will the fires consume the entire island?

With normal flame, burning fuels like wood fed them, but with Solomon's demonic fire, it transformed any type of matter it touched, including the stones and rocks of the mountain.

"Sir!" a voice called out from above his head, and with his eyes drawn upwards, he didn't anticipate the explosion until a shower of deadly slivers blasted through the decking a dozen yards ahead of him.

It only took one canon shot to identify the location of their enemy, but the fiery dragon began firing relentlessly upon them. The next several shots fired over the ship, but by the tenth cannon, the aim lowered and the ship began to take damage.

Sixteen canons—a warship!

But whose?

"Prepare to return fire!" Drummond shouted to his confused crew.

In the end, not a single shot was fired.

The mountain exploded in a billowing green cloud from the remaining vats left in the wagon.

Parked along the shore, waiting in ambush, the foreign warship found itself engulfed by the plume that swept down from the mountain. The explosion itself created such a violent gust of wind that Drummond thought the masts might snap.

He'd never felt a ship move so hastily or so suddenly.

In moments, the surge of energy took them miles to the northeast away from the island.

By the time the wild ride ended, dawn had arrived.

Eos—a true rebirth.

"Ship on the horizon!"

Drummond knew Newton's plan. After the Black Feet took out the heart of the Free States, a fleet of merchant ships would arrive to intercept any Eos survivors.

"Lure them in and then blow them out of the water," Drummond told his quartermaster.

"Sir, unless I'm mistaken, that is Captain Woods," the quartermaster answered.

They think we're all on the same team still.

"Woods Rogers has betrayed us. The East Indian Trading Company means to hang us all. Who do you think fired on us back in the bay?"

The lie worked.

I'll need to replace this crew at some point, Drummond realized. *For now, I'll have to make do.*

He signaled to his navigator and went into his cabin. His heart fluttered when he saw the first chest that'd been evacuated—the translated texts. Beside the chest filled with secret knowledge was a large wooden crate—the ancient *Al Marakk Map* created by King Solomon during his quest for the Philosopher's Stone. It combined knowledge of the old world, including the ancient language of old. A third crate held an even older relic—*the Odin Stone.*

"What's our course?"

"I need to understand our options first," Drummond said as his navigator unrolled modern nautical maps. It soon became apparent that it'd be an 8,000 mile journey back to Madeira, which no longer

served as a safe port. To get back to Eos allies in either Montreal or the Gulf, it would take him another 4,000 miles.

"How many miles is it to here?"

His navigator hesitated. "To the Black Sea?"

"Yes, I have allies along the Danube River. What's the fastest way to get there?"

"There isn't a waterway from the Red Sea to the Mediterranean Sea. To sail there, we'd have to go around the whole of Africa."

Edward Drummond's duty had almost been performed. As soon as he secured the relics, he'd be free to return to the Caribbean. Global war had broke out between European allies, which made the trip west risky. Heading into the Red Sea meant entering the Ottoman Empire.

Not allies, yet they could certainly be bribed.

His cannons opened fire on Woods Rogers' merchant ship.

"Chart a course to the Port of Aqaba," Drummond said.

Revenge will have to wait.

CHAPTER 60

As day broke, the island of Madagascar seemed afire. Smoke from the battle of Antongil Bay continued to pour out onto the cold surface of the Indian Ocean like a wound that would not clot. The sudden gale had pushed them away from their observation of the battle, and it'd taken most of the dawn to return.

As the *White Zombie* tracked north, Louis-Armand Guerin had not been able to pull his eyeglass away from Bannockburn Palace.

No army alive could have inflicted so much damage overnight.

At first, he thought the bluff might have turned into an active volcano—if not for the bizarre blue-green hue of the cloud.

Explosions sent fragments out into the air, and the hill seemed to grow smaller, as if melting within itself.

When they reached Antalala Beach, more smoke greeted them.

"Sail on the horizon!"

The call pulled the focus away from the shore and off to the northeast--toward open ocean. Although several miles away, Guerin could see it was one of the warships from the Black Fleet.

Then why does it flee?

He snapped the scope back around, finally understanding the source of the smoke.

A few minutes later, the news rippled through the crew of the *White Zombie.*

The Adventure Galley burned to the waterline.

What happened to LeSueur?

With Long Ben Avery locked away in the brig, the second phase of the plan had been to ambush the ambush. For that purpose, Queen Rehena returned the collateral given to her years ago—Captain Kidd's hobbled ship, the *Adventure Galley*.

The plan had been for LeSueur to lead an attack on the back-door of Bannockburn Palace, waiting for the Templar treasure to be brought into the open before revealing their position. With the *Adventure Galley* anchored a few miles from the port of Antalala Beach, they could load and fly at first light, reuniting with Guerin and the *White Zombie*.

Now, the ship burned where it anchored.

Quartermaster Del Torro barked out orders, and the *White Zombie* prepared for battle against an unseen foe. Master Gunner Benjamin Horne readied the cannons and supplies to keep the fight going.

Naro Bonn stood by his side. "Is it a trap? Should we anchor here and let search parties investigate?"

Through the eyeglass, the scene grew worse by the second. Half-burned, half submerged, the *Adventure Galley*'s short-lived restoration ended just as Kidd predicted—on the seafloor. From the gaping wound upon her flanks and masts, it was clear that the ship had not been boarded.

It was attacked in the dead of the night while anchored—a sitting duck. With flames still rising in three areas, the ship looked to be entirely abandoned—an obvious course of action after it flopped onto its side. Bodies littered the water and shore, and a few dozen men dragged bodies off the beach.

The young men were those given to LeSueur by Queen Rehena.

"Drop anchor," Guerin said. "We need to be ready to depart on a moment's notice."

"Aye, captain," Del Torro responded, and the ship obeyed.

"Naufragio, Papa Bones, Murray!" Guerin called out, dropping his lens when they approached. "Three boats, glean what you can from the wreck. One hour, understood?"

No one knows what happened except those men.

"Barrow, Bon, Horne!" The three rushed over. "Horne, are the cannons loaded and supplied?"

"As ordered."

"I want the three of you to bring boats to the shore. Horne and Bon, I want you to gather up all the able-bodied. Let them know it isn't safe to remain here. Barrow, I want you to give the burned a merciful end after the others depart. Is that understood?"

It was grim business, but they understood why it needed to be done. Guerin restlessly paced back and forth between the open ocean of the starboard side and the disaster along the shore on the port side. The departing warship continued to get smaller and smaller as it raced off to the north, and he kept an eye on the distant peninsula forming Antongil Bay.

We need to leave this place before anyone knows we're here.

Far off in the distance, the bluff that had once been Bannockburn Palace continued smoldering.

What sort of sabotage occurred?

Papa Bones returned first, his boat filled with a small pile of harvested supplies. Back on shore, Horne gathered up the survivors, at least twenty of them, into two of the ships, and he and Bon began rowing back.

"Horne, I want a briefing on what happened!" he shouted to the starboard side and the boats waiting to be unloaded.

It's taking too long. We needed to be gone an hour ago.

His glass once more studied the bluff and then slowly dragged over the green canopy of the jungle until the blur ended with the sand of the shoreline.

Dr. Barrow stood and walked toward the jungle's edge.

Guerin adjusted his scope, his jaw dropping at the sight.

"*Cho djab,*" a voice muttered beside him, it was the voodoo cook, Papa Bones. He could see it with his eyes.

"Is that Charlie?" Del Torro asked.

What happened to him? Not a stitch of clothing, or even hair, remained on LeSueur, who stumbled forward to be balanced by Dr. Barrow, who led him back to the remaining rowboat.

The crew rushed to the port side to see Barrow struggling to row back to the ship.

"I've brought the survivors to the mess hall for food and rest," Horne explained, also staring off at the approaching boat. "The survivors claimed to have heard explosions come from the bluff,

both at the top and the base. They were firing upon another warship when the flames engulfed them."

Impossible.

When the rowboat pulled up to the port side, half of the crew peered over the edge, but LeSueur needed no help, nor did he even show any ill effect from the explosion. Without eyebrows or a lick of hair upon his body, LeSueur looked strange enough, but none of the scars earned by Pierre-Charles LeSueur, burns or battle wounds, could be seen on his polished flesh.

"What happened?" Guerin asked.

"The damndest thing," LeSueur said softly. "I felt like I was dropped into a boiling cauldron so hot that even the water evaporated around me. I thought I'd died and gone to heaven or hell, but then darkness returned, and I found myself like this."

"Find Charlie some clothes," Guerin said, the first to snap out of the stupor. "We need to leave."

"We need to go after that bastard with the black beard," LeSueur said. "He's got half the treasures already loaded onto his ship."

"What about the other half?"

LeSueur looked at what Papa Bones had scavenged from the wreck of the *Adventure Galley*.

"I'd advise not opening up that lead vat," LeSueur said and then looked to the ruins of

the mountain.

"I think the men expected gold and jewels," Louis-Armand Guerin added. "Let's get out of here, and then you can tell me all about what happened."

"Where are we going?" LeSueur asked.

"Before our great adventure can continue, we need to rid ourselves of Captain Avery and convince Emperor Aurangzeb to give up his favorite new toy."

THE END OF PART THREE

PART FOUR
THE LION DEN OF EMPEROR AURANGZEB

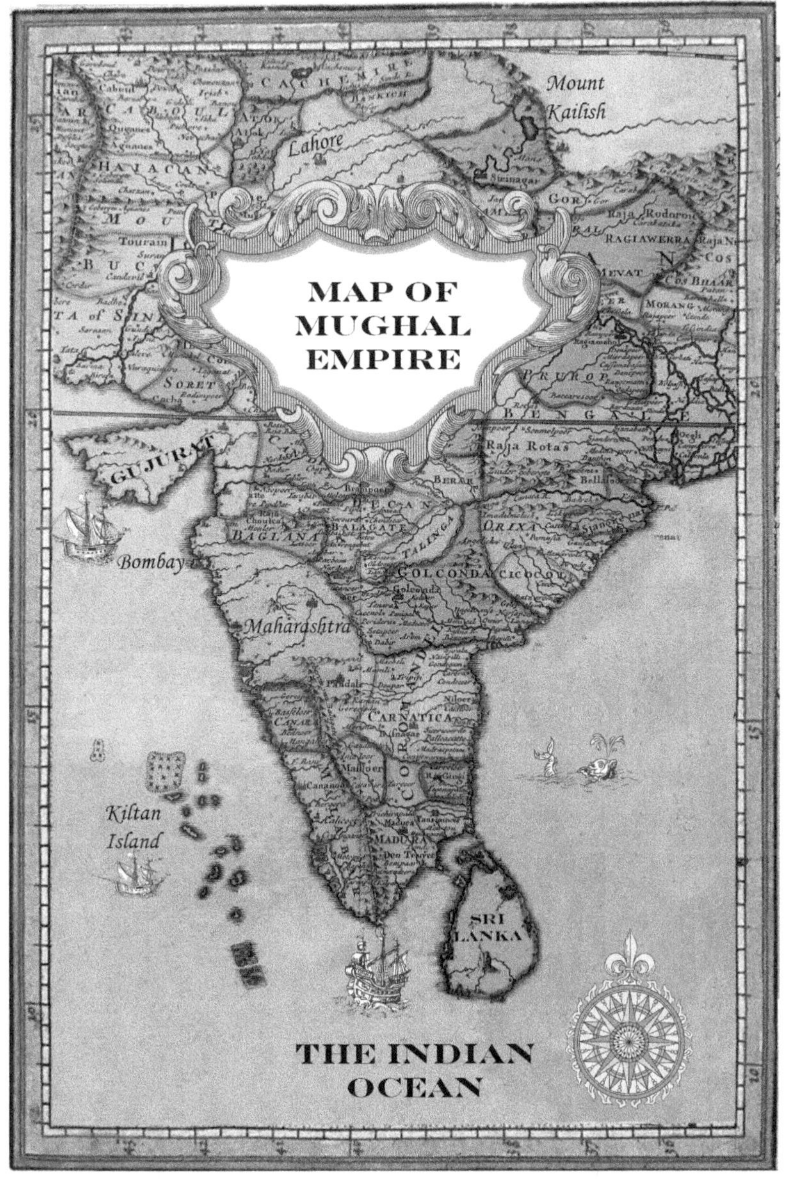

CHAPTER 61

Sir Isaac Newton shivered but not just from the cold—he was afraid. *Too many unknown variables. How have I bungled things so badly?*

Catherine Barton, his niece, seemed oblivious to the peril that waited for him. She leaned forward and kissed him on the cheek. "You'll be fine."

The carriage door opened, and he flinched at the sight of two royal guards outside the doorway. He stepped out into the cold and into the palace.

Angels closed the mouths of the lions to save Daniel, Newton reflected as he followed the queen's guard through the ornate halls. *I must deliver myself from this peril.*

He steadied his breathing and reviewed the rules of protocol for his meeting with Queen Anne. One misstep and the lions would tear his flesh from his bones.

Studying came naturally for Newton, but social customs were a science very foreign to him. While he'd met her several times in recent years, he'd never met with her alone and in private. A royal meeting did exactly what it was meant to do—terrify him.

Queen Anne rested upon a sofa like a walrus upon a melting chunk of ice. It surprised him to see how much weight she'd gained in only the several months since he'd last seen her at his knighting ceremony. Her blue and gold gowns had ballooned and her double chin rolled over her pearls. Her dark hair had been re-placed by a golden wig and her pale skin contrasted with the rouge upon her cheeks and lips. Her fingers were swollen from gout, which is why she lounged upon soft velvet. Although Queen Anne's appetite was legendary, she was not the lion Newton feared.

In a chair beside the queen, her royal husband, Prince George of Denmark, looked almost dainty in comparison. As consort to the Queen—and not an acting king—he'd been given the title of Duke of Cumberland and the title of Lord High Admiral.

It is not as husband, prince, or duke that he will devour me.

In another chair on the opposite side of the couch, the lion sat with crossed arms. George Churchill, while not as obese as the queen, still filled his velvet chair, which matched the burgundy velvets he wore. As a longtime friend of the royal couple, Churchill had been granted the title Admiral of the Blue, giving him command of the royal fleet. Newton heard whispers about the two Georges, as well as Queen Anne's own relationships, but he understood the three heads were tines of the same trident.

Newton passed the first test with flying colors, and after being introduced by the title given to him from Queen Anne, he sat in the chair across from the triumvirate.

Like any great apex predator, they lured their prey to them with flattery.

"Is that the new medal design?" Queen Anne asked.

I'm still the Master of the Mint, aren't I? Surely, this can't be the purpose of the meeting. "Freshly minted, your majesty. Would you like to inspect its craftsmanship?"

With a nod, Prince George rose and carried the leather box to his wife, who politely raised eyes and even guffawed when she saw her likeness. "Thanks to the craftsmanship of your mint, Sir Newton, my likeness will be preserved by history rather than by reality."

Prince George remained standing, and then in rehearsed orchestration, she handed it back to her husband, who then passed in front of the couch to hand it to the Admiral of the Blue.

Once accepted, Queen Anne continued, "Your work will be presented to a fellow Whig, Captain John Norris. Georgie, remind Sir Newton why we've decided to knight Captain Norris."

Why are they belittling me?

"Captain Norris is single-handedly winning the War of Spanish Succession for the Protestant nations," Prince George explained. "Perhaps the Admiral of the Blue can better explain it."

"Yes," the other George continued, "Captain Norris commanded the vanguard in the Battle of Malaga and most recently, showed cunning and valor at the capture of Barcelona."

What does any of this have to do with me? Norris knows nothing of Madagascar.

"There you are," Queen Anne ended the summary. "As we did with you, we chose to knight a prominent Whig whose public exploits are openly celebrated. The scientific community knew your name, even if the Tory politicians failed to understand how beneficial your time at the mint had been to us. Captain Norris earned his knighthood for his naval exploits and for his ambition."

Newton found himself reflecting on the play *Macbeth*.

'I have no spur to prick the sides of my intent,
But only vaulting ambition.'
Perhaps my sins have not been discovered.

Newton kept his mouth shut and smiled.

But the longer their smiles lingered, the more he knew they were playing with him. Finally, Admiral George flinched. "We recently hosted Captain Norris and your name was brought up on two separate occasions."

"Yes," Newton conceded. "I first learned of John Norris when he was known as Foul Weather Jack during the War of the Grand Alliance, when he was tasked with harassing the French in Hudson Bay. He was a friend-of-a-friend, who provided victories, both great and small, that helped bring France to the negotiation table to end that war."

"It was your shared friendship that turned our conversation in an unexpected direction," Prince George teased with raised eyebrows.

Newton remained calm. "I have many friends in many fields, which is how I was able to bring financial stability to the kingdom."

"Captain Norris explained that he frequently received correspondence from you through a certain William Kidd."

"We executed Kidd for piracy," Queen Anne added.

I labeled him a pirate and now that is being used against me. "My friendship was with Governor Bellomont of the Massachusetts Colony, who not only recommended Captain Kidd but later helped secure his arrest when he exceeded the mandate given to him by King William, your predecessor and brother-in-law. I did utilize the services of men outside of the Royal Navy to relay messages, conduct business, and gather valuable intelligence." Newton opened his eyes widely as if expecting a specific chemical reaction to occur even though he had no idea where it was about to go.

Too many variables. Too many unknowns.

"It could be inferred that you helped direct Captain Norris to attack French outposts in Hudson Bay," Prince George asserted.

I thwarted an Eos plot. "I wish I could take credit for such an endeavor. Securing outposts in Hudson Bay has given England a foothold to acquiring the vast resources of Canada." *If we could not go through the Great Lakes, we had to find a way around,* Newton remembered from studying the maps. Taking Hudson Bay, and then Lake Winnipeg, offered a back door route from the north. *Is this conversation leading to my failed gamble with LeSueur?*

Prince George continued, "Foul Weather Jack certainly did make a name for himself during the Nine Years' War, and before we could knight him, we needed to understand an accusation of insubordination, where he received orders to retake Newfoundland and Labrador."

"Such an action certainly would have weakened the Sun King's hold on New France," Newton assessed, knowing he'd given the order that would have caused chaos and rekindled the war prior to peace treaties. *How are they onto LeSueur? Did Kidd confess prior to his execution? Or…'Two separate occasions.' What don't I know?*

"Let me be clear," Admiral George began. "Captain Norris believes you were orchestrating foreign policy at a time when you were only Warden of Mint. Is this true?"

"Absolutely," Newton grabbed ahold of the lion's mane instead of running in terror. "The financial networks for the Kingdom of England are vast, and corruption ran wild for decades. I made inquiries into bankers, investors, governors, royal houses—anywhere I suspected corruption, and I utilized the resources given to me. During periods of war, corruption often goes unchecked. For me

to investigate accusations, I could not afford to do it through official channels, and I was forced to use spurious resources, such as men of notorious character like Captain Kidd. Considering the reputation of Captain Kidd, I cannot imagine what he might have said in my name to Captain Norris."

And luckily for me, Captain Kidd now cannot answer these questions.

Queen Anne pursed her lips, looked at her two Georges, and sighed. "I've been told besides being a world class scientist that you are a religious scholar as well."

"That is true, my step-father was a Reverend, and in order for us to converse, I had to learn his language. Prior to my commission at the mint, I had an obsession with antiquity and prophecy."

"You must be aware of the parable about a House Divided."

A metaphor He used when talking about the House of Darkness. "Yes, I am familiar."

"We've called you here today because England is just a few decades removed from a civil war that almost caused the empire to collapse from within. I wish to continue the work begun by my sister and brother-in-law, William and Mary, but even now my Anglican Tories fight against Protestant Whigs while my half-brother, the Old Pretender, rallies his Catholic support against us. Along with the chaos of religious strife, I seek to bring Ireland and Scotland into a union that will unite us as Great Britain. While juggling these domestic threats, England is participating in the War of Spanish Succession which will either elevate or destroy England as a global empire. To survive the days to come, we risk financial ruin, and I learn that my Master of the Mint is funneling funds to support a fleet of pirates. Explain yourself."

Ah, there it is. "I am a servant of England, acting under orders from King William," Newton began, knowing what he held in his jacket pocket. "I am the left hand belonging to one body, the body of England. I can assure you that the management of funds during this time of war is beyond reproach, and personal funds afforded to my office have been made through legal grants belonging to men upon whose shoulders unite the crown and the right arm of the military. We are a House United, even if the right hand does not always know what the left hand is doing." *A vague confession without any details. Let's have them reveal what they know.*

"So Captain Norris spoke true?" Prince George asked.

"I am not aware of Captain Norris's claims, but I am certain any actions I have taken promote only the welfare of England and not any personal projects."

"Our concerns go beyond associations with the notorious Captain Kidd," Admiral George began. "There are rumors from the Indian Ocean far more troubling."

Rumors from a traitor. Could it be Bellomont? Now I must rewrite history. "Yes, rumors have been whispered in my ear as well about a terrible disaster near Madagascar. I believe it is called a tsunami, a giant wave created from an earthquake deep in the ocean. I heard the Great Storm of 1703 paled in comparison to what this storm did to the coastal villages on the eastern shore."

"A storm?" Prince George's brow wrinkled. "A giant wave?"

They know about the Black Fleet, but its destruction has not been factually established. I will decide the facts and let them deal with rumors. "Yes, a British Merchant ship traveling from Bombay passed by Madagascar shortly after it happened, describing the devastation caused by the earthquake."

"We heard of another disaster," Admiral George added, showing frustration. "Escort ships in the northern Indian Ocean encountered a surviving vessel from a private fleet. Although it was affirmed this was not a typical pirate ship, its only identification was a black flag with—"

"Crossed thigh bones? Yes, our missing ship has been found. May I present you with my commission, instructions given to me by both of our predecessors."

Prince George snatched the letters from his hand. He walked it over to Queen Anne who began to read it. "Thomas Neale was your predecessor at the Mint. Who is this Robert Boyle fellow who signed next to King William?"

"Robert Boyle was the left hand for King William, a gifted scientist, a devout Anglican, and the leader of an organization he dubbed 'The Invisible College.'"

"Yes, I see mention of the Invisible College in the letter," Queen Anne admitted. "Explain it."

"Upon Robert Boyle's death, I assumed control of his commission, and in the second letter, you will see that King William

directed me to deal with the coalition of pirates gathered in the Indian Ocean. As Captain Norris correctly assessed, I did enlist Captain Kidd and other ambitious men to deal with this shadowy threat in Madagascar, and my financial supporters, understanding how Indian Ocean piracy threatened commerce, funded the creation of this covert fleet. During the commission of its duties, however, this great tidal wave brought ruin to both sides. The fleeing ship you spoke of has more likely than not turned rogue, or else it would have remained in Madagascar for subsequent orders. Does this satisfy your majesty?"

A few sheets of paper have closed the mouths of these lions.
But which of the eight captains fled Madagascar?
I'll have the traitor's head set on my desk.

Queen Anne handed the letters to her husband, who then walked them over to Newton. A bell summoned the footmen back into the room. "Sir Newton, from this time forward, please keep the Royal Navy informed about such grand endeavors."

Newton bowed, "Yes, your majesty."

As Newton walked out of the lion's den, he smiled. *The great fat fools thought they could eat me. Now I've ensnared their support and learned a valuable truth—a ship fled.*

Once outside, back in the cold, he almost began trotting back to the waiting carriage. When the door opened, Catherine scowled. "It's about time. So how did it go?"

"It took them fifteen years, but I think they finally understand I am more than a scientist. They knew I arranged for Captain Norris to take Hudson Bay but had no imagination for the reasons I did it. They also knew about the Black Fleet but had no idea what to say when I effectively sank it with a lie about a tsunami."

Catherine chuckled. "My clever Uncle. So you're not going to be arrested and thrown into your own tower?"

"No, but I have a task for you, my sweet—find out which of our eight captains has been spying for the crown this whole time."

"An excuse for more parties," Catherine smiled. "I'll deliver his head upon a plate, dear uncle."

CHAPTER 62

N A T C H E Z   T E R R I T O R Y

1 7 0 6

Two hundred miles upstream from the mouth of the Mississippi, Gaspar continued his mission, blindly unaware of anything that took place in the Indian Ocean.

And what have we caught in our nets today?

In the distance, he could hear the excited voices of his Natchez soldiers, who were mostly teenage boys given to him for seasoning.

Gaspar worked beside the young men in the trap he fashioned, and his post was at the center of it all in the big cypress tree. The trap was set at two islands opposite of a large meander that had almost filled in. Deep in the meander, the scouts made camp, but here, along the river, the scouts hid in the trees overlooking the two islands that divided the river.

"Sir, we've caught a Frenchman," a Natchez warrior said with a wide grin.

Gaspar didn't want to have to climb all the way down from his lofty perch. "A fur trader?"

"Yes, but he didn't come from the south like the others," the young warrior stated. "He came from the north."

Before Gaspar could even press further, another young man came running up to the base of the tree. "We were about to kill him, but he recognized the word you'd given us."

Penicaut!

"Go back and make sure he isn't harmed," Gaspar said.

A moment later, he found himself breathing heavily at the base of the big Cypress. Except for getting to know his new Natchez allies, Gaspar had served the Periphery for almost a year without any news. Six years after LeSueur left Penicaut behind at Fort L'Huillier far upstream, the secret agent of the Periphery finally came down the river.

By the time Gaspar reached the prisoner, a dozen young Natchez warriors surrounded the ragged Frenchman, who looked at him with curious but doubtful eyes. His European clothes were in tatters, patched and replaced by furs and leathers. Despite a ragged beard, the young man looked relatively healthy.

Gaspar, however, had to let his heart and lungs calm.

"You're not from around here, are you?" Penicaut said.

Thirty years earlier, the Periphery had sent a spy to the Mississippi in search of allies. The Natchez had accepted the news, hoping to survive the coming colonial tide. LeSueur had almost murdered the spy, believing him an enemy. "DuBois," Gaspar said, invoking the name of the elder Periphery spy who'd cultivated Natchez relations before retiring back to Europe.

Penicaut nodded and then collapsed in relief. "Phillip Fucking DuBois," he repeated the keyword to identify himself as the lost Periphery agent described by LeSueur.

Gaspar quickly explained the situation to the Natchez and he embraced the stranger.

Two men to hold back an entire nation, Gaspar realized. *But it's more help than I had when I woke this morning.*

Soon, Eos and France would send more than just a few squads into the nets.

I can only hope I last until Guerin and LeSueur return.

CHAPTER 63

Across the street, the elm trees budded, filling the branches with a tinge of green. The marketplace already bloomed with tulips and spring grass.

My enemies move while I stand still, watching days, weeks, and months slip by.

Remembering pieces of a late-night conversation, Newton turned back to his bed, straightening the sheets and pulling the red mohair blanket back into place. His old friend, the mohair blanket, kept him warm through another cold London winter, but with the full arrival of spring, he'd pushed it down to his ankles before dawn.

After declaring crimson as his favorite color to his niece, every fabric he now owned seemed to be crimson, from his bedspread to his curtains to his chair. Most of the jackets in his closet were also crimson, but today, he slipped on a heavy blue robe and slippers. Since he'd transitioned from science to politics, she'd been his most trusted aid.

Walking down the stairs to his office and library, he found his coffee and newspapers waiting on a small table beside his...crimson sofa. Memories of a late night visit kept him from sitting down, and he continued to the staircase that led to the main floor.

There, in the kitchen, he found Bernard Clairval hunched over a plate of bacon and eggs. He asked, "Yes?"

"Catherine has an answer," Newton said. "Gather everything, including maps, and bring them upstairs to the library."

"Good, this sedentary life bores me," Bernard said with a crooked grin.

Beyond the kitchen, the spacious entertaining room remained pristine except for articles of clothing leading to the small apartment on the far side. He'd given Catherine six hours to sleep and for the alcohol coursing through her system to filter. Her body sprawled out on the bed, with just a thin gown covering her form. He sat at a small footstool beside her bed. "Catherine, my mind has been spinning for hours while you sleep. It's time to get dressed and join me upstairs in the library to discuss your discoveries."

Catherine groaned as if dying, and opened one eye. "I was dreaming of tattie scones."

"Considering the hour, you might want to fancy something for lunch."

"Can you mix a concoction for a headache, dearest uncle?"

"Take your time, we'll be sorting through things upstairs."

THIRTY-THREE MINUTES LATER, Catherine walked into the room, perfumed, powdered, combed and dressed to dazzle. Newton extended the cup which she snatched as she walked by. She perched down on the loveseat opposite of his reading chair. Bernard sat in a corner of the crimson sofa.

She finished her beverage to the last drop as she continued her habit of letting the men in her life spill their secrets. Finally, she asked, "So what in the world does Bilocci mean?"

Bernard leaned back on the couch, crossing his arms and kicking up his feet.

"The hunchback knows but I'm kept in the dark?" Catherine asked sternly.

"Go ahead and tell her," Bernard said.

"I thought the whole point was to keep the two of you separate from one another," Newton argued. "My right hand and left hand, so to speak."

Bernard rolled his eyes. "She's shown discretion since we invited her to London. You served, without question, for several years

before *gnosis* was given to you. As far as I'm concerned, Miss Barton should know more."

I almost lost my mind when I learned the truth, but keeping secrets from her will only endanger our relationship. How could I bear losing her? "Tell me about our song bird and I'll tell you all about Bilocci."

"An abuse of office," Catherine began. "Not as the Master of Mint, they are more than delighted with your financial work, but they've known for quite a while that you're the president of the Invisible College, as you put it."

"How much do they know?" Bernard asked.

"If this was a Catholic monarchy, you might need to worry," Catherine said, fiddling with her fingernails, "but they seem to view it as a scientific club, even if they don't have a name or clear understanding. It is Admiral Churchill who wanted your blood, especially when he found out resources for warships were not going to him during the War of Spanish Succession."

"How long have they known?" Newton asked.

"Since you ordered the fleet built shortly after the attack on the *Ganj-i-Sawai*. They were willing to look the other way when you hired privateers like Kidd to do your bidding, but creating the Black Fleet crossed the line. Luckily, your handling of Kidd's trial proved enough to them. In a way, both of you were on trial, and luckily, Kidd hung instead of you."

I am the public face for a secret enclave. Now I understand why—I am expendable. "So did they court one of my captains or was he one of them from the beginning?"

"A double-agent, apparently," Catherine added. "Like you, the Crown wanted an ambitious young man willing to get his hands dirty to advance his position—Edward Drummond."

Newton turned to watch Bernard's reaction, whose face twisted until he realized he was being watched. "What?" he snapped. "He was the only one who could positively identify Henry Avery."

My calculated risk failed. "And that fact is what he used against us. I take it our Scottish queen got a hold of him before we made our move?"

"The royal investigators wanted to know as much as they could about Henry Avery, so when Drummond returned to England, he was quickly caught up into the conspiracy to spy on you. Again,

both Georges took offense at the creation of the Black Fleet and wanted to find ways to entrap you."

"A complete naval disaster should have given it to them," Newton said. "I doubt if I'll be given another opportunity to spend such vast sums of money."

"Yes, luckily Edward Drummond's true loyalty did not belong to Queen Anne. What do you know of the Order of Eos?"

Bernard grinned, "See...I told you she is too clever for us. Your brain might have ten times the information in it, but she is quick witted and clever."

"I take it you old men already know about the Order of Eos?"

Both nodded. "It will explain Bilocci," Newton said. "but please continue."

"Edward Drummond had sworn loyalty to the Order of Eos before he left his home in the Caribbean, and as an agent of Eos, he collected information while working his way up the ranks, until the day Henry Avery mutinied."

"And Drummond had a card to play, selling information to the highest bidder, which would have been me if I hadn't brought financial stability to the English Crown."

"When you were summoned to the meeting at Kensington Palace, they already knew all about the Black Fleet, but then suddenly...nothing. Drummond vanished."

"He's quite adept at double-crossing," Newton added. *At least I picked an impressive young man, even if he is my enemy.*

"Now Queen Anne and her Georges want what they paid for, and the main branch of the Drummond family are distancing themselves from him," Catherine said. Her lovely gaze fell upon Bernard just as it did for her social victims. The misshapen creature, once deposited on the slopes of Mount Grauspitz as a form of post-birth abortion, nervously adjusted his position on the loveseat. "If I was to ask where Edward Drummond took his warship, I'm assuming the answer will involve Bilocci."

Newton glanced to Bernard. "Yes, before explaining Bilocci, I'd like Bernard to tell you what happened on Madagascar."

"Long before you were born," Bernard said, looking down, "there was an alliance of men seeking the truth, and when the alliance had run its course, one side betrayed another. Along with the

philosophical betrayal, thievery was involved, and the stolen goods were shifted from stronghold to stronghold until—"

"They ended up in Madagascar?"

"Yes. The previous Grand Shepherds focused mostly on maintaining power within the courts of Europe, but your uncle is determined to recover what was lost so long ago."

"Under the guise of hunting pirates."

"Oh, no. The pirates and the thieves are one and the same even if they were unaware of their own identity. In the past, entire armies marched on strongholds, allowing our enemies to slip away with the stolen goods. This time, we sent a smaller force of eight ships filled with elite soldiers to snatch our prize before they knew what happened."

"And Edward Drummond betrayed us."

"Yes, my dear, and as a result, our plan failed in very strange ways. Instead of securing the treasure, Captain Drummond, working with the Order of Eos, managed to evacuate it, and once again, it vanished into the night."

"And then came the tsunami, the tidal wave," Catherine repeated his lie.

At this, Newton interrupted the tale. "The tsunami is a fabrication told to Queen Anne to explain what happened to my fleet. Tell her the truth, Bernard."

"Your uncle's fleet smashed the defenses of Fort Wallace before finding themselves in a trap. Against overwhelming odds, the Black Fleet triumphed thanks to its modern weaponry and stronger design. None of the seven warships left the bay, but a small armada of merchant ships led by the late Woods Rogers secured control of Madagascar's waters. Despite our losses, this allowed us to control the narrative."

"The story of the Tsunami."

"It was an unholy disaster of another kind. Betrayal is a two-edged sword, and those willing to betray often find themselves betrayed. Eos is utterly routed, and our new ally, Queen Rehena, rules the island. What do you know of the French Cathars?"

"My modest education has left me ignorant of the Cathars."

"Of course. Your specialty is current events, not four hundred year old massacres. The Cathars were a religious group with close

ties to our thieving friends, and when the might of the Catholic Church decided to exterminate the threat to Christendom, they did not stand a chance. Locked away in their strongholds, the Cathars chose the ritual of Endura, or suicide. All across the highlands of Madagascar, the colonists took their lives by the thousands. Many men, women, and children died, yet many were liberated."

"How?"

"Queen Rehena sent envoys to tell us of her active involvement in the revolution upon the island. She's even managed to secure some of the lost relics, which she wants to trade for the return of her son."

"Her son?"

Bernard had created the cruel plot with John Yarland. "A political prisoner to coerce her obedience, yet it turns out she's willingly aided us against Eos. The twelve cities were dead by the time our allies set foot to conquer them."

Years of planning. So much went according to plan, but the victory was tarnished by Edward Drummond. "Tell her about their capital."

"They called it Edinburgh Castle, where their elected monarch ruled. During the battle of Antongil Bay, we assume shortly after Captain Drummond helped evacuate the treasures, the entire complex dissolved."

"A volcanic explosion?" Catherine asked.

"Evil unleashed, from the descriptions we received, a vaporous cloud that dissolved anything it touched—rock, metal, organic. For three days it swirled around, transforming the terrain into melted butter. The men withdrew to the battered ships until it cleared."

"What was it?"

"Simply put—magic. But acquired magic. Stolen magic. These zealots saw it as a way to destroy the old while sanctifying the new. As you can see, we succeeded in dislodging them root and stem from Madagascar but only because they chose it. If we can find that ship, we can crush the seed before it can germinate."

"Apparently the seed will be planted in America," Catherine smiled and shrugged.

"America?" Bernard questioned. "Immediately after the battle, Drummond was seen sailing north from Madagascar."

Catherine smiled confidently. "A lot can change in a year. As an outlaw from the British Empire, Captain Drummond sailed home, ahead of the news of his betrayal. By the time news of Madagascar reached you, he was already home in the Bahamas. From there his destination is uncertain. Some reports have him going north to Bermuda; others say he went to Jamaica and joined a crew under the alias Thatcher. The most credible involves him abandoning his warship at a place called Bilocci, which means nothing to me. Care to explain?"

Newton explained. "It is an indigenous tribe that lives along the Gulf of Mexico, which the French called Biloxi. He most likely brought his ship directly to Fort Maurepas, where one of the LeMoyne brothers commands."

"Jean Baptiste?" Bernard added.

He's been my source of information for so long he is threatened by my amazing niece.

"No, the elder, Pierre," Newton corrected Bernard and turned to Catherine, "Pierre LeMoyne fought against Captain Norris, and when that path was stolen from him, he went to the Gulf to find a southern route for our former operative, Pierre-Charles LeSueur. Bermuda or Biloxi? Fort Maurepas is controlled by the Order of Eos, which would make sense. But Bermuda? That is strange." *LeSueur's ship sank along with the Philosopher's Stone near Bermuda.* "You've done very well, Catherine."

"Thank you," Catherine said, "So the Order of Eos is our enemy."

"Drummond represents a group of religious zealots who would sacrifice thousands to wake the old gods and open the abyss to the evils within," Newton explained. "Our truest enemy remains the Catholic Church and its Jesuit Order. The three of us are the defenders of humanity."

"So was it the church who contacted Queen Rehena about our operation?" Catherine asked.

"Why do you say that?" Newton asked.

"Rumors," Catherine shrugged. "Now that your net of merchants have returned, I've heard a couple strange tales involving the queen."

"Such as?"

"Accounts from the survivors claim that prior to our arrival, a single pirate ship arrived at Queen Rehena's palace at Foulpointe. I can only assume it wasn't one of our captains."

"If it was an agent of the Catholic Church, it'd likely be a French or Spanish vessel," Bernard added, and then showed deference to his young rival for attention. "Did your contact get a description of it?"

"Apparently, it was a ghost ship."

"No," Newton dismissed. "Our enemies speak like this. We deal in facts. Give me the facts."

"The eyewitness claimed that Captain Kidd returned in the *Adventure Prize* and sent his First Mate to the queen, a man wearing a red eye patch."

"But Captain Kidd is dead," Bernard protested. "I saw him executed."

"Hopefully he will stay dead this time," Newton said, "But I worry about this loose thread unraveling everything. We've expended vast resources taking Madagascar from our enemies, and now we must find new agents and new funds for our operations. Obviously, we must find and deal with Edward Drummond, but keep your ears open about a rogue pirate ship captained by a man with a red eye, would you?"

CHAPTER 64

What's taking them so long? Louis-Armand Guerin worried as he waited for the skiff to return to the disguised *White Zombie*. His looking glass studied the frenetic port along the western shore of India. Two mighty empires—the Mughal and British—shared the port. Dozens of other countries used the harbor also. Although surrounded by hundreds of vessels, Guerin felt no security as he nervously studied the waters for dangers.

"There they are," Guerin muttered to himself upon seeing the skiff. A moment later, Jimmy Duke announced it to the crew after spotting it himself.

Impatience had soured the mood of the crew. The treasures collected from the burned wreck of the *Adventure Galley* turned out to be a small deposit on what most of the crew had hoped for. Certainly, they stayed for the adventure, but none of them were Periphery, and Guerin gravely worried about pushing them too far, especially with the latest gambit.

Pierre-Charles LeSueur still sat apart from the crew, who still looked at him with wide eyes months after he walked out of the mouth of hell without a scratch. If anything, the divine intervention bought Guerin more patience, but the miracle didn't put any money in the pockets of the crew.

Benjamin Horne also sulked. Following the fall of Madagascar, he'd begged two courses of action: to scour the smoldering ruins of the Madagascar vault or to pursue Blackbeard's fleeing warship. Instead, Guerin ignored Horne and plotted a course to India.

The skiff bounced into the side of the *White Zombie*. While not Indian, Naro Bon had been chosen for the covert mission into the busy city. His aging navigator nodded in affirmation that the terms had been delivered to Emperor Aurangzeb's men.

So close yet so far away, Louis-Armand Guerin mused. "Duke, lift anchor. Del Torro, get us underway."

"The course?" Del Torro asked with a sour expression.

"Bon knows the course."

Dr. Barrow stood at the cabin door, his arms crossed. All his officers understood the brazen plan, but none of them liked it in the least, especially the doctor, who often acted as if he'd be able to one day retire to a country cottage.

So Guerin avoided all of them and went down to the brig.

There, in the same cell that held the arcane symbols and ancient language that began the side-quest, archfiend Avery played cards with himself beside a chess board waiting for Guerin's next move. Seeing him, Avery slid it to the bars of the brig.

"The fuse has been lit," Guerin said as he sat down on the stool outside of Avery's cell.

Avery's face grew solemn. "I don't see another way."

"Neither do I," Guerin agreed. "Still willing to do your part?"

"When Halyburton showed up at my home, I wasn't ready to die. In lieu of you dropping me off on some tropical island, this is the best plan—but only if you survive it to do your part."

"I plan on surviving," Guerin said with a chuckle.

"It'll be a good death," Avery assessed the plan hatched over the past several months. "A death of my choosing—it's all a man could ask for. I'd hate to think of what the Emperor would do to me if I were taken alive."

"We'll make sure that doesn't happen," Guerin promised. "I just hope Professor Josiah Faero is worth all of this."

"Oh, he's worth it. Get him out of the clutches of Emperor Aurangzeb and I'll gladly give you my death."

CHAPTER 65

Mount Kailash is a 21,778 foot peak located near the borders of Tibet and India. West of the Himalayan Mountain Range, Kailash uniquely stands alone on a plateau that feeds four of Asia's longest rivers: the Brahmaputra, Sutlej, Indus, and the Karnali, a tributary of the Ganges. Along with being the source of four rivers, it is also a sacred place in the religions of Hinduism, Bon, Buddhism, and Jainism.

For the Tibetan Buddhists, it is known as Kangri Rinpoche, or 'Precious Snow Mountain,' and is considered to be the navel of the universe. Another Tibetan religion, Bon, has several names for it in their sacred texts that recognize its place as a watershed for the continent: Water's Flower, Mountain of Sea Water, and Nine Stacked Swastika Mountain. The Bon also believe it is the abode of their sky goddess Sipaimen. The Jains, an ancient Indian religious group, share the idea that it is a home for a deity, and for them, it is where their first leader gained enlightenment. For the adherents of Hinduism, it was a gateway to Heaven and is a home of Shiva, who once trapped Ravana in the mountain for his crimes.

Along with being a watershed, the ancient Hindu text *Vishnu Purana* described the mountain as a pillar of the world, with its four faces made of crystal, ruby, gold, and lapis lazuli, a deep blue volcanic stone.

For Professor Josiah Faero, Mount Kailash was now his prison. Nine months into his year-long expedition, he still marveled at the mountain each time he stepped out of his tent.

Ngari, a local old man who now cooked for the royal expedition, sat on a stone beside the campfire and prepared a warm breakfast. Now that it was summer, overnight temperatures stayed above freezing, and many of the locals slept under the stars. Faero still wore his wool and leather, even to bed. Although he'd grown up in the northern climate of the Massachusetts Colony, the Harvard professor had never experienced the cold he felt over the previous winter, and he stood with his face to the sun to find warmth to thaw his frozen core.

His captors stirred also.

The Grand Mughal's men were also being punished.

For months, none of them bothered to wear their uniforms or arm themselves, despite being royal guards of Emperor Aurangzeb. All had once been trusted, all had since failed, and each wanted an opportunity to redeem himself. Even though Professor Faero knew them all by name, they were all the same—his captors.

Only Aqueel Kam welcomed him with a smile and a wave. Also a thin man, Aqueel was a decade younger than Faero, who was fifty. He woke each day at peace with his royal father's lot in life for him. Aqueel showed up with a beverage, this time a steaming cup of tea. "It's going to be a beautiful day," the cheerful royal bastard said.

"I suppose it is," Faero agreed. "With such clear skies and light winds, we should be able to finish our reconnaissance of the eastern slope. Is it time to break camp and move to the northern slope?"

"We'll see what the day brings us. The weather in June can still bring terrible surprises. There are a few places I'd like to revisit before breaking camp," Aqueel denied his request politely. "Get some breakfast and we'll head out."

Faero scratched his blonde beard and walked over to Ngari. "The lotus blooms in summer," the cook said, passing him a bowl. The good weather seemed to lift his spirits also. "Perhaps she will open her petals to you today. She knows how you've suffered at the base of her slopes."

"I appreciate your kind words," Faero answered. "But you and I both know the Holy Mountain would not reveal her secrets to a man like Aurangzeb."

"But it is not the Emperor who is here looking for secrets. Instead, a Holy Man from the far side of the world has come with his own questions. Perhaps she will reveal some of her ancient secrets to you alone."

"Anything she reveals to me will be seen by Aqueel—or our escort. What is it? Day two hundred ninety three? I doubt today will be any different."

"I don't understand why you don't vanish in the middle of the night. I've told you all about the villages north and west of here— why don't you run away? Do you want to go back to prison?"

"I was only in prison a short time, and I was brought to Lahore for the knowledge in my head. I was imprisoned in a library, an interpreter of legends, which is ironically the same thing I did before I left my position at Harvard."

"Emperor Aurangzeb is an old man. Even if you do find the cave that holds the…"

Faero grinned and finished, "Prima Materia, the building blocks of life. You don't believe the tales of Mount Kailash being the Navel of the Universe?"

"My navel never held anything other than filth."

Faero laughed, finished his bowl of broth, and handed it back to his greatest pupil, a retired herder who'd learned English in only six hundred lessons over meals.

Back in his shelter, he found his insulated, fur-lined cap that covered his ears with a strap that tied under his chin and also covered his thinning blonde hair. He double-checked his knapsack for the proper maps and sketchbooks and then found his faithful walking stick. Although fit and healthy for fifty, he knew his body could not afford an injury, so he walked with a stick wherever he went. He held it as he knelt down on his knees to pray.

Born to Puritan parents in Massachusetts, Faero still felt he was a Calvinist at heart, even though his ever-expanding world views led to his removal at Harvard, which brought him into the service of another former pupil, Thomas Tew. His private research into old conspiracies swept him up. Tew brought him to the Well of Initiation, where he laid eyes on something that was not made by the hands of man—the Odin Stone. It was only the corner of an

ebony slab of stone, shattered at its center, and at first, appearing to be engraved with ancient runes.

But the runes were not made by hand or tool. They floated at different depths within the black mineral. "We believe this stone contains an ancient language. It has been guarded by Eos for generations," Thomas Tew had once explained.

"Do your legends tell who made such a thing?"

"It was made by a sorcerer, an alchemist, who wrote magic within it—magic that would be used to save the world," Tew claimed.

"But it is broken," Faero stated. "It's incomplete."

"The other fragments are known to us, scattered around the world lest they fall into the hands of our enemies," Tew added. "The black stone is so old, however, that we no longer know the language or how to sing it."

"Sing it?"

"We believe it is a song," Tew explained. "We'd like your help in translating the song."

So Josiah Faero spent a summer in Madagascar trying to decipher the language. It has been so exciting that Faero and Tew had been reckless in their enthusiasm to unlock it, and their interest in Egypt, ancient Aksum, and the ruins of Jerusalem caught the attention of another great predator—Emperor Aurangzeb.

For my sins, I suffer here at the top of the world.

His morning prayers complete, Faero walked out to the waiting expedition members.

The base of Mount Kailash formed a near square with each slope spanning five miles. Over the past nine months, the expedition team had methodically explored the western, southern, and now eastern slope of the mountain, leaving the northern face for the summer months when the sun was highest in the sky. The hike to the northeast corner took them an hour, and once they passed the rusty patch on the slope and found the aqua pool at the foothill, they all took a short break before eyeing the next section.

It was another two mile hike to the peak overlooking Toeprint Glacier, which began at the dead center of the peak and sloped to the northern base. With it being the north-facing slope, the mile

wide depression filled with snow and ice that never melted and fed the raging rivers flowing north.

An entrance covered in ice, Faero theorized. *How many of the old myths and legends tell the same story with different names?*

With their breath caught, they began their walk up the rocky ridge that led to the top of the glacier. "Ngari," he said to the slowest member of the expedition, who lugged his cooking equipment. "Tell me the story again of the thumbprint."

"It happened during the conflict of Shiva and Ravana."

Ravana, the demon god. Shiva, known both as the Great God as well as the Destroyer.

"The telling varies, but in all of them, Ravana wanted Kailash for himself and conspired to keep it."

"Why?" Faero pressed. "What value did it bring him?"

"It was Shiva's home," Aqueel answered, despite being Muslim like his father.

"Actually, it was the place where Shiva entered our world," Ngari corrected.

"Ah, the navel of the universe."

"Yes, but Shiva and his wife Parvati had long ago left for a better home, yet he left behind great magic within the mountain itself and a great sword which Ravana used to unfasten the roots of the mountain."

"Yes, but why would he do that? What purpose did he have in stealing the mountain?"

"Mount Kailash collects the winter snows, and when the time comes, it releases the waters for the great rivers. If Ravana took Mount Kailash for himself, he would stop the seasons from happening."

"Time would cease and all prophecies would be hindered or forestalled."

"Yes, well, whatever his selfish intentions, Ravana used his twenty arms to lift Kailash from its foundations, which threatened to disrupt the entire world. Both humans and gods trembled at the menace posed to them, and sweet Parvati convinced mighty Shiva to intervene, so Shiva pressed Kailash back into place with his great toe."

"Don't forget the army of monkeys," Aqueel added.

"Oh yes! An army of monkeys overwhelmed the base of Kailash, distracting Ravana and keeping his attention on the valley. I've heard versions where Shiva and Ravana battle with their magic swords. In the end, Ravana was trapped inside of the mountain."

"For a thousand years," Aqueel finished.

"Yes…"

"But?" Faero prompted.

"Knowing he was defeated, Ravana manufactured his own release from his prison. First, he composed a song that he gave to Parvati upon a stone tablet; when the song was sung, he would be released from his earthly prison. Next, he cut off one of his heads and buried it in a secret place outside of Mount Kailash."

Veritas Caput—the truth about the head. "Why did he cut off his head?"

"If the song was sung, he'd be released and given a new body, but if the song was never sung, and his body remained trapped inside of Kailash, then when his head was eventually found, it would open its mouth and sing the song, bringing about his own release."

"Ngari's version is much more interesting than your southern version," Faero teased. "So if we do find the navel, will the demon king Ravana still be locked away?"

Aqueel looked at Ngari. Clearly, neither had a conclusion to the ten-headed demon god of the Hindu.

Eos searches for a fallen god. Is this the answer to their riddle? "Well, first we need to find the entrance, don't we?"

Once they reached the marker from the previous day's work, the guards produced their eight foot metallic pry bars and began to hoist and flip stones while he and Aqueel used rope and stakes to mark the search area.

Two years earlier, Emperor Aurangzeb gave his theory: the entrance was covered by a rockslide or by ice. Along with the imprisoned Ravana, Mount Kailash hid the magical stones used to bring the universe into existence. *Now, my penance for befriending pirates is serving a madman.*

As the two began to place the string marking the Y-axis for the search grid, Ngari called out from his small fire.

When Faero turned, he saw a caravan of at least a hundred Marwari horses.

"Perhaps my father has died and the country has erupted in war between my brothers," Aqueel offered.

Or perhaps they are here for me, Josiah Faero worried. *Sold to the higher bidder.*

CHAPTER 66

SRI LANKA

1706

I've been pretending to be a pirate—it's time to truly become one. Louis-Armand Guerin lowered his scope. Beside him, Naro Bon watched the same ship as it pulled out of the busy Colombo Harbor.

"She's flying a Dutch East India Company flag," Bon added, and Guerin's scope flew to his good eye.

Show me the seal. Show it to me.

The feet of Quartermaster Manuel Del Torro appeared below the eyepiece of the scope. "The ship is ready on your command, sir."

The boys are ready for a chase, but we only get one chance.

From the crow's nest, Jimmy Duke hollered to his anchoring crew. Guerin lowered his scope for a moment to see his boatswain scampering down to the deck. Raising the scope again, he now saw the second flag—the Mughal Imperial flag. Seeing the green and gold flag, Guerin knew the odds were in his favor, but Colombo was an international trade port with hundreds of ships departing a day.

"It's the golden sun," Bon confirmed. "The ship flies an Imperial Seal."

The crew cheered.

"Let's chase her down," Guerin said, and from the far side of the bay, the predator prepared to hunt its prey.

A few miles from the bay, the Dutch ship continued to track to the northwest, and the spirits of the men increased as the odds increased dramatically of it being the right ship.

LeSueur's shadow fell on him.

"I can't believe this is working," Guerin said with just a trace of giddiness.

"An overly complicated gambit."

"Yes, but Naro was right," Guerin said of the officer beside him. "If we'd simply handed over Avery, we might have been able to collect the reward money. Might. When we asked for a prisoner exchange...we've insulted the Emperor. We need this gambit to get Faero."

"Will we ever return to the Mississippi River?" LeSueur muttered.

"In good time. Once we've collected Faero, we will soon make the turn for the Land of the Blue Woman. First, the gambit. Remind your men about the nature of this attack. I don't want things to go awry."

Just the sight of LeSueur should make those Dutch sailors surrender. Nothing of Pierre-Charles LeSueur remained. Charlie Johnson still had the monstrous frame of the fearsome fur-trader, but the hair that finally regrew had been bleached of all black ink, leaving him with a beard and head full of white hair. With his flesh again having a bronzed hue, he looked much younger than fifty. Between Papa Bones' voodoo christening and surviving the explosion, Charlie was a god to his men. *Perhaps Gaspar was right about this man being marked by God.*

A FEW HOURS went by as the distance narrowed. Benjamin Horne readied the cannons, and Charlie stood with his boarding parties.

"Raise the flag," Guerin said, "and fire a few warning shots. With the cargo they carry, they shouldn't want a fight. Would you?"

Surprisingly, the ship fired a few shots back at them. One cannonball sent a sliver into the forearm of LeSueur, and half the crew

stopped fighting when he pulled the splinter out and blood oozed from the wound.

So he is not immortal. Guerin spotted Giovanni Naufragio at the front of the ship as part of the defensive measures if things went horribly wrong and the enemy decided to fight to the death. "Sharpen those chisels, Giovanni."

The carpenter nodded.

"Take down those masts, Mr. Horne!"

The guns of the *White Zombie* sunk its teeth into the masts and sails, crippling the Dutch merchant vessel in minutes, prompting the white flag of surrender. Unlike most pirates, the *White Zombie* hunted for a specific purpose.

The *White Zombie* slid up next to the Dutch ship. Master Horne's guns were ready to split her in half. Most of the Dutch crew stood at the rail, a sign of surrender. When the hooks flew from the *White Zombie*, the Dutch crew helped secure them.

Well done, boys, well done.

"I am Gareth LaGrande, Captain of the *White Zombie*, and I hold your lives in my hand. Surrender your ship and its possessions, and all of you will be allowed to live."

From the poop deck, the Dutch captain presented himself. "I am Captain Adrian Van Broeck, captain of the *Starling*. You imperil yourself with this act. While we carry a load of cinnamon for Bombay, we also carry an Imperial Ambassador for the Mughal Empire."

"Yes, I am very aware of this fact, which is why we are boarding you," Guerin continued speaking in Dutch. "How is his health?"

Captain Van Broeck turned to his officers.

No one wants to die for a dead man. To help them arrive at a logical conclusion, Guerin added, "May I speak to Ambassador Abdi Tariyy. I heard his health has suddenly worsened."

Again, Captain Van Broeck spoke discreetly to his officers, and a moment later, three Mughal men dressed in fine clothes joined him on the deck. "Here is Ambassador Tariyy. What is your business with him?"

Guerin turned to find Dr. Barrow standing in the doorway of the cabin door. "Is that the Ambassador?"

Dr. Barrow shook his head.

Guerin turned back to the *Starling*. "That is not the man we poisoned back in Colombo. In fact, we recognize the imposter as the ambassador's servant." A ripple of unease covered the men of the *Starling*. "You carry the body of the ambassador, don't you? Tell his men that if you peacefully surrender, we will see that the ambassador's body is brought home."

The Mughals and Dutch conferred for a moment. "You may board."

The planks were readied, and Guerin called down to his deck, "Charlie, remember the gambit. Secure the Mughals and any paperwork they have."

The seizure of the Dutch ship happened without another shot. During his time with Captain Kidd, Guerin had seized dozens of ships while gathering intelligence for Isaac Newton rather than gathering plunder. In the early months of this enterprise, Guerin boarded the captured ships while Kidd stood where he now stood.

I could have been a legendary pirate.

The crew of the *Starling* took prostate positions on the main deck as Charlie's gun crews stood over them while other crews searched the ship. After half-an-hour of waiting, Charlie climbed the stairs to stand beside Captain Van Broeck. With everything secure, he signaled to Guerin.

"Here is what will happen next," Guerin shouted over. "You and select officers are going to be brought over to my ship, where you will be kept as hostages. Half of your crew are going to be marooned on Kiltan Island, with enough food to last them a month. If all goes well, you will personally be able to rescue them when this ordeal is over. Do you understand so far?"

"It's your death sentence that you request," Van Broeck said.

Guerin laughed heartily. "Then it will make me the most wanted man on four continents, if Madagascar is considered part of Africa. I've made worse enemies than Emperor Aurangzeb or Prince William of Orange. I will need my man to lock the Mughals in your brig. I'll explain the whole thing when you're brought over. It's rather complicated. Charlie, bring him over."

Both decks flowed with motion, and tensions remained high, even as Giovanni Naufragio found his Dutch counterpart to immediately begin repairs.

With the Dutch crew divided, LeSueur returned from securing his Mughal prisoners with Captain Van Broeck at his side. "The ambassador's identity is verified. Here is the official correspondence proving it," LeSueur offered. "Your gambit might get you in the front door, but then what?"

"I wish I could unleash you and your ax upon the whole of Bombay, but to get what I want, deception will matter."

"All for one man?" LeSueur asked.

"You're here today because of this man. I could put you back in your Cuban grave. Show some patience, Charlie. Whatever's waiting for you in the Land of the Blue Woman can wait. We might only get one shot at doing this properly. Now, go inspect your new ship with Naufragio. Pick your men wisely and send half over to the White Zombie. I'll escort our new friend to the brig."

The officers were chained together in Guerin's quarter and half the crew were chained on deck. Guerin separated them to avoid any attempts at mutiny until they reached Kiltan Island. Guerin led their captain to the brig where boatswain Drake Murray met them with the keys.

"Captain Van Broeck, I'd like to introduce you to the most wanted man in the world, apart from yours truly, the infamous Captain Henry "Long Ben" Avery."

Van Broeck gasped at the name.

"So you managed to get the ambassador?" Avery asked, raising his eyebrows.

"Captain Van Broeck is a rational man who might end up surviving this if he plays nicely," Guerin explained.

Avery winked at Van Broeck as he entered the cell. "I bet you're wondering what's about to happen to your ship and crew. My plan required both, and if you comply, you'll get them all back when this is over."

"Or you'll end up as dead as Captain Avery," Guerin said, prompting an eye roll from his prisoner. "And don't be taking credit for my plan."

"Our plan," Avery said. "You might've come up with the sleight of hand trick, but I'm the one that came up with the big finale."

"Our plan then," Guerin conceded. "The Lord preserves the fool, the Good Book says."

"Just as he punishes the wicked," Avery added. "And I'm ready to atone for my sins with a final act of wickedness."

CHAPTER 67

By privately serving Emperor Aurangzeb, Corgi Baba had become a fat, wealthy man, but he'd also struggled to live down a public shame—losing his ship to Captain Kidd a decade earlier. Now he had an opportunity to restore his importance to the Emperor—by identifying a man's face.

And soon I will have the head of Captain Gareth LaGrande.

Several other men joined him at the table. Following a ransom request involving Henry Avery, all five of them had a part to play in the Emperor's response. The British host and military man William Burniston held the meeting at the military post used to secure the interests of the East Indian Trading Company. Today, the British possessed the island on the other side of the Ulhas River. *Tomorrow...who could tell?*

The Imperial Admiral Daud Khan Panni sat beside him, and despite being a guest of the British, he ran the meeting as Emperor Aurangzeb wished.

Prison warden Konhoji sat beside, bringing with him the subject of the ransom, Professor Josiah Faero. Baba's jaw dropped when he learned Faero was still alive. Twelve years earlier, Baba captained the *Quedagh Merchant*, which lingered behind the convoy led by the *Ganj-i-Sawai*. His part of the mission had been a success—killing Captain Thomas Tew and capturing the religious scholar, Josiah Faero.

Across the table, Bombay's Governor Gayer sat, slightly disinterested by a crime that happened long before he arrived. Had former governor Thomas Pitt sat there, the British involvement would have been more motivated. Next to him, local religious leader Imam Shah sat, very interested by the strange coalition of people.

Corgi Baba already knew the last man who sat across from him, Augee Peree Callendar, an East India Company trade representative, who knew Henry Avery prior to the *Ganj-i-Sawai* incident. Several months earlier, Callendar stepped out of his factory office to receive LaGrande's letter.

"This is how the trap will work," Admiral Panni explained. "While Captain LaGrande might think he has the advantage by setting the date and place, Emperor Aurangzeb will not negotiate with infidel pirates, regardless of what they offer."

Admiral Panni referenced the map of Bombay on the table. Bombay was a series of islands stacked lightly against the delta of a river. At its widest, the British had a fort overlooking the bay, which was large enough to make it an international port. "These cowards have chosen the island, thinking the British will somehow offer immunity, but Commander Burniston will have a company of men lying in wait once Henry Avery is revealed."

"Why does it have to be a Mosque?" Burniston asked. "Tensions between the British and Muslims are still high. If this doesn't go smoothly…"

"Captain LaGrande knows Emperor Aurangzeb to be a righteous man, which is why he chose a holy place for the meeting. Warden Konhoji will have four Imperial troops within the Mosque to make sure the transfer of prisoners happens in a pleasing manner, and Mr. Calendar will also be there to make sure we are receiving the real Henry Avery."

As if anticipating objections, Admiral Panni added, "The ground between the shore and the mosque is not holy."

Imam Shah added, "The Mosque is built upon a high hill facing east. While it seems isolated from the water, the hike up the hill takes several minutes, and on the backside of the hill, the streets of Bombay are crowded."

"That is how we'll hide Commander Burnistan's men. We'll have them hidden in two alleys, and when the signal is given, we will cut off these pirates from returning to the bay. Regardless of

what happens on the island, Captain Corgi will help identify his former ship and its red-eyed captain, Gareth LaGrande." Admiral Panni took a moment to drink his wine. "If this arrogant man had simply brought Captain Avery to us, the Emperor would have made him a wealthy and celebrated hero, but when he gave conditions to the exchange, he became complicit in the crimes. Don't think of this as a prisoner exchange but as capturing *two* dangerous fugitives—Henry Avery and LaGrande."

At this, Corgi Baba found his voice again, "Captain LaGrande was part of Captain Kidd's crew. At his insistence, my ship, the *Quedagh Merchant*, was illegally seized and stolen. He is a menace to civilized society."

"Then why go through this charade of bringing the prisoner?" Governor Gayer asked. "As soon as they sail into the harbor, blow them out of the water."

"As much as Emperor Aurangzeb enjoys his American magi, he wants vengeance for his murdered daughter. Acquiring Henry Avery alive is our first priority."

All eyes went to Callendar. "It's been a decade, but I should be able to identify the scoundrel."

Admiral Panni nodded. "We expect Captain LaGrande to be wary. He won't put Avery at risk until he believes the situation is under control."

Warden Konhoji shook his head. "Then why are we putting Faero in the Mosque at the start?"

"The Emperor must appear to operate in good faith," Admiral Panni explained. "If the terms are not met, Captain LaGrande could cause international damage by crying foul and keeping Avery. We assume he'll send some minion into the Mosque first, identify Professor Faero, and then send a signal to bring Avery. Even this act must be shown patience. If they send an imposter, and we go for the bait, the real Avery could vanish forever. We must make sure Avery is delivered before we act."

No one has asked why LaGrande wants Faero.

Or why the Emperor is willing to double-cross to keep him.

A decade earlier, Corgi Baba sat with a different admiral as they discussed plans for a different trap—capturing Tew. The Emperor's spies knew the truth about Madagascar: that instead of pirates a secret society grew in isolation. With the young American serving as Presider of the Free States, a new religious revolution was building. By this time in the Emperor's life, his obsessive mind had already moved from Islam to understanding foreign religions, especially one of the oldest beliefs—alchemy. So the Emperor publicly offered a trade of religious artifacts with the Sultan of Arabia, knowing Presider Tew would risk his own life to obtain a treasure far more valuable than an earthly princess. Captain Baba and the *Quedagh Merchant* hunted down the tail of the pirate armada. Unfortunately, Thomas Tew died in the capture, but once Aurangzeb learned the truth of who and what Professor Josiah Faero was, the enterprise momentarily paid off. Years later, Corgi Baba was on another covert mission for the emperor when he crossed paths with Captain Kidd.

"With the British as our ally," Admiral Panni concluded once the meal ran its course, "the guns of the fort will prevent any ship from leaving the harbor, and I will have warships hidden behind the shield islands and smaller crafts ready if the men abandon ship and flee. By agreeing to do the prisoner-exchange in Bombay, they are already trapped, they just don't know it yet."

Just as I trapped the King of the Templars...only to see the other rats gnaw their legs off and take the Ganj-i-Sawai.

I just hope there is something left of my ship when the dust settles.

CHAPTER 68

Josiah Faero smelled the ocean through the stench of the slums, giving him hope that he wasn't being led to an execution. The men who accompanied him from Mount Kailash did not speak English, or any language for that matter, bringing a strange silence to the end of his prison sentence.

As with his previous trip, Faero counted the rate of passage. Now, the passage was slow through congested city streets where he visualized one block at a time. Over the past month, travel had been on open roads, where dozens of miles passed under hoofs. With Kailash as the axis, the length of travel could have brought him in any direction, but based on the direction of the sun, he knew they'd traveled south—to either freedom or execution.

If the elderly emperor had indeed died, the expedition should have ended with Faroe's blood being spilled along the base of Kailash. If the emperor was dying, the journey most likely would have ended hundreds of miles earlier, at an imperial palace. When Faero smelled the sea, and then the stench of Bombay, he began to dream of freedom.

The carriage door opened, and he found himself on a hill. A quick glance back at the carriage revealed a sprawling city below the hill. A glance forward revealed a brilliantly blue Islamic mosque, with two soldiers standing at the doorway. His eyes darted to the side, spotting a soldier hiding in the nearby alleyway. To the other side, he noticed another alleyway with another conspicu-ous soldier.

I'm bait for a trap.

Yet a large cemetery, with dozens of small mausoleums, sepa-rated the mosque from the city by hundreds of yards. Even though the mosque blocked much of his view, he could also see past it—to a large bay on the eastern side of the hill.

Bombay. He'd last seen it twelve years earlier after his capture.

Warden Konhoji led him forward. The exterior of the mosque was skirted with pillars, each capable of hiding men in ambush, but as he passed, each of them proved vacant. Inside of the mosque, he passed through another series of pillars that supported the tall, domed ceiling, but aside from a well-dressed Englishman and his two guards at the front doors, it was empty. Finally, he saw anoth-er person, an Imam, standing on the opposite side of the cavernous space, in front of an ornate mihrab. His head spun to both sides, confirming there were just the four of them.

In front of the Imam, a small chest waited on the floor.

Surely not severance pay. Is this an exchange?

The warden addressed the Imam. "Any sign of the pirates?"

Pirates! Has the Order of Eos found me?

"No, but the sun has just set," the Imam said. "Per written in-structions, we vacated the Mosque at sunset, leaving only the guards and me stationed at the door. For all we know, the pirates had men faking the evening prayers in the crowd."

"And the signal?" the warden asked.

"I placed the torch in the eastern doorway, as instructed."

Faero located the burning torch, but his captor's eyes intercept-ed. "Don't hope for rescue. You'll be back—with company—in a British jail cell in Bombay Castle by midnight."

After a few minutes of waiting, Faero learned the name of the Englishman—Callendar. Both Callendar and the Imam drifted to the open door overlooking the bay. Two more soldiers flanked the eastern door, but Faero remained unattended in the center of the mosque. Just as had been the case in the Himalayas, space provid-ed its own kind of guard. The entire facility was being watched from a distance, so he did not entertain foolish thoughts of run-ning.

He looked back to the chest—*payment.*

The moment Thomas Tew died upon the deck of the *Amity,* Faero's importance to the Free Clans grew more valuable, but within minutes of capture, he'd been whisked away on Captain Baba's *Quedagh Merchant,* never to learn what happened to the rest of the convoy or the leadership of the Free Clans back in Madagascar. His time in the Gujarat prison led him to conclusions based on the questioning, but it had been a decade since his transfer to the palace, a living book placed in the Emperor's vast collection of ancient texts.

What has transpired to this moment?

"May I join you?" Faero called out. All four guards stepped into view. Callendar stepped back into the doorway and waved him over. The warden escorted him step-for-step.

Once in the doorway, Faero understood the strategic location of the site. A quarter-mile slope descended to the busy harbor below. With the ports further inland, or across the bay on the mainland, and the British port at the tip of the island near the mouth of the bay, the shore below was undeveloped, which was why it was easy to spot a single vessel approaching.

"Who is it?" Faero asked.

"More likely than not, just a messenger," Callendar explained. "Do you see those ships in the distance? They are there to make sure you do not leave India. Ah, and that patrol down there? They are going to find out if we are dealing with fools."

Who would want me after all of this time?

The folks at the bottom of the hill were not fools. A small rowboat separated from the vessel, and upon landing, the patrol advanced on it.

Ten minutes passed, and then a solitary figure began walking up the hill away from the stationed patrol.

It was too dark to make sense of the figure carrying the torch, but he advanced at a leisurely pace, as if strolling through a park. A wide-brimmed hat further hid the face in shadow.

"Your weapon, sir!" the warden said when the man transitioned to the lowest stone balcony connected to the complex.

The man's belt was unbuckled and the sword set down upon the railing. The man called out in English, "May I approach or is there another patrol waiting to ambush me?"

"Approach," the warden said.

The man continued his approach up the stairs, and even though a small man, his presence filled the mosque. The fellow looked around the high ceilings of the mosque instead of at the men fearfully studying him.

"Where is Captain Avery?" Callendar asked.

Long Ben? My God, is that what this is about?

The question brought the gaze of the pirate along with his eye patch, which had a red gem sewn onto the patch. The man continued to look around the mosque, and said, "When I give the signal…"

"We've done our part. We've brought Professor Faero as requested. We've brought the chest of money, as requested. Where is the captain?"

"We had to make sure there was not a double-cross," Red Eye said and began to stroll about the mosque. He checked behind pillars and looked in alcoves until finally going all the way to the door leading to the city. He stood there for a few minutes, as if taunting the Mughal's men. Next, he stepped to the side of the western entrance, dramatically flinging open the side doors one-by-one, pausing when he found a dark room lit by the glow of wicks burning incense. On the floor, a coffin. Finally, he turned back to the warden.

"How am I to know if this is the real Professor Faero?" At the men's silence, Red Eye approached, standing almost toe-to-toe with him. He had a surprisingly youthful face with blonde hair under his hat.

Who is he? Faero cleared his throat and swallowed hard. "I can assure you, Captain, I am the one and only Josiah Faero."

"Just like I am the one and only Captain LaGrande? It wouldn't surprise us if the Emperor scoured the jails for a man matching your likeness and coached him. Let's put you to the test."

LaGrande reached into his pockets, retrieving a cigar. He held it in his hand for a moment longer while his other hand searched the

interior of his jacket. "I seem to have misplaced my matches." Then his eyes widened, "No, but this will do."

In his other hand, he held a sheet of paper. "I have a few questions for you, to prove you are really Josiah Faero. When I am convinced, I will give the signal for Captain Avery to be brought to us."

"I can assure you," Warden Konhoji said. "This man is Josiah Faero. I've personally escorted him from Emperor Aurangzeb to Bombay."

LaGrande turned back to Faero. "When Thomas Tew was slain and you were captured by Captain Baba, I believe, what personally happened to you?"

"I was immediately taken off the ship, along with my possessions, and brought aboard an Indian vessel."

"Yes, the *Quedagh Merchant*, it turns out."

"It happened so fast, I never learned the name of the ship," Faero answered.

"And you were kept in Captain Baba's cabin until you were brought to Gujarat."

"No, I was locked away in the brig."

LaGrande smiled. "Good answer. And during your journey across the Indian Ocean, locked in your cell with your possessions, you took it upon yourself to carve...inscriptions...upon the walls, correct?"

Faero felt his heart racing. The runes had saved his life. "Yes."

"Why?"

"I knew any men put in the brig would most likely be either European or pirate, and if that was the case, I wanted them to know what happened to me. I wanted news to travel. I didn't want to just vanish from the face of the earth."

"And here I am—your rescuer. Last question, along with your manifesto carved onto the wood, you left a few symbols. I'm going to show you these symbols, and if you can tell me what they represent, you'll have proven that you are indeed Professor Faero."

How bizarre? He nodded and tightened his eyes. LaGrande pointed to a symbol on the paper. "That is the symbol for the Philosopher's Stone."

LaGrande flashed another.

"The symbol for copper."

A third.

"Ursa Major and Ursa Minor."

A fourth, which gave Faero pause. "The signet ring of King Solomon."

LaGrande ripped off his eye-patch to reveal a healthy blue eye. He extended his hand, "Pleased to meet you Professor Faero, I'm Jimmy Duke of Boston. I've heard a lot about you."

CHAPTER 69

Jimmy Duke tossed the imitation patch to the ground. "I am convinced you've brought Faero, but I am still not convinced you're operating in good faith. Twice you've intercepted us with intent on stealing Avery and keeping Faero," Duke said in reference to the patrol at the shore and the soldiers waiting in the mosque. From the look in their eyes, they showed disappointment that he wasn't really Captain Gareth LaGrande. *Guerin was right about the trap.* So he called them out. "In this holy place, the Emperor is prepared to break his word and act like a thief?"

The three officials nervously looked at each other. "Yes, we have guards posted to ensure the safety of Faero, and yes, we intercepted your arrival, but only to make sure some random citizen was not interfering."

Duke scoffed. "Your men only allowed me passage when they thought I was Captain LaGrande. I'm betting one of you is here to help identify Avery. This is all a trap, isn't it?"

"No, no," they protested.

Duke grinned. "If the Emperor is operating in good faith…convince me, and I'll give the signal to bring Avery here," Duke said, stripping off most of his clothing. "Professor Faero, I need you to strip down also, but not to your skivvies."

Faero began to strip down.

"If you want Avery, convince me," Duke repeated.

"How? What do you request?"

"Two requests, call in the guards from the western doors, and send the guards from the eastern doors to the two adjacent alleys where your soldiers are lying in wait. Tell them they are to remain where they are until Avery is brought up to the mosque, and then they are to remain where they are until Professor Faero and I have traveled back down the hill to our waiting ship, understood?"

They must have ships waiting to capture us in the harbor, Duke realized as they discussed the proposal. When they agreed, Duke knew it. A moment later, the eastern guards trotted off and the western guards stepped into the mosque.

"Thank you," Duke said. "I will now give the signal for Avery."

Duke walked over to the eastern doors facing the bay, and with the adjacent torch, he lit his cigar and then removed the torch from its holder to wave it three times.

Stepping back in, he puffed away at the cigar for a moment. "Now, if you'll come with me, we need to visit the coffin of the recently deceased Ambassador Abdi Tariyy."

Out of curiosity, the men followed him all the way to the open doors along the rear of the mosque to the one where incense burned. He paused in front of the coffin, glancing at the small holes along its base. The details of Louis-Armand Guerin's plan had been moved into position days earlier, including the dead ambassador. "Right now, all eyes are following a slow moving rowboat traveling to the shore when the real Long Ben Avery is already here. Come, I'll show you."

Duke watched the guards slip their hands into their tunics. *Unarmed? Doubtful...*Guerin spent weeks working out what he'd do if he were the Emperor. Arming the guards seemed obvious.

Duke sat beside the coffin and glanced up at the men watching. "Captain Avery has had a rough few years—especially the last two days—but I can assure you he is very much alive—in here."

Jimmy Duke slid off the lid a few inches, and his hands reached under the feet of the wrapped body to find the smooth handles of two familiar friends.

Two pistols pointed at the face of the guards, temporarily ignoring the Englishman, warden, and Imam, who he didn't worry about. "Move, move, move, over to the coffin. I need your help getting Long Ben out of there."

The guards hesitated, for just a moment, until they recognized the threat posed to them by the pistols. The shrouded corpse wiggled, pausing the efforts of both men as they stood along the edge of the coffin.

Finally, the white burial fabric was torn away, and the head and torso of Henry Avery emerged from beneath a death shroud believed to belong to Ambassador Tariyy. Jimmy Duke remained ready, watching the stunned warden and cleric as Avery fully emerged from the coffin.

So far, so good. Sending Henry Avery to the mosque in a coffin had been the most outlandish—and necessary—part of the plan.

Avery's ashen eyes showed no emotion, passing from his former captor to his new captor until he locked eyes with Josiah Faero. "All of this just for you…"

"We don't have time for reunions," Duke barked. "All of you except Faero need to sit on the floor against the wall. Now."

Even Henry Avery sat down, his shackles still secure on his wrists and ankles. "Quickly, Professor. You're about to witness my greatest heist. Now use the fabric to bind their wrists and hands."

Faero obliged while Jimmy Duke stood in the doorway. Once completed, he immediately set down the pistols and began to change into the uniform of the guards and then retrieved his guns. "You, too."

"This is madness," Faero said when Duke pointed to the extra guard clothing.

"Yes, which is why I volunteered to be the one," Duke said with a wink.

In just a few seconds, Faero transformed himself also, including a turban upon his head.

Finally, Duke walked over to where Captain Avery sat beside the coffin. "Are you still willing to do this?"

"Or what…get tortured to death in front of the Emperor? I died the moment I set foot on the *Ganj-i-Sawai*. Yes, I am willing."

Duke set the pistol on the floor five feet from where Avery sat. Next, he took several quick puffs from the cigar and then examined the embers inside before placing it in Avery's bound hands.

Another sweep of his remaining pistol reminded the prisoners to keep their place as Avery struggled to stand. *Avery deserves a hor-*

rible death. When Avery just stood there, he looked at the pistol on the ground and then to the coffin. "So?" Duke asked of the two choices.

"I am no coward," Avery said of the pistol. "Give me Odin's death."

He'll take out his enemies during his own death, Duke thought and sighed. *Could I do the same?* Duke leaned over the coffin, found the discreet looped fabric along the edges, and lifted the bottom platform from the coffin, revealing the explosives and their detonation fuses. "If you want to live, Professor, stay on my heels."

Duke grabbed Faero and jogged to the western doorway, standing in it. *They will think we're the guards.* He heard Avery light the fuse. Then he shouted in rehearsed Farsi, "It's a trap!"

Duke ran through the cemetery; Faero ran behind him. Benjamin Horne emphasized they'd only have ten seconds to get away from the mosque.

"It's a trap!" He shouted to the confused troops waiting in the alleys.

Chaos would be his shield.

It was closer for the troops to run to the mosque than to the central entrance of the cemetery, which they did.

No sounds came from the mosque. A single pistol shot meant Avery shot himself or had to fend off the Emperor's men within the mosque.

The streets of Bombay would shelter him.

And the dark streets waited just a few yards ahead.

If he couldn't get to them before the soldiers intercepted him, he would stop and wait for the explosion.

Ten seconds, Horne had promised. The central gate loomed.

The stunned troops began to emerge from the wings and headed to the mosque.

Did the fuse go out?

Then a thunderous explosion reverberated through the still Bombay air, filling the cemetery, eastern slope, and even the distant bay with dust, debris, and shards of blue.

CHAPTER 70

Louis-Armand Guerin could see the two figures running through the cemetery. Even with one eye, he could see the uniforms of two Mughal soldiers running straight for the central gate. Even though his men insisted on a LaGrande decoy inside of the mosque, Guerin insisted on being close should the plan work.

He rose from his hiding spot, stepping out of the shadow along the edge of the building.

If need be, he was ready for a footrace to the ship.

Although he couldn't see it, he knew the captured staff of Ambassador Abdi Tariyy would either be rowing an imposter Henry Avery to shore or walking up the hill. If the Emperor's men didn't zealously kill them, they would be able to explain how Henry Avery wound up inside of the mosque.

The local Bombay wharf rats, already criminals in the eyes of Imperial law, would lead the naval blockade deep into the bay on a fruitless chase, for they knew how to abandon a skiff and swim to safety.

The distant net of warships filling the bay would catch nothing—for neither the *White Zombie* nor the captured *Starling* came anywhere near the mouth of the bay or the British fort. Bombay, after all, had a western shore behind the bay.

Guerin gasped. *Sweet Heavens, Duke has him.*

At fifty yards, Guerin saw the face of Jimmy Duke and a Caucasian that was certainly not Henry Avery.

A flash momentarily lit the interior of the mosque.

A moment later, the dome lifted.

The walls buckled out.

And then a cloud of chaos grew, swallowing Duke and Faero just as they cleared the central gate.

An act of revenge from Long Ben Avery.

During the months Henry Avery spent locked in the brig of the *White Zombie*, Guerin had spent countless lunches with his valuable prisoner, devising plans with the doomed man. Years earlier, when Guerin first realized he needed Faero's help unlocking the great alchemy puzzle given to him, the only bit of leverage he had was to find the most wanted man alive for the Emperor. Once he procured him, he needed a delivery method that could guarantee a prisoner exchange. During these discussions with his officers and Avery, Long Ben always reminded them that it ended gruesomely for him.

Once in the possession of Emperor Aurangzeb, Long Ben would face some of the most horrific tortures found in the archives of the Imperial library. Merciful poisons were discussed and denied. Time in the brig allowed Long Ben to imagine what he would do in the Emperor's place, and his hatred for his imagined torturers grew until he came up with his own death plan.

"How about I take some of them out with me?" he had offered. "It will be my penance for unleashing the beast Dalziel upon those women."

It took a week to devise the exploding coffin concept, a plan which left a malicious grin on Avery's face.

Now, Guerin had to shield his face from the full effect of Henry Avery's revenge.

He heard footsteps before he could see anything.

"Over here," he called out to the approaching figures. Jimmy Duke chuckled as he bolted past him. Guerin grabbed Faero by the fabric of his shirt and began running down the dark street, away from the chaos.

Two blocks passed by in seconds. Naro Bon and a group of twenty Hindu men and children flowed out of the evening shadows.

"Follow me, Captain," Bon said to the crowd. "The rest of you do your part."

Their part—an insurgency of chaos—quickly followed as teams of four to five spread into different streets, setting trash on fire and drawing attention to themselves with shouts of anarchy and protest.

It had been a month since Guerin had seen his sailing master after leaving Bon in the city of Bombay with two purposes: to find a route and to create another diversion. For two hundred years, the Mughal emperors had waged war upon the subcontinent of India, bringing one small kingdom after another into the empire. But oppression also followed, and with it, sharia law followed the Islamic emperors, leaving a large population of Hindu followers desperate and willing to follow a radical voice like Bon.

Plus, a little of the Captain Kidd loot helped make friends.

With each stride Guerin took running from one side of the peninsula to the other, chaos and riots followed behind him. Having studied the map of Bombay for months, he could picture the scene already. The troops back at the destroyed mosque—those meant to kill or capture Duke—were now tasked with sorting through the rubble for answers. Even if a quick-witted sergeant spotted Duke and Faero running from the mosque (disguised as soldiers), his men had a lead in the footrace. The southern island creating the western side of the large bay was only a few miles wide, so as the Imperial navy used the British Fort and its hidden ships to serve as a net, open water of the Indian Ocean was on the other unguarded side of the island.

Young Hindu boys joined the four men as they ran, taking them through a maze of streets and alleys. All the while they ran, Guerin felt the streets begin to slope downhill—to the western shore—to freedom.

CHAPTER 71

Captain Charlie Johnson—formerly First Mate, formerly the Bear Man, Paul Bonjean, and Pierre-Charles LeSueur—stood in the darkness of night facing the east toward India. *Dawn comes. Where are you, Guerin?*

The divided crew didn't sleep either as they waited to find out the fate of their bold captain.

There were so many things that could have gone wrong, LeSueur decided, but Guerin insisted their plan was the only path forward.

The deck boards of the *White Zombie* creaked under his weight as he paced from one end of the railing to the other. After his encounter with Blackbeard's men, LeSueur fully believed what Guerin told him privately. The substance being taken from the mountain stronghold and placed upon Blackbeard's transportation wagons was shamir, something few in the world knew existed, according to Guerin. The dangerous substance had once been a successful failure, an unintended mistake from its creator, and instead of being destroyed, it was kept hidden in storage. When the container broke open, it didn't explode in a flash like gunpowder; instead, it rose from the ground like a vapor, and like an entranced cobra being led by the music of an invisible flute, the strange vapor flowed against the laws of physics—and then began to feast on any flesh or substance in its way.

How am I even alive?

LeSueur looked down to his hands, remembering a similar heat he had encountered back in a deep pit at Mahkato.

Perhaps Wenonah was right. If I am the Wishwee, then I need to get back to the frontier to save her people.

"A ship!" one of the men up in the crows nest called out in a muffled tone. "Heading right towards us." The entire crew shifted nervously in their position. To be sailing at night, so close to land, it would either be an Imperial patrol or…

Keeping his own voice harnessed as he gave out instructions to the crew, he remembered the words of Jimmy Duke, "Don't let anyone else touch my anchor." Master Horne's cannons were loaded, even though he wasn't on the ship to give his powder monkey's commands. If it was an Imperial patrol, they would fire all of their guns and then return back to Kiltan Island to wait."

"It's the *Starling,*" another crewman shouted out.

"It could be a trap," LeSueur reminded them. "Wait for the signal."

After taking command of the *Starling,* Guerin and his team took the Ambassador's coffin, staff, and Long Ben Avery to a minor port on the north island of Bombay, where the Dutch ship anchored anonymously with its cargo of cinnamon. If the prisoner exchange happened, Guerin and Professor Faero would escape away from the mosque to the western shore, to be ferried back to the *Starling.* Any attempts to spot the former *Quedagh Merchant* would prove futile since LeSueur anchored miles away.

If Guerin was captured and tortured, Imperial troops could be on the Starling right now, his pessimism argued. *No,* his optimism countered, *Guerin wouldn't give us up.* Even so, LeSueur worried for his friend. Without Guerin, everything would fall apart. LeSueur wondered where he would even go—Pierre-Charles LeSueur was dead, after all, and he had only an unfaithful wife waiting in the New World, more likely than not, already married to another.

Without Guerin, there'd be no reason to return to Wenonah either, and the dark secrets hidden in the Land of the Blue Woman would stay buried.

Lanterns illuminated the deck of the *Starling.* Hats began to wave, including the large hat of Captain LaGrande.

Thank God! He's alive.

The *Starling* didn't even wait for the *White Zombie*, blowing by it as cheers erupted on both sides. The anchor was raised, sails were dropped, and both ships chased the darkness west into the vast space of the Indian Ocean.

Perhaps I'll still be able to see Wenonah again after all.

CHAPTER 72

At thirty-one, Marguerite LeSueur remained the most beautiful and wealthiest woman in the Alabama colony, whose cemetery outpaced the growth of residents. A year after she'd sent a letter to Montreal asking for help, a large merchant ship finally arrived with an answer. Her four children ran down the hill to the docks, along with all of the other colonists, but she took her time in the mirror preparing her makeup and hair.

I must be the Queen of La Mobile even if my title has been taken away.

She lived in a sturdy but simple two-story wooden home built on a hill that overlooked the colony and fort. Like the other eighty single-story homes along the banks of the Mobile River, her home was freshly painted. It had been built out of courtesy, despite the fact that her husband had died while she was traveling south from Montreal. Her hired servants—François Benoît, Julien Choquet and Antoine Foisy—helped build the house out of pity, for they knew she also had lost a daughter and brother on the trip down the Mississippi River. Once the largest home in the colony was built, all three servants, having fulfilled their contracts, returned back to Montreal. For two years, she lived at the mercy of the other colonists and Commissary Nicholas de la Salle.

Marguerite turned from her mirror, and out of the window, she saw the tall sails of the big ship that'd arrived that morning.

Stepping outside her home, she noticed a swarm of canoes and small sailing vessels surrounding the anchored ship. All in all, almost three hundred figures lingered along the long boardwalk that led from the base of the hill and over the marshy bank.

A young slave girl came running up the hill to her house. "Your cousin is on the ship."

Oh, thank God. Thank God! Marguerite straightened her back and held her head high. "Tell my cousin he can find me in the cemetery."

She turned her back on the river and walked up the street that led to the cemetery to be with the dead. Although the *Pelican* left La Rochelle with dozens of eligible young women, only twenty-three reached La Mobile alive. Marguerite walked through rows of dead dreams. She stopped in front of the marker for the colony's founder, Pierre LeMoyne Sieur d'Iberville, her cousin, who'd died the previous summer in Cuba.

She vividly remembered when her mother Anne brought her to visit Uncle Charles and the dozen cousins that filled his mansion. For a brief moment in time, the LeMoyne family had positioned itself to become the monarchs of New France, and Princess Marguerite would rule the Louisiana Colony with her ambitious husband, Pierre-Charles LeSueur. War with England changed everything, and now nine of the twelve LeMoyne cousins were dead, so were her dreams of being a queen.

The slave girl came running across the spongy ground to stop in the shadow of the tall grave marker. "Your cousin is coming to see you. Do you need anything?"

The little orphan girl had been brought back after a recent battle with a tribe up the Mississippi River. Marguerite understood her melancholy. While bringing life-saving supplies, the big merchant ship likely carried disease as well. "Find the children and have them go back to the house."

Her children with Pierre-Charles would soon begin flying the nest. Mary Ann was 14, Mary 11, Margaret 8, and her son and heir, Jean-Paul, was ten and yet looked like a full-grown man. If Louise had lived, she would have been 13 in the summer.

Marguerite looked up from her feigned prayers when she heard footsteps reach the soft ground of the cemetery. The shocking sight caused her broken heart to tear in half. One face and figure she recognized immediately—Nicholas Chauvin. The brash Montreal soldier had once served her husband in the Battle of Quebec, and despite having married a local native woman, he acted as her surrogate husband the past two years.

The other two figures were phantoms of dead men.

The ghost of Pierre-Charles LeSueur towered above the other men just as he'd done in life. Marguerite clutched her chest and tried to find her balance with her other hand grasping the grass. The long black beard and broad shoulders looked the same from a distance, but with each step, the giant shrunk a little until it became painfully obvious that the stranger was not her husband.

But the other phantom only gained reality with each step he took, and soon, the face of one of her dead cousins, Joseph LeMoyne, smiled at her. "Marguerite?"

She tried to rise to her feet but stumbled awkwardly, prompting him to rush forward to pick her up from under her arms and to lift her into the air before crushing her in his strong embrace. "We were told you had died at sea," she said through her tears and laughter.

"I thought I *had* died also," Joseph LeMoyne added. Eight years her senior, his face was weathered and scarred at the cheek, his hair gray and thin, yet his arms and stature were still strong. He glanced at the vacant grave of his elder brother Pierre and then set her down. "I've returned to help set things right again."

She stepped back, still clutching her chest, and nodded for him to explain.

"This is my friend and companion, Captain Edward Drummond, a loyal servant and *Son of the Morning*," Joseph LeMoyne added.

Captain Drummond extended a hand to hers, which he kissed as he bowed.

Perhaps I won't have to settle on marrying Mr. Chauvin.

"Captain Drummond and I have spent the winter raiding English settlements in the Caribbean, and along with money and supplies, we've also brought back Jean-Baptiste who'll be establishing a new colony more suited to such a beauty as yourself." Jean-Baptiste LeMoyne, 27, had been unceremoniously sent out as a scout following the departure of colony founder Pierre LeMoyne in 1702.

"It is so good to see you," Marguerite said, throwing her arms around her cousin for a second hug. Behind them, standing at the boardwalk, she saw the slave girl, her four children, and her servant, Charles Poiter, who'd been sent back to Montreal a year ago to sell her house and two properties that would've gone to either Pierre-Charles LeSueur or her brother Michel Messier. Instead, Mr. Poiter likely carried a chest of money.

Marguerite shed tears of joy.

My prayers have finally been answered.

CHAPTER 73

KILTAN ISLAND

1707

With the two ships anchored off the shore of Kiltan Island, Louis-Armand Guerin stood at the railing of the *Starling* and quickly shook hands with the freed Dutch officers as they returned to their ship. On the shore of Kiltan Island, the marooned Dutch crew watched the whole ordeal. In the water, a crewman from the *White Zombie* held onto the rowboat floating beside the ship.

"I certainly wish we could have met under better circumstances," Guerin said, repeating the sentiment he'd told them a dozen times in recent days. "I wish all of you safe travels."

The Island of Kiltan stretched only two miles north-to-south and was only a third of a mile wide. Located over four hundred miles south of Bombay, and 150 miles off the coast of India, it served as the final stage of the Henry Avery plot.

Guerin turned, seeing the *White Zombie* anchored fifty yards away, with LeSueur standing at the railing and a rowboat at its side. There'd been whispers from the true pirates in his crew of keeping the *Starling* and abandoning all the Dutchmen, but Guerin— despite all the roles he had to play—wanted to be a man of honor, a man who'd make his mother proud.

He'd been born a bastard and had no memory of his mother, Jeanne Guerin. The servants in his father's household told him how Isaac Lom D'Arcy, the Baron of Lahontan, had dearly loved Jeanne, but their relationship was consummated out of wedlock. When Louis-Armand was born outside the bonds of holy matrimony, the only heir of Lahontan remained illegitimate for the first few months. His mother Jeanne died shortly after his birth, and he was raised by a wet-nurse until his father married Françoise Le Fascheux de Couttes, who became the only mother he could remember. With his foster-mother's loving consent, he was baptized at the age of three, turning him from bastard to heir of Lahontan. Religious protocols had kept his parents from marrying, and the shadow of his mother's devout legacy fueled his own religious studies. By the time he was a young man, the heir with a servant's humility went to Rome for more than just training—he went looking for answers.

Hidden in Rome, he found the Periphery, and when the priests and agents of the organization that existed prior to the founding of Rome discovered his talents, he became an acolyte. When his father died and he was called back to France to play the part of the Baron of Lahontan, Louis-Armand had already sworn his life to the Periphery.

Now, as his mother's son—he was on the verge of unlocking an ancient mystery.

The son of Jeanne Guerin climbed down the rope ladder and into the rowboat. The crewman held the boat steady, and once he took hold of the oars, he turned back to his ship.

Across the way, Captain Adrian Van Broeck rowed back to reclaim his crew and ship. When the two rowboats met in the waters between the ships, they paused for a moment.

"I see you have the promised treasure," Guerin said. "What will you do with your share?"

"Captain Kidd's blood money? I haven't decided how to spend it, but you've effectively destroyed my life by using my ship in this ruse. The name of Adrian Van Broeck has been stolen from me."

"Yes, but you're also alive. If you ever use your name again, the Emperor's men will find, torture, and kill you to learn more about me. Whatever you do, don't make port until you're a thousand miles away from India. Start again in the New World. You're Dutch. You'll find a home in Montreal or New York. Take a new name and start a family. Or...sail to the Caribbean, build a shack, and drink away your small fortune—just not as Captain Van Broeck—that name belongs to me."

Van Broeck laughed. "I supposed I must first gather my crew."

"I have been a man of my word, and your crew has certainly been loyal to their word. Has my first mate treated you well during your time on the *White Zombie?*"

"He has. The crew thinks he is a demigod. From the tales I've heard, I almost wish to join you on your new adventures. Where will you go now?"

A lot depends on Professor Faero. "I am riding the maelstrom, and it is hard to say where it will take me. I only hope the Lord has further need of me and will forgive me my sins. I have left a new manuscript in your cabin. If you manage to find a way to bring it to the address of the publishing house in Amsterdam, another small fortune will be given only to you."

"A manuscript?"

"A false narrative about the life of Henry Avery. Some of it is true, other details have been embellished. Men like Emperor Aurangzeb often determine fact and fiction, and this account, written in your name, will further muddy the water about what transpired at Madagascar."

"You stick a dagger into a man and then apologize for killing him," Van Broeck shook his head dismissively.

"Fate put you on my path, and I've done what I can to rectify it. Publish the manuscript and you'll be able to start a new life."

Van Broeck laughed again. "You are a vile and amazing man." He began rowing back to his ship.

"I look forward to reading about Long Ben Avery," Guerin shouted as they faced each other with their backs to their respective ships.

"I only wish I was writing about the exploits of Captain LaGrande," Van Broeck said. "Good luck, LaGrande."

The crew of the *White Zombie* began to cheer for their captain's return, bringing a wry smile to Guerin's face.

Guerin. I am from this time forward Guerin.

When the nose of the rowboat struck the side of the *White Zombie*, Guerin slumped down in exhaustion.

CHAPTER 74

Edward Drummond heard all he needed to know—*we're at war with a third enemy.* He emptied his cup, set it down upon the table with a long sigh, and then pushed himself away from the table. He dined with Eos men at the abandoned fort, first built to aid in LeSueur's expedition up the Mississippi River to search for the Philosopher's Stone. After he returned with it, the location was abandoned in favor of the more secure La Mobile.

"You're not leaving tonight, are you?" Jean-Baptiste LeMoyne asked. Apparently, he'd lost the trust of the local colonists following the death of their older brother, the Sieur d'Iberville, Pierre LeMoyne. While almost the same age as the twenty-seven year old Drummond, he'd lived the soft life of an aristocrat.

"Here on land," Drummond began as he rose from his place at the officer's table, "time moves slower than it does on the ocean. Our enemy is not the Priory of Ormus, the Periphery, or even the Jesuits; it certainly is not the Spanish, the Natchez, or diseased creatures of these swamps—we are in a race against time." He picked up his hat, his cutlass, and his thick leather belt that had four pistols strapped to it.

"We could use you here," Joseph LeMoyne added as Drummond secured his weapons.

The officer's table was filled with men who served Eos. He looked to the rogue who'd once served Baron Lahontan on the frontier. "Gather as much wealth from the Caribbean as you can in the coming days. The war in the northern colonies has stalled, and we have good men like Etienne Delhut and your elder brother Charles there to protect the interests of France and the Order of Eos. Here in the swamps, we are weak. The traitor LeSueur has already proven how feeble the Eos leadership is down here in the Gulf."

Two weeks in Alabama taught him all he needed to know about the monstrous man that almost took his life back in Madagascar. Even though the widow and the LeMoynes insisted Pierre-Charles LeSueur had died in Cuba, Drummond now had a name for the face that had come out of the jungle. With Baron Lahontan vanishing onto a pirate ship near Oak Island, Drummond finally understood what went so wrong. Eos had only been focusing on the Priory of Ormus. The men who ambushed him certainly belonged to the Periphery, the ancient enemy that existed in the shadows.

"Where will you go?" Nicholas Chauvin asked. The fools in Montreal had almost set-up Pierre-Charles LeSueur as the leader of the Louisiana Colony, only to be discovered by chance by Bartolome St. Clair, who exposed LeSueur's connections to the theft of the prized Abbaron Map. Charles LeMoyne selected a loyal Eos man, Chauvin, to accompany his niece to the southern colony.

Apparently, I have an Empire to build before I crown myself. "I'm sailing back to Scotland. First, I'll visit the Sinclairs and return the Odin Stone to them. Then, I'll pay a visit to my ancestral home to make sure the Al Marakk Map remains in safe keeping."

"Won't you imperil yourself by getting so close to England?"

"The Priory has its hands full with the war," Drummond said. "Morrison managed to cripple their attempts at building a fleet, so we need to be quick before they regroup. Our forefathers underestimated both England and the Priory. We will not do the same."

"When will you return?" Antoine LeMoyne, the youngest of the three brothers in Louisiana, asked him as he began to walk away.

"As soon as the sea allows," Drummond said earnestly. "I mean to search the ruins of your brother's sunken ship. If the Philosopher's Stone is indeed beneath the waters of Bermuda, it will be found—although we now know LeSueur to be a liar, don't we?"

The three LeMoynes, who'd once worshiped the man, nodded.

"It is not a coincidence that there is an organized resistance up the Mississippi River," Drummond finished.

"The Natchez?" Jean-Baptiste asked.

"While I am away, root them out. I would suspect agents of the Periphery are supplying them with the resources needed. Chauvin, you need to press them hard. Make alliances with other tribes and overwhelm them. While preying upon the Spanish and British colonies in the Caribbean," he said to the other seafaring brothers, "keep an eye on the mouth of the Mississippi. I suspect the Natchez are being aided by outside agents."

For saving his life and preserving the Order of Eos, Grandmaster Marco Alvorez had promised him a great reward.

Soon, the Order of Eos will be mine to control.

CHAPTER 75

Professor Josiah Faero woke that day a free man for the first time in over a decade. No more shackles. No more cells. No more guards. The Island of Socotra could be seen in the glow of the rising sun. At any time, he could hop onto the dinghies transferring supplies or even jump into the water and swim to the sandy shore.

As promised, Louis-Armand Guerin had taken him to neutral waters. Socotra was situated in a shipping lane between the Indian Ocean, the Red Sea, and the nearby Persian Gulf. Countless nations sailed the waters, allowing him to find a port of his choosing. Captain Guerin had also given him an ultimatum, and he expected a decision to be made by the time they crossed from Kiltan Island to Socotra Island.

Where do I go from here?

He chose to walk up to the captain's quarters.

Three men stopped eating their breakfasts when he appeared in the doorway. Guerin gestured to the empty chair beside Pierre-Charles LeSueur. Opposite of them, the Abyssinian, Benjamin Horne, watched him with wide eyes.

"I'm glad you've decided to join us for breakfast," Guerin said as he finished his last bite. "I really didn't want to see Charlie have to slice up your genitals to get the answers we wanted."

Guerin laughed but LeSueur didn't—a harrowing sign. *Is he being serious?* "I want to be part of this…investigation."

The word made Guerin smile and lift his eyebrows. "Very well. No torture. No murder. Just an…alliance of minds. As you know, we went through a great deal to acquire you. We could've returned to America with our heads held high knowing that we'd foiled the plans of our enemies, but that's not what I was put on this earth to do."

"You were put on this earth to torment me," LeSueur said.

"I've made promises to these two men. Important promises. The four of us, however, all seemed to be given different pieces of the same puzzle. I believe the Lord brought us together to solve a great mystery. Let me begin with my piece of the puzzle."

Guerin wiped off his mouth and pushed his plate away. "I'm an advance scout for the Periphery. It's a religious organization, of sorts, established long before the Catholic Church took root in Rome. We're wardens of humanity. We fight against the darkness, which means we protect the Lord's people, great and small, from evil men like those in the Priory and Eos. We don't evangelize. We don't preach—"

LeSueur cleared his throat.

Guerin ignored it. "We protect. I was trained as an advance scout. Rumors reached the Periphery that both the Jesuit Order and the Order of Eos were fixated on news of an ancient relic out on the frontier—the Philosopher's Stone."

Then my carvings in the brig certainly drew his attention, Faero decided. "Yes, I supplied plenty of books on Alchemy to buyers from Montreal."

"That was me," LeSueur muttered and continued working on his plate of food.

And here we sit together years later.

"I fulfilled my mission prerogative by thwarting the interests of my enemies and confirming the resting place of the Philosopher's Stone."

He found it?

"But before I could return home, I ended up being swept up by pirates. Like yourself, I was driven by curiosity and followed the clues to where they led: a secret colony of Templar refugees. Your turn, Charlie," Guerin concluded.

LeSueur cleared his throat twice. "I didn't have a choice in the matter. Fate just took a massive shit on my life. When I was a kid, my family sent me to New France to make a name for myself. At first, I worked for the Jesuits as a linguist. I learned the languages of the local tribes and helped the priests in all manner of communications. The most gifted and brilliant of the priests I worked with was Father Marquette. At first, it appeared he'd simply been tasked with exploration, but…at the end…he revealed his real purpose. He'd been given an ancient map that purportedly described the location of the Philosopher's Stone. Because of his efforts, the Order of Eos poisoned him. I kept the map."

"Apparently," Guerin added when LeSueur emotionally withdrew, "The map once belonged to the Priory of Ormus, was stolen a century ago by the Jesuits, and now is in the hands of Eos, but not before Charlie made a mess of things. Tell the Professor what happened."

"I led a secret mining expedition into the frontier, dug it up, but lost everything when the ship carrying it sank off the coast of Bermuda. When I returned to France, instead of punishing me for my private and public failures, they chose to reward me with a new colony on condition of returning to the Land of the Blue Woman."

Faero chuckled knowingly. *Blue Woman…vitriol…Undine. It all connects.* He grew self-conscious of his misunderstood reaction, so he refocused. "They sent you back."

Guerin pointed a finger at him and grinned. "Ah, you're beginning to see the larger mystery also. What else is out on the frontier? Luckily, Mr. Horne came into my life around the same time I found your coded distress message. Tell Professor Faero about your piece of the puzzle."

"Like Louis-Armand, I was sent out into the world by a religious order with ancient roots. The Order of Eos has been our enemy since the days of the dawn, but in recent centuries, it tried to steal the knowledge we've long protected. When I found your marking inside of the brig of this ship, then the *Quedagh Merchant*, I believed you were the thief who stole our holy relic."

"Me? I've never stolen a thing in my life," Faero insisted.

Benjamin Horne nodded. "I now know that it was Eos, but once we filtered through the lies surrounding the *Ganj-i-Sawai* incident, Louis-Armand and I understood why Eos fixated on the legends of King Solomon. The Abbaron Map that LeSueur witnessed was created by an Abyssinian mapmaker and navigator employed by the Queen of Sheba. She gave him to King Solomon's expedition to find the Philosopher's Stone on the lost continent. Although the expedition failed to bring back the Philosopher's Stone, it nevertheless created a map that led back to LeSueur's Land of the Blue Woman."

LeSueur rose, walked over to a locked cabinet, and produced a lead canister that he set on a table. "The shamir of King Solomon."

Louis-Armand waited for him to sit down. "When the Order of Eos called themselves the Templar Knights, it discovered a cache of Solomon's attempt at replicating the Philosopher's Stone. This same material devoured much of the mountain months ago back in Madagascar. Some of it still exists thanks to LeSueur's rival Blackbeard. This canister remained unopened, and for now, a dead end. Besides raiding the ruins of the Temple in Jerusalem, the Templar knights briefly invaded Benjamin's homeland. Tell them what you seek, Master Horne."

"Do you know what we keep in the sacred churches of Abyssinia?" Horne instead chose to quiz him.

Faero nodded. "If the tales are true, Queen Makeda made eleven replicas of the Ark of the Covenant, and twelve sacred churches kept them, with only a secret order of priests who knew which one was the true ark."

Louis-Armand clasped his hands. "You are indeed the right man. Regardless of *which* Ark was taken by Eos, I knew there were three locations it might be kept. It was not on Madeira, and it turns out it was not on Madagascar either, which leads me to a final destination. After all of our time together, Master Horne and I are in agreement with what we need to do next, but before we do it, we'll be visiting Abyssinia to collect a necessary relic, especially after LeSueur dropped the key into the Atlantic. Of course, you know what we're going after in the ancient Kingdom of Sheba, don't you?"

Faero nodded. Had they not fallen into Emperor Aurangzeb's trap, he and Thomas would've scoured the ancient lands for a mysterious relic that could command demons to do its bidding. *"Khātam Sulaymān…*King Solomon's ring, the *Seal of Solomon."* The two unlocking triangles in alchemy, known commonly as the Star of David, was the central etching upon the mysterious ring.

"Now it's your turn," Guerin added. "Tell us what piece of the puzzle you possess."

Like Daniel in the lion's den, Josiah Faero had prayed earnestly to God for delivery from his enemies. After passing from Eos to the Emperor, his prayers seemed to finally be answered. "In creating the Seal of Solomon and the shamir, King Solomon researched an ancient legend involving the Sorcerer who created the Stone. What piece of the puzzle do I have? Thomas Tew knew I was working on the ancient language used during the time. Solomon engraved what he knew of it upon his ring. The Arabian sarcophagus lusted after by Tew and the Emperor held phrases of that language still upon it. To command the evil spirits within either the shamir or Stone, the ancient words needed to be uttered."

"So will you come with us to help unlock these great mysteries? You now understand our rivals and enemies. We can leave you behind on Socotra, or…you can come with us on the next leg of our great adventure."

He'd probably kill me rather than risk me falling into the wrong hands again. "I'll come with you willingly."

"Wonderful," Guerin said and then loudly clapped his hands together to say, "Open Sesame."

Faero grinned. "When the time arises, you might want to try Abracadabra instead."

CHAPTER 76

Catherine Barton sat in her private box at The Queen's Theater. As the mistress of the Earl of Halifax, she was quite used to whispers. As a regal beauty since her teens, she was used to lustful eyes watching her. As the niece of Sir Isaac Newton, she understood his lessons in alchemy on how to transform fame into power. But as a new leader within the Priory of Ormus, she took her social status to a whole new level. The comedy was well into the second act when a handsome gentleman entered the box from the rear and sat down beside her.

"Miss Barton," he whispered softly.

She extended her gloved hand, which he accepted and kissed lightly. Not yet thirty, she wore a velvet gown that showed plenty of cleavage. "Sit, Governor Rogers. We have much to discuss."

Rogers lightly chuckled at her playful use of the title governor and sat down meekly beside her. "You tease, Miss Barton."

"Oh do I?" she said gaily. "This play has put me in better spirits, I suppose, after hearing so many bad reports in recent weeks. I hear you are a companion of bad news also. Your father recently died?"

"Several months ago," he said and then cleared his throat. "That is correct."

He knows who I am, and he certainly knows my Uncle. "Which leaves you a grieving yet wealthy man. I forget…is your name spelled with or without the e?"

"My father was Woods Rogers, and I am Woodes Rogers with an e."

"Then our paperwork is all in order," Catherine Barton said, handing him the portfolio. "Our offer is summarized on the top sheet. Take a moment to review it."

Even though Woodes Rogers was a handsome, robust gentleman, he was only a new pawn in the game, and thus, held no interest for Catherine. Even so, she dressed as if she planned on seducing him away from his young bride. With the death of his father in the Madagascar debacle, young Woodes inherited a shipping business, making him an formidable ally.

She ignored him as he read, and after a proper amount of time, she began talking. "Did you hear that the director of this play died a few weeks ago. Is it morbid that audiences pack the theater?"

"Not at all," he answered, his forehead wrinkled. He kept his eyes upon the stage as she studied him. "If anything, it immortalizes him after his death.

Perhaps he has the makings of a knight or a rook instead of just a pawn. Woodes looked strong and sophisticated. "My uncle makes plans for his work to continue after his death, so in that matter, Mr. Farquhar the playwright has attained a small measure of immortality. I doubt his play will be remembered as long as my uncle. It's titled *The Beaux' Strategem*. What do you say, Mr. Rogers, will you be our beaux?"

"It's…shocking, to be honest with you, but I have recently agreed to accompany Captain William Dampier on a two-ship expedition to the Pacific. If only this offer had been made a few—"

"Yes, and it's the reason why we chose you. We want you to go on your three-year circumnavigation of the world, but we want you to be our eyes and ears. My uncle has had his pride wounded, and I've tempered his wrath for the time being. You've lost a father, and have no recourse for your grief and wrath either. When you return in three years, we will unleash you on our shared enemies. We will fund your every need, and you will become a bane to these pirates who sail the Seven Seas—the ones who killed your father. If you punish my uncle's enemies, I will greet you earnestly with the title of Governor. Read through the rest of the proposal, but at the end of this play, I want an answer."

"You won't have to wait until the end of the play, Miss Barton.
Give me the names of the men who killed my father."
Where shall I begin?

THE END OF PART FOUR

PART FIVE
A KINGDOM OF UNHEWN STONE

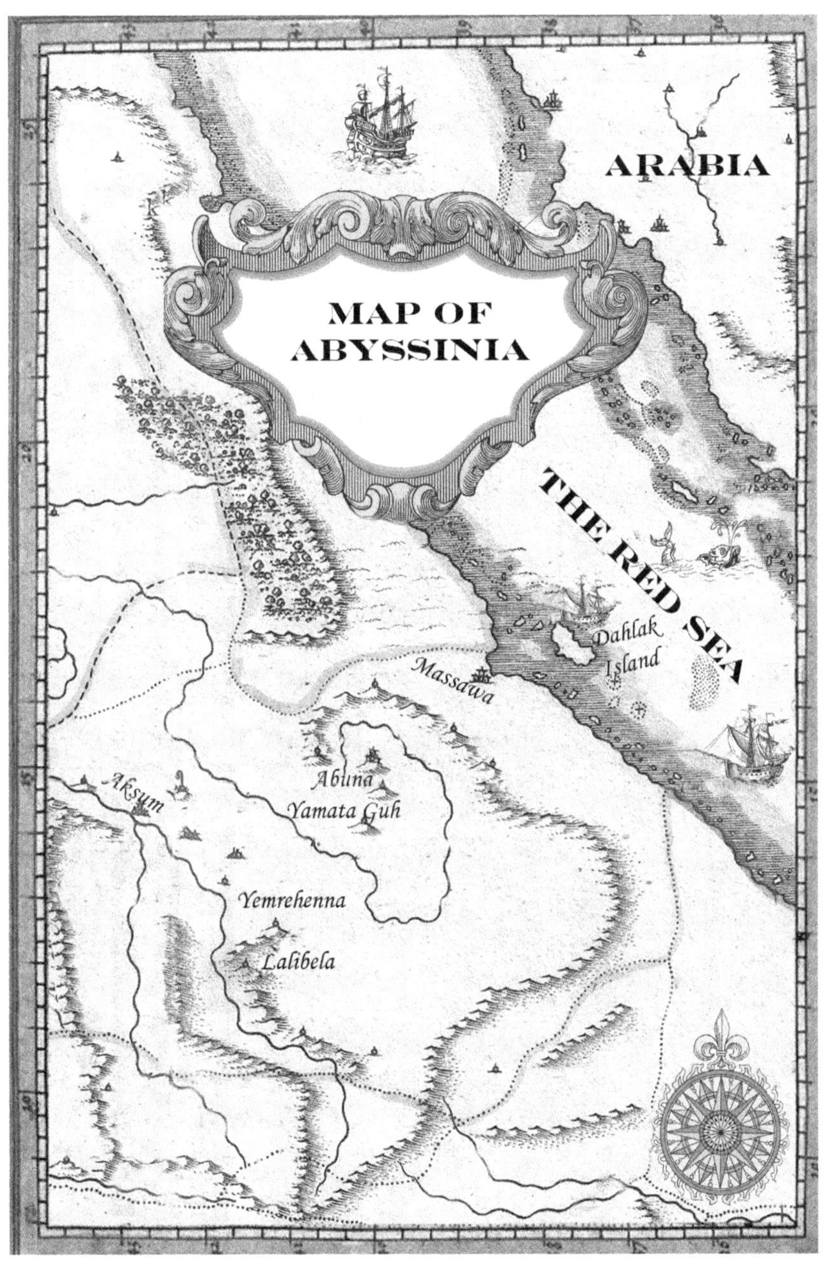

CHAPTER 77

Of all the islands of the Caribbean, the island of Bermuda is the northernmost and is located six hundred miles off the coast of North Carolina. Bermuda forms the top of the triangle that spans between the tip of Florida and Puerto Rico. The British Empire established a colony in 1612, which began developing agriculture before quickly shifting the economy to whaling, shipbuilding, and privateering. Its unique hook shape made it an excellent harbor for ships crossing the Atlantic.

Six years earlier, two French ships departed Bermuda for La Rochelle. One of the ships, guarded by Pierre-Charles LeSueur, abruptly burst into flames, taking its precious cargo down to the depths.

Now, Captain Edward Drummond anchored near the place where the ship was lost. *If I find the Philosopher's Stone, I win.*

"A ship approaches, Captain."

Edward Drummond abandoned his spot at the railing of the ship, looked up at the crow's nest, and then found the line of sight for the approaching ship.

Spanish.

"Quartermaster, to arms."

The ship came alive after hours of hushed silence, and Drummond rushed up the stairs to the quarterdeck for a better view.

The ship came out of the Great Sound, a protected harbor almost ninety percent enclosed by a thin arm that wrapped around from the main part of Bermuda Island. The *Pretender,* Drummond's stolen warship, was anchored almost fifteen nautical miles from the mouth of the harbor, between the outer edge of the reef and the Bermuda Rise, where the ocean floor met the island.

"She's small and she's alone," Drummond said to himself more than his crew. "Master Gunner, load the cannons and stand down. I want to hear what they want."

"Sir?" his anchoring boatswain called out from the edge of the ship where divers were submerged.

"As is," Drummond ordered.

"The time, sir?"

Drummond pulled out his watch. The diving bell had been under for thirty-six minutes already. *Dammit.* "Let them stay, but if the time expires, be discreet about it."

He found his looking glass and studied the approaching ship. It was a small vessel, armed with just a few cannons. *A patrol boat— more bark than bite. Perhaps I should snarl a bit.* "Show him our teeth."

A shout went out from the crew, and just the order raised the blood lust. The white skull on the black flag had attacked enough ships for rumor to circulate the Caribbean Sea.

Surprisingly, the ship did not change direction, but a white flag climbed up the pole to join the Spanish flag. *What do these fools want?*

As the Spanish ship came into range of the guns, Drummond heard the diving bell release air behind him but knew the hull of the *Pretender* blocked the view of their activities.

"State your business in Bermuda," the Spanish captain called out.

"I am Captain Edward Thatcher of the *Pretender*," he partially lied. "We are wanted fugitives by the British government and seek safe harbor. We anchored off the coast of your island so not to raise alarm and to show our good faith. We'd heard that the French and Spanish had taken the island away from England last year, but wanted confirmation, lest we fall into a trap."

The Spaniard nodded. "The rumors are true. Spain now controls Bermuda. I am Captain Hernandez, harbor patrol, but for the safety of our people, we will deny your entrance into the harbor."

"My ship is in desperate need of supplies." *Another lie, but I'll play along.*

"Until our defenses can be rebuilt, the port is closed, especially to English ships, whose loyalties are often doubtful. Another English fugitive told a similar story, and when we allowed him into port, he raised *el miembro*, attacked the port, and killed a dozen residents before he was driven off."

El miembro? Drummond kept a serious expression but reveled at the thought of a penis upon a flag. *Does Patrick Dalziel live after all these years? He'd be a valuable ally in the Gulf.* "I understand your reticence, but know that I have Catholic allies. I have letters from the LeMoyne family, including the governor of Mobile colony. If that helps I can send—"

"I am only enforcing the policy chosen by the administration of the island," Hernandez interrupted. "But we will gladly supply any requisitions in exchange for your compliance."

They are begging to be pirated. Alas, I have no time. My interest is beneath the waters. "We have no interest in attacking your island, so I accept the terms you offer, and I will send my provisions boatswain to supervise these requisitions. If we are properly outfitted, we will depart peacefully from your island within three days."

A deal was struck and his provisions boatswain quickly loaded onto a skiff.

No sooner had it departed than Drummond rushed to the side of the ship. He looked over the railing to see his crew of Greek divers staring up at him from beside the suspended metal bell.

"So?" Drummond asked.

"It's a French vessel with damage from a fire. Another few hundred yards, and it would have been much too deep to reach."

"But you can reach it, right?"

"Oh yes, we've already begun exploring the ship. We'll have to clear away some of the old rigging to move the bell into position, but she's not as deep as you'd imagine."

Drummond looked back to the Spanish ship and the island of Bermuda. The location was close enough to shore to be witnessed and rescued yet far enough from shore to sink it in the depths of the Atlantic—*LeSueur wanted it to be seen.*

Witnesses confirmed his account of the disaster.

Drummond felt reinvigorated and pounded his fist on a railing. "How much time will you need?"

"It'll take us a day to remove the rigging, but once we do that, we'll be able to scour that wreck from nose to stern."

The explosion had caused the ship to sink so quickly, according to the reports, that Pierre-Charles LeSueur barely had time to free his prisoners, let alone obtain the treasure securely locked away in the hold.

I would've saved the Stone. Too suspicious to believe—unless he wanted to be rid of it.

Drummond called to his navigator. "I want you to create a chart; marking a triangle-shaped grid from this point back to the island—a map of the sea floor."

A few years earlier, Pierre-Charles LeSueur had reported the disaster to King Louis and Farmer-General Alexander L'Huillier, an alchemist who served the Order of Eos.

After reviewing the court records and the accounts from the LeMoyne family, Drummond now understood how Eos had been duped by a monster of a man who was capable of ripping up trees with his bare hands and whose feet were so large they created lakes where he stepped.

Like the giant I faced in Madagascar.

If Pierre-Charles LeSueur did not die in Cuba, then what truly happened to the Philosopher's Stone?

CHAPTER 78

The Sublime Ottoman State, as it called itself, was founded at the end of the thirteenth century in modern day Turkey. After crossing into Europe in 1354, and parts of Africa shortly after, it became a global power on three continents. During the reign of Suleiman the Magnificent, who ruled from the capital of Constantinople, the Ottoman Empire reached its zenith with thirty-two provinces and numerous vassal states. With its powerful military, flexible economy, and strategic intercontinental location, the Ottoman Empire ruled in relative stability in the region despite conflict along the Habsburg and Russian frontiers.

Because of its presence in the Mediterranean Sea, Black Sea, Persian Gulf, and Red Sea, European empires developed trade routes around Africa to avoid Ottoman control. Like its powerful neighbor, the Mughal Empire, it also supported the religion of Sunni Islam. With its northern arm reaching as far north as Kiev, and its western arm reaching as far west as Algiers, its southern reach grasped the Red Sea all the way to the Horn of Africa. Possessing mostly coastal lands, it had vital ports such as Jeddah, Suakin, Adulis, and Massawa.

Thirty nautical miles from the port of Massawa, the *White Zombie* anchored in the shallow waters of the Dahlak Islands. Surrounded by 123 other islands in a bay whose mouth was hidden from view by smaller islands, the *White Zombie* allowed trade vessels to cruise by at a distance without being seen.

Captain Guerin and Master Gunner Horne took one of the skiffs to first scout the area and then scout the port, leaving Pierre-Charles LeSueur trapped on an island with the overly-inquisitive Josiah Faero. Just like freshly washed white linen, LeSueur's flesh and hair had returned to a normal, but still unusual, condition. Faero couldn't let it go.

As Papa Bones prepared breakfast for the men sleeping on the soft sands of the warm island, Faero came up with a plate of freshly cooked eggs and offered it to LeSueur.

Accepting meant he'd be stuck answering questions all morning.

"Strange word, Wishwee," Faero began. "You say it's a Sioux word."

Wenonah used it. He nodded.

"Any Sioux words similar to it?"

LeSueur sighed and nodded. "Wichapi is their word for star."

"Oh, oh," Faero got to the connection quickly. "The Comet of 1682—the one the natives believed summoned a hero to fight the shape shifting monster in the cave. Wishwee… Wichapi… fascinating." Faero took a few moments to eat his eggs. "The cook is an eccentric fellow, too. He believes you've been marked. He thinks he could see a glow about you even before the meltdown at the island. So why do you think you were spared by the 'vaporous cloud' that destroyed so much of the island?"

Faero transitioned from his question to his food in a blink of an eye.

He'd idolized Father Marquette's Jesuit oath, yet LeSueur had murdered men in war and in peace. He tried to remain chaste yet gave himself to Wenonah out on the frontier and then refused to name her as wife. Even worse, he replaced her in his bed with Marguerite Messier, who ended up being his Delilah. He, like Samson, chose to live with his enemies. To survive, LeSueur had made pacts with two enemies—Eos and the Priory. "It obviously has nothing to do with my moral quality."

"Ah, like the sinful Israelites standing beneath Mount Sinai while Moses was made pure by the fires of God," Faero said while scooping up each tiny bit of egg from his place. "The Philosopher's Stone lore tells how Nicholas Flamel managed to replicate

the original in a way that prolonged the lives of his wife and him. I've been reflecting on that theory, but according to your anecdotes, both the Philosopher's Stone and the shamir felt…unholy?"

"When we unearthed the Philosopher's Stone," LeSueur began telling the story that had unfolded seven years earlier, "my colleague reached for the stone, and the flesh from his hands sloughed off as if he'd grabbed a white hot coal. Another time, Keoxa, my…uh…a warrior of renown amongst the Sioux, had the Stone slip right through his hands, which were left burned and bloody."

"Yet the Stone recognized you—that is curious," Faero set down his plate, rolled up his sleeves, and gave his undivided attention to LeSueur, who self-consciously looked down.

"Louis-Armand held a theory that the Philosopher's Stone had somehow imbued you with magic. Imbued means that—"

"I know what imbued means," LeSueur snapped. "Remember who purchased so many of your books on alchemy."

"Yes, but you didn't purchase my whole library, did you?" Faero retorted playfully. "I had a collection of 'alternative' versions of Genesis, one which even came from the ancient land of Sheba. That account gave a fuller description of Eden, which included a lake that translates as Crystal. Although it sounds a little fanciful, anyone who bathed in the waters of Crystal Lake found themselves purified both physically and spiritually, washed white."

"You think that's what happened to me?"

"Oh, no. I dismissed Louis-Armand's 'imbued' theory since you obviously held the ability to hold it prior to holding it. See? Plus, there was no physical change to your two states of being," Faero chuckled at his own phrasing.

He mocks me for being a killer? "So what is your theory about what happened?"

Faero took a moment. "Wutach."

I never should have told him that part. I was delirious from loss of blood. "Wutach?"

"Take the Biblical figure of Abraham as a comparison. He was a Babylonian warrior before he settled in the Promised Land to raise his flocks. Yet when God looked out upon humanity, he chose Abram and then placed his seal of approval upon him, and

for generations afterwards, anyone who held the mark received the glory of God. Generations of Jews received God's glory because of their connections to Abram. The shadowy figure that stood between you and the blast—it called you 'Child of Wutach,' didn't it?"

"Yes, but I don't know what that means."

"If I were to venture a guess, I'd say it was an angel that stood in front of you, and with the immortal nature of angels, it likely recognized you just like Abraham's descendants were recognized in the Bible. That crazy Haitian chef might be right about *cho djab*. Both relics, the Philosopher's Stone and the shamir were crafted with evil spirits that can harm mere mortals, but you, Child of Wutach, there is something in your blood that makes you different."

LeSueur scoffed. His aristocratic blood resulted in him being shipped away from France since his older brother would inherit all the property. "Perhaps I'm descended from the Alchemist."

"King Solomon?"

LeSueur shook his head. "I jest. But no, I was referencing the original Alchemist, the one who crafted the Philosopher's Stone, as we call it. If the Stone is real, then he is also real. Solomon went looking for him, Eos searches for him, and now, Louis-Armand Guerin searches the earth for clues about him. While I understand the Periphery serves as wardens for humanity, what if our efforts to thwart Eos leads to something worse."

"Worse?" Faero asked.

"Guerin has referenced the Stone as a key. Right now, we search for the ring to command the shamir, but for what purpose? To act as a key. I've sinned enough in my life. I'm already responsible for unearthing one unholy relic. I don't want to be responsible for unlocking something worse."

Faero pondered quietly for a few moments. In the distance, the camp began to stir, drawing his attention away. Then suddenly his eyes widened. "The key to the bottomless pit? Is that what concerns you?"

LeSueur nodded about the prophecy about the end times. "We know what Eos believes about buried Norse gods. The Book of Revelation describes a key that is used to unlock—"

"Apollyon the Destroyer," Faero finished. "That is a disturbing thought."

The words were swallowed up by excitement in the distance, and even LeSueur's concentration was broken by the sight of his master gunner and captain walking into the camp. "The whirlwind has returned to us."

Faero took the plate and cup and scurried back to join the others.

LeSueur methodically began to pack his tent and belongings. No sooner had he finished than Guerin himself walked up.

"Let me guess. You found the ring, it's in your pocket, and now we can depart for America?"

Guerin felt into his pocket, found it empty, and then shrugged. "No such luck. We'll be departing soon. We're going to be leaving the ship here with Naufragio and Del Torro. Seabird eggs, turtles, and food from the mangroves will sustain the crew, and we'll leave them with a rowboat just in case they need to supplement the supplies. The African mainland is just 10 miles due west from here."

"And where will we be?"

"Forty-seven miles due east at the busy port of Massawa. Horne and I have just returned from it. It's far too busy a port to pull up in a stolen Mughal vessel, even if the *White Zombie* no longer resembles itself."

"How long will it be anchored here?"

Guerin chuckled. "How long will we be gone? Along with Horne's original Abyssians, I'm only taking a handful of our best men so that we travel quickly and discreetly. From what Faero and Horne tell me, I hope it'll only take a few months."

"And then we'll return home?"

"To France, hell no."

"To America?"

"Yes, it seems as if we have unfinished business. Almost two years ago, the locals reported a foreign warship docked for supplies with a destination of Aqaba next. It seems as if your Captain Blackbeard docked in Aqaba for a few months before sailing away to unknown waters."

"You and I both know where he's heading."

"Oh, I know. I just hope you trust me. Once we acquire Solomon's ring, we'll be able to turn the tables on the Order of Eos."

LeSueur extended a hand, which Guerin took, and with a loud groan, he helped him to his feet. "Lead the way."

CHAPTER 79

The port city of Massawa, shielded by numerous islands along the African coast, had once been part of the ancient Kingdom of Axum. Possession of the key African port shifted from the Umayyad Caliphate, the Kingdom of Bejag, Portuguese, and finally to Ottoman control in 1557. The nearby mountainous Ethiopian country of Abyssinia, with its borders just thirty miles from the coast, repelled foreign influence for centuries and maintained robust trade at the Red Sea port.

Even though the port didn't belong to Abyssinia, it signaled home for Benjamin Horne.

My mission is only a failure if I stop now, he told himself as the three skiffs approached the docks. Following the *Ganj-i-Sawai* incident, his superiors determined the time was ripe to attempt to regain the missing Ark of the Covenant. Ultimately, his superiors had been right about Eos moving their relics, but everything else about the mission fell apart.

With the sun on his face as he rowed, Benjamin Horne returned to Massawa with his head held high. He'd shed all of his tears when he returned a few days earlier with Guerin, and now he watched the survivors of his expedition return home.

I must continue for those who died.

They cannot have died in vain.

Men who were only boys when they departed thirteen years earlier now set foot upon the docks of Massawa as freed men. In the other two skiffs were members of their sailing family: Drake Murray, Jimmy Duke, Dr. Barrow, Naro Bon, LeSueur, and their newest and final master, Louis-Armand Guerin.

The cross left Horne exhausted, but his men were a generation younger. Most of the original crew died in the first attack. Horne was kept because of his skill on a ship and the younger boys for their gunnery skills. Most were in their late twenties now.

They don't know what to do, Benjamin Horne realized as they fanned out onto the platform, suddenly surrounded by men who looked similar to them. "I will go speak with them again," Horne shouted back to Guerin, who paid the harbor master a fee to keep the skiffs safe.

Horne walked past his team, who were trying to reconcile childhood memories with what they were witnessing as men, thirteen years after they'd last been on Africa soil. "Come, follow me."

Having followed Horne for almost half their lives, the gun crewmen fell in line as Benjamin walked from the busy docks to the marketplace and finally to the shade of the mangrove trees that line the coast. They'd departed with Horne as their leader, then found themselves captured by an Eos pirate ship, later to be captured by Corgi Baba, and finally by Captain Kidd and the *Adventure Galley*. Louis-Armand Guerin freed them and returned them home.

"You are all free men now," Horne told them, "and from this moment on, you follow me by your choice. As Guerin promised we would long ago, he has brought you back to the land of your birth. I will stay with him as an equal, not a servant, because the road we walk must be walked together. We need each other to face the perils ahead, but this is far from the end of my journey. You've all served with honor and fought with bravery. Somewhere out there might be family members: brothers, sisters, nieces, nephews, and for a few of you, parents. Each of you has money to start a new life. You can find work right here in Massawa and put your own name on a ship. If you stay with me, I can guarantee many dangers ahead—possibly even death—but I can also promise you adventure and wealth. This is where you must choose."

Of the seven who'd survived the journey, six stayed with Horne. They said their goodbyes to the one and then stayed shoulder to shoulder with their aging leader. "Then let us unload our supplies."

On the platform, the motley crew of pirates loaded supplies upon their shoulders and backs and walked into the city. Benjamin Horne led the way, with the six white foreigners following at the rear of the procession.

As decided, Horned acted as leader of the expedition into Abyssinia. Under Horne's feigned leadership, they purchased more supplies and transportation horses. In just a few hours, the tasks were accomplished. "And now we walk," Horne declared and led the men out of town.

"How far is it?" Jimmy Duke called out.

"Two days until we reach the mountains. Then we will see how you fare."

CHAPTER 80

AKSUM, ABYSSINIA

1708

For Josiah Faero, the mountains of Abyssinia looked the same as the vassal state of Habesh Eyalet, yet Benjamin Horne insisted they looked quite different.

The region was dry, yet they crossed through river and stream beds that indicated the rainy season had to be quite intense. The mountains were a series of peaks with deep valleys and a sprinkling of short tree and shrub growth due to the seasonal droughts. Faero understood how the people of Ethiopia had repelled foreign invaders and interlopers for thousands of years: each mountain was a defensible fortress overlooking fertile ravines,

Over the past several days, their expedition had traveled almost two hundred miles with no notice or fanfare. At each village or town, Horne would walk ahead, speak with the authorities, and women and children would bring out so much food that their sacks of supplies began to feel superfluous.

Who is this man? Faero wondered, trying to discern how Horne parted the figurative thickets of thorns with ease.

Another man who fascinated Faero was Naro Bon, a fellow sailing master. In a way he reminded him of Ngari, the prison cook from his Kailash expedition. Each day, Bon would find time to walk with him for a few minutes—and then press for anecdotes about his life.

Coming out of the mountains, they paused once again for Horne to clear the path for the large village below. It was unlike any other mountain village in the area. Aside from the span of the large valley, which tripled the footing space for anything of recent note, the city was nestled in between several volcanic lumps. While the Tigray Mountains continued on the opposite side of the valley with a distinct wall that indicated days of mountainous travel ahead, from the relatively flat valley floor, rocky boils rose up like festering acne upon youthful skin. The only one with tree growth had a top that appeared leveled off by God's trowel. The city flowed around three of these large mounds, which rose as high as the mountain pass from which he emerged.

Naro Bon approached once again for another exchange of tales.

Bon sat beside him, and together they watched Horne descending the road toward the nearest of the seven volcanic lumps.

"This reminds me of a place from my home," Bon finally said. "It is a shame you spent all those years in a prison because just a few hundred miles from Delhi are mountains so beautiful and tall, they would cause you to weep."

Oh, dear, he's under the impression I was in a prison the whole time.

"And beyond the Himalayas," Bon continued, "in the land of my birth, there is a mountain just like those small rocky plumes, which rises from the earth like a stairway to heaven."

"You're speaking of Kailash, aren't you?"

"You know of Kailash?" Bon asked, the wrinkles in his brow doubling.

Faero had kept his time on the mountain mostly to himself. "My study of ancient religions is extensive, which is why the Templar pirates abducted me in the first place. Yes, I am very familiar with Kailash; in fact, it filled my thoughts in my final years as a prisoner of the Emperor." *Truth disguised.* "So it rises in a similar fashion?"

Faero could still picture the regal mountain as he was taken away to be traded for Henry Avery. Despite being a prisoner, he knew there were secrets to be found at Kailash.

Bon nodded. "If you are a professor of ancient religions, then you know how the Greek god Apollo drove his chariot across the sky, or how Ra and Apophis chased each other across the sky to create day and night." Naro reached down and picked up a medium sized rock, which he held with his thumb and middle finger. "Do you see how I have two fingers, two small points, which sup-

port the weight of the rock. Now, with my other hand, I can spin the stone upon these two axis points. Instead of a chariot, now imagine that my face is the sun, and as I rotate this stone, it goes from light to dark, doesn't it?"

Who needs Galileo when I have Naro Bon to explain modern astronomy? He smiled and nodded, waiting for the point to emerge. If information had value, he kept the currency gained during his trip to Kailash to himself. He'd spend it only if needed.

"Mount Kailash is the place in which our world is held, which is why it is a sacred place. It is where heaven and earth connect," Bon concluded, tossing the stone aside. With his finger in the dust, he began to draw a shape. "From Kailash, four rivers flow, each in a different direction."

"A place where water flows in all directions," LeSueur said from several feet away, his finger pointing to Naro's diagram in the dust. "I've seen such a place on the far side of the world."

LeSueur—still a mystery. Despite being fifty, LeSueur had the muscular body of a gladiator and the mind of a wizard. While no longer a prisoner of the Emperor, Faero still yearned to know more. "You called it the 'stairway to heaven,' why is that?"

"It is the place where Tonpa Shenrab came down from Heaven to earth, thousands of years before Buddha or Jesus the Christ."

"Thousands of years before Christ would mean Tonpa Shenrab came to humans during the Dawn of Humanity, as the Templars saw it. Tell me the story of Tonpa Shenrab," Faero requested.

"You would be disappointed by my tales, for Tonpa Shenrab is not an epic hero as in other religions. His example is the opposite, a peacemaker, for his stories deal with enlightenment and introspection—an example for regular humans to follow instead a life of madness like the one I've been living. Shenrab renounced his royalty at an early age, chose to wander the world, and lived in nature. It is said that when his natural life came to an end, the mountain opened up to take him into her bosom."

And there it is...strange confirmation of the ancient theory. Faero glanced down to the valley, where the pied piper Benjamin Horne led another throng of children as they followed him back up the mountain pass. "In your stories, does Shenrab receive stone...tablets, with sacred words written upon them?"

Or perhaps runes like the Odin Stone?

"The ten commandments," LeSueur scoffed. "You think Shenrab is Moses, rejecting his Egyptian mother to wander the world seeking enlightenment?"

Faero chuckled. *A brute but not a fool.* "Hearing it aloud, I see your point, Charlie. Let me rephrase the question, Master Bon. I've read ancient stories, predating Moses, from the Dawn Era, where the secrets of the universe were written upon large rectangular blocks of stone, and after a great cataclysm, the stones were brought to Kailash, carried into its interior through a secret entrance."

"The one used by Shenrab?" Bon asked. "Is that your theory?"

"Many legends share common truths. Perhaps these two accounts share a common item—a secret entrance."

LeSueur leaned back. "Where are you going with all of this?"

"I'm chasing after a shadow, a figure without a name, even if he has a thousand different names. Across our earth, a thousand pieces of him remain, and I've spent my life trying to understand the puzzle." Faero looked to confirm that it was only him, Bon, and LeSueur. All of the others were thinking the dull thoughts of a warrior-soldier as they sharpened blades and cleaned weapons, except for Louis-Armand Guerin, who walked to where they talked.

"Who is he?" LeSueur asked.

The first alchemist? "If you are telling the truth, he is the one who created the thing you held in your hands."

"You're searching for Charlie's father?" Guerin called out from a distance. "I've seen what Charlie holds in his hands each time he relieves himself."

Faero and LeSueur laughed while Bon only wrinkled his forehead.

Guerin waved Faero to him. "This village...is unlike anything we've seen before, and I'm going to need your help understanding some of the clues left behind."

THE EXPEDITION FOLLOWED Benjamin Horne into the ancient city of Aksum. As they neared the first bluff, a crowd of old men, women, and children came out of the homes to study

them as foreigners but also celebrate them as sailors, one of which was remembered from years earlier. At first, the children studied LeSueur with wide eyes, but after a few blocks, they were climbing all over him as he gave rides upon his broad shoulders.

Guerin paid it no attention and kept his gaze upon the path.

Once they passed by the first bluff, a peculiar sight came into view between the central bluff and the western wooded bluff.

Are those pillars?

Faero was so focused on the gray stelae that he almost jumped when he saw a series of Christian churches at the beginning of the cut between the two hills. From one of the churches, the local priest focused his attention on Horne.

Benjamin Horne conversed with a gray-haired priest for several minutes in their own language. Upon seeing Faero's reaction, he translated. "Aksum has been a Christian city since the third century, the tallest stele ahead is the Obelisk of King Ezana, who brought Christianity to *all* the people of Ethiopia, not just those who dwell in caves."

While ornate and quite old, it didn't explain what had rattled Guerin. "Cave dwellers? What is that supposed to mean?" Faero asked.

Horne pointed to the wooded bluff. "On top of that hill, there is an observatory, where the ancients studied the stars. It is said that one of the magi, a godly man born centuries before the rest of the heathen in Aksum became believers, visited the Christ in Judea and lived upon that very hill."

And the kings of Tarshish and of the isles shall bring presents: the kings of Sheba and Seba shall offer gifts, Faero remembered the passage from the Psalmist. *Princes shall come out of Egypt; Ethiopia shall soon stretch out her hands to God.* Faero knew of many theories about the origins of the Magi.

Horne continued chattering away with his guide as they walked down the streets. Three hundred yards from the field of stelae, they turned toward a small church. Barrow, Duke, Murray, and the others all pressed closely in shared wonder.

Horne explained, "Inside that church is an ancient relic that every man, woman, and child would die to protect, and few foreigners have ever been this close."

Faero's eyes noticed the squadrons of men upon the hilltops, guardians who watched their every move.

"Although there are grander churches, the church at the center of this city holds the special honor of being the resting place of the Ark of the Covenant."

Or at least one of the replicas, Faero smirked.

"The Ark of the Covenant is, er, was in Jerusalem," Dr. Barrow said faster than Faero could process. "It was taken up to Heaven by God following the destruction of Jerusalem by the Babylonians. Why would it be in this place?"

Guerin shared glances with LeSueur, Horne, and Faero. The four already knew the full story.

Horne explained, "Each church in Ethiopia holds an Ark of the Covenant, just like churches in Europe have replicas of the cross that held Christ. The folks in Aksum claim theirs to be the original. Only God knows."

Guerin interrupted. "Our tour is not over, gentleman. Master Horne and our guide have other wonders to still show us."

"You're saying that the tablets written by God's finger are inside of a golden chest with angels atop it?" Jimmy Duke added. "Inside of that little church?"

"I can assure you, Jimmy, that it is quite safe, and will continue to be quite safe," Guerin added. "Our friends here have watched us for the last few days, but even now, knowing that we are allies, it is quite secure. Look around you."

Guerin pointed to the hundreds of eyes looking down from the bluffs.

"Come there is much more to see," Horne explained, and just two blocks later, he stopped at an intersection of roads. "Centuries before King Ezana brought Christianity to the masses, the people of Aksum already worshiped the same God as the Hebrews, and down that road, on the edge of town, are the ruins of Dongar Palace, where countless kings and queens ruled. You asked why the Ark of the Covenant would be brought to Aksum? Do you see that large pool on the far side of the Garden of stelae? That is the Pool of Makeda, once Queen of Sheba."

Who came to Jerusalem to test the wisdom of King Solomon.

"The Queen of Sheba from the Bible?" Barrow asked. "The same one?"

Horne answered, "When she departed Jerusalem, she returned with much more than answers."

"She stole the Ark? That timeline doesn't make sense," Barrow added.

"No, she did not steal the Ark, but she did return bearing a child, who became Menelik the First, ruler of Ethiopia and father to the nation of Aksum and now Abyssinia. He was one of several heirs, including the line that brought forth the Christ, which is why the magi came from the east—and also Ethiopia. When Jerusalem fell, the Ark was brought here for safekeeping so that it did not fall into the hands of the Babylonians. For two thousand years, it has been safely kept here, despite attempts to claim it."

It fits the narrative found in the Bible without any proof, Faero realized. *The only way to prove it was real would be to touch it—and drop dead, according to the Bible.*

"To understand, you must see something important," Horne said. "It is not far."

He led them through the intersection of streets to the short wall that surrounded the narrow Garden of Stelae, where more than a dozen gray stelae pointed to the sky, and another dozen lay upon the ground in a state of shattered collapse.

The largest obelisk, almost eighty-feet tall, had ornate carvings over its facade. "Much like Emperor Constantine is celebrated for making Christianity the religion of the Roman Empire and creating the Catholic Church, so too is King Ezana celebrated here for bringing Christianity to all the people."

"But you referenced a connection deep into the Old Testament times," Faero said.

"Yes, but before that, it was…underground." As Horne walked toward the large obelisk, the gunners stayed with the priest, and only the five foreigners continued. "For as long as our people can remember, obelisks have been used for royal grave markers, and below the spire, the leader is laid to rest. We've been granted permission to visit the crypts in order to explain why we must be allies in the day to come."

After lighting torches and lanterns, Horne led them to a small, square opening in the ground, and although he could crouch down and fit through, LeSueur almost had to crawl to enter. Once they reached the bottom of the stone-carved stairs, the passage opened up, yet LeSueur still had to hunch over.

"The stone around Aksum is volcanic, and with limited effort, hammer and chisel can create tunnels. The ones you see connect the crypts together."

Faero counted his steps, understanding the general distance and direction they traveled. Sure enough, they stopped at a place where water leaked from the wall into the floor.

"We're under the Pool of Makeda," Faero said.

LeSueur flinched when he understood the implication. "There is enough water in that pool to flood these tunnels, isn't there?"

"Yes, it is possible to use the water to flood the tunnels, which means our lives are in the hands of someone above us...right now. But we are being allowed to enter here with knowledge we are not thieves. However, the water serves two purposes—death and re-birth. While the water can be used to kill our enemies, it can also be used to hide the truth from our enemies also."

"A valve," Faero said. "A way to evacuate as well as to trap."

"Yes, I wanted you to see it first, so you can understand the significance of the next two things you are about to see."

Horne continued his tour, torch in hand, taking them through the twists and turns of the sealed crypts. Finally, he stopped, letting the men fan out in front of a tomb.

Templar symbols, Faero recognized. The images appeared roughly cut as if a vandal had hastily marked them. The chiseled graffiti desecrated the older art and decorations. Aside from the most obvious marking, the Templar Cross, two riders on a horse, and the pentagram symbol created the horned goat of Baphomet lore.

Horne knelt down to change angles for the men to view what Faero saw immediately. "When the Great Crusades reclaimed the Holy Lands, Palestine was much different than the accounts described in the Gospel, for the Romans did everything in their power to erase Judaism from the earth, especially the Holy City. For some reason, the Templars foolishly believed the Ark would

be sitting pristine in the Jerusalem Temple, and when they could not find it, they were left with two realizations."

"It had been taken to Heaven by angels," Barrow offered.

"Or it had been relocated by men. Within a few decades of exhausting all efforts in the rotting corpse of Jerusalem, the Templars struck out for Aksum, and with a relatively small force of Templars Knights, traced the legends back to the Obelisk of Queen Makeda, which they toppled. Can you imagine the restraint it took the Aksumite guardians to stand back and let it happen? These "Sons of Solomon," as they saw themselves, did not look kindly upon the bastard heirs of their Master Mason, which is why we let Queen Makeda's tomb be discovered so easily. The Templars found their way down here and left these marks on our walls."

"Like a dog pissing on a tree," Duke added.

"What did they come down here for?" Doctor Barrow asked.

"I will show you," Horne said, hustling down a narrow corridor.

Faero understood where they stood in relation to the surface just from the footsteps it had taken him, but Drake, Duke, Guerin, Charlie, and Dr. Barrow looked up at the ceiling for a few moments before he explained to them, "It's a trap door to the church."

Drake stepped backwards, as if in danger.

"The Ark of the Covenant rests above us?"

"Possibly," Horne said coyly. "For poor Ethiopian Christians, the church is only a simple shelter for what lies within, for now each and every one of our churches holds a replica of the original Ark of the Covenant. Only our high priest knows the location of the true Ark, and the rat took the cheese, these Templars."

"Did they steal a fake?" Faero asked.

"Perhaps," Horne answered, "but only the high priest at the time knew the truth, didn't he? The Templars took a treasured relic and showed their true colors in the process. Within a century, they surrendered Jerusalem to Saladin and returned home more powerful than any individual European nation. Shortly before the papal bull destroyed their order, the Templars were making plans to invade Ethiopia, just as they were planning to do in recent days. What does that tell you?"

"They suspected they were tricked?" Murray added, still looking around the tunnel nervously.

"Or...they were searching for something of greater value," Horne explained. "Luckily, such a relic is not kept in such an accessible location. I wanted all of you to see this place before we continued."

And a magical ring would be quite easy to hide, Faero decided as they found their way out of the tunnel.

CHAPTER 81

Pierre-Charles LeSueur thought back on a lifetime of Christmas celebrations. He remembered the Cathedral in Artois, France, when he was just a boy. The choir and pipe organ filled the space with such melody that he felt as if he were a shepherd on the night of Christ's birth.

He remembered a Christmas celebrated on the shores of Lake Huron when he frantically gathered up symbolic items for the better part of a day before Father Jacques Marquette turned the mundane into holy symbols to act out the Christmas story for a crowd of three voyageurs, two Metis, and a family of Wyandot converts.

Once, in the deep snows of Mahkato, he and a crew of thirty men sang carols together around a large bonfire. Each man dressed with a pelt of a buffalo—a bellowing herd of carolers. At the time, he'd smiled, unaware of the daggers in the smiles of the others.

For another Christmas, during a winter in Montreal, a heavy snowstorm forced him to load his wife Marguerite and his children onto a sled, which he pulled like a pack mule through three blocks of snow packed streets until he brought his family to the church. He'd expended so much energy that his young wife had to elbow him during mass.

His favorite Christmas, until now, had always been the one he spent with bare-breasted Wenonah. The trading outpost on Mackinac Island had a small population of men who were baptized

Christian but only professed their faith privately, leaving him without anyone to lead a traditional church service. So that Christmas Eve, he brought in a double-stack of firewood, and soon the heat of the fireplace forced both of them to wear nothing but loin cloth as they laid on a bearskin rug with only a Bible between them. He told her the nativity story that night, and she would counter with comparative details from her own Dakota traditions. It was the deepest exploration of Biblical text he'd ever done.

Until he arrived in Lalibela.

From the tallest peak of the mountain village, LeSueur sat with the rest of the foreigners. From the north and east, hundreds of white-robed pilgrims flowed together like a river of humanity at the bottom of the hill. As the two currents crashed together, singing and dancing presided. There was no choir director or pipe organ to guide the pilgrims—only the collective will of the people. Somewhere, a southern road and western road brought in two other veins of pilgrims, but LeSueur could not see them, for all along the western slope of his perch, a great sea of white covered the mountain village like a glacier.

Like Zacchaeus in a tree, he watched the joyous throngs as they crushed together into the churches below.

Their timing had either been terribly or divinely ordained, for no sooner had they begun their climb up the hill to the sacred city than the white-robed pilgrims began to arrive. As always, Benjamin Horne found food, shelter, and a warm welcome for them, but their tour of the site would have to wait until after the Christmas celebration ended.

So they camped upon the hill overlooking it all and watched.

While Horne spoke with the church elders, LeSueur only caught the translated names for the churches, but he quickly locked those details away in his head.

Farthest away, to the north side of the sea of white, there were five churches, or *bietes* as the local priest called them. House of the Savior of the World, House of Mary, House of the Cross, House of the Virgins, and House of Golgotha Mikael were so tightly constructed that it almost looked like the pilgrims were vanishing into an underwater cistern. Yet the bodies continued to pour into the spaces of worship.

The River Jordan divided the complex.

Of course, LeSueur knew immediately that it was neither *the* Jordan or even a river, for that matter, that divided the complex in half. It only took a few minutes to understand that the channel had not been formed by water—or any other *natural* process.

"Later," he was promised by Guerin. "We'll get a thorough explanation later."

Sitting on a hill overlooking it all, he understood why it was called New Jerusalem. Just as the ancient Holy Lands had been divided between the twelve tribes into Israel in the north and Judea in the south, a symbolic Jordan River, etched into solid rock, which was now filled with waiting Ethiopian pilgrims, divided the two regions.

A solitary church to the extreme west, House of St. George, was symbolically disconnected from the Holy Land metaphor, something he also intended to ask about later.

LeSueur observed that the House of Emmanuel, House of St. Mercoreos, House of Abbot Libanos, House of Gabriel Raphael, and House of Holy Bread revealed a bit of magic. All eleven churches were built below ground level into the stone of the mountain. If they'd been above ground, they would have risen as high as any cathedral, but instead, the subterranean structures filled with celebratory pilgrims.

I shall never have a more glorious Christmas celebration, LeSueur decided, and even though separated from the crowd by distance, language, and culture, he joined his prayers with theirs, hoping the short distance to heaven would help them be heard.

If God will still listen to the prayers of this sinner, he concluded.

Guerin, the man who forced him to leave that little cabin he once shared with Wenonah, and all the other pirates seemed to be sharing their own private reconciliations with God.

In a few more days, the quest would resume, and Guerin and Horne would be leading them to the next mystical location. Long ago, LeSueur had released himself to the wind that blew him from place to place, and unlike Guerin, no longer tried to steer his way through the storm.

Yet one question suddenly troubled him, so he counted again.

And he confirmed it following the quick tour he'd been given around New Jerusalem.

If ancient King Lalibela fashioned the complex on the Hebrew Holy Land, all the way down to a fabricated Jordan River, then why were there only eleven churches yet twelve tribes...or twelve disciples?

Where is the twelfth church?

CHAPTER 82

Louis-Armand Guerin couldn't shake the idea. *A city revealed.* Below his feet, cut from solid rock at the top of a mountain, the churches of Lalibela stood, surrounded by the stone that once surrounded them.

Sculptors would begin by looking at a block of marble and trying to imagine what existed within. Instead of creating art like a painter, a sculptor revealed what had always been there. In the same way, the designer of the churches of Lalibela stood where he stood and imagined a city below the rock that supported his feet.

He kept his thoughts about the complex to himself during the private tour.

They descended the same steps used by the pilgrims a week earlier. His hands reached to the rock walls that still belonged to the mountain, feeling the texture, grain, and density of the stone. Upon the ridges of his fingers, he felt dusty residue, a sign that the stone was relatively soft. When he reached the bottom of the stairs and looked up at the towering walls of the House of the Savior of the World, it took his breath away.

The others in the party peppered Horne and the local priest with predictable questions, which brought predictable answers, as well as the history of the place.

How old is this place?
Who did this?
How was it made?

THE ALCHEMIST'S RING

With the fall of the Holy Lands in 1187, King Lalibela determined a new Jerusalem needed to be built. Modeled on Israel, the subterranean churches were cut, inside and out, from solid stone, along with the artificial channel for the Jordan River and also a tunnel system that connected all the churches. Each church was a masterpiece unto itself with ornate pillars, doors, windows, roofs, and floors.

Above, in the village, stacked stones and thatched roofs served the people well for centuries. Here, in the mountain itself, something divine existed.

While the exterior of the churches looked like giant sand castles, the interior of the churches inspired reverent awe. Guerin looked past the decor, medieval art fitting the era of King Lalibela, to the precision of every wall and dome. The longer he stayed, the more agitated he felt. Everything was too perfect.

Supernaturally perfect.

He imagined a thousand hired workers with hammer and chisel.

Then he imagined a dozen workers, skilled mathematicians with the finest technology to follow angle and plane.

While his rational mind struggled, his heart knew the answer to the mystery.

He'd first learned the theory as a Periphery student back in Rome, years later, contemplated the theory after his visit to the frontier, and finally accepted the theory after he met the prisoner Benjamin Horne.

The finest engineers in Rome, Greece, or Egypt did not build like this, for they would assemble archeological masterpieces block by block, and if error was detected, a block could be dismissed and another fashioned.

At Lalibela, there were no blocks.

Each church, with its straight walls, began from the top and worked down. A single lapse of judgment or missed hit ruined everything, like a sculptor knocking off the nose of a bust.

Flawless.

A single church would take a lifetime to shape to such perfection, for fear of error would inhibit the workers with constant measurement. Then, after achieving external perfection, to bore into the solid block to create rooms.

"How long did this take to make?" Guerin finally asked.

The tour guide paused. "King Lalibela did not become ruler until 1181, and upon his death, in the year 1221, he was laid to rest in Bet Abba Libanos. Would you like to see his tomb?"

Guerin contemplated the answer as they walked through the underground tunnel under the pseudo Jordan River and emerged in a courtyard of three churches. Bet Abba Libanos was one of the smallest but no less grand.

"You avoided my question earlier," Guerin said after the guide finished his description of King Lalibela's resting place.

"But you already have the answer," the guide countered. "King Lalibela determined that after the fall of Jerusalem, Christians needed a new home for pilgrimage and when he died, he was laid to rest—"

Such perfection in such a short amount of time was almost inconceivable. "Four decades? You're telling me that the entire complex was begun and completed in four decades?"

The guide's eyes twinkled before saying, "If not faster than that."

From the second complex, they once again returned to the tunnel, which led them on an even longer expanse, once again under the Jordan River, to the isolated House of St. George.

Like the others, it stood within the space of the stone from which it was carved. Equally beautiful, it distinguished itself by being the tallest, or deepest, structure with walls forty feet high. The guiding priest led them up the stairs that skirted the church. The men removed their footwear as instructed and stepped inside.

Their bare feet found ornate, colorful rugs, by themselves a work of art, yet drab in comparison to the paintings on the walls. The largest painting showed St. George upon a horse and slaying a dragon crawling upon its belly. The men studied it, perhaps finding personal meaning, but Guerin soon fixed on the green curtain behind it. A white-robed priest sat comfortably in front of it.

The Christmas celebration had been funneled to the northernmost complex while this church stood isolated.

"Please kneel," the priest in the chair said.

Guerin did as instructed; followed by his men. Their guide stepped toward the chair and stood beside it.

"Before you continue on your quest, you must be purified, for your journey will be both perilous and divine. If this is God's will, then may His blessing and grace follow you when you return out into the world."

Could it be this easy?

Will the priest present us with King Solomon's ring and wish us well?

The priest stood, and together with the other priest, they parted the heavy green curtain. Within, the tabot stood upon the altar.

A replica, or is it the real Ark of the Covenant?

Does Horne even know?

Guerin readily received the blessing, knowing why they were there and where they were going. He also reflected on his own answer to the question he posed.

The curtains were again closed, and in silence, the men walked out of the church. An almost imperceptible staircase led them back to the surface, where they stood on the edge of the mountain, overlooking the valley below.

The priest departed, and Jimmy Duke summarized the mood of the group when he plopped onto the ledge with a muttered, "Holy shit."

The rest also bent their weary knees and dropped to the ground as well, including Benjamin Horne, the last to sit.

"So you're *from* here?" Drake Murray asked Horne incredulously.

"I was an acolyte of the church in my youth, selected and trained. When I was a young man, I was tasked with a purpose, and to achieve this purpose, I had to become a navigator upon a sailing vessel."

"To be led by the grace of God on your quest to find the stolen Ark," Faero speculated.

"There is no way these churches were carved during the span of a single king's reign," Dr. Barrow said. "Each one, if carefully monitored, would have taken a hundred years, and with that, there would have been mistakes made."

Benjamin Horne glanced over at Guerin, who shrugged for a bit of information to be revealed to the crew. "What the priest didn't say is that the construction of these churches is not credited

to the work of men. The legend says that angels shaped these churches."

"Angels?" LeSueur repeated, then looked to Guerin. "Is that what you think?"

Guerin looked over at Horne. "No. I don't think this place was built by angels, but I do think King Lalibela built this place in the same manner and fashion that King Solomon built the original temple in Jerusalem. During the reign of Cyrus the Great, the priest Ezra oversaw the rebuilding of the Second Temple around the year 537 BC, and while it was functional within seven years, King Herod was still refurbishing it right up until the time of Christ—five centuries of remodeling. We have eleven churches around us as grand as the Second Temple. How did Solomon do it?"

Faero locked eyes with him. "He shaped unhewn stone with the shamir."

"But what controlled it?" LeSueur asked.

"King Solomon's ring," Faero admitted. "It's what Tew and I were going to pursue before he was killed."

"In order for us to retrieve a treasure," Guerin said, turning to Horne, "we will need a treasure." *A skeleton key to pick a lock: Solomon's ring.*

Benjamin Horne nodded. "Then we will travel to the twelfth Church, the Church of Adam, and you can make your request to my superiors."

CHAPTER 83

The oldest of the twelve churches was only a day's journey away from the other eleven. From the village of Lalibela, Louis-Armand Guerin and his crew followed a high mountain path that led due east, and then along a high ridge that extended for almost five miles.

All the men were careful and deliberate, watched by the Heavens above, for on either side, one misstep near the steep slopes meant certain death.

When they woke the next morning, the Ethiopian mountains were blanketed by a dense fog, hiding the valley into which they descended. Once they reached the valley floor, walls of fog and mountain kept them cutting back and forth until they had no sense of which direction they were even walking, yet Benjamin Horne and his team of young acolytes steadily led the way.

By afternoon on the second day, they hiked out of the fog as they scaled a mountain. This mountain was not nearly as formidable as the spine they'd walked before, or as grand as the one upon which Lalibela was built, but it was most unique of all they'd seen so far in Ethiopia, for tucked high in the mountains was a dense forest.

They entered the hidden forest on its steepest end of the elevated ridge, following a trickle of water that grew as it slowly descended. With the thick canopy of juniper trees, the Ethiopian air was strangely humid, and Guerin found himself touching moss upon the oldest trees along their path. With ridges rising on both sides of the sheltered woods, Guerin realized the path they took was marked with small trinkets and colorful ribbons, and on several occasions, he sensed movement—unseen eyes followed them. Yes, there were colonies of small monkeys that watched from the trees, but humans also watched, guarding.

Soon, the creek expanded over the marshy ground, caught in a ladle that collected the water at the lowest part of the small forest. In fact, Guerin could see the far side of the little ridge that collected the water and revealed the end of the mountainous paradise, where the ground dropped away to the dry valley below. In the rainy season, it would have been a lake hidden in the clouds.

Standing on the shore of the marsh, Guerin could see how vegetation filled the depression, and he knew crossing the expanse by foot or horse meant sinking into the depths.

Benjamin Horne neither looked at the marsh nor at the descending valley beyond it; instead, he looked sharply to his left, at the side of the depression.

At first, Guerin thought Horne only appreciated the beauty of a rock facade draped with a green curtain of vines, but where the longest vines dangled down, he saw darkness, like a crescent moon on its side.

In the dark smile of the crescent, teeth—a man made wall stretched from corner to corner. *What could a wall so far back be guarding?*

"The wall has only stood since the time of Christ," Horne said, "but the church is the oldest in the world. The monks that live inside can trace oral history to the days of the dawn, and what we seek will be known here."

Beyond the wall, a deep darkness extended as the natural overhang of the cave sheltered the wall, a structure within, and even more. As a military installation, the walled structure could have been defended effortlessly by a dozen men, who Guerin had to assume were watching from the trees. As the party grew nearer, the wall took on another purpose—preservation.

A trickle of water came down the dark gray facade of the mountain, dropped onto the deck of the cave floor, and leached away to the marsh. The wall shielded the cave from any intruder, including the elements.

Three simple but solid gates divided the wall into sections—*Father, Son, and Holy Ghost.*

Once inside, a small monastery stood in the opening of the massive cave. Built horizontally, dark wooden beams and light mortar created a striped appearance, and judging from the architecture of the doors and windows, the structure was several hundred years old.

"This was the first church to be built in this area, prior to the eleven built by King Lalibela," Horne explained. "It is now called Yemrehanna Kristos, built in reaction to the Crusades upon the Holy Lands. Jerusalem was no longer safe for pilgrims, whether possessed by the Roman Catholic Church and its Templar Knights or by Caliph Saladin and his Muslim warriors, so it was decided that a new, safe home needed to be built."

"Who decided?" Faero asked.

"Indeed?" Guerin speculated aloud. "A moment ago, you said this place is the oldest church in the world yet built after the Crusades."

"The structure in front of you is only a few hundred years old, but the cave has been a place of worship and sanctuary far, far longer."

The ground itself was artificial instead of stone. Between the stone wall and the monastery, a fabric of slender wooden reeds formed a woven mat that stretched for yards in all directions. Under his toes, Guerin could feel the mat give slightly as they moved across it, a strange buoyancy that made their approach quiet.

Colorful monks nodded and smiled as the small band of men approached. Cups of coffee were offered to the travelers, along with a small offering of food, and soon they entered the structure. From the regal paintings to ornate ceiling tiles, Yemrehanna Kristos was the most magnificent and meticulously kept church Guerin had seen, but he had to push his feelings of awe back down in his soul as he kept a critical mind for a keen observation—he recognized it was all a visual ruse.

The church and monastery was as real as the monks who lived there—of that he had little doubt. It was a truly divine place of worship, worthy of pilgrimage from all of Christendom.

When the tour ended, Horne led them out of the back door of the temple.

Deeper in the cave, the light crawled over the ceiling, above the wall and monastery, where a span of several yards remained. Each step they took, as the soles of their feet slid over the wooden platform, echoed inside of the massive space. Horne walked into the narrowing space until the wooden platform ended and the stone floor of the cave rose to accept them.

Soon the angles of the floor and ceiling came together. LeSueur reached up and touched the ceiling, but the angle continued for countless yards as if leading into the underworld itself. At the place where a normal man could touch floor to ceiling, a pile of stacked rocks formed a low wall.

Horne stepped aside so his friends could stand at the wall and peer into the deeper recesses.

Corpses.

Guerin paused. The scene was not macabre but nevertheless surprised him. Hundreds, if not thousands, of corpses stretched out into the darkness. The acrid stench of death hung on the air, corralled, seemingly by the low wall. Back at the entrance of the cave, light and life abounded, yet here, hell itself opened its mouth.

"These are the saints of our faith, the guardians of the sacred, the keepers of the truth. One day, I hope to pass beyond this low wall, and have my weary bones join the bones of those who came before me."

A catacomb of sorts.

Horned turned and walked back toward the opening of the cave, but before he brought them all the way out, he stopped and sat. The others followed.

"Shortly after the rebirth of the new world, when humanity began to go forth over the face of the earth, there were no countries, cities, villages, or even houses to shelter the earliest travelers from the storm. Whenever a cave was discovered, it was viewed as a gift from God, and those places, like this one, became centers of worship and sanctuary. A network of caves served humanity in those days, and generation after generation flew away from their nests and out into the unknown world.

"It did not take early mankind long to learn how to fell trees and create thatched roofs, and then how to create brick and how to cut stone, but the monks who came to the caves remained. As time passed, some caves fell into disuse, others were attacked by the ignorant and violent, but some remained, still networked together in common purpose. Despite being the guardians of mankind, these wardens of peace quickly became misunderstood, even feared. Although spread out over continents and nations, they retained a common tongue, and from the ignorant, earned a name—the Cave-Divers. For living in caves, the title seemed appropriate, and when hunted, yes, my people certainly would dive back into the caves to vanish in the protective womb of the earth. Thus began a silent vigil.

"When darkness descended upon Egypt—and the world—during the days of Moses, our people already understood how to live in darkness. Just as you and I found ourselves together on a ship, Moses crossed paths with our kind as well. The young Prince of Egypt, during a war against Nubia, found his way back to the light by walking into the darkness. He sat where you sit now, and worshiped God in a church of unhewn stone. Later, during his exile from Egypt, he found another priest, and a smaller cave, at a different mountain. For forty years, he trained and prepared in a way the Egyptian court could never prepare him until God called him from Midian back to the land of Egypt. As young Christians, I am sure you know this part of the story."

Guerin wasn't sure if his crew had such an understanding, yet they listened reverently.

"While this cave was not the first place of worship, it remains the oldest place of continued worship. When Makeda traveled to visit King Solomon, monks were here. When the magi were summoned to bring the holy treasures to the Christ child, monks were here. When Crusaders invaded the Holy Lands, monks were here.

"As time passed, it was decided that a new home needed to be built, a new cave, located in the heart of society but tucked away, out of sight."

"On the periphery," Guerin muttered aloud, thinking of the underground complex in Rome that housed his order. *This is why Horne allied himself with me. He wanted to bring me home.*

"Yes, the Periphery," Horne affirmed. "Rome became a new complex with a new purpose while we remained here at an old cave with an old purpose. Now, our two branches have come together, and you and I will go together to make our request."

Benjamin Horne stood back up, and the rest of the men followed. "The rest of you must wait here. Guerin and I must go together, for each of us has a separate request to make."

"Where are you taking him?" LeSueur asked, suddenly protective.

Horne pointed to the left wall of the cave. "There is an inner cave that is only accessible to those who know the secret path. To enter it, we must receive a special baptism."

Horne gestured to the Church of Yemrehanna. "They are waiting."

CHAPTER 84

As Louis-Armand Guerin rested upon his knees beside Horne, the priest who'd been feeding syllables of prayer paused. Instead of rising, the old man simply leaned forward and grabbed the small rug between them.

Pulling it away, he revealed a wooden, thatched door.

It was similar to the construction of the decking in the front of the cave, but when he lifted it and set it aside, a pool of water reflected a mirror image of them.

Having seen dozens of baptism fonts in a dozen churches around the world, Guerin understood that his cleansing would not be with a cup of water within a hand.

Horne nodded, stood back up, and began to strip away his clothing. The three men were in an inner room, not much larger than a closet, where modesty was not an issue. Horne stopped disrobing while still wearing a small loin cloth whereas Guerin had baggy breeches.

"We must submerge ourselves in the water. The priest will take us by the hair and not release us until the proper time. Is that understood?"

Obviously, this isn't a typical baptism. "I think so."

"I will go first," Horne said and sat down next to the hole in the floor. He put his feet over the edge of the dark water, kept his hand on the side, and then slid in.

He bobbed into the water past his head, and then his right hand reached up to the other side of the opening. With both hands balancing him in the water, he looked up to the priest and nodded. The priest reached out his hand and placed it upon Horne's head. With a nod, Horne took a deep breath and submerged.

The priest kept his hand in place, just a few inches below the surface of the water. He looked up and smiled warmly.

After a few moments passed, Guerin realized the submersion was a test of sorts. He began an internal clock for his friend, whose fingers quivered slightly upon the edge of the opening.

The darkness of the water alarmed him, for its depth not only provided for a grown man to submerge but also held no reflection of light to indicate the side or bottom of the baptismal chamber.

A deck…

The path that led them from the highest part of the hidden forest steadily descended for almost a mile until they reached the depression in front of the cave. While the marsh in front of the cave was filled with vegetation, the depth of the swamp could not be determined. The wall, the deck…built at the surface level of the marsh to insinuate that it was built upon solid earth but—

A floating sanctuary?

Guerin's mind reviewed the construction of the cave and suddenly felt short of breath.

Did the waters below Horne's feet descend for six feet or sixty?

Was the pool built up thousands of years ago to flood the area for security reasons, a moat for an ancient castle?

Of course… the cave-divers.

This is no baptism—this is a test to see how long I can hold my breath.

Finally, the hand came off of Horne's head, and he burst to the surface with a gasp. He pulled himself out of the opening, allowing Guerin to take his place.

The water was not frigid, but it certainly had a chill that took his breath away for a moment, indicating the true depth of the water under his feet. He let himself slide quickly into the abyss, not even holding onto the edges, but his feet did not find anything below, and when his hands reached back up to the edges of the opening, he felt his heart pounding in anticipation.

The priest looked down at him, and Guerin nodded in affirmation, submersing himself into the water. As he counted in his mind, he opened his eye.

The dim light from the church filtered into the water around him, and he could see the bottom of the hidden lake. At the deepest, the clear water descended for twenty feet. Along the sides, he could see the sharp accent that formed the walls, as well as the rear wall of the cave that held the bones of the saints. To the left, though, he saw a dark opening just below where the floating timbers anchored to stone.

Is that where we're going?

In the center of the dark eye, he saw a faint light, indicating another chamber beyond.

The pressure on his hair released, and for good measure, he stayed for a few more seconds before bursting to the surface.

Benjamin Horne slid in beside him.

"Have you ever done this before?" Guerin asked.

"No, but there is an old man beyond that wall who keeps vigil. If we wanted, there is a place outside, past the cave, where the monks can remove a series of boulders to drain the water so we can safely pass, but I told them we are both strong swimmers. You are a strong swimmer, aren't you?"

"Let's race and find out. I'll meet you on the other side, or else in the afterlife."

CHAPTER 85

Benjamin Horne paused when his hands touched the opening to confirm Guerin was on his heels. He was.

The light at the surface now seemed as if a window of Heaven had opened, but the chill of the water and the ache in his lungs reminded him of his mortality. Once Guerin caught him, he finished the turn toward the surface.

He opened his mouth slowly, releasing his spent air and taking a controlled breath; Guerin breathed like a panicked newborn.

The water in Horne's eyes kept him from seeing clearly. First, he saw a pair of feet and ankles just a few feet from where they rose from the abyss. The irregular rocky walls behind him came into focus next—not sandstone, mortar, timber, or tapestry, but unhewn stone.

The original cave, now hidden from the world.

But it wasn't cut off from the world.

The aging monk with white, patchy hair, a thin beard, jovial eyes, and a lean but healthy body was surrounded by texts, creature comforts, and even a tray of fresh food. Then Horne noticed the most peculiar thing about the bizarre world they'd entered—holes.

The holes acted as windows to the open sky above, but most were only a few inches in diameter—and perfect. Each was a shaft meant to catch the light from the sun as it passed above in the sky, a strange clock that illuminated the chamber with both diffused light and also a direct beam of light. From the comments of his childhood mentors, Horne suspected places like this existed, but now as an older man, he had confirmation.

While he hadn't yet found the lost Ark, he'd brought back an ally.

"Looks like we've come to the right place," Guerin said, observing the same holes.

They climbed out of the watery passage, just a few feet from where the priest smiled at them. Although isolated from the outside world, the priest could still be reached both vocally and with written messages via the tubes.

Horne spoke in Amharic, "I am Genet K'enidi, a trained disciple from Washa Kokebi, and I have come with my friend to ask a favor."

"Who is your friend?"

"He is Louis-Armand Guerin, from Washa Tekula."

"I am Father Dewili. Does your friend come directly from Rome?"

"No, he has traveled to the far side of the world and sailed upon many seas to come here. He has not been to Washa Tekula for many years. We found each other by chance, and common purpose has brought us together."

"Common purpose?" Father Dewili said with a tone of suspicion. "It has been more than a thousand years since we have had a common purpose with Washa Tekula. What does he want?"

"He has found the stone the mason rejected."

This took the smile off of Father Dewili's face. "Your ancestor Kokebi claimed to have found the Stone in a mystical land where the water flows in all directions and the earth bleeds blue. Have you seen this place? Have you witnessed the Stone?"

"No, the one who pulled it from the earth has thrown it into the depths of the ocean," He said in reference to LeSueur.

"Perhaps that is for the best. For the one who made it was evil, and his works, even more. We might worship the same God, the same Holy Spirit, and the same Christ as our northern brothers, but they do not understand the past the way we do. What does he know about Zik'itenya?"

At this, Horne paused, looking over to a patient Guerin, who understood little of what they said. "Father Dewili asked me what you know about the Alchemist and his stone."

"What name did he just use for the Alchemist?" Guerin pressed.

"Zik'itenya," Horne repeated. "It's not a proper name as much as it is a title. It means the Low One."

"Low One? The Hebrews used a similar name for the human king who was brought low. I'm familiar with the legend of Zik'itenya, who is known by many other names," Guerin answered.

Horne nodded and began to translate.

Guerin interrupted to add, "Tell him that our shared enemies wish to find him, and that the Periphery—um, Washa Tekula—intends to stop this from happening. Explain to him what we did in Madagascar, and then explain how our plan will cripple the efforts of the Order of Eos from ever attaining their purpose. Tell him that is why we've passed through earth and water."

Horned nodded and returned to his native tongue. "I've spent many years with this man, and he understands Zik'itenya even if his people do not use the same name."

"Of course, no one should speak his cursed name, which is why we created the name Zik'itenya."

Horne continued his explanation. "As a representative of Washa Tekula, he said their intention is to stop our common enemies from reaching the tomb of Zik'itenya, which is why they cast the key into the depths. Our enemies are resilient, however, and either by technology or sorcery, they intend to resurrect their dark messiah. The secret knowledge to do this is kept in a locked vault, which cannot be accessed by natural means."

Horne explained what happened in Madagascar and also what they intended to do. While he explained the plan, the old priest seemed to nod in approval.

"And where is this vault?" the monk finally asked.

I have no clue. I can only hope Guerin told the truth. Horne turned to Guerin. "He wants to know more about the vault."

"Tell him I visited it during my travels to the far side of the world," Guerin said. "It is found on a sacred island. Only those

who built the vault can access it, which is why they keep their greatest treasures locked away inside of it. Tell him the Periphery has always known about the travels of Kokebi during the reign of King Solomon, and that our enemies have maps that led them to the area, but they do not understand the map, nor do they understand the truth about Zik'itenya."

Horne translated.

The priest now frowned. "If I grant your request, it could be turned against us for foul purposes. If Zik'itenya's Stone has been cast into the sea, then why do we disturb the sleeping lion?"

Upon repeating the question, Guerin exhaled and hung his head. "Another enemy is coming to destroy the prophecies by destroying the relics."

"The Priory?" Horne confirmed.

Guerin nodded. "The prophecy doesn't just include the 'key' which is the Philosopher's Stone, but it also mentions the Ark of the Covenant. Once the Priory discovers the vault on Oak Island, they will have no qualms destroying everything in it, including the lost Ark. Tell him the sleeping lion will wake one way or another, but if it is killed while sleeping in its den, then the prophecies will crumble like ash."

Horne explained it to the priest, who asked a question. "And he will return the missing Ark to us when this is over?"

Guerin confirmed he would.

"The item you seek is dangerous," the priest added. "It corrupted King Solomon to the doom of Israel. What makes you think it will obey your commands?"

Horne translated and waited for Guerin's answer.

Guerin nodded. "We have a ring-bearer."

CHAPTER 86

ABUNA YEMATA GUH, ABYSSINIA

1709

Pierre-Charles LeSueur had been born of flesh in Artois, France in 1657. Hiding along an earthen bank of a Wisconsin river, he was transformed into the vengeful Paul Bonjean, scourge of the Great Lakes. Later, in the fires of a Sioux pyre, he became a treasure-hunter for evil men. In the waters of the high seas, he transformed a third time into Charlie Johnson, First Mate and namesake of the *White Zombie*.

Now, almost nine-thousand feet above sea level, he did the exact opposite of what he was told to do—he looked down at the 1,000 foot drop below him.

Will air transform me into my final self?

His bare feet shuffled along the sandstone cliff while his hands searched for any tangible hold to keep his body from tumbling backwards to his death. Had he been a younger man and not an aging relic of the previous century, he might have been able to turn away from the wall as Duke and Murray did, but the climb had turned his legs to jelly, and he doubted any of the great strength left in his body. His girth, too, inhibited his passage, for his shoulders, belly, and chest filled the narrow passage high up in the sky. While the others certainly carried their fears, he could see from their eyes that they worried about him falling over the edge.

"Take a breath, Charlie," Dr. Barrow said behind him. "You are barely breathing, and your muscles need air to function.

LeSueur realized it was true. He was holding onto his breath.

So he forced himself to take a deep breath, but that only caused spots to appear, and the wobbling in his legs doubled.

I am going to fall.

I'm going to pass out and tumble backwards to my death.

"Keep shuffling your feet, Charlie. The path widens just a few feet ahead, and you can rest," Dr. Barrow said. Ahead of them, Professor Faero reached the wide area and turned back around to watch LeSueur clinging to the wall. The others kept on going, vanishing around the bend. "Just a few yards more."

The slippery residue between his toes grew for he did not lift his feet for those final spans, and as the space between the wall and the ledge grew, he slowly crouched down, his head against stone the whole time, until he panted like an animal on all fours.

Faero waited and offered him water; Dr. Barrow patted him on the square of his back. After catching his breath, LeSueur rotated his hips and sat down against the wall, his bare feet pointed toward the open sky.

Earlier in the morning, all nine of them woke at their camp upon the valley floor. LeSueur had eaten three eggs, gobbled down a local breakfast meal called chechebsa, and tried a strain of Ethiopian coffee, which had fueled him for much of the leisurely stroll up the narrow paths. Even though they climbed a mountain, it had been easy to focus on the path, even when they had to climb up and over boulders. Ascent allowed him to put one foot in front of the other like he was climbing stairs.

Then they reached a balcony of stone.

The local priests had used a pointed finger to show the path they would take up the mountain. They'd pointed out the balcony—a narrow passage across the sheer cliff face that led to the final leg of the ascent—but LeSueur tried to focus his eyes on the spire atop the mountain, the place where a tiny church had been carved from stone.

Abuna Yemata Guh was named after a Christian monk who'd established the secret church more than a millennium ago. At the time of its shaping, the Romans had driven Christianity underground and Jerusalem had been leveled. Even in Ethiopia, threats from Nubia and Arabia required a stronghold, an island, to be es-

tablished for the flowing currents of political upheaval. Father Yemata spent a lifetime designing the ascent and the church.

"It's times like this that a fellow can look back on his life with regret," LeSueur said with a sigh, the shaking in his legs over and his breath in his lungs back.

"Strange," Faero said, "I was just thanking the Creator for leading me on a path that brought me to this time and place. What do you regret?"

"All of the lies I have told—to myself and to others," LeSueur began, and then realized that perhaps God had buckled his knees to force a confession out of him. *Perhaps if I lighten my load, let go of the burden I carry, I will be able to reach the top and unpack my great lie.*

Instead, Dr. Barrow made a confession. "I paid a gang of ruffians to bring me mortally wounded men from bars and taverns—men who had no chance of survival yet clinged to life—so that I could operate upon them, and in doing so, understand how the body functioned. Only later did I learn that these ruffians preyed upon innocent bystanders, inflicting the wounds themselves, knowing I would pay them."

"I have worshiped false gods," Faero next confessed. "I tried to rationalize that humans worshiped the same god in many different ways—that the little details shouldn't matter because my Creator would know it's all the same. It only allowed me to pick and choose a faith that suited my sins, and the god I created was fashioned in my image."

"I once had a chance to become the husband of a beautiful Dakota woman," LeSueur revealed. "She'd been born a princess to a mighty king, but during a battle, she was taken prisoner, sold, and turned into a slave whore. For rescuing her from slavery, she wanted to express her gratitude in the only way she knew how—and I denied her."

Dr. Barrow scoffed. "How is showing virtue something worthy of guilt and confession?"

"Wenonah—that was her name," LeSueur continued. "I should have made love to her until my arms and legs were weary. Why didn't I love her fully? I could have built her a home and lived the rest of my days in happiness. Now, I am a world away on this damn mountain with a bladder full of piss."

"I agree with Barrow," Faero said. "I still don't understand your sin or your lie."

"I lied to myself that I had honor—that I had virtue. I ignored the whore so that I could save myself for a chaste young lady, who turned out to be the real whore—a Delilah that betrayed me. What a fool. Pierre-Charles LeSueur! My truest name and my biggest lie. To believe I had virtue? To judge myself better than her. Oh, my sweet Wenonah, I am sorry."

"You should save your confession for the priest at the top of this bloody mountain," Barrow said. "We're no better than you."

Will you forgive me my other sins?

Will you forgive my great lie?

"Yes, that's what I'll do," LeSueur said aloud. "The Lord has brought me to my knees, and now I will make my confession right outside of his window, where he is certain to hear me." LeSueur rose, followed by the other two. "If you wouldn't mind doing me a favor, though."

"Absolutely," Faero said.

"Could I bother the two of you to place a hand upon my shoulder while I piss off the edge. I can't hold it any longer, and I wouldn't feel right pissing upon a church, even if it is a mountain. Everyone would see the puddle upon the descent."

"As long as I don't have to look at it," Faero laughed.

"I'd insist you look away," LeSueur said, and with the support of his friends, he stood, swaying yet restrained, with his toes to the ledge. Soon a burden was released over the edge of the cliff, and in a short time, another burden would be released when he confessed another sin to the priest at the top of the mountain.

CHAPTER 87

It is smaller than I expected, Louis-Armand Guerin thought. Although the mountain towered above the valley below, now that they reached the top of the climb, the actual church seemed small and modest—*if you didn't look down.*

Like fingers reaching for heaven, the mountain divided into separate spires, turrets of a castle, where a small bridge connected the platform of their ascent to the spire that held the church. On the other side of the natural bridge, a monk stood, and another looked out a window. To the side, an open path led to the main door of the church, where a third priest stood grinning.

"What a strange journey we've shared," Guerin said. "Are you ready to see what's on the other side of those walls?"

Josiah Faero and Benjamin Horne both nodded. The five gathered around LeSueur also nodded in affirmation.

As had been the case for the past few hours, they precariously crossed the final stretch. No castle in Europe was as defensible as Abuna Yemata Guh. First, it had a full view of miles upon miles of valley floor, which gave it the advantage of time. Even if a conqueror knew the path to take, which seemed impossible to the untrained, a hurried ascent took hours to make. A shower of gravel or unleashed arrows could defeat an army. Now facing the church itself, a single monk could defend it from the window facing the narrow bridge.

Yet they were greeted with smiles and quickly brought into the sandstone opening.

Horne translated, but after weeks in Abyssinia, Guerin knew enough phrases to understand that the priests spoke of an omen.

While the exterior of the church appeared to be tiny, the interior opened up to a surprisingly large space comprising three areas. The first, where they greeted the priests, was a small area for music, typical of churches in the area. Then they were led into a larger space, where 80 worshippers from the area would crowd every Sunday.

Here, the priest explained the sign.

The murals on the wall rivaled anything from Constantinople or Rome, and the conditions of the cave had kept them preserved for the past fourteen centuries.

"Nine saints," the priest said, tucking in a thumb as he stared at his nine guests and then at the ceiling and walls. When the church was founded, nine saints, including Father Yemata, came to this mountain to establish a church where there had already been a sanctuary.

While Guerin marveled at the ornate art, Horne and the priest discussed the significance of nine guests coming to a place where nine saints built a church, but when the words "Washa Tekula" were mentioned, Guerin's head snapped back to the priest. "Washa Tekula?" He confirmed.

According to Periphery legend, the great she-wolf of Rome had actually suckled nine pups, which were represented by the nine levels of their subterranean headquarters, where nine different types of agents were trained for service in the world. As one of their trained secret agents, Guerin went out into the world as a sheep in wolf's clothing decades earlier, yet the priest standing in front of him knew well the symbolism of the Periphery.

Through Horne, their story and purpose were shared, and when the request was made, the priest took it in stride, unflinchingly.

Which led to prayer.

For the quiet hour of music and mediation, Guerin indeed praised the Lord, letting his weary legs rest in one of the most glorious places on earth. When the worship service ended, the priest sat with the visitors for a few minutes.

"After King Lalibela rescued it from Jerusalem and finished creating the eleven churches, he ordered it to be sent to this lonely

mountain. We have simply been its caretakers. After your purpose is fulfilled, hide it where it can do no harm."

Then he rose and walked to the third part of the church, the Holiest of Holies.

A thick curtain partitioned this area from the place of worship, based on the original concept of the first temple in Jerusalem. As had been the case in Aksum, Lalibela, and even the small village churches, an Ark of the Covenant rested behind the curtain. In the days of Moses until the reign of King David, the real Ark had been kept in a tent. During the reign of King Solomon, the chest that held the Ten Commandment was brought into the stone temple, where it rested for the better part of four centuries—until the day it vanished from history.

When the priest returned from the Holiest of Holies, he carried something in a wrapped box. Upon removing the outer covering, a small lead box appeared. Once the lid was removed, a small ring rested within.

The Seal of Solomon.

Instead of gold, it was dark, an amalgamation of brass and iron. Upon its face, it bore strange etchings instead of holding jewels.

"Do not wear this until it is needed," the priest explained, "for no man is righteous enough to bear it without risk of corruption."

"We will use it wisely," Guerin said in Amharic.

The priest and the men with him rose, leaving Guerin squatting on the floor with the ring. Placing one hand on the stone floor, he rose and walked over to LeSueur. "I can think of no other who could bear the weight of this burden. For if you were worthy to hold the Alchemist's Stone, you are worthy to the ring's keeper."

"No," LeSueur said, stealing the smiles of the others.

"No?" Guerin recoiled. *We've come too far for him to ruin this now.*

"Keep it, for I must first make a confession to this priest. Now go, wait outside."

So Guerin kept the ring in its lead box, carrying it with him as they walked out the small doorway, onto the final deck, and across the bridge to the other spire to wait for LeSueur.

CHAPTER 88

ABUNA YEMATA GUH, ABYSSINIA

1709

Unable to converse with the foreign giant, Father T'ebaki held up his finger to halt the frenzied words coming from the man. He poured his visitor a small cup of tea, which got the big ogre to stop talking for just a few minutes. While the visitor sipped his tea, Father T'ebaki did his best to relate an important message for the man the others told him would be the ring-bearer.

"I came to serve here after my wife died," Father T'ebaki began. "My family lives in the area, and I'd visited here many times in my youth, so it seemed an obvious place for me to confront my grief while also serving. I didn't eat properly in those days, and once, when I rose, I stumbled and fell. My hand reached out to keep myself from falling, and I touched the Ark." He pantomimed himself tipping over with his forearm. Then he showed the palm of his hand to the giant. "I should have died. The ancient texts describe another fool who stumbled, touched the Ark, and fell down dead. God either spared me for a greater purpose, or it was only a replica of the real Ark of the Covenant."

Father T'ebaki put a finger to the ring-bearer's chest. "You must find our missing Ark. I don't know if the stolen Ark is the real one or another replica, but whatever the truth, it needs to be brought back home." He lifted his finger to point at the curtain and the hidden Ark. "Bring it back."

The giant nodded in understanding and then proceeded to babble incoherent phrases, ending with him bowing low enough that his head was inches from T'ebaki's feet. He touched the man's head to calm his penance.

When the giant rose, he had grit teeth and had tears in his eyes, an attempt to assuage his guilt. After pursing his lips for several seconds, his eyes grew wide. He shuffled to the edge of the room and picked up a loose stone, which he set between them.

The giant pointed to himself. Then he pointed to the stone.

He began moving his hands through invisible dirt, separating it until he reached the stone. When he took hold of the stone, his shook his arm dramatically and even covered his eyes with his other hand. Then he turned over his palm to show the stone.

He pointed to his friends who waited across the narrow passage. Then he gestured a throw to the other window, as if tossing the stone into the valley below. Shaking his head, he revealed he still held the stone.

The giant then pointed directly at him and said. "Wenonah." He extended the stone to him, and just as he was about to grab it, the giant pulled it away, shaking his head.

Then he pondered, closing his eyes and holding the stone to his forehead as he thought. The giant stood and looked out the window to where his friends stood. Pointing to them, he shook his head.

Then he walked over to Father Dilidiyi, who greeted arriving pilgrims outside the church doorway. The giant cleared his throat and then handed him the innocuous stone before returning to his spot in front of Father T'ebaki. He resumed his lowly bow.

Once again, he placed his hand on the giant's head. "It seems as if you are filled with doubt and regret, and while I do not understand your confession, it seems contrite and worthy of forgiveness. You have traveled the world to visit me, and we do not understand each other at all, but we know why you've come. Come, let me share a secret with you."

Father T'ebaki took the giant by the hands and pulled him back to his feet, leading him to a window. "Somewhere far out in the distance is Aksum, where another sacred treasure was kept for generations. When the time came, my countryman, a man named Balthazar, took this sacred treasure on a great journey very similar to yours. On this journey, he met other men, just like your friends

outside. Some were gruff, some were mighty warriors, and some were wise. They all came together and trusted that the Lord would guide them to the right place at the right time."

Taking the ogre by the arm, he led him into the inner room, stopping short of the thick curtain that separated the room. Instead of showing the man the Ark, he turned to show him one of the many paintings created centuries ago. Three men stood together, each holding a chest. "That is my countryman, Balthazar," he said, pointing to the man on the right. "The other man is named Gaspar, a foreign king from the East. The third man came from the north." Father T'ebaki pointed to the height and the dark beard of the man. "His name is Wutach."

"Wutach," the giant repeated and then pointed. "Wutach."

Father T'ebaki nodded and put a finger into the man's chest. "Wutach."

He pulled the giant out of the inner chamber and back out to the main room. There he found a picture showing Mary and the infant Jesus. "It is said that all three laid their gifts before the Christ child, but when Wutach presented his, the child reached out a hand and touched him."

The giant squeezed his eyes tight as if struggling with the concepts. He shook his head.

"Your blood is special. Seventeen centuries ago, Wutach the Northman served another prophecy, but only because it was his duty as a blood heir."

Father T'ebaki took hold of the giant's two hands. "One hand was touched by the Christ, but the other hand brought evil into the world. You were able to hold the sacred Stone because you are an heir of Zik'itenya."

"Zik'itenya?" the giant repeated, referencing his left hand.

Father T'ebaki closed both hands together to unite their hands together in the bond of prayer. "I will pray for you as you finish this terrible journey, for you have the capacity to serve good and also unleash evil. May you choose the right path."

411

CHAPTER 89

The city of Philadelphia witnessed four significant population shifts in the 1600s. Originally home to the Lenape people, later known as the Delaware, the settlement was devastated by smallpox, leaving the river valley and port open for settlement. Fort Christina was built by Swedish settlers in 1638, but Dutch settlers quickly moved into the river valley. By 1655, Dutch General Peter Stuyvesant claimed the colony yet allowed Scandinavian colonists to remain in the area in what became known as New Sweden. By 1682, England had taken claim of the colony and renamed the settlement Philadelphia, a Greek phrase meaning "City of Brotherly Love."

Under an elm tree, William Penn made a pact with the surviving Lenape, Scandinavians, and Dutch: the new English settlement would be a place of religious tolerance where anyone could worship freely. By the time the global War of Spanish Succession broke out, known in the colonies as Queen Anne's War, Philadelphia had become home to Germans, Scot-Irish, Scots, and French settlers along with minority Christian groups such as the Huguenots, Puritans, Calvinists, Mennonites, and Catholics.

With Queen Anne's War raging most fiercely in the south along the Gulf of Mexico and in the north in Acadia and Newfoundland, Philadelphia suffered financially when trade was mostly cut off to the English colony.

Unbeknownst to Queen Anne, three ships of refugees, mostly children, arrived in 1706. The new colonists built a large school for the orphans that was open to the diverse melting pot population of Philadelphia. Its headmaster, a vibrant man of Portuguese descent, found himself embraced by the community due to his philanthropic nature.

Yet headmaster Denis Falcoa had his secrets.

Today, instead of supervising the students and teachers at Jacob's Well Preparatory School, Headmaster Falcoa put on his jacket and went down to the docks where three ships prepared to depart. The two merchant ships, renamed *Adam* and *Eve* instead of *Lif and Lifthrasir*, hadn't left port due to the frequent military patrols. The warship, now named *Jonathan*, had been stripped of most of its provisions, especially the cannons. Its captain and first mate stood upon the dock.

"So it's true," Falcoa called out to them. "You're leaving Philadelphia."

Robert Culliford smiled upon recognition. "Likely for good. After returning these three ships to the Bahamas, Swan and I plan to withdraw to a quiet little island and retire. I've had enough of piracy for a lifetime. Swan and I have enough money hidden away to live four lifetimes, and after our dedicated service to Eos, we intend to live a simple life now."

Culliford and Swan protected the children during the crossing from Madagascar, and after remaining to safeguard them for the past three years, they were leaving. "The Bahamas?"

"Edward Drummond is gathering pirates there, and Eos has need of ships. Patrick Dalziel is there, and Joseph LeMoyne and his younger brother too."

"Why not defend Acadia?" Falcoa asked. "There's nothing of value in the Caribbean."

"Acadia will fall. If Eos fights too hard to keep it, the Priory will believe there is something worth fighting for. They'll never find the vault. In a few years, your students can discreetly deal with the vault."

"It's probably a good thing for the school that you're leaving. I talked to a local merchant who thinks there is pirate treasure buried up the river from the school."

"In Philadelphia?" Culliford scoffed. Even John Swan rolled his eyes. "The only thing of value in Philadelphia is the children."

Falcoa shrugged. "I know. If you've received correspondence from Drummond, surely you must've heard how the extraction of the relics went."

"All I know is that it went well. Some treasures were left within the mountain, but the most important treasures have been secured. Men like you and I will never learn the exact details."

From the ashes of the Phoenix, Eos rises again. "To think…In just three short years, Eos has taken root again. Montreal had survived another war, and the fledgling colony in Louisiana had grown feathers. And now the Bahamas?"

"Pay attention to what you read about the Caribbean," Culliford said dismissively. "It is only subterfuge to distract the Priory of Ormus and our other enemies," Culliford instructed. "Ormus will poke around the corpse of Madagascar and then turn its attention to the epidemic of piracy. This place. This is where all of the stolen funds will be directed. The dreams of Thomas Tew will flourish here. Within a generation, the Free States will be reborn. Teach these children well, Headmaster Falcoa."

Falcoa extended a hand, but Culliford pulled him in for a warm embrace. Never gregarious, John Swan crossed his arms.

"I wish both of you a healthy retirement," Falcoa said before turning to his school. As he strolled back up the streets, he smiled, knowing that James Morrison would eventually have his revenge.

CHAPTER 90

Giovanni Naufragio's command of the *White Zombie* came to an end with a smile. As a young man, he'd spent enough time up in the rigging to suite him, but today, he had no problem climbing up the mast to the crow's nest for a better view. Putting the looking glass to his eye, he saw three mostly full skiffs crossing the Red Sea channel.

Charlie's hulking frame and the crew's mixed ethnicity made their identities fairly obvious.

They survived the journey.

He let out three shrill whistles.

Farther away from the ship, in the makeshift camp, dozens of men rose from their shade to face the ship. Naufragio let out three shrill whistles again.

Men began to run.

His crew of carpenters ran to the port side of the *White Zombie* for a look. Compared to the long, challenging stay on Tortuga, Naufragio had barely fallen into a new routine. Most of the Caribbean crew stayed on the island with Del Torro in charge, and he kept men to maintain the ship and steadily improve it.

If Captain wants to lift anchor tonight, the White Zombie will be ready.

THAT NIGHT, THOUGH, the men feasted on fresh food after stuffing the ship for the next journey. The officers gathered together around the central fire to share tales. Things had gone well,

Naufragio learned, much more exciting than staying on the lonely island. As Guerin and Duke told the tales of Aksum, Lalibela, Yemrehanna, and Abuna Yemata Guh, Naufragio couldn't help but notice a harrowed expression on Charlie's face.

What happened to him?

Finally, the journey ended with Guerin's grin. "Show the others the ring, Charlie."

LeSueur produced the small lead box, and taking the gold ring in his fingertips, he showed it for all the men.

"We all witnessed what happened to Charlie back in Madagascar," Guerin said. "It seems as if Papa Bones was right about him having *cho djab*. In the spirit of Odysseus, let me be clear: no one is to even breathe on that ring except for Charlie. It's powerful but dangerous."

For many, it was their second decade with Guerin. For the rest, they knew the mission was special.

"Tomorrow, we'll lift anchor and begin our long journey west. With Professor Faero's command of the ancient language, Charlie wearing the ring, and a canister of shamir to unlock, we'll rob the Eos vault—and then begin to set things right."

THE END OF PART FIVE

PART SIX
THE GHOSTS OF OAK ISLAND

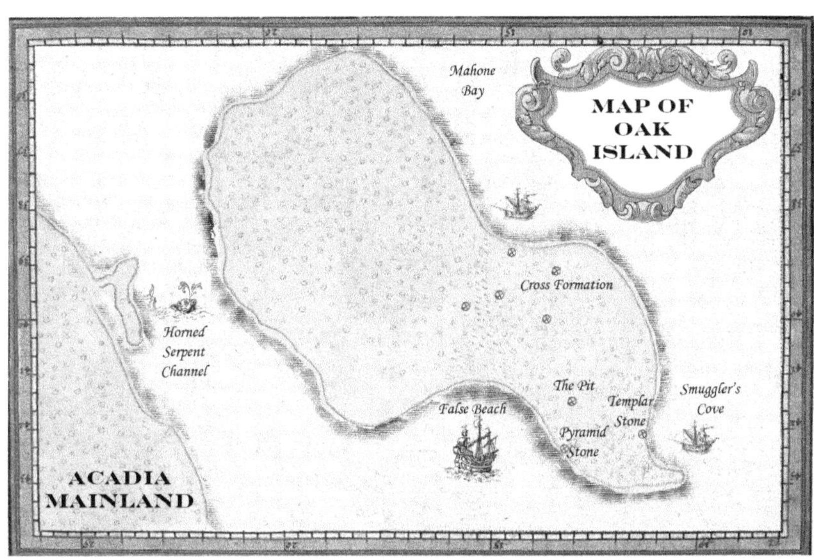

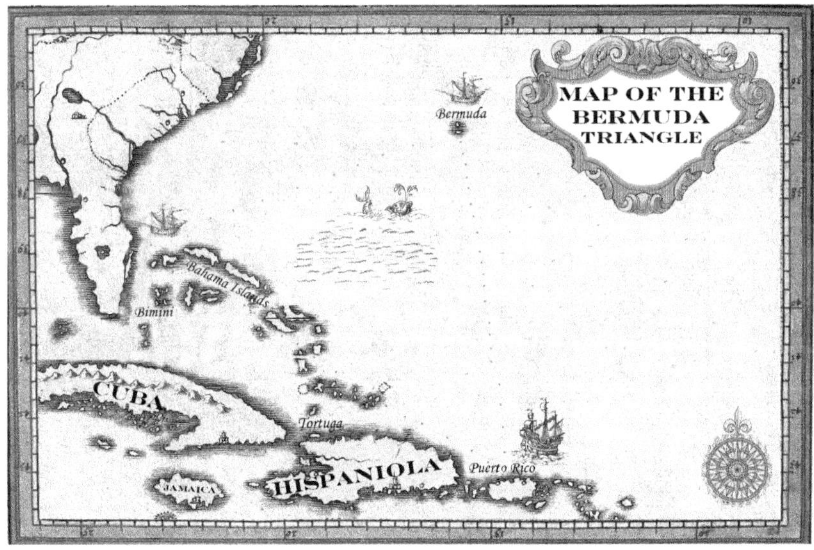

PART SIX

CHAPTER 91

LONDON, ENGLAND

1709

Michael Sikkar double-checked the address and then walked around to the front of the building. The grand, four-story home seemed appropriate for one of the world's most powerful men who wished to hide in plain sight. Even the address seemed duplicitous, for there were two street addresses.

The front of the house was facing posh St. Martin's Street, the political facade for Sir Isaac Newton. The backdoor, to which the directions led him, was Ormond Square, a courtyard with a single elm tree.

Sikkar slipped the piece of paper into one of the pockets not already stuffed with mechanisms of death. He ran a hand through his thinning hair and opened the metal gate separating the home from the cobblestone street. Potted geraniums grew on both sides of the entryway.

He knocked firmly.

When the door opened, a female servant stood and blocked his entrance.

"Hello, I am Michael Sikkar; I have an appointment with Sir Newton."

"Please excuse me for one moment," she said, closing the door.

Enter through the front door, and all is well. Enter through the back door, unseen, and you could leave in little bits and pieces in the trash.

When it opened again, a beautiful young woman stood at the bottom of the stairs behind the maid. "Mr. Sikkar, please come in," she said, her brow wrinkled as she studied him curiously.

She's in the Priory, too. How times are changing. "Miss Barton, you are even more lovely than the rumors suggest."

She giggled and rolled her eyes. "Come, my uncle is upstairs."

He handed the maid his jacket, fully aware she'd find the weapons once he walked up the stairs. *Newton knows what kind of creature I am.*

As he was reaching the top of the stairs, another figure came up the stairs from the rear of the house—*The hunchback.*

Bernard Clairval could not hide his agitation. The twisted mass of sinew and muscle had undoubtedly been powerful in his youth, and from his reputation, quite cunning. *Could I take him in a struggle? How does one earn his way into being Newton's right hand man?*

As a professional assassin, Sikkar kept himself fit and strong for times when poisons, powders, and blades failed.

Powerful men expect absolute obedience, including when to arrive for a meeting and which door to enter, but I've sworn no oaths to him—only the Priory.

"Ah, good to finally meet you in person, Mr. Sikkar. We eagerly await your personal report, however enigmatic." Clairval turned and began his ascent up the stairs, working twice as hard as an average man. As if noticing this, Ms. Barton walked beside him, attempting small talk as they slowly followed.

Finally, they stopped at a large library, with more art than artifacts. *A lie to remind his other guests that he is a politician and not an alchemist. I wonder where your secret lab is hidden?*

Isaac Newton sat on a couch with a blanket over his legs. He wore a yellow robe with a blue silk collar and a basic white shirt underneath. His hair was fine silver with enough length to cover his balding scalp and brow. His pale complexion was reddish around his angular nose and cheek, making him seem jovial despite his emotionless stare. "Bernard tells me your investigation has taken a sudden turn. Have a seat."

Barton, leaning back into the corner of the red sofa, sat atop the edges of the blanket next to her uncle.

Clairval poured from an open bottle of wine and offered the first cup to Newton, a second to Barton, and then lifted the last two and carried both to where Sikkar sat.

He's letting me choose, proof of no poison. These bastards could have developed a tolerance or have an antidote. Cie la vie!

He accepted the cup.

"To what shall we drink?" Newton asked genteelly.

"Hang all pirates," Barton said with a flash of dimples.

"Child," Newton chided.

"Death will have his day," Barton countered.

"Shakespeare." Newton smiled and raised his cup higher, "Death will have his day."

Sikkar repeated, swallowed, and began. "Adrian Van Broeck, the assumed pseudonym for the author of *The Life and Adventures of Captain John Avery,* is the name of a real Dutch captain. He worked for the Dutch East India Company for the past nineteen years, primarily on a route between Bombay and a cinnamon plantation on the island of Sri Lanka—until a few years ago, late 1705, when an earthquake off of Madagascar claimed his ship and crew."

"Madagascar?" Newton muttered.

"Yes, small world. I want to apologize, for I understand my mandate was to investigate the veracity of the text. The colony, Libertalia, is a fiction. The pirate utopia described in the book, replete with a naval armada, a 15,000 man army, and an impregnable fortress, also does not match reality. Yes, there were settlements and colonies on the island continent, but the author made obvious changes. The most dramatic change involved the events of the *Ganj-i-Sawai.* Instead of the brutal rape of the Emperor's daughter, Henry Avery fell in love with her, preserved her honor, and ran off to Madagascar with her, where he created a royal family in a fantasy kingdom. While the text is a fabrication, ask yourself who it serves?"

"Obviously Henry Avery," Newton said.

"That was my first reaction also, for the yarn tries to rehabilitate his ruined name. But hidden under the lies is a strange truth—a princess of Madagascar. In truth, there is a Queen Rehena, who once was a princess, whose royal son and heir, Ratsimilaho, is of mixed blood. Rumors say he is the son of a pirate."

"But not Avery?"

He's quite keen. "No, but I believe the real author of the text might be the father or perhaps even her lover."

"Adrian Van Broeck? The Dutch captain? But he's dead, you claimed."

"Rumors claim it—not I—but no, I do not think the prince's father is Dutch. I believe his father is French, a pirate known as Gareth LaGrande."

"Not Thomas Tew?" Newton asked.

"An obvious pseudonym," Catherine Barton mocked. "So who is this pirate?"

"When you squeeze an orange to extract its juice, whether it is a light squeezing or enough to get every last drop, the orange cannot be restored. Left alone, the orange might have continued as it was for weeks, but with even the lightest squeezing, it quickly rots. In my profession, I've learned to simply get all that I can and then toss the rind and pulp away. This is how I deal with people on my list. I extract all that I can and then leave them in the ground."

Despite Barton's obvious annoyance, Newton sat up straighter to listen.

"I recently squeezed an orange to extract juice. After sixteen years of relative silence, the name Avery emerged in a tell-all new book. So after a few months of investigation into Madagascar and Van Broeck, I stopped looking for the author and instead searched for the acquisition agent, whom I found in Amsterdam."

Newton nodded his head in anticipation.

"After a little squeezing, I learned that the complete manuscript was brought to Amsterdam by a Dutch captain who was seeking a new life in America, his pockets lined with gold. He only fulfilled his end of a bargain by...dropping off a manuscript he didn't write."

"So you killed an innocent man?" Barton asked dismissively.

"This French agent has several publications to credit, so I won't bore you with those details except to highlight his most successful manuscript—*New Voyages to North America: Volumes One and Two.*"

Newton said it aloud for the others. "Baron Lahontan."

"Our fugitive fur-trader has stuck his head up for air, and instead of fanciful tales of the Long River and exotic tribes that live

in a land where the earth bleeds blue, he writes a love story about a Madagascar princess. Obviously, just the origin of the two texts was enough to convince me, but upon examining them, both hyperbolic distortions of truth, I understand now why the Baron has so easily evaded capture by King Louis' bounty hunters."

Newton hummed.

Bernard Clairval took longer to understand. "Baron Lahontan wrote a book about the life of Henry Avery—how would he even know him?"

"The French king drove him underground," Barton assessed, "and where's a better place to evade justice than on a pirate ship? The text isn't the story of Avery, it's Lahontan's tale. Remind me about his African queen."

"Rehena? She recently won a war in her country against southern tribes who were poised to invade the lush eastern region. Just prior to the outbreak of war, she entertained a pirate known as Red Eye or Gareth LaGrande."

"Gareth LaGrande?" Clairval repeated. "Isn't that the name of the fellow wanted by Emperor Aurangzeb and the East India Trading Company?"

Newton did not respond; he only blinked.

Obviously, I've given them valuable information. I wonder what connection Baron Lahontan had with India?

"Should I know this Baron Lahontan?" Barton asked.

Clairval explained. "He is a minor French nobleman who came to New France in the 1680s as an adventurer, or so it was thought. All the known powers clashed and spied while this brash young man went right to the heart of the matter and set the frontier on fire. Two decades later, things are just beginning to calm again."

"The heart of the matter," Barton repeated, to which Clairval nodded. "So after leaving the frontier, he went all the way to Madagascar to—"

"Enough!" Newton snapped, causing everyone to jump. His glare shut all mouths, and then in a heartbeat, he put on a smile. "My apologies, Catherine, and to you also, Bernard. I focused all of my attention upon Eos and I failed to factor in another variable in the equation—the Periphery."

"The Periphery?" Clairval repeated.

"We had the solution to this problem and we let it slip right through our fingers," Newton said and then buried his head in his hands. The other two held their tongues. "Our collateral."

At this, the hunchback gasped. "The prince."

Barton's eyes grew wide. "He was just released and sent back to his mother."

"Queen Rehena sided against Eos but secretly dealt with a Periphery agent," Newton muttered with his head still hidden. He dropped his hands to pleasantly add, "From his time on the frontier as Baron Lahontan to his time as a pirate as Gareth LaGrande, it is clear this Periphery agent has been two steps ahead of me."

Sikkar watched as Barton and Clairval tried to catch up. Lahontan's tampering on the frontier created a roadblock to both Eos and the Priory, and then he quickly returned to keep England from dislodging the French in Quebec and Montreal. A few years later, as Newton prepared to crush Eos in Madagascar, an anonymous pirate meddled once again, creating another stalemate.

An impressive fellow, whoever he is.

Newton turned to him, "Mr. Sikkar, your efforts in this matter will be rewarded well, and I wish to enlist your efforts again: when Baron Lahontan makes port again, I want you to be there to eliminate him. Is that clear?"

A challenge worthy of my talents.

CHAPTER 92

Gaspar looked out over the Mississippi River valley, now a mixture of blood and ice. He cleaned the blood from his hatchet by chopping into the edge of the frozen river, leaving behind French blood while also creating a gap in the ice. He set the hatchet aside and splashed cold water onto his face.

The Muskrat has emerged to strike his enemy.

Unlike in his youth, Gaspar did not relish the slaughter of his enemies. Now, he prayed for their souls. The Frenchmen he'd killed were not evil men—only misled.

But Guerin had been right in his prediction. To the north, the French were fortifying Haute-Louisiane with several forts and colonies around ancient Cahokia. To the south, the French were establishing Basse-Louisiane with colonies at Biloxi, Mobile and Fort Maurepas. The Natchez were the only thing keeping the French—and Eos—from a conquest of the Mississippi River.

One of his Natchez warriors came running up to him.

"Did we hold the flank?" Gaspar asked.

"We did, and we managed to capture their leader."

"And the rest of the French?"

"Eliminated."

"Bring me their leader—alive and unharmed."

As Gaspar waited, he thought of the others doing their part in the great drama. He thought about his Petun people living near Fort Detroit, where the colonists promised would be the extent of their interests. He thought of the Chippewa, who relentlessly pressed to fulfill their prophecies. On the other side, he thought of Wapasha, Keoxa, and sweet Wenonah, who defended the Lands of the Blue Woman from the inevitable.

Gaspar turned to the carnage around him where the blood of three dozen dead men melted through the snow and ice to join with the great river. The young men celebrated another victory, but Gaspar yearned for the days of violence to be over.

Where are you Guerin? How much longer must I play the part of Samson, holding back the Philistine hordes?

The prisoner brought to him was a Frenchman in his mid-forties. When they tossed him onto his belly, the man rose slowly onto all fours before sitting on his haunches. His eyes did not look up from the ground.

"What is your name?" Gaspar asked in French.

"Nicholas Chauvin," he muttered.

"Well, Monsieur Chauvin, fate has smiled on you today. We are going to send you back down the river with a message to the men who sent you. Tell them the lands of the Natchez will never belong to the French."

Finally, Chauvin looked up, locking eyes for just a moment before flinching and looking back down.

Was that fear or recognition? It'd been almost a decade since Chief Kondiaronk died in Montreal, and aside from aging, Gaspar dressed in the manner of the local Natchez. *It must be fear.*

"Escort Monsieur Chauvin safely back into Choctaw territory. He carries an important message for his friends," Gaspar said.

Chauvin glanced up one final time before being led away.

The first step of my new strategy.

"Gather the men, but only the young men without families," Gaspar insisted. Even though he had promised Guerin to hold the position as long as possible, the southern colonies grew stronger by the day. Doing the same thing again and again was a recipe for defeat.

I have to try something different.

Within moments, his other officers, wondering what the next move would be, began to gather.

"I sent their leader back, which will only harden their resolve," Gaspar explained. "They will be resolved to hit us with twice as

many men next year, but by that time, we'll be hundreds of miles from here."

"Are we going north?" his officers wondered, also sensing the relentless tide of French bodies being thrown at them.

"No, the French are even stronger in the north. We're going to flank them through the territories of the Atakapa and Chitamacha. When they come up the Mississippi River in force, we'll destroy their unguarded territories. We'll crush the egg in the nest."

It'll be a decisive victory—or a good death.

CHAPTER 93

The War of Spanish Succession, which began in 1701 after King Charles II of Spain died without children, saw a shift in power in 1710. For the early parts of the war, France championed the Bourbon heir Phillip of Anjou and seemed to impose its will; however, the Grand Alliance (England, Holy Roman Empire, Dutch Republic, Prussia, and pro-Habsburg Spain) endured the early years as they stood behind their choice for the Spanish Empire throne, Charles VI. The stalemate began to inevitably crumble when England tired of the war and elected a pro-peace Tory government in 1710. The Grand Alliance quickly began negotiating treaties that would lead to peace.

Despite the political shift at home, England managed to secure a key victory in North America. While attempts to gain territory in the Gulf of Mexico failed since France maintained Louisiana and Spain kept Florida, American Colonists first won the Battle of St. John in Newfoundland and then took the capital of Acadia, Port Royal. Although the French navy remained strong, the American ground forces led by Sir Francis Nicholson effectively established a new English colony of Nova Scotia.

For boatswain Jimmy Duke, the winds off the coast of New England brought memories of home. Even though Boston was only a few hundred miles southwest of Acadia, it still felt a million miles away.

I've spent more of my life on a ship than I ever did in Boston, he reflected. When he left with Captain Kidd in 1695, he assumed he'd spend the winter in the Caribbean before returning to a dreary life as a fisherman.

What fishing crew would hire me now? I'm almost forty. I could buy a spot along a bar in some tavern and tell tales for the rest of my life that no man would believe. Or...I could finish this adventure and buy a tavern.

The *White Zombie* blindly approached Acadia from the deep waters of the Atlantic. Duke had helped Naro Bon navigate the fishing grounds to Sable Island, where they encountered fishermen who updated them on colonial news. Now, after spending the last two nights taking careful astronomical measurements, they chose a sliver of continent for their approach.

According to Guerin, they'd only get one chance to do it right.

It had been the fugitive Lahontan who fled the continent at Acadia two decades earlier. The crime? Although the talk around the Boston taverns had been that the young Baron fled with his tail between his legs after putting his tail between the governor's daughter's legs, Louis-Armand Guerin later told a far more sinister tale of why a death warrant had been issued for his head. After all that Duke had seen, he knew Guerin told the truth.

Yet looking upon the dark, wooded shore, the tale seemed unbelievable.

An ancient treasure vault?

Who would bother to put anything here?

The spotters shouted out confirmation of the required landmarks to the forty-mile window of the horizon. To the north of the large bay, the presence of a fishing village was noted. To the south of the large bay, a wide, deep river came rushing down to meet the Atlantic. Ahead of them a hundred islands spread across the deep bay.

Guerin, Faero, LeSueur, and Bon gathered together on the rear deck as they used their looking glasses to note the islands and compared them to charts. The *White Zombie* came straight toward the continent while the crew looked for any nearby vessel that could bear witness to the former Mughal warship entering American territory. Even though Port Royal, the largest settlement upon the peninsula, was on the inner shore, Guerin did not want to risk being spotted by a British patrol.

Looks like we got it right, Duke assessed when all of the scopes were lowered and Captain Guerin quickly walked back to his cabin.

Confirmation made, the *White Zombie* pivoted back to the deep waters from whence they'd come, and Duke prepared his crew to make deep-anchor on the Emerald Basin.

When dusk came, they'd return to Acadia under cover of darkness, and then, for the next two days, he'd become the newest captain of the *White Zombie.*

Despite the promotion, Jimmy Duke grit his teeth in frustration.

I wish I could be with them when they land upon Oak Island.

CHAPTER 94

Under cover of darkness, the three skiffs landed upon the uniform gravel of the small cove. Louis-Armand Guerin turned back to where the *White Zombie* anchored a few hundred yards away. As instructed, no light came from the ship. Starlight and a sliver of moon created enough to silhouette the ship against the backdrop of the Atlantic, but in front of them, a deep darkness hid the contents of Oak Island.

To his left, LeSueur, Horne, Naufragio, and Papa Bones began to unload the equipment from their skiff. To his right, Del Torro, Barrow, Murray, and Bon began to pull their skiff further onto shore. Along with Professor Faero, Guerin rowed with two of the original Abyssinian boys, now grown men.

Once the twelve stood upon the shore, Guerin knelt down, drawing all eyes. "Notice anything strange, gentlemen?"

LeSueur kicked at the gravel.

Horne scanned the dark horizon of the night.

Only Faero noticed, commenting, "The gravel is very uniform...as if it has been poured."

"Three hundred yards of false shoreline," Guerin declared. He stood and pointed up and down the cove.

"Is the treasure below us?" Del Torro asked.

"No," Guerin chuckled. "Naufragio asked how deep the pit was, and this gives his answer."

"I don't understand," the carpenter admitted.

So Guerin asked, "Why would you build a false shore with poured gravel?"

No one answered.

"Okay then, I'll ask another question. If you had the most valuable treasure horde known to the world, why would you keep it unguarded?"

"It's booby-trapped," Faero said. "Just like the Well of Initiation back on Madagascar."

"When I was last here, it was daylight, so excuse me if I miss the mark on the first attempt. Master Bon, I want you to count off the paces from the beach. Follow me gentlemen."

Shaped like a young elephant, Oak Island stretched less than a mile from trunk to tail. Beginning at the neck of the cove, Guerin walked the men into the heart of the island. Part of the brilliance of the vault was that no signs of civilization had been allowed. Only upon close inspection did the first clue become obvious—the sessile oaks.

Now protected by the curtain of trees, the men lit the lanterns and continued walking.

"Do you see those tree branches above our heads?" Guerin asked.

The men looked up to the twisted branches.

"Oak trees are not indigenous to these islands, so to make it easier to find this island, they razed all the cedar and pine and planted oaks."

"How do you know this?" Dr. Barrow asked.

"When I fled Montreal, I was forced to wait for a ship to extract me. While I waited, I took the opportunity to come explore this island. The Periphery had heard rumors of it for some time, but most of my superiors dismissed the legends of an ancient king from a forgotten kingdom, despite the obvious signs when settlers began to cross the Atlantic."

"What signs?" Naro Bon asked.

"Tell him about the Newport Tower, Professor Faero."

"Oh dear. It's the bane of my existence. It's what drew me into this mess." As they walked, Faero explained the Norse tower built in the colony that now bore its ironic namesake, Rhode Island. He then added several other anecdotes that supported Norse explora-

tion centuries prior to Columbus. "If I were to guess, I'd say the Templars came in the 1300s with the belief they were about to build a new colony."

Naro Bon, the navigator, understood. "And the Templars knew the latitude of the Lost Kingdom?"

"44 degrees north latitude," Guerin added. "Of course, they had different systems based upon star maps, but it led them across the Atlantic and right into the continent of America. At first, Oak Island became a landmark. Much later, it became a symbolic vault. I'll show you."

After a short walk, the oak canopy opened to a clearing about the size of a home. "My guess is Eos sends some sort of 'maintenance crew' that visits on a regular basis, those branches were cut so they could find the pit, and every few decades, they put more dirt over the pit and reposition the flagstones just below the surface."

He knelt down and reached out his hand, his fingers gently touching fallen leaves before he aggressively pushed it away, taking dirt and debris with it.

"We should have brought shovels," Del Torro muttered.

Already complaining and we've been ashore for ten minutes, Guerin observed. *That is the reason why I left you with the ship in Africa. But you've earned this honor.* Digging like a dog, Guerin quickly removed enough dirt for confirmation.

"There you are," he said once his fingers felt flat stone. He stood back up, allowing the shuttered light of the lanterns to illuminate the hole for the others to see. "It's flagstone."

He looked back up to the monstrous oak with three overhanging limbs that had been neatly hacked off above the place where they stood.

He'd stood in the same spot before, years earlier. *Have I lost eighteen years of my life to this quest? Eighteen years since I fled the continent.*

The men who'd seen the church in the clouds, the floating church, and the churches carved from stone stood with those who hadn't—Del Torro and Papa Bones. Their collective hands cleared away the rest of the dirt to reveal three exposed flagstones.

Del Torro didn't seem impressed.

"They placed the flagstones a few feet below the surface to keep subsidization from revealing the pit," Guerin explained, stepping back.

"Didn't seem to work," LeSueur said, stepping back to the perimeter of the depression. It wasn't a large depression, only ten yards in diameter.

"It's been over three hundred years since the pit was made, Charlie; the flagstones have done their job. The rest of this island is slate and bedrock. Except for here, of course."

"Carved out by shamir," Faero muttered.

The entire crew now understood the shamir. It'd been a long journey from Abyssinia to Acadia. The first experiment had been conducted off an unnamed, uninhabited island near Socotra. With Solomon's ring and a lead container of shamir, LeSueur used a lead cup to extract a small amount before quickly resealing the container, which was immediately brought back to the ship for safety. The small cup transformed into a vaporous whirlwind that violently lashed around, kicking up wind and debris that reached the ship anchored hundreds of yards away. LeSueur had been once again left unharmed but had failed to command anything, leaving him ankle deep in the Indian Ocean.

A second experiment was conducted weeks later on Madagascar. Returning to the spot where the *Adventure Galley* had ambushed Blackbeard's ship, LeSueur repeated the experiment at the base of the mountain. Once again, the small extraction of shamir attacked everything around it—except for LeSueur, who failed a second time to command the spirits within the substance. The failed experiment led them to the literal breakthrough.

The unleashed shamir ate away at jungle, foliage, and stone, opening a crevice into the underground structure. There, Faero found the prize that had eluded both Emperor Aurangzeb and Thomas Tew—the sarcophagus.

The third experiment did not happen immediately. After leaving Abyssinia, Guerin privately visited with Queen Rehena, who anticipated the return of Prince Laho after pretending to be Newton's loyal servant over the past few years. He'd left her with more promises, and she in turn supplied them for their return voyage to the West. Once they sailed, Professor Faero worked on his transla-

tion, focusing upon the foreign words carved into the ring. Off the coast of Morocco, LeSueur tried the experiment a third time, this time uttering the same words Solomon had uttered. The demons obeyed, leaving a cylindrical hole at LeSueur's feet when it was over.

Guerin had stood beside LeSueur for a fourth experiment and afterwards set his course for Oak Island.

"If I were to venture a guess," Guerin responded to Faero. "I'd guess the Templars of old had a superior knowledge of the shamir, and even without Solomon's ring, they used it to bore through the slate and bedrock. Remember, Templar Knights trace their lineage back to the stonemasons of Hiram Abiff of Tyre."

"What about the treasure?" Del Torro asked.

Guerin turned to Naro Bon. "How many paces did we walk from the cove?"

"Approximately three hundred paces," Bon answered quickly.

"This central chasm would have been used to lower down treasure into a vault, much like the Well of Initiation was built. Faero, tell these men how the central chasm was constructed."

"A spiral staircase surrounded the central chasm, and at the bottom, chambers were built off to the sides of the chasm."

"The men who built the Well of Initiation in Madagascar were likely the same generation of masons. Covering up the vault was their way of locking it, and as Newton and the Priory discovered, trying to rob the contents of the vault ended up locking it up even more securely."

"Ah, the booby-traps," Del Torro said in understanding.

"The false beach is used to collect water to flood the pit," Faero both explained and concluded.

Guerin nodded. "Exactly, and based on the distance, slope, and angle between this shore and the pit, I'd guess the two met almost a hundred feet underground. A foolish intruder would trigger the release valves and flood the pit with seventy feet of water, but more than just the volume of water—"

"It was connected to the ocean itself," Dr. Barrow answered.

"And not even Thor could drain it," Faero finished.

"If the pit was the opening to the vault, it was also meant to be the focus of attention, and if someone went through all the efforts

of creating a vault of such complexity, he had to value the treasure he kept. Why would he let it be destroyed by seawater?"

"A gopher hole," LeSueur said. "It goes deeper into the ground than the nest, so that when the rains come, the gopher and its babies are protected in a pocket of air."

"My thoughts exactly. Yet there is no backdoor to reach this gopher nest, and the front door is a death trap, which means, we will do something the Templar's did not anticipate."

Guerin took measured paces away from the center of the covered pit, and standing near a rooted tree, he stomped his foot down. "Here. We'll create a side tunnel here. Are you ready, LeSueur? It's time to command demons."

CHAPTER 95

OAK ISLAND, ACADIA

1711

Fie on it, LeSueur thought, channeling the dark side of his mixed ancestry. He took out the lead box, pulled out the ancient ring, and once more, slid it onto his finger. Aside from a strange feeling of euphoria, nothing dramatic happened.

Except for Guerin and Faero, the others all stepped away from him, giving him dozens of yards of room. Guerin held the lead vat of shamir. Faero held the translation.

"Remember, measure out only a small amount. Once the first measure is exhausted, we'll need the second measure to close it back up."

"Why do we care about closing it?" LeSueur asked.

"I don't want Eos to know we were here," Guerin said with a shrug. "It'll be funny if one day they go to open the vault and find that it's empty."

"Do you really think it is down there?" Faero asked.

"I hope it's down there," Guerin said. "But I'll take whatever we find. Are you ready, Charlie?"

LeSueur nodded. "Be ready with the rope."

Guerin stepped back to the others, leaving just Faero, who stood midway between. LeSueur cracked the seal and opened the lead vat, scooping out a small amount of the strange liquid. He quickly resealed the larger vessel and took several strides away from the open container.

Guerin rushed forward, hustling the remaining shamir to safety.

Once again, Faero stood alone, lantern in one hand and the translated pages on the other. While Thomas Tew had been quite wrong about the safety of standing on the deck of his ship, he'd been equally right about the ancient sarcophagus found in Arabia. Professor Faero immediately recognized the Hebrew language written upon it, and after extrapolating the missing vowel sounds, matched it up to the language that Solomon had also managed to crack.

Now, with an imperfect knowledge, Faero began to feed the syllables of the dead language.

A wave of hatred swept over LeSueur, and he found himself grimacing in emotional agony. *Not my hatred…it's the demons within the shamir.*

On the crossing, Professor Faero chronicled how wise King Solomon fell from grace and worshiped the gods of his foreign wives. In folklore, a more explicit tale was told involving a demon named Asmodeus, and depending on the telling, Solomon duped the demon into acquiring the secret knowledge once used to forge the Philosopher's Stone. Enslaved by King Solomon, Asmodeus, in turn, tricked his captor once the Temple was complete. "Take the chain off me and give me the ring," Asmodeus baited King Solomon, who acquiesced, only to have the demon attack him and cast him far from Israel. Solomon learned the powerful nature of his ring. With his ring as a catalyst, Solomon commanded the demons into a new prison—the shamir.

LeSueur watched as a cup full of the vile substance began to expand. As before, he repeated the syllables to command the substance. The vapor spread out around his feet like a large cobra, but before he'd finished the first command, it snapped out like a whip to strike Faero. The lantern tumbled from his hands, resulting in a fireball that ignited the professor's wool jacket.

Chaos ensued. Some ran away. Others ran forward.

Slimy little bastard, LeSueur thought as his heel crushed the vapor. Then his mouth opened to continue the next syllable. As a literate boy, he'd learned several languages as an aid to the Jesuits and then as a fur trader. Even though he knew little about the ancient king or his lost kingdom, LeSueur continued to utter all the words written down on Faero's burning piece of paper.

His commands took hold of the raging cloud, which returned back to a small sphere around him.

Down, you filth, down.

The shamir obeyed, and whatever divine spark that had been given to the Morning Stars during creation still allowed the demonic shamir to transform the elements from under LeSueur's feet. Like standing upon quicksand, he descended past the horizon of horrified friends into a confined darkness, where the bluish-green glow of the nebulous shamir reflected off of solid stone.

How far down do I descend? To the Gates of Sheol?

LeSueur's answer came when his slow descent ended in an abrupt drop.

Traitorous whore! LeSueur thought the shamir had turned on him, but he felt cold stone against his throbbing cheek, ribs, and knee. Above him, he saw the shamir still swirling near the ceiling in the cavity it'd just formed.

Enough, he ordered, and with a glance at his ring, he uttered the final syllables.

The shamir vanished like smoke, leaving him in total darkness.

"I'm through, dammit!" he shouted. "Where are you sons of bitches? Send down a torch or something, you bastards."

LeSueur felt his hands clenched, and then remembered the ring. As soon as he removed it, his fear, rage, and hatred vanished like the shamir.

"Charlie?" Guerin asked.

"I've found a chamber."

"What do you see?"

"It's dark," LeSueur stated the obvious. "Send down a lantern on a rope."

As the lantern appeared, the light looked like an angel descending from the heavens, but when it crossed from chasm to chamber, the light revealed a room filled with the flickering light of gold. LeSueur's heart fluttered with joy and despair.

The room extended in a rectangle that stretched about twenty yards wide by sixty feet long—an astonishing feat of masonry. Within it, though, were two-dozen golden relics. The wrong relics. Each and every one of them appeared to be Egyptian.

"What's happening, Charlie?" Guerin's voice called down. "Is it safe to come down?"

LeSueur untied the lantern and answered back. "It's a vault full of treasure, but…"

The men on the surface rejoiced. LeSueur began to walk away. His gopher theory proved to be true. At the narrow end of the chamber, a small ramp descended.

LeSueur followed it.

It led to the narrow, spiral staircase anticipated by Faero, which meant the false door of the covered central chasm was likely a trap. LeSueur took a few steps around the arc of the staircase and found another opening.

This one did not lead to another room. Instead, it was a sloping ramp leading up to the surface. *A secret entrance.* From the angle, it likely was hundreds of paces from the obvious center of the pit and small enough to be discreetly hidden.

Returning to the spiral, he continued to the next opening. Inside, he found a collection of prehistoric art, sculptures and rune stones.

His pace hurried, and in the fourth opening, he almost dropped the lamp as he paused in the entryway. He found himself breathing hard as his heart thumped within his chest.

A new light appeared from the first chamber. "Where are you Charlie?"

"Here," he said with a dampened voice.

He glanced once more and closed his eyes.

Guerin rounded the staircase with a grin on his face. "Can you believe it?"

LeSueur shook his head.

"What's wrong?"

"Look inside," LeSueur said.

Guerin stopped in his tracks, and his free hand reached for the edge of the opening to find his balance. "It's…it's…"

"Looks like we're going to make Benjamin Horne a happy man."

CHAPTER 96

Josiah Faero realized he'd been curled up in a ball, still smoldering a bit, and he unwrapped himself to crawl on his hands and knees to the opening in the earth. Giovanni Naufragio, the ship's carpenter, was the first to climb up out of the hole. His breathing was labored from more than just exertion.

Faero extended a hand to Naufragio, who grabbed it and said, "It's beyond reason," before crawling out on all fours, collapsing onto his chest, and then turning back to look at the gaping hole in the ground. "Unbelievable," he muttered and patted Faero's shoulder. "I could use your help."

Faero rose and followed him through the darkness of the small oak forest to the northern shore. Still tucked into the rocky shore, the three boats waited.

"Hold this," Naufragio said, and a great bundle of rope filled Faero's arms. For a moment, he wrestled with the cluster until he slipped an arm into the center and then held the weight upon his shoulder. A moment later, a hammer, saw, and canvas bag balanced the weight.

Naufragio paused from his efforts to lift the lantern, opening its shutters four times in slow increments—a sign to the anchored ship that things were underway. "I can't believe we're doing this," the carpenter muttered. With a bundle of small beams upon his shoulder, he carried the lantern with his free hand as they crossed back through the oak forest.

As they walked, Faero recalled a story from antiquity, a Persian tale about a boy who is ensnared by an evil sorcerer who uses him as a sacrifice to gain entry into a booby-trapped cave. *Have I lost my mind? Am I insane, stuck on an island, dying of thirst, imagining that I am Aladdin?*

If anything, he'd had too much water as he watched his friends descend into the pit. The weight of the ropes felt real, as did the tools he carried. The man in front of him, his shipmate for the past two years, also seemed authentic and not just some shape-shifting Jinn who took on human form.

Returning to the opening that looked like the Gateway to Hell, Faero could see the open lanterns below, casting strange shadows and reflections in the chamber.

The carpenter began barking out orders, and Faero gladly followed, if only to quiet his mind. In the tale, Aladdin was tricked by the sorcerer into entering the cave to retrieve a treasure and then found himself trapped on the inside.

With a ring.

The irony was too much, and Faero refused to recall the tale further.

"Now help me drag it over the pit," Naufragio said.

The wooden tripod fit over the top of the hole in the ground, which Faero had helped create with only the syllables from his mouth. The ring worked, as Guerin long ago predicted, and the elements—Earth, Air, Fire, Water—obeyed.

Thomas Tew had promised an adventure, which hadn't been a lie, yet the all-expenses paid trip around the world had come at a steep cost—his stolen life.

The ropes and pulleys were now in place, and Faero could hear the men below.

Risking a view, he leaned over the hole.

"Dear Lord, what have we done?" Faero muttered when he saw what filled the hole below them. "Be careful. Don't touch it or you will fall down dead!"

Louis-Armand Guerin leaned into the illuminated space below, showing gloved hands. "Don't worry, Professor, we're taking all precautions. It's only a replica, remember? The real one and its location is kept secret."

If that isn't the real Ark of the Covenant, I don't know what is.

The golden box seemed to emanate light, but with the open lanterns, the polished surfaces could have simply been reflecting the light.

Men scaled the sides of the pit, and soon, LeSueur and the others gathered around, each taking hold of the rope connected to Naufragio's rigging.

Once out of the pit, the chest seemed diminished, smaller.

"We must get it to the ship at once," Horne said, assuming command.

His mission is over, it seems. The treasure stolen by the Templars centuries earlier was now being returned to Abyssinia, where only the high priest knew the truth.

Faero escorted the relic to the rowboat where they loaded the chest into one and towed it with the other. Horne and Naufragio steadily took the treasure toward the anchored ship, which came to life as Del Torro opened and closed the shutter of his lantern, giving another signal everything was clear.

"You just going to stand around gawking or are you going to help?" Del Torro asked and walked back to the opening.

When they returned to the chasm in the earth, Faero did not hesitate this time. He followed, shocked at how slippery and perfectly smooth the walls were. Although the golden glow had left with the Ark, the lantern light still cast surreal illuminations in the chamber below.

Charlie and Papa Bones dragged a chest to where Faero dropped onto the floor. Surrounding the single chest were dozens of other treasures.

"We're going to need a larger ship," Papa Bones flashed a toothless grin.

Guerin stood a few paces back with arms crossed. "Nice of you to join us."

"This is...all a bit much. I've been investigating mythology and legend for my whole life, but I never imagined that—"

"I need your help prioritizing the rest of this treasure. Come, let me show you what I'm dealing with."

For the next hour, Faero walked through time as he tried to identify the stolen treasures of the legendary Templar Knights.

Guerin ordered most of the Egyptian artifacts to be loaded onto the ship, knowing he'd make a fortune in selling them.

"The Odin Stone?" Guerin asked.

"Some of it is certainly early Goth, but I don't see anything as critical or unique as the Odin Stone. I would guess these are ancient family heirlooms."

"Unfortunately, our hold cannot carry much more of this loot," Guerin said with a shrug. "Our crew will certainly leave fortunes to their descendants, won't they?"

"If we live long enough to spend it."

"Good point. Let's leave a message for Eos to discover."

"A message?"

Guerin secured a hammer and chisel. "One day, when they believe the time is right, Eos will come for their treasure, so let's leave them an idea who got the better of them."

Guerin handed Faero a hammer and chisel and the two quickly went to work leaving their names etched in stone at the bottom of the pit.

CHAPTER 97

Edward Drummond understood how the great explorer LaSalle missed the Mississippi River Delta. The mighty river that ran through a continent fanned out into several muddy fingers of a peninsula that jutted into the gulf. None of the little fingers seemed substantial enough to matter. For that reason, LaSalle kept sailing west, where he died in a mutiny in Texas.

The issues led the LeMoyne family to build their Gulf colonies a hundred miles away from the delta, where a deeper bay allowed much better navigation to Fort Maurepas, Biloxi, and Mobile.

The mud flats also prompted Drummond to anchor two miles past the silty water to be sure his hull wouldn't get stuck.

Three factors led him to return to the colony. First, Culliford and Swan returned to the Caribbean with three ships that could join the pirate fleet in exchange for, as they put it, their "retirement." Drummond granted them their wish.

The second factor had been an empty hull. Back in Bermuda, his divers scoured the wreck of the *Berger* with no success, leading Drummond to an obvious conclusion: LeSueur lied. Yes, the ship sank. Yes, there'd been a fire. But the Philosopher's Stone could not be found.

The third factor had been a cry for help. Two major attacks had occurred over the summer from the Natchez Indians on the colonies. Instead of simply defending their territory, the Natchez came down river to uproot the colonists.

To strike quickly, the Natchez used canoes.

Despite a clear autumn sky, Drummond heard the thunder of cannon fire. He smiled, thinking of Patrick Dalziel's ambush location in the mud flats. His orders had been clear: wait for the flotilla to pass by and then unleash hell behind them.

Before spreading out in a thirty-mile fan, the Mississippi River passed through a muddy neck just three miles wide. That was where Dalziel waited.

Now, trapped in the Delta, the Natchez had no other choice than to try to flee forward, where Joseph LeMoyne's *Griffon* and Antoine LeMoyne's *Salamandre* guarded the other large outlets.

Drummond nodded to his Master Gunner, who had the cannons ready to fire. Knowing the Natchez canoes posed no threat to a warship, all four vessels kept only their gun crew and loaded a fighting force of four hundred men into skiffs that now waited at every turn for the fleeing Natchez.

First, I win the battle of the Delta. Then I conquer the whole continent.

CHAPTER 98

Pierre-Charles LeSueur did not sleep that night, and he found himself at the railing of the rear deck as a gray dawn greeted the *White Zombie*. He, along with Naro Bon's crewmen up in the rigging, waited for a sign of Bermuda.

Guerin's cunning and patience is far beyond what I gave him credit for, LeSueur decided as he shivered in the cold morning air. Even after extracting the Templar treasures, they lingered near New England, leaving Jimmy Duke and Drake Murray behind for a covert mission. Even after leaving the two trusted officers behind, they lingered in New England for another two months. Just like with the crossing from the Indian Ocean, Guerin made use of every port to send out letters to his mysterious superiors. *Twenty years ago, I thought Guerin fled the continent a beaten man, but even in defeat, he knew how to best his enemies.*

Instead of spotting the island, the call came down from the rigging about spotting a sail. LeSueur strained his eyes to match what was seen, but before he could find it, another call went out spotting a second sail.

The entire crew came to life like an angry nest of ants.

A third call went out before Guerin stepped onto the deck—land.

Seven hundred miles straight west of the continent, Bermuda remained a vital port in Atlantic travel. As the northernmost "Caribbean" island, it had been selected by Guerin as a rendezvous. During the War of Spanish Succession, it had fallen into French and Spanish control for a time, but now it was back in British control as the war wound down in Europe.

In passing, Guerin gave his familiar nod and wink.

We'll see if he's smiling after I tell him.

Now, Guerin pointed to the two ships anchored off the northern tip of Bermuda just as he promised.

The lucky bastard.

The two ships were the *Meliae* and the *Daphne*, both known to senior crew members. The *White Zombie* approached and then anchored. A few hours later, from the port of Hamilton, the *Phoebe* and the *Eurydice* joined them a few miles from the island.

LeSueur knew where they anchored even if no one else, except for Guerin, understood why and where they met. As the five ships came together, LeSueur pulled over the elder member of the crew, Naro Bon.

"Can we trust these people?" LeSueur asked.

"No," Bon answered too quickly. "Luckily, none of them know what's in our hold, do they?"

"Why don't we just sail back to Abyssinia?" LeSueur asked.

"Guerin always has several irons in the fire," Bon said with a shrug. "He befriended Athena while he was still First Mate to Captain Kidd. You know how he is with the ladies."

"Athena?" LeSueur repeated, remembering how close he'd come to death during torture at her hands.

"The only woman captain I know of," Bon said and tapped his temple. "She's some sort of mathematical genius if you can believe it from looking at her. I'm just glad Guerin never replaced me with her. She's a skilled navigator, apparently, who warms a bed even better."

Seeing her boarding the *White Zombie* gave LeSueur chills.

"She's been passed around by several captains until she became a Sylph."

"A Sylph?"

"It's what they call themselves. They all have Huguenot loyalties."

French Protestants—bound together by faith. "They're refugees."

Bon nodded. "The Huguenots back on Tortuga helped hide us after Captain Kidd was arrested, and in turn, Guerin made them promises as only he can."

"What did he promise them?"

"Help. They helped him, so he promised to help them in turn. The poor Huguenots are being crushed between the Catholic nations of Spain and France and the Anglican British Empire. They've no one to protect them from pirates on either side of the war."

"He's giving them some of the treasure?"

"Oh, I hope not. Do you remember our stops at the Gold Coast? He's planning something big, I think. He asks me frequently about the lengths of trips to places all over the globe. Do you know why we've come here? This isn't a safe port for us to linger."

LeSueur knew. Naro Bon deserved an honest answer. November, 1701. He told of his former ship the *Berger* and the escort ship *Nautioneer* departing Fort Maurepas in the new Louisiana Territory, established by his LeMoyne in-laws. Then LeSueur explained how the heavily armed convoy resupplied at Bermuda prior to taking a route-less-traveled back to France. Just as he'd done for men far more powerful than Bon, he told the harrowing tale of how the ship burst into flame and took everything down into the depths of the Atlantic.

"Including the Philosopher's Stone," Bon said, and with raised eyebrows, looked over the edge of the ship.

By noon, LeSueur sat at a table filled with Captains Vincent Galloway, Archibald Vero and Willow Thomas, Wart Jacobs, and Athena McCormack—all criminals yet allies. Also at the table sat Guerin's guests, Josiah Faero and Benjamin Horne.

"While I certainly have important news, I'm curious about any news from Europe," Guerin began. "Particularly from Königsberg Castle?"

Prussia? LeSueur's head hurt as he transitioned from supernatural thoughts about the Ark, ring, and Stone to that of politics."

"Curious you should mention that," Captain Vero coyly added. "I've just returned from a trip to the Baltic Sea and happened to make port in Gdansk."

"You did? Do tell?" Guerin grinned.

"The old Brandenburg Navy is no more," Captain Vero explained. "King Frederick of Prussia, as it is now called, has none of his father's interest in his recently built merchant navy, and even in being a colonial power. His focus on developing an army to contend with his northern rivals required an influx of finance, and he decided to sell off his father's legendary fleet for pennies on the dollar, even the new warships."

"Indeed?" Guerin continued toying. "Who had the resources to make such a purchase?"

Vero shrugged. "No one knows. It's all quite mysterious."

Then Guerin grew serious. "How soon until they arrive in Bermuda?"

A fleet of warships?

"Assuming your envoys safely traveled from Boston to London," Athena McCormack said in reference to Jimmy Duke and Drake Murray's covert mission across the Atlantic, "and assuming your Brandenburg allies were ready to sail, they couldn't possibly arrive for another nine days, but that could be nine weeks also."

"Can you give me ten days?" Guerin finally asked after all the concerns were given.

"Before you arrived, we spotted salvage ships in the area," Wart Jacobs added. "They didn't move when they saw us, but whenever the British Navy showed up, they bolted like scared rabbits."

"Eos ships," Guerin theorized. "Most likely former Madagascar pirates." He turned to LeSueur, adding, "I'd bet your Captain Blackbeard or Dalziel. Hopefully, it was too deep to recover anything of value. What of it?"

Wart Jacobs continued, "We can't just anchor here for ten days. It isn't safe. We're a target for all enemies."

When the Sylph captains hesitated, concerned about being gathered together in one place for too long, Guerin conceded, "Fine. I don't want all of us anchored together like this either. In fact, I'd prefer it if the four of you circled the island at a distance, making sure none of our enemies come from America or from the south. For now, we have time on our side."

They agreed to two weeks.

I shouldn't feel bad about keeping my secret when he keeps plans to himself.

Finally, Guerin did explain the next step. "When our new fleet, the former Brandenburg Navy, eventually arrives under the guidance of Admirals Duke and Murray," he said with a wide grin, "I will accompany Benjamin Horne and the treasure on a return trip to Africa, where I promised Queen Rehena help in ridding her country of the remaining pirates. In my absence, I'll give Charlie command of the *White Zombie*, and with the support of the Sylphs, they will return to Tortuga to await the final stage in the mission."

LeSueur had heard enough. "Final stage?"

"Surely, you must understand why we are meeting in Bermuda. Did you think the quest was over? As long as we have the ring, we can finish this fight with Eos and—"

"The ring will return with me to Abyssinia," Horne insisted.

Guerin shook his head slowly. "That was never part of the deal. I helped recover what was stolen from your country by the Templars. That was the promise I made to you. I only promised the priest that we would use it wisely, which we did and we will."

"It's not your relic. It belongs back at Abuna Yemata Guh."

"It belonged in Jerusalem, but your King Lalibela had no qualms using it to build his "New Israel" did he? I have need of it also. I need it for several reasons, in fact, beginning with a special purpose here in Bermuda."

He expects the ring to retrieve the Philosopher's Stone from the depths. LeSueur exhaled, and even though it was inadvertent, he drew the attention of everyone, including Guerin.

"Is there something you wish to tell us, Charlie?" Guerin asked.

"There is something you need to know," LeSueur said, "but I must tell it to you first in private."

CHAPTER 99

B E R M U D A

1 7 1 2

Louis-Armand Guerin folded his arms as he sat on the edge of the table in his cabin. LeSueur looked back and closed the door.

I thought we had this all sorted out. "What did you do, Bonjean?"

LeSueur shook his head. "No, I first need to understand your intentions."

"My intentions?" Guerin laughed, flashing a bit of anger. "Aren't my intentions obvious?"

"Then be clear. Say them."

"Okay, I intend to find the wreckage of the *Berger*, and once located, use the ring to command the elements, or even the Philosopher's Stone itself, to rise to the surface. They both use the same dark magic even if they do not share the same maker. If the ring can penetrate stone, I don't see why it can't open the depths."

"And then?"

"*My* mission is complete. I came to the continent two decades ago with orders to investigate the rumors of the Stone. I ascertained, and now I mean to acquire."

"You're doing it for your own glory. I don't believe you."

Guerin scoffed. "If there's anyone with credibility issues, it's you, Bear Man. You've been carrying around your secret like it's a warm buffalo hide. I already have a good idea what you're going to tell me."

"Fine, but I do not understand what *you're* hiding," LeSueur said, pacing around the room while Guerin sat in one spot. "Let's say the Philosopher's Stone is resting on the table behind you. What happens next?"

"Are you worried I'll drop you over the side of the ship? Don't be foolish. While I might not have liked either Bonjean or LeSueur, Charlie and I are friends. If the Stone rested on the table, my mission would be over, and I could follow the advice of my friend rather than any oaths I swore to the Periphery."

"Here's what I understand: A phantom fleet is arriving to take Horne and the Ark back where it belongs. Will the Philosopher's Stone go with it?"

He's bluffing, but why? "I suppose that depends on what we find on the ocean floor."

"No, we've already established that it's sitting on the table behind you. Where does it go next?" LeSueur asked.

Guerin talked slowly as if to a child. "The Order of Eos, as we speak, is creating a new Utopia in the American colonies, and down in the Gulf, they've already established a position at the delta of the Mississippi." *Surely he understands the lore surrounding the Low One.*

LeSueur shook his head. "Here's what I don't understand: I publicly failed. I privately failed. I limped back to France with my tail between my legs, having lost a ship, and more important, the Philosopher's Stone to the depths of the Atlantic. The copper vitriol I returned was discredited as worthless, and my public mission to establish a copper mine was viewed with ridicule and—"

"Don't forget that Fort L'Huillier was burned to the ground by the Fox shortly after your departure."

LeSueur looked down. "Despite all of that, I was rewarded with a leadership role in the new colony. Tell me...why was I being rewarded? You seem to have all the answers. Why was I being sent back? Why did you send Chief Gaspar to block the Mississippi?"

Is he daft? Or is this rhetorical? "I suppose there are some who doubt whether you found the Stone."

"No, trust me, it has been found. It's sitting on the table behind you," LeSueur insisted sternly.

Guerin walked around to the other side, feigning that the hypothetical stone was real. "Okay, Charlie, we'll be honest. I'd

consider risking the dangers of bringing it back to Rome or even Abyssinia."

"But you have the might of the Brandenburg Fleet. You can do whatever you want."

"Tempting, yes, but I also know that with the War of Spanish Succession distracting the whole of Europe, now is the right time to strike—if it was right in front of me. Perhaps I'd send the Stone with you, back to Tortuga, where the Sylphs make port while also providing reasonable levels of protection. Once the Ark is returned, I could return with the fleet. Gaspar is already waiting for me in the Louisiana Territory. He's been leading a coalition of Native forces who harass the French forces along the Mississippi and keeping them in a defensive position. When the time is right, Spain will seize control of the gulf."

"Spain?"

"Not truly Spain; it'll be me. The Brandenburg Fleet will be dressed up as Spanish warships."

"So you're not planning on returning to Rome." LeSueur said with a nod. "If you returned with the Brandenburg Fleet, what would you do with this power?"

"While France is trying to surround the English colony, Spain is doing the same thing to France with its colonies in Florida and Mexico. They are allies in a long war that is drawing to an end. By the time any real military forces arrive, we'll be gone, for I'll take the Stone back up the river and finish things before anyone knows better."

"Finish things… " LeSueur repeated and then added. "I cannot allow that."

Is he getting senile in his old age? Surely he understands Eos is after more than just a key.

LeSueur did not act senile, and with narrowed eyes, he asked, "And what if the Philosopher's Stone is not on the table between us? What if it is so deep in the ocean that it can never be found."

"Same plan, different key," Guerin said flippantly. "I need you to understand something. The Order of Eos will not stop. There is no reasoning with them, and there is no snapping them from their religious delusions. Their actions will either hasten the arrival of the fires of the End Times or shatter the prophecy, delivering the world into the hands of a risen deity. Neither of those options sound pleasant, do they? While securing the Philosopher's Stone would certainly thwart their immediate plans, they would find another way. But just like I've emptied their vault, I mean to empty a tomb."

"Whose tomb?"

"It depends on who you ask. The Hebrews, the Phoenicians, the Priory, the Jesuits, the Chippewa—

"The Dakota," LeSueur added bitterly.

"Even Horne and the Abyssinians have a name for it…him. Eos seeks the tomb of one they refer to as Surtur's Bane. It's a bit complicated, but they believe they can resurrect or unearth this…buried god who will lead them into a rebirth of humanity. With either Solomon's ring or the Philosopher's Stone, we could help dig up this crusty corpse and steal him away from our enemies before they can, uh, wake him."

"And how would they wake him?"

Guerin swallowed hard. "Professor Faero and I worry it has something to do with the Odin Stone, which contains a spell, verses, some sort of…song. You saw how the ring and shamir responded. The Philosopher's Stone is much more powerful than either."

"The Philosopher's Stone never left the Land of the Blue Woman."

It felt as if LeSueur had scooped out his other eye. Guerin grimaced in pain. A decade earlier, he would have killed LeSueur for the lie, but now, he knew LeSueur to be something special. "So you're telling me there's nothing on this table," Guerin calmly said.

"I carried a locked chest along with barges of vitriol from the mine," LeSueur explained. "One look at the vitriol was all it took to convince the LeMoynes. I waited until we were to Bermuda before I personally sabotaged the ship."

"Why?"

"I had to protect Wenonah from the Order of Eos and the Priory of Ormus. I wanted them to believe it was at the bottom of the Atlantic. I wanted them to think all was lost."

Guerin let out a long groan. "The Periphery would have come to your aid. Wait, wait…you left it with the Sioux?"

"The priest back at Abuna Yemata Guh was right…the Stone was evil. I couldn't put it back and I didn't want to leave it with her people to see it poison their hearts. So we did something not even Newton would suspect. We willingly gave it to the Fox Indians to protect."

"So you have no idea where the Philosopher's Stone is right now?" Guerin asked.

LeSueur shook his head. "It was a shortsighted plan to keep her safe, but I had to trust it was the right thing to do."

This certainly changes things, Guerin decided. "I might have underestimated your cunning, LeSueur. Well played. Well played indeed."

CHAPTER 100

L A N D   O F   T H E   B L U E   W O M A N

1 7 1 2

Wenonah shivered in the dark. Her buffalo blanket had slid off of her legs as she slept, and winter's chill kept her from returning to sleep. Now fifty, she slept alone without child or husband to help keep her warm. It'd already been two years since her husband White Raven died, and both her boys had grown up and taken wives, leaving her surrounded by a new family but still cold at night.

At night, she felt old—when dreams and memories of countless winters came back to her. Instead of hoping for sleep to return, she dressed and stepped out of her teepee. Her family camped at the base of Bear Lodge, a solitary butte on the north-eastern edge of the Black Hills. It had been her home since her father Wapasha gave her to White Raven in 1689. Their camp was nestled into the base of the mountain, sheltering them from the north wind. A canopy of stars filled the night sky, and glancing east, she saw not even the faintest glow of dawn yet.

A walk will help. A walk will warm my body and clear my mind.

Even though as a Mdewakanton—a Dweller of Spirit Lake— she'd been born alongside water, she now considered herself a Blackfoot Lakota, dwelling in the shadow of Inyan, the god who gave his life to form the stone foundations for mankind. Of all the tribes, bands, and camps of the mighty Seven Council Fires, her new family belonged to a long line of priests and philosophers known as the Five Lodges. Pilgrims from lake, forest, river, and plain came to their home for spiritual guidance and to pray atop the great stony butte.

Even in the dark hour before dawn, her feet knew the path to the top of the mountain.

By the time she sat down upon its ragged top, she once again felt the heat of youth pulsing through her veins. Even though her heart and lungs were agitated by the exertion, her mind was clear.

LeSueur needs my prayers.

Looking up at the expansive cosmos, she stared at the constellation that held so many meanings. To Pierre-Charles LeSueur, the seven stars represented the Great Bear, Ursa Major. To the people who waged war upon her eastern brothers, the seven stars represented the Chippewa hero of the Fisher Cat, who dared to battle the evil sorcerer known as the Wintermaker. To her people, the seven stars were Tun Win, the Blue Woman. As a child, she knew her star was the top right and that somewhere far to the left—across the Great Plains—the seventh star was the Lakota people. Now, she not only understood all seven stars of the Blue Woman, but she also understood the reason she was blue.

She fell in love with LeSueur the first moment she laid eyes upon him, for it was as if the Great Spirit had shaped the perfect man and dropped him onto earth as her rescuer. The Serpent Star appeared in the heavens to announce the arrival of the Wishwee, manifested in the form of a modest woods runner named Pierre-Charles LeSueur. Yet fate had torn the two lovers apart after she brought him to see the place where the earth bled blue. After a decade apart, fate had brought both of them together again, and this time, she was his rescuer. The French miners might've unearthed the sacred White Egg known to LeSueur as the Philosopher's Stone, but only her Bear Man could hold it without being burned—confirmation he was indeed the Wishwee.

But the white stone swirled red with cursed blood, a sign of its evil presence.

Some wanted to put it back in the ground.

Others wanted to take it west, to keep it away from the Chippewa.

LeSueur even offered to throw it into the Atlantic Ocean—to protect her and White Raven's children.

"No," she'd told him. "I agree that we cannot put it back into the ground. My husband is right about it being a weapon, but the Serpent Star has left, and you are no longer a young man. The elders at Bear Lodge felt the Serpent Star would bring a series of prophets to us until the time came for the final prophet, who would face No Soul."

"I thought I was supposed to face No Soul," LeSueur had said since he'd been able to handle the fire of the stone. "I'm the Wishwee, right?"

"You are one of the Wishwee. It was your destiny to unearth the stone, but to destroy it or throw it into the ocean would rob another of his destiny. If No Soul must be faced, we must make sure everything is in order when the time is right."

"I don't understand. If you don't want me facing No Soul, if you don't want to bury it, if you don't want to take it west, then what is your plan?"

"Isn't it clear what must happen?" Wenonah asked. "All nations have a part to play in this prophecy. For generations, the Seven Council Fires have guarded it. For generations, your people have searched the globe for it until you…unearthed it. For generations, the Chippewa have pressed west searching for it."

"We can't give it to the Chippewa; they are currently allies with Eos," LeSueur insisted.

"I agree with you—this White Egg is evil, and thus, I will not let my husband White Raven take it back to infect my children with its darkness. There is only one nation who is the enemy of all."

LeSueur scoffed. "The Fox?"

Wenonah had been a slave of the Meskwaki when LeSueur freed her. "By putting it into the hands of the Meskwaki, we will be putting our trust and faith into the hands of the Great Spirit. The last appearance of the Serpent Star signaled the end of an era for my people, who will no longer guard over this evil spirit."

LeSueur pondered her plan for a few minutes. "And you think another Wishwee will come?"

"When the Serpent Star returns, the Great Spirit will summon another Wishwee to do his will. We must trust in his plans."

"My enemies know I've found it here," LeSueur insisted. "They will destroy the Fox, Chippewa, and Sioux to find it."

"Then they must continue to believe you have it. You will pack it up in the eyes of many, you will load it onto your barges, you will take it personally down the Mississippi River, you will load it onto your ships in front of your enemies, and then, in the eyes of all, you will cast it into the Atlantic Ocean."

LeSueur shook his hands. "But all the while, it will be in the hands of the Meskwaki."

"Will you return?" Wenonah had asked.

LeSueur slowly shook his head. "These people will most likely kill me when they learn the truth, but if I can give you time to raise your children in a world free of evil, then…it will be worth whatever happens to me."

IS MY BEAR MAN still alive? Wenonah now wondered, staring up at the stars. At the foot of the butte, her sons would soon raise a new generation. *How much time has he given us?*

Somewhere in the cosmos, hidden behind the bright stars, the Serpent Star slithered into its dark hole, destined to return again.

But what form will the Wishwee take?

Will my grandchildren and great-grandchildren recognize him?

CHAPTER 101

A storm answered the prayers of Chief Bakinis. It rolled in from the north, bringing billowing thunderheads and fierce lightning from Lake Huron. Although a foreigner to the region known as Michigan, Bakinis knew his Chippewa forefathers had once inhabited the place they called Waawiyegamaa but was now known by the French as Detroit, or *the straits*. Although an old man well over sixty, Bakinis had gathered his most loyal warriors from distant Mooningwanekaaning, or Madeline Island as the French called it, to retrace the steps his people had taken on the Seven Fires migration.

Thank you, Great Spirit, for calling your Thunderbird to my aid. Your will be done...

For almost three weeks, Chief Bakinis and his band of fifty warriors waited on the large island at the mouth of the Detroit River, where Round Lake drained into Waabishkiigoo-Gichigami, or Lake Erie. The thunder of gunfire and cannon to the south came from several hundred warriors from the Ottawa and Potawatomi who fought alongside the French in a great battle against the Meskwaki tribe just five miles away.

Wiyipisiw, his youngest son, entered the shelter. His face was painted black—a sign he wanted to join in the slaughter of their enemies. "The Fox are finished. If we joined our forces with our Anishinaabe brothers, we could rout them."

"It is not my destiny to share glory with lesser men," Bakinis muttered. "I will trust the path set before me."

"If the Fox are defeated tonight," Wiyipisiw pressed, "the glory will go to the unfaithful. Where will that leave us?"

"Perhaps we are suffering dark times to be tested," Bakinis countered. "My faith has been rewarded. By returning to the Third Stopping Place, we will find what has been lost."

"The Sacred Shell?" Wiyipisiw asked.

So my obstinate son does listen to me. "No. Do you know why the Meskwaki went to war against the French?"

"The Red-Earthers are inbred fools," Wiyipisiw scoffed.

Bakinis knew better than his son. The Meskwaki were not only fierce warriors but also were iron-willed men when motivated. Two months ago, Chief Lamyma and Chief Pemoussa brought a great force to Fort Detroit to lay siege to the new fort and cast out the foreigners. Something emboldened them. Something gave them confidence that they could produce a miracle.

And I suspect what they possess.

"They might be fools, but they are also deeply religious," Bakinis continued. "Before you were born, when I was still a young man, a strange star appeared in the sky. The Meskwaki saw it as a sign to return to their homelands. Our people refused to listen to me, and instead, chose to listen to the French traders. The faith of the Meskwaki was rewarded, though, and rumor reached my ear that the star delivered to them a sacred treasure from the days of the Dawn—the original Water Drum."

"From the story of the Seven Grandfathers? The story of how the Old Man used it to heal the boy on the brink of death?"

Wiyipisiw remembers the stories I told him. "The story I told you explained how the Old Man created the Midewiwin lodge to honor the Creator. His faith in creating the Lodge and the Water Drum did indeed save the boy's life, but he did not create the original Water Drum. He only honored what was once used to create physical and spiritual life."

"Are you saying the Fox found the *original* Water Drum?" Wiyipisiw asked with wonder.

"It gave them confidence to overthrow the French, but it is not the destiny of the Meskwaki to use the Water Drum in the era of the Seventh Fire."

"That right belongs to the Wijigan Clan," Wiyipisiw finished.

THE ALCHEMIST'S RING

For generations, since the time when the Anishinaabe dwelt along the Great Water known as the Atlantic, the Wijigan Clan served the prophecy given to the boy-hero Iyash, who was visited by several prophets after a visit to a remote island. His faith led the People from the coast to Mooniyaang, now the French city of Montreal. Bakinis meant to keep the faith of his forefathers.

"I believe the prophets that visited our ancestors generations ago wanted us to find the Water Drum, so that in the era of the Seventh Fire, we can help restore the world to what it was meant to be. Our people might have found the Seventh Stopping Place far to the west, but it won't matter if we don't have the tools needed to save humanity. I've prayed for most of my life for answers, and in my darkest hour, I discovered that I needed to retrace the path we took. It was never our destiny to defeat the Sioux in open war, and my faith meant leaving our friends and family, but here, at the Third Stopping Place, the Great Creator is about to reward my trust."

"How did the Fox end up with our Water Drum?"

Bakinis shook his head. "It never belonged to us. The current Water Drums of the Midewiwin are made of deer hide, wood, tobacco, hoop, hair, and stone, but the original Water Drum was most likely formed by Manabozho himself when the god walked in the form of a man upon the earth. It was not crafted by human hand. The Sioux described it as a white egg."

"And eggs are symbols of creation," Wiyipisiw added.

Perhaps he will make a great Wijigan priest after all. "The prophecies describe a young boy who led the people to the proper path. I will put my trust in the Great Spirit—and in you."

"You honor me, father. What do you want me to do?"

Shortly after the Meskwaki began their siege of Fort Detroit, an alliance of Ottawa and Potawatomi came to the aid of the local Huron and Petun, who'd been granted the area in the 1701 Treaty of Montreal. Chief Bakinis and his Wijigan warriors also arrived but remained hidden upon the island several miles from the fighting.

Now they would end the fight.

"After nineteen days of fighting, the Meskwaki will use the cover of the storm to flee. Their only path to escape is north, where you will be waiting in ambush.

Wiyipisiw nodded obediently but his eyes filled with worry. "What do I do if I…find the…the Water Drum?"

"If the Creator determines for you to have it, then we will return west and defeat the Sioux together."

CHAPTER 102

B E R M U D A

1 7 1 2

Louis-Armand Guerin stood upon the deck of a German ship legally owned by the Netherlands, commissioned by the Italian-based Periphery, and currently flying Spanish flags.

The *Nau de Refuerzo*—the *Reinforcer.*

Standing upon his new ship, Guerin indeed felt reinforced for the first time in more than two decades. He didn't know the new crew, but he knew where they'd come from.

With Bermuda buttoned up and ready for an unexpected invasion, the two small fleets took their time off the coast of the island.

I have enough firepower to claim this island for myself, he decided as he took measure of the Sylphs as well as the ten new warships. *Am I making a mistake by not attacking?*

Beside him were Murray and Duke, both now familiar with the new crew after spending months with them while the *White Zombie* hid in Canada. Drake Murray now captained a ship he dubbed the *Son of the Sea,* a reference to a Celtic sea god; Jimmy Duke captained another warship he dubbed the *Mary Dyer,* a reference to a relative who'd been hanged in Boston.

Climbing aboard, Benjamin Horne and the last of his original gunners followed the large wooden crate as it was lifted onto the deck. Unlike the rest of the smaller, more agile warships of the fleet, the *Reinforcer* was a 300-ton cargo ship, which now took on the cargo of an emptied vault.

The Ark of the Covenant—or one of the arks—is going home. Who truly knows?

None of them were foolish enough to directly touch or open it—a task left for Horne and the Ethiopian priests.

Fifty yards away, Pierre-Charles LeSueur stood with crossed arms on the captain's deck of the *White Zombie*. Beside him, Professor Faero, having been told of his part in the impending Mississippi River Expedition, nervously paced.

The rest of the old crew—Dr. Barrow, Naro Bon, Papa Bones, Manuel Del Torro, and Giovanni Naufragio—also stood at the *White Zombie's* railing, waiting for the transport skiffs to return. They'd all wait back on Tortuga, and upon Guerin's return, they'd begin the final mission to the Upper Mississippi River.

Murray barked out orders for securing the cargo, and soon Duke gave his orders also. They were staying with Guerin. Several thousand miles of Atlantic Ocean remained until they reached the tip of Africa, followed by another four thousand miles past the scene of the crime in Madagascar.

Will Rehena still be there?

When the anchor came up and the ship began to drift, Guerin gave a hearty wave to the *White Zombie*.

In turn, the crew affectionately dropped their drawers, slapping their cheeks as they mooned their former captain.

LeSueur saluted with a smirk.

Will I ever see them again?

THE END OF PART SIX

PART SEVEN

A GENERAL HISTORY
OF PYRATES

PART SEVEN

CHAPTER 103

T O R T U G A   I S L A N D

1 7 1 3

Each morning, Pierre-Charles LeSueur brewed a pot of Ethiopian coffee, spent half-an-hour sharpening his ax blade, and then for an hour, transformed himself back into Paul Bonjean, lumberjack of the Great Lakes by chopping wood. Compared to the pine forests of the great north, the wood was spongy and soft, but it relented nevertheless.

By noon, he dragged back the timber that Naufragio would transform into a new facet of their little colony of religious refugees. Except for Papa Bones, who saw everything through the lens of Voodoo, all the men found it easy to take on the guise of being religious refugees instead of pirates—they'd seen enough. Young women took an interest in the younger crewmen, but LeSueur frightened them, which left him with only dreams of Wenonah.

On occasion, thoughts of Marguerite filled his mind, especially thoughts of his children. Knowing his blood contained the ancestry of both sinner and saint, he thought about ways of forgiving her. Time also let him realize his true love had always been Wenonah.

Tell yourself a lie enough times and it becomes true, LeSueur decided as he watched the men make homes for themselves, losing bits of their former selves every day they lingered.

LeSueur's blade remained immaculate as he waited for a final chance at redemption.

No, I will not marry again. Father Marquette swore an oath to chastity, and because of me, his life was cut short. I'll finish his oath—and the oath I swore to Wenonah.

He'd loved two very different women, and unlike the rest of his restless crew, he had no room in his heart for a third.

Each day, after exhausting himself chopping down trees, he'd sit in his hammock and picture Guerin and Horne sailing the open seas. More recently, he'd mentally retraced his trip through Abyssinia.

It would be another year before Guerin returned—*if he returns.* Spending his final years on a Caribbean Island would content him, but Guerin needed to finish his fight with Eos, which meant LeSueur needed to protect both Wenonah and Marguerite in the days to come.

So one day, standing along the beach that faced the larger island of Hispaniola, he broke routine. With his ax on his shoulder, he just stared out into the waters.

Dr. Barrow joined him.

"Something troubling you? The children came to me saying you'd been like this for almost an hour."

"Something's not right," LeSueur said flatly.

"Are we talking weather, digestion, or something more nefarious?" Barrow asked.

"I just feel the hairs on the back of my neck rising, like I'm in danger, but I don't know where it's coming from. I've been watching the port, and I saw a Sylph ship depart just like clockwork."

"If you're worried about Guerin, I can assure you he'll find a way back to us...or we live happily ever after on this island. Is that so bad?"

"No, my worries lie to the northwest. We've been out of contact with Gaspar for far too long."

"He's waging a campaign of terror upriver. And it's working. The Natchez allies he's made are blocking the French from going up either the Mississippi River or the Alabama. You heard Captain Galloway—he made contact as recently as three summers ago. Are you really worried about him or something else?"

"I can't stay here any longer. This foreboding feeling is overwhelming. I should investigate. I can scout ahead, see what is happening, and if possible, make contact."

"It sounds reasonable," Dr. Barrow said. "Guerin left the *White Zombie* behind for a reason. But you should speak to Captain Johnson about it." Barrow slapped LeSueur's shoulder and winked at the irony of his complaint.

TWO WEEKS LATER, a partial crew of the *White Zombie* sailed past the delta of the Mississippi River. LeSueur gave Del Torro command of the settlement. Josiah Faero, Dr. Barrow, and Naufragio remained in Tortuga in case Guerin returned unexpectedly soon. From information gathered by the Sylphs, the settlements of Mobile and Fort Maurepas remained only a few hundred souls.

While there were no stories of Marguerite LeSueur, he did receive news of a Madame Langlois, a widowed cousin of the LeMoyne family.

She's dead to me, just as I am dead to her, he decided.

His former in-law, D'Iberville, had died several years earlier, but another of the LeMoyne brothers, Joseph—now Lord Bienville, inherited the French Colony.

Which means the Order of Eos remains.

Naro Bon approached, studying the sketched map given to him by the Sylphs marking where they secretly met Gaspar. "There will be two more small rivers, very close to each other, before we reach 'Marsh Island' as it is called. At the rate we're going, we could be there tomorrow."

"But?"

Bon hesitated. "Nothing. I'd just love to sail up that river. I've been mapping the earth my entire life. I've heard so much about the Riviere Espiritus Sanctus, the Mississippi, that I'd love to see how far we could sail up."

"It's a death trap," LeSueur explained. "The French use their Choctaw allies; the British use their Chickasaw allies, and Gaspar sabotages them all. LaSalle couldn't sail down from the north, and Bienville can't go up from the south. Until war sorts it all out, we will need Gaspar's help getting us upstream. Besides, a ship this large wouldn't get far. The Mississippi drains an entire continent, and sandbars and mudflats would stop you quickly."

"Even so, I'd love to see where Chief Gaspar commands the Natchez forces. I'm working on a map of the region."

"Believe me, it probably is more subdued in reality than in your imagination," LeSueur chuckled.

NARO BON'S CALCULATIONS were correct, and by the next afternoon, they'd sailed past Two Deltas and found Marsh Island guarding Vermillion Bay.

LeSueur certainly didn't expect to find an old friend camped on the island, nor did he expect to find several of his Natchez companions.

Bon pointed and asked, "Do you know this white man?

LeSueur held his gaze until he was certain. "Yes, but it's been a dozen years. I can't believe he's still alive." Saying those words suddenly made him worry about Gaspar, who was nowhere to be seen.

Andre Penicaut stood but didn't wave.

CHAPTER 104

*W*hy *didn't he go back east?* Pierre-Charles LeSueur asked himself. *What is Penicaut doing in Louisiana?*

"This could be a trap," Naro Bon said as LeSueur strapped his ax to his back in order to climb down the rope netting to the dingy below.

"If he's here instead of Gaspar, something has gone terribly wrong," LeSueur snapped.

"Don't you see the grave markers?" Bon asked. "It could be the plague."

"Penicaut is here to warn the Periphery about something happening on the frontier. This isn't a trap. The trap has likely already been sprung."

LeSueur checked the horizon one more time before handing the looking glass to Naro Bon and climbing into the dinghy.

Penicaut anticipated the Periphery, but he didn't anticipate me.

Fourteen years earlier, the young carpenter had only been a teenage boy begging for a job. At the time, LeSueur juggled the interests of the Priory and Eos as he loaded a ship full of miners whom he'd taken deep into the frontier. In the end, Penicaut had been his only true ally, and after saving LeSueur from the men in his expedition party, LeSueur in turn saved Penicaut from the flames of Chief Keoxa's pyres. Together with Wenonah, they crafted the lie: months after LeSueur descended the Mississippi with barges of vitriol and an empty chest, Penicaut began spreading false reports of a Fox Indian attack upon Fort L'Huillier.

"I thought you died from smallpox in Cuba," Penicaut said once he recognized him.

"I thought the Meskwaki took your scalp," LeSueur countered.

"It's hard to believe anything you hear these days," Penicaut teased. He had a ragged beard and filth that grew upon his skin and clothing like lichen on a tree, but the eyes were the same inquisitive ones that begged to be brought to the New World.

"Are these Gaspar's allies?" LeSueur asked as the dinghy made ground on the small island.

"He told me the Periphery sent allies to this island at certain times during the year. I just didn't expect it to be you."

"Louis-Armand, um, the Baron of Lahontan…we've found common cause. The allies you speak of are the Sylph pirates of Tortuga. They are my allies now. Anything you would have told them you can tell me."

"Gaspar and the Natchez suffered a stunning defeat," Penicaut answered. "These Natchez men witnessed it. Gaspar and his Natchez war party, surrounded by several pirate ships that fired upon the river from the sea, were ambushed as they passed through the Mississippi Delta. Those who weren't killed were captured and taken as slaves upon the ships."

"Including Gaspar?" LeSueur asked.

"We returned after the ships left and gathered the dead here to receive a proper burial. Gaspar was not found amongst the dead, which is why I—"

"Came to warn the Sylphs." LeSueur finished. *If they have Gaspar, they can learn about Tortuga and Guerin's plans.*

"I can tell from your expression that my instincts were correct. Are our affairs in the Caribbean in danger?"

"They are," LeSueur answered, feeling rage growing within him. "Did the Natchez identify the men who took Gaspar prisoner?"

Andre Penicaut repeated the question to the Natchez survivors. One pointed to his groin and the others added their observations. "One ship flew a, uh, penis on its flag. That was the ship that attacked first. The man who commanded them was a large fellow with a large black beard, and on his flag, he had a skull over two crossed bones."

Blackbeard. It's the man I faced in Madagascar.

"The other ships had a red and blue crest with three—

"The LeMoyne crest," LeSueur finished. "I know it well."

"So I gathered," Penicaut said with a slight chuckle. "I trust you'll get word to Baron Lahontan and the Periphery."

"Where are you going?"

"To help the Natchez regroup. Eos is sure to take advantage and secure all of the Louisiana Territory. I will return to help those in need. Your family believes you are dead."

"Keep it that way," LeSueur said. *I doubt if I'll be able to ever return to either Wenonah or Marguerite now. My men are in danger back on Tortuga.* "Stick to the narrative also. Tell the world I sailed down the river with the vitriol"

Penicaut shook his hand vigorously. "It'll be an honor to tell your story, even if we're the only ones who know the truth."

Wenonah knows. So do all my friends.

Once LeSueur parted ways and returned to the *White Zombie*, he privately told Naro Bon about their need to make haste.

I only hope it's not too late.

CHAPTER 105

CANAL DE TORTUE

1713

Edward Drummond double-checked the strait with his looking glass just to confirm what his eyes told him.

One, two, three, four.

I see you.

All four ships had returned to protect the settlements on Tortuga, unaware of his trap. "Raise the black!"

Moments later, the familiar black skull smiled down upon him with the two thigh bones crisscrossing behind it.

An ancient calling card, Drummond remembered, *and a declaration of our intentions.* Back when Eos wore the cloaks of the Templar Knights, the skull represented the lost king from the lost kingdom far beyond the Atlantic. Newton had known this when his Black Fleet flew the headless flag. Now, he flew the head to remind his enemies of their true pursuit.

For years, the Flying Sylphs, as they were known, had avoided the authorities by using tactics shared by insects and vermin—scattering to the darkness. Smaller and more elusive than the predatory warships that hunted them, they never got into a fight they could not win. Because of this, they ruled the area for the better part of a decade.

Now I will rule these seas.

For the past two days, Drummond kept his own warship anchored and hidden twenty miles from the canal behind a peninsula. Thanks to his deceitful partnership with Newton, he captained one of the finest warships in the Caribbean, and the sight of it would cause any fleet to piss down their legs and run.

The *Pretender* slowly built speed as it caught a westerly breeze, and the crew, with a hired boarding party of another fifty men, began to work themselves into a frothy bloodlust.

They've spotted us, Drummond confirmed as anchors raised and sails dropped. *All four will now scatter in different directions.*

He licked his lips, the little bit of tenderness not covered by his massive black beard. Like a Nazarite, he'd neither touched alcohol nor let a blade touch him since the ordeal in Madagascar. He swore to not cut it again until Eos returned to power in England. Although far from Catholic, Eos had the ear of the Catholic kings until the recent coup supported by the Priory of Ormus, who supported the Protestant William, Prince of Orange. Thanks to the Priory, rumors went out that James Francis Edward Stewart, dubbed the Pretender, was an imposter for the real prince who died at birth. While Queen Anne, James's half-sister, now ruled, the rightful king lived in exile. Before that wrong could be righted, Drummond needed to win the Caribbean. His Eos masters in Montreal, Boston, and Philadelphia gave him one purpose—terror.

I am an instrument of death, he reminded himself as his anxious hands found their way to two of the six pistol handles strapped to his chest. His belt, which held multiple scabbards, was supported by leather suspenders that passed over his shoulders.

His jaw dropped when one of the Sylphs, the smallest, turned her nose toward the *Pretender.* The others had already made a fatal blunder, unaware that his small flotilla of gunboats and fire ships was stretching across the eastern end of the canal from Anse a Foleur and St. Louis du Nord.

"Cannons ready," he barked even though the blade of war was already sharp and waiting.

A suicide mission, he thought as the single ship headed toward his powerful warship. In reality, the truest danger came from the other side of the canal. After the success of crushing the Natchez in the Delta, Drummond's men now had confidence in the newest battle plan. A net of small ships continued to fill the four-mile gap between Haiti and Tortuga. Relying on rowers instead of sails, the vessels took only a few minutes to assemble. Already, the sharpshooters were picking off men from the rigging while rowers in lit fire ships began placing themselves in the path of the ships, with buoys extended that would snag the bow of a ship.

The single Sylph fired its small forecanons. Normally used in chase, the smaller cannonballs could disable a rudder. Today, they simply bounced off the thick hull of the *Pretender*.

Still she advanced.

"Let her have a volley," Drummond said, studying the ship for identification. He'd been patient with this plan, gathering up information about this elusive enemy before attacking its base.

Thunder, smoke, and splintered wood filled the air, and by the time it settled, the *Eurydice* had taken a new course, angling toward the shore of Tortuga. *Captained by the sea bitch, Athena McCormack.*

By now, he knew the other three captains as well. Vincent Galloway captained the *Meliae*, Archibald Vero captained the *Daphne*, and Wart Jacobs captained the *Phoebe*. "Fire again, hit her ass!" Drummond said when he saw her exposed rudder.

As the *Eurydice* tacked to the north, Drummond adjusted his own approach. The three other Sylphs still didn't understand the danger of the small ships. Even if they did fight their way through the tangle, Joseph LeMoyne and his other allied warships were positioned off the coast of Turks and Caicos, and when the plume of smoke rose into the air, they would advance, crushing any final resistance. For the past few years, he'd avoided direct contact with any of the Sylphs, so they didn't know they were being hunted. After capturing the leader of the Natchez, he knew he needed to root out the Sylphs next.

Now I've got them.

The brazenness of the *Eurydice* caught his men off guard. "What are you waiting for? Fire!"

The first cannon missed, a signal to the captain of the *Eurydice* to do the unthinkable—she reversed course and pointed her bow right back toward the *Pretender*.

Drummond laughed at the foolish bravery being shown. *Does she think she can ram us?*

"Ready the boarding parties!" Drummond bellowed, and the hired mercenaries echoed his barbaric yawp. He snatched up a handful of fuses and stuck them into his beard, personal motiva-

tion to drench himself in the blood of his enemy before the fuses ignited his beard.

The vanguard, grappling hooks ready, rushed to the port side of the ship.

The cannons tore into the *Eurydice*, and her sails dropped unexpectedly. *She's ready to fight to the death, apparently.*

"She's dropped her drawers, boys. This is it!"

His gunners made quick work of her mast even as momentum kept her streaming toward them under full speed.

Drummond glanced back to the east. His swarm of fire ants were already on one of the three ships, and the doom they posed made itself known to the others. But it was too late. Changing course meant getting entangled.

He glanced back to the *Eurydice*, a small, hardnosed ship whose hull remained solid despite damage to the rigging. *Which will change when we get her broadside.*

"Put us alongside her," Drummond said to his navigator. He began to descend the stairs to the cheers of his vanguard.

He'd no sooner reached the bottom stair than the *Eurydice* sharpened her turn, directly at their own nose. A volley of cannon fire sent up a cloud of smoke, but by the time it cleared, her intentions were known.

Drummond rushed back up the stairs, but he was too slow.

The *Eurydice* struck his *Pretender* cheek-to-cheek, and the mass and momentum of collision nearly bounced the smaller ship out of the water and knocked her back several feet.

The vanguard, unaware of the brilliance of the physics, cast lines immediately, and when she hit, those closest, about eight men, jumped ship.

The impact to the nose took the momentum of the smaller ship and effortlessly turned the nose of the *Pretender* away from the impact, while simultaneously, the *Eurydice* absorbed the momentum of the larger ship, pushing her away in opposite angles.

Like billiard balls, they bounced in opposite directions in such a violent manner that the men at the grappling hooks either flew off the deck or had their riggings explode in splinters before their eyes.

A woman captain appeared, correcting the rudder and firing a pistol directly at him.

By the time Drummond reached the top of the deck, the *Euryd-ice* not only slipped behind him but she also revealed what was under her skirts——a second main mast. Although smaller, the dropped rigging quickly rose back upon the undamaged mast.

Giving chase would allow the other three sylphs a means to escape.

Drummond roared as he had to let her go. His net was meant to catch a bigger fish.

Because of his poor choices with the *Eurydice,* he wouldn't get as close to the others.

He'd pivot in the channel and blast away at the other three ships with his cannons.

The giant wasn't on board, he reminded himself. *Which means he's either on one of the other three ships, or he's waiting on shore.*

Where are you, LeSueur?

I'll put you in the grave for good.

CHAPTER 106

T O R T U G A

1 7 1 3

From the shore of Tortuga Island, Manuel Del Torro suddenly wished for someone to bark out orders. Captain Guerin and then LeSueur left him in charge of the crew and settlement. Not knowing what to do, he stood in front of the cabins, watching in spellbound horror as a line of fire ships ensnared their allies.

Captain Galloway's *Meliae* snagged and burned on the eastern end of the canal as the crew battled flames and flocks of small boats that boarded her.

Captain Wart Jacob's *Phoebe* managed to avoid the snares, but with its momentum stalled, it took on heavy fire from the smaller vessels coming from the shore.

Now, the big warship that came from the west began blasting away at Captain Vero's *Daphne* as it turned toward the lesser of two evils.

What have I done?

A week earlier, they'd caught two spies, who gave vague answers about their purpose upon the island. Alarmed, and without Guerin or LeSueur, Del Torro sent word across the canal to the mainland of Hispaniola that the Sylphs needed to return for a possible extraction from the island. The four captains answered his call—to their demise.

"We need gun crews on the beach!" he barked to both crewmen and villagers. "Keep these bastards from landing."

Captain Vero angled sharply toward Tortuga and the settlement, and with it came the big warship, the *Pretender,* closer to shore also. *It's the ambush ship from Madagascar. It's Blackbeard.*

"On my mark!" Del Torro, finally taking charge, shouted.

Hidden behind trees and shelter, his snipers waited for the *Pretender* to come within range. With miles of shoreline looking the same, he had no idea that Vero drew him into a vice. The *Daphne* traded punches with the larger ship, but its rigging was cut to tatters and the two ships drew closer to intercept.

"Ready on the canons!"

Hidden in the center of the village, two shore-mounted cannons faced the water, and as the *Daphne* slid in front of them, the nose of the *Pretender* came into view.

Scattered gunshots filled the air.

"Hold!" Del Torro repeated as the scene worsened by the second.

Far off in the distance, the thunder of canons intensified as three other warships blasted away from the opposite side of the right.

As the *Daphne* slid by the shore and past Blackbeard's *Pretender,* another Eos warship entered the western side of the canal, blasting away at Vero.

Shrieks filled the trees, and for a moment, Del Torro turned away from the naval battle. Dozens of hazel-skinned warriors came running down the hill toward the camp, each with a hatchet in his hand. *Where did they come from?* The gunshots he'd heard came from the men closest to the unexpected swarm.

The canons of the *Pretender* opened fire, not to create damage but instead to direct the swarm of invaders to the beach.

Del Torro lifted a rifle to his shoulder and fired, hitting one of the bare chested maniacs rushing toward him. Before the cloud of smoke even cleared, three more filled the space.

He grabbed his pistol.

Why? Why? Where did these men come from? All around him, dozens of alien attackers swept over the village. Dr. Barrow wrestled one to the ground. Giovanni Naufragio turned to run but was quickly chopped down by a hatchet.

Del Torro squeezed the trigger and turned the face of the closest attacker to a red pulp. Then two other men, in a full run, knocked him off his feet. His hand reached down to his belt and as he rolled, he punched at the muscular solar plexus of the nearest man.

The other attacker swung a hatchet, which crushed a rib but proved ineffective against his thick leather vest. Del Torro tried to stab down into the man's neck, but hands intercepted.

Fingers fought fingers, and in the struggle for control of the blade, Del Torro realized it was ten to five. His attacker only had a stump for a right hand, all the fingers had been cut off. In fact, every attacker wielded the hatchets with their left hands.

Slaves, Del Torro realized as his own blade began to turn. *It's an army of slaves.*

His arms were no match for the strong arms of the slave, who pressed down on the hilt of the blade with his full weight. At first, the tip of the knife caused his whole body to convulse, but about the time he was ready to surrender to his fate, a pistol fired, splattering him with his attacker's hot blood.

Professor Faero extended a hand, pulling Del Torro to his feet.

And then they were running with a swarm of attackers on their heels.

CHAPTER 107

Pierre-Charles LeSueur rushed to the prow of the *White Zombie* as soon as land was spotted, and now, as the island of Tortuga loomed larger in his scope, he studied the shore closely.

He risked the threat of the Spanish over his other enemies and spent the whole night sailing around the northern shore of Cuba, which was eighty miles from the northwestern corner of Hispaniola and the island of Tortuga.

He'd already weighed the implications of Gaspar's capture—including the demise of the entire plan to send an expedition back up the Mississippi. *Eos will learn we had a staging area.*

Nothing hid along the open northern shore of Tortuga, but in the canal, it could be another story.

"Prepare the ship for a quick change of course," LeSueur said to Naro Bon. "We need just a peek into the canal, and if necessary, to bounce right back toward the tail end of Cuba. Do you understand?"

Naro Bon nodded and rushed back to the wheel.

Be careful. Had he brought the full crew, he could both sail and defend, but without the manpower or Benjamin Horne's experience, the *White Zombie* was all but toothless. *I just need to spot where the danger lurks.*

LeSueur's scope turned from the northern shore to the western point. Unlike the lush greenery of the rest of the island, the western point had almost an orange hue as waves peeled away all the topsoil and revealed the jagged underbelly of the orange limestone bedrock. At the extreme end of the peninsula, a large boulder had a peculiar-looking anomaly protruding from it.

As they grew closer, LeSueur could tell it wasn't a geologic formation.

A man sat in front of the rock.

"Be ready!" he shouted across the ship to Naro Bon.

Holding his scope steady, he took measure of what he saw—and who he saw. A pair of dark suspenders crossed from shoulder to belt, and the sleeves of a long sleeve shirt remained white even though the torso was stained with dark blood. The source of the blood came from a scalped head. The bloodied corpse hid in plain view from one sailing but was invisible to a hunter upon dry land.

Professor Faero died trying to warn us, LeSueur realized.

Then the corpse raised a hand to wave.

Shit, he's alive.

"Captain!"

LeSueur dropped the scope away from his wounded mate and spotted the caller, who pointed to an object in the water. Just three feet of wooden shaft protruded from the water.

The mast of a ship.

"Slow us down, Bon. Don't let us get closer to the channel, or we'll be spotted. Hold us in place."

Then, turning to a quartermaster who was not Manuel Del Torro, he commanded, "Four of our strongest men, get in a rowboat and go get him. As fast as humanly possible. Go, now, while we pivot for a turn."

The ten-year veterans responded without question.

The skiff launched on the starboard side, and as soon as it touched the water, Naro Bon skillfully spun the wheel, pivoting the ship 180 degrees in the water. By the time they turned and stopped, the rowboat had reached shore.

LeSueur rushed to the back of the ship and then turned his scope to the channel, looking for a white sail coming out of hiding. Luckily, Bon stopped them before they entered the waters between the two islands.

Is it Spanish? Or Eos?

When he heard the pulleys lifting the skiff back up to the main deck, he moved again to the center of the ship.

Professor Faero's scalping had not removed the hair, but instead, left a long knife wound across the top of his forehead.

"What happened, Faero?"

Faero slumped down next to an empty cannon. "Del Torro died saving me. The savages caught us. One jumped on my back and grabbed hold of my hair, but Del Torro wrestled him off me so I could escape."

Savages? "What of the others?"

Faero shook his bloody head. "Warships attacked the channel. Slaves poured onto the island from the north. I've been hiding here for two days."

"Get us out of here, Bon!" LeSueur bellowed, and the ship careened on its side as it pivoted directions. He jogged back to the rear of the ship, passing by Bon at the wheel until he stood upon the railing of the rear deck.

Instead of focusing on Tortuga or the sunken ship off the point, he again scanned the channel.

His instincts were rewarded.

A couple small schooners came rushing from hiding spots on both sides, and a moment later, a big warship came out from a cove on the main island of Hispaniola.

It's not the Pretender, dammit. Even if it was, I'd need a full crew.

"We need speed. We're going to have to outrace these bastards. Hang the shirts on your backs, if necessary. We need to catch the wind."

Another day, Blackbeard.

CHAPTER 108

Dipping his pen into the ink, Isaac Newton knew his true enemy was time. Now seventy, he'd die before seeing the defeat of his other enemies—the Catholic Church and the Order of Eos. It didn't matter if it was a Julian calendar or Gregorian calendar (both systems had indeed been taken into account) since each day that passed signified a defeat of sorts—humanity was one step closer to destruction.

Newton's hand paused as he crossed off the previous day's task written on his calendar. He'd been actively at war with the future for two decades—*and what do I have to show for it?*

He next looked at the schedule for the day, and two initials told him what he needed to know: CB. His niece would be returning with a list of updates, defeats, and hopefully a few victories to lighten his burden. He flopped into his oversized loveseat, pulled a blanket over his feet where his robe didn't reach, and calculated the time until Catherine arrived: 128 minutes.

It gave him time to think.

How many days does humanity have left?

Approximately 127,020 days. That was when the Great Comet would chime the final hours of humanity. Newton knew there was a deviation of exactly how many days, but his approximation was based on the median of his numerous theories.

How many days do I have left?

His ailments were multiplying by the day—if not hour—and the thought of living to eighty seemed incredulous. Even if he reached eighty, he only had 3,650 days remaining on his ticking clock.

How shall I spend this day?

So as he waited, he devised a plan.

WHEN CATHERINE BARTON blew into the room two hours later, he knew she had no idea why he was smiling or why he greeted her with "You are a goddess."

"Please," she scoffed. "I looked at myself in the mirror before I left."

"How is Halifax?"

She huffed again as she prepared for the briefing, and after several moments, she muttered, "I am surrounded by old men." In typical fashion, she then answered the question with layers of meaning: "Things are in order."

Now thirty-four, she was as beautiful and voluptuous as she'd been when he unleashed her upon the aristocracy of England. The two had conspired together for twenty years. As the primary mistress of Charles Montagu, Earl of Halifax, she'd spent the better part of a decade gleaning information for Newton. She'd even managed to enter into the Earl's legal will despite her unofficial presence in his life.

Tabloids, fearing her influence in British politics, called her Bartica. *I will give her a new moniker befitting the goddess she has become.* He was still Master of the Mint and intended to use the power he had to make her an immortal.

He watched her as she gave an update on "Queen Anne's War," which began as the War of Spanish Succession in 1701. Born a Protestant, Newton had always vilified the Roman Catholic Church, so hearing Catherine talk about the war's cost to the Catholic nations of France and Spain to maintain their status quo brought a smile to his face.

"This pleases you?"

"The chaos of war has been our ally," he said. "If the mighty nations are indeed inclined to peace, then we must have our pawns in position for the next stage."

"Speaking of pawns, I've recently met with Captain Rogers."

Really? She is taking the bull by the horns. "I thought we were going in another direction," Newton countered.

"He took his spanking like a man once he realized how easy it was for me to ruin his life. While his ego was certainly stroked by his popularity in the press after his trip around the world, losing his wife, his profits, and his business partner made him quite amenable to our request."

I failed to properly read the people I selected for private commissions. Catherine has always understood people so much better than I. "So we are sending him to Madagascar?"

If Queen Rehena lied about her involvement in the conflict, she likely lied about other things, so another venture to Madagascar was warranted.

Catherine explained her plan. "His public commission is to purchase slaves in Madagascar and bring them to the colonies in the Dutch East Indies, which will allow him to hunt down any remaining vestiges of the Order of Eos in the region. If he succeeds, which I trust he will, we will then bring him back to the West Indies to deal with our enemies in the Caribbean."

"What about the injuries he incurred on his circumnavigation of the world?" Newton asked. Even though he gave more and more responsibility to her, he still kept abreast on the news.

Catherine grinned. "I find his new visage quite—terrifying. Surviving a musket ball to the face gives him a new aura of invincibility. He'll strike terror in our enemies, especially when we unleash him on the pirates."

"Well done, but now we must talk about your legacy." From what he knew about the Priory of Ormus, the Shepherds had always been male and served until death. The mysterious enclave that had voted him as the newest Grand Shepherd after the death of Robert Boyle in 1691 would likely vote for another male replacement. They'd sent him Bernard Clairval, which meant the hunchback served the Priory before serving its current Shepherd. Newton, however, had another plans.

"Oh please, I don't want to talk about husbands again."

"I agree. My life is coming to an end, but my legacy must continue long after my death. For centuries, men have been selected to guide the Priory of Ormus, and the invisible college that elected

me will find another victim from society to bear the burden of responsibility. In that same way, I choose you to play the part of a goddess."

"A goddess?"

"She will be our invention. God gave the world the Christ, yet Catholics venerated the Virgin Mary. Eos gave the world Columbus, but I will give the world Lady Columbia."

"Lady Columbia?" She laughed at the idea at first, but he could see her mind wrapping around the concept.

"She will be a guiding light in a dark world. While Eos and the Catholic Church look backwards to the past, Columbia will be a guiding light for the future of humanity. As a defender of humanity, she will find a way to stop the world from ending in 2060 and will stand in opposition to those who worship the religions of doom. You will be the manifestation of this goddess and then will pass the mantle onto another impressive woman who will help guide the destiny of mankind. Will you become Lady Columbia?"

The Priory of Ormus offered the world to me and it almost drove me insane.

She put a hand to her chest and looked up to gather herself. "You've grown quite eccentric in your old age, Uncle. If I say yes, can we then return our focus to Captain Rogers hunting down pirates?"

"First we'll finish discussing my vision for Lady Columbia, and then you can plot the destruction of our enemies."

CHAPTER 109

Fifteen years earlier, Louis-Armand Guerin threw himself at Queen Rehena's feet as a one-eyed beggar; now he returned with his head held high, ready to fulfill his promises.

Through all the turmoil, she remained upon her throne. Where there was joy and attraction, resignation now lived. Sadness filled her eyes, creating wrinkles that had not been there before. Her smile no longer lit the room, and her shoulders and back seemed bent by burden. A British flag had flown at the docks—a worrisome sign.

Yet Prince Andriana remained at her side. Both had been youthful teens when he came to them after being marooned by Robert Culliford, and now, the prince also carried the wariness of adulthood. *Have they remained loyal?*

Guerin's eye went to the court. Most were Malagasy, proof that Queen Rehena had indeed united the largest tribes of the island. Although a few lighter skinned Zana-Malata representatives could be spotted, Guerin didn't see any full-blooded Caucasians. *Although assassins could be lurking behind any pillar or curtain.*

Knowing a trap could be set, he'd arrived in Foulpointe with the might of the Brandenburg fleet. Unlike the fast, nimble pirate ships that frequented the Indian Ocean, his ships were lumbering war elephants capable of leveling a port. The *Reinforcer* alone could take on several pirate ships, so returning with large war ships protected him from any uncertainty on land.

At his side, Captains Jimmy Duke and Drake Murray also wore their finest attire. Benjamin Horne also risked the appearance but left his Abyssians captains on the *Reinforcer* to protect the Ark. Dutch Captains Daalman and Kikkert, who captained the other Prussian ships, stood on the flanks. They'd been chosen by Periphery agents, but even though Guerin could trust them, he didn't know them well. Over the past year, they'd only gotten to know each other when making port.

Along with the procession of captains, Louis-Armand brought holds full of goods to trade, and most importantly, a sampling of ancient treasures stolen from the Oak Island vault.

He knelt down, followed by his companions, and hoped for the best.

"I am your humble servant, Queen Rehena," he added.

"Seeing warships off the coast concerns my people," she began. "What are your intentions?"

"To fulfill a promise I made years earlier. For centuries, foreign pirates have plagued your waters and ports. I have come to rid you of these threats so that your reign might prosper even greater than it has already."

"You're late," she said, standing up from her throne. "When you first came to me, when you had two eyes, you promised to return with pirate loot in a few weeks, yet three months later, you showed up in a skiff begging for more aid."

Captain Kidd had taken them into a trap set by Robert Culliford, who killed and tortured the crew before stripping the *Adventure Prize*.

"And then, I didn't see you again for…what? Seven years? Then, as before, you came to me empty handed yet expecting something in return."

She'd given him Henry Avery.

"But you were the harbinger of death and chaos," she continued. "While two ancient enemies tore each other apart, I took control of my country. We freed the people from their tyranny while you were off on another adventure. Now, eight years later, you strut in here offering to rid me of threats. I've ruled Betsimisaraka for two decades without any help from you."

Guerin saw her quickly hide her emotions as she returned to her chair.

"My Queen," he asked softly. "Why does a British flag fly in the harbor?"

"It came from the men who brought back my son from his education in England."

A sigh of relief came over him. "The prince is here?"

She didn't answer, and the longer that she thought about her words, the more nervous he became. Finally, she said it. "You are being hunted."

Oh dear. "Yes, that was the case the first time I met you."

"The kingdom of France and the Mughal Empire seek your head, but now the British also want your head. I had no other choice."

Choice about what? "Am I being arrested?"

"When they returned my son, I had no choice but to feign loyalty to England. He's a young man, but he lives far from Foulpointe with his Imerinese wife. Despite all of his mother's political meddling, he has a chance to rule for many years in a united Madagascar."

"I'd very much like to meet the prince." *My son.*

She scoffed at the suggestion. "For all I know, you'd take him away and I'd never see him again. I must protect my son just like I had to protect my people from its enemies."

"Are you saying I'm an enemy?"

"Of course not, but our enemies know you. You once gave me your true name, and now it is being used by your enemies who know the names Gareth LaGrande and Captain Redeye are only aliases for a French Baron."

"If they know my name, and know you had dealings with me, then why would they return…your son to you?"

"Luck. They released him while they still believed I'd been a willing accomplice in the destruction of Eos. They learned the truth after he'd been sent home. A few months later, they came blustering threats if I didn't help them find you. That is what I meant when I said you're being hunted."

"Who is this man sent to hunt me?"

Rehena looked to her brother. Prince Andriana, who answered, "He is Woodes Rogers, son of a man who died at the Battle of Antongil Bay. He pressed for information, and now he holds you and the surviving pirates responsible for what happened to his father. He's pledged to spend the rest of his life hunting them down."

Fed by Newton's lies. "And where did he sail when he left your palace?"

"He'd just come from the Dutch East Indies," Andriana finished. "And he sailed for England in December of 1710."

Because of my two books, Rogers logically thinks I'm affiliated with the Dutch and hiding in Indonesia. The moon of England waxes strong while the other empires begin to wane. Soon, there will be no place for me to hide in this world.

"Captain Rogers claims he will return with an expeditionary force to claim Madagascar as a British colony," Queen Rehena added. "And it's already been two years."

"No, for the love I bear to you, my queen, no. My fight with the puppet-master is not over, and I will not see your land become a colony. May I speak with you in private?"

She looked to her brother, who shook his head.

"I'm not a foolish girl any more," she said with a faint smile. "Our dealings will remain public."

"This is my offer. I must help my Abyssinian friend return home, but while I am away, I'll leave my trusted officers here to show you I am a man of my word. They will root out any vestiges of Eos and will make sure this Captain Rogers does not lay claim to your country."

"And what do you ask for in return?"

"I've had enough of a life of adventure," Guerin admitted honestly. "All I ask for is a chance to meet the prince."

A chance to meet my son.

CHAPTER 110

T O R T U G A

1 7 1 3

Athena McCormack knew the risks, but she returned nevertheless. Together with the *White Zombie,* she piloted the surviving Sylph ship into the channel. Through her looking glass, she carefully watched the far shore of Hispaniola for any ambush ships, but two months after the attack, Blackbeard's ships had all departed.

All three Sylph captains had died, yet she'd been able to find three-dozen survivors who'd made it to Hispaniola. Those survivors willingly volunteered to serve for Captain LeSueur, who pledged to get revenge for the slain. Now, with both ships repaired and manned, they anchored off the shore of Mare Rouge.

Little remained of the former Huguenot village, and no one greeted them.

"I need to see for myself," she said to her quartermaster. "I'm going ashore also."

A short ways away, she saw the towering figure of Pierre-Charles LeSueur joining the men sent to scout the island.

Once she stepped into the surf, she saw movement in the jungle. Three men, all armed, stepped out into a clearing a hundred yards away from the beach. When she saw a yellow and red flag bearing the unique "Huguenot Cross" upon it, her legs almost buckled. As a girl, she'd lived in a similar settlement as Mare Rouge until it also fell under attack and she was taken away to a new fate.

When the kids appeared, she almost shed a tear, but the barnacles that grew around her heart kept her wary for the next threat.

The survivors, around eighty souls, relocated Mare Rouge up the hill for better defense. They told the story of what'd happened. The pirates used cannon fire to destroy the settlements along the canal, and simultaneously, used a slave army to sweep in from the north. For the first day, the attack had been relentless, but then the slaves withdrew into the jungles, allowing the survivors to regroup. Now, they were clustered together on the far eastern side of the island. After destroying Basse-Terra and scouring Trou Basseux, the bombardment stopped. The pirates cruised the area for a week until Spanish ships chased them off.

"I'm going to tend to my dead," LeSueur said once the explanation had been given. He walked off to Basse-Terre, leaving Athena to a similar task.

By later afternoon, Athena McCormack better understood the cruelty shown by Blackbeard in his attack on Tortuga.

"I buried Dr. Barrow, Giovanni Naufragio, Papa Bones, and Manuel Del Torro," LeSueur said. "You and I have lost many good men."

"I've uncovered the mystery of Blackbeard's army," she said. "He took hundreds of our Natchez allies as slaves. He unleashed them upon Tortuga with the threat that it was kill or be killed. Once the Natchez wore themselves out, they better understood what Blackbeard had done to them."

"Yeah, we ran one down," LeSueur added. "The poor devils had no idea we were allies. I released our prisoner and told him we'd bring food and supplies."

"Should we evacuate the island?" Athena asked. "Bring everyone to another location?"

LeSueur shook his head. "He's made his move. Queen Anne's War is over, and now Spain will protect what it has kept. Blackbeard knows this and has likely withdrawn to friendlier waters. Besides, Louis-Armand will return here, unaware that his plans have been crushed."

"So you will stay?" Athena asked.

"For now," LeSueur nodded and sighed. "Savagery."

"Then let's unload supplies for these poor people. You can tend to the Natchez. Keep them on the far side of the island for

the sake of these poor families. Then tonight we'll organize a plan."

Part of her wanted to just sail away and leave the troubles behind.

Another part, however, wanted vengeance.

CHAPTER 111

Edward Drummond anonymously ruled the colony as Blackbeard. He stood at the window of his cabin and looked over the sleepy town and distant harbor filled with dozens of pirate ships, many that now flew the black. His alliance with several key scoundrels turned the seven hundred islands of the archipelago into a confederacy of pirates.

But he didn't sit on a throne.

Two local scoundrels, Benjamin Hornigold and Henry Jennings, sat in the spotlight for him. Both men had gained a fearsome reputation during the War of Spanish Succession and now used that reputation to gain a stranglehold over the Caribbean, for the next fight would not be over a rotting throne in Europe but for control of a new throne—America.

For his part, his new gang of pirates brought in funds that could be funneled to the growing Eos colonies. Already, the Order of Eos used fire and water to temper the steel of its new home. While Hornigold and Jennings were necessary allies, he still had Patrick Dalziel's *Earl Mar* and Joseph LeMoyne's two warships, the *Griffon* and the *Salamandre,* in his pocket also. With visible leaders in Louisiana, New England, and even in Nassau, Drummond helped behind the scenes. *And I can choose who will sit on that throne just as I chose the right pirate to lead my kingdom here.*

He didn't bother saying a word to the whores still sleeping in bed, nor did he attempt to be quiet as he dressed and armed himself with enough guns, swords, and knives to kill a dozen men. His last act was to tuck an old newspaper under his armpit. He didn't wear a crown or sit on a throne, but all men knew who now ruled in Nassau.

"Where is Vane?" Drummond asked of his new First Mate, Charles Vane.

"He's gone into town to gather news," the quartermaster answered.

"When you take the ladies back into town, be sure to send a messenger to retrieve Vane. I'm getting restless with all of this inactivity."

Months earlier, when he anchored the *Pretender* in the harbor, he created a plan. The *White Zombie* and the *Eurydice* had escaped his grasp, and while the gutting of Tortuga pleased his Eos masters, he wanted to find his true enemy, so he initiated a practice of slowly torturing the Tortuga captives each night upon the deck. The screams and cries for mercy echoed over the still waters of the bay, forcing the musicians to play louder to keep the chill away, but late into the night, the screams would continue, and now, there wasn't a man upon the island that didn't look away as he walked down the street.

The spectacle told everyone who they were and where they'd come from—which was the purpose. He'd even give them food and water if they shouted out a man's name. He wanted his enemies to know that their friends were taken to the Bahamas.

His prized prisoner, however, he kept locked safely in his brig.

On his way there, he stopped by for a plate of breakfast, which he carefully carried all the way downstairs to his treasured captive.

All men break under torture, even the mysterious strategist with so many names. Charles Vane had helped extract the information, and as a result, received the promotion.

"Good morning, Adario," Drummond said as he set the breakfast in front of the metal bars. Granted, he wasn't sure if Adario was the man's real name, but after the torture stopped, the two settled into the routine of conversation each morning. Drummond even let the man read the newspapers that found their way to Nassau.

Adario rose and walked over to retrieve his food. He no longer had toenails or fingernails. His torturers used razor blades to re-

move a few patches of skin—along with a few unique tattoos—but those wounds had healed nicely, thanks to the ship's doctor. Joseph LeMoyne refuted the man's claim to be Chief Kondiaronk of the Huron, insisting the real man had died a dozen years earlier, but the Canadian did support the idea that the man had once been part of the Petun.

"Peace has finally returned to Europe," Drummond paraphrased the newspaper. "France and Austria signed the Treaty of Rastatt, and the Holy Roman Empire will soon end hostilities with France as well. While these global powers lick their wounds, my pirates will prepare for the next fight."

Adario hastily gobbled up his meal and opened up the newspaper. "The King of Babylon conquered the Hebrews and brought them back as prisoners. The great king asked the Hebrew prophet to interpret his dreams. One day, instead of seeing events generations into the future, Daniel interpreted the king's doom."

"The writing on the wall," Drummond finished. "See, Adario, this is why I like to start my day with you. You, sir, are wise. So do you see any omens or portends in the newspaper that spell my doom?"

Adario shook his head. "No, the only dreams of doom are in my head, and I've done everything in my power from delaying its arrival."

"Ah, I like this topic. My ancestors called it the Ragnarök. What do your people call it?"

Adario's eyes narrowed. "Armageddon."

"Oh, that's right, you're a baptized Catholic. What about your tribe? What do they believe?"

Adario didn't answer.

"You understand that I only keep you alive as bait for my enemies. I sent that patch of skin to my allies in Montreal. If I keep you alive long enough, I'll eventually learn who you are and where you come from. Do you see yourself as a warrior of light, preventing the doom of man from coming?"

"There is nothing I can do to prevent the doom from coming, but if I am a faithful and true servant to God, I can hope to protect the innocent and delay it for as long as God wills it."

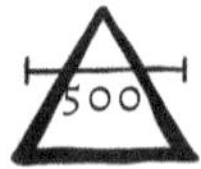

Drummond chuckled. "Well said. So you must see me as an emissary of darkness for wanting to be an agent that hastens it?"

Adario nodded and shrugged.

The floorboards above them shook as a man ran. The sound grew louder until Charles Vane came rushing down the stairs to the brig. "We've got news of the giant."

The White Zombie has finally come out of hiding. "Please tell me he's locked in chains, waiting to be interrogated."

Vane's steely eyes did not flinch, but he also hesitated. "No, he is not in custody, but we know he was in Puerto Rico just a few weeks ago."

"And how do we know this?"

"He attacked three ships anchored in San Juan. He crippled two and boarded one as it fled. He took hostages."

The White Zombie is hunting me? Drummond laughed aloud. *Perhaps it is time for a hunt.* "Let's go visit Puerto Rico, then. Prepare the ship for departure. I will have a word with the captains."

Drummond rose, but not before Adario came to the bars. "It seems the writing is indeed on the wall."

"Someone will die soon; that's for sure," Drummond said and followed Vane up the stairs.

CHAPTER 112

The *Reinforcer's* gun crews waited for his command.

Louis-Armand Guerin steadied himself at the railing as he scanned the bizarre sight of a British ship anchored off shore. None of the Periphery's four warships under command of Duke and Murray could be seen.

What has happened?

The British ship remained quite still.

No alarms, no sails, and the anchor remained set.

Just because it flew the British flag didn't mean it wasn't Eos or the Priory, Guerin reckoned. As he grew closer, he spotted the ship's name: *The Delicia.*

"Sail!" The cry came from the Crow's Nest. A deep-water cove had provided cover for two warships six miles north. *They'll be on us in minutes.*

Guerin turned his looking glass to the south. A small river six miles south of Foulpointe created another deep anchor channel near shore.

Four ships—a good omen.

Guerin looked to his navigator, who was ready at the wheel to pivot and head for deep water. On the way to Abyssinia, the crew of the *Reinforcer* tangled with African pirates off the coast of Somalia, and on the return trip, Arabian pirates twice attacked off the coast of Yemen. Although it'd been mayhem on deck, the *Reinforcer* had enough firepower to easily fend off the attacks. Five against one—not even with his veteran crew and the *White Zombie* could he fend off an attack like that.

"Who is it?" Guerin shouted.

The watchman dropped his looking glass. "Captain Jimmy."

Duke. Clever boy to hide along the coast.

As they neared the *Delicia,* Guerin's looking glass spotted an entirely dark-skinned crew. *Queen Rehena's men.*

THE MYSTERY OF the British ship was answered a few hours later when Queen Rehena brought out Captain Woodes Rogers in chains. Ironically, his mission had almost been identical to Duke's mission: eradicating any remaining Eos pirates. Duke left Murray's ship to safeguard Foulpointe and took the other two warships to scour Antongil Bay, St. Mary's Island, and the other former haunts of the pirate colony. By the time Captain Rogers rounded Cape Town, Duke had finished his offensive mission and turned to a defensive strategy for any visitors.

"A servant of Newton," Prince Andriana explained as he escorted Rogers into court. "His public commission was to eliminate pirates, turn any Eos colonists into slaves, and then look to establish a friendly port for an English colony."

"How many Eos colonists did we find?" Guerin asked.

Duke answered first, "We rounded up a few hundred on the islands."

"And where would you have brought these slaves?" Guerin asked Rogers.

Rogers appeared to be in his thirties. Life at sea had weathered his skin and a gruesome injury to his face made him a formidable looking fellow, even in chains. "I'd sell them to the Dutch East Indies."

"The Dutch…a fitting end for the Eos colony. My Queen, has he avoided taking any of your people as slaves?"

"Your men certainly didn't allow it," she said, with a rediscovered playfulness in her eyes. "You can do with Captain Rogers whatever you see fit, especially since the last time he visited, he specifically searched for you."

"Me?" Guerin grandstanded. "What did I ever do to him?"

Her smile appeared. *Obviously, I've delivered on my promises to her.* "He's looking for a man named Edward Drummond, known for his long black beard, and Baron Lahontan, known also as Gareth LaGrande and Captain Red Eye."

"Then you'll be relieved to know that you're not standing in the presence of either Edward Drummond or this Baron Lahontan although even if I was this French aristocrat, I certainly would not be your archenemy. Even though we've never met, Captain Rogers, I feel as if I know you…or at least your master."

"I don't have a master," Rogers retorted.

"We all have masters." Guerin chuckled. "How did Newton acquire your services? I'm just curious."

"He offered a chance to avenge my father, who was killed by traitorous men after the battle of Antongil Bay."

"I saw it happen," Guerin said, remembering Blackbeard's ship heading off to open ocean. "You see, I am a servant of many masters, including Queen Rehena. But I do not serve Eos, and I do not serve the Priory. The man you seek, Edward Drummond, is my enemy also."

"Then we have a common cause," Rogers added.

"No, I only have cause to kill you. Your master is a different sort of villain in comparison to the Men of the Dawn, yet he is a villain nevertheless. I stand in opposition to him and his plans."

"I only want to avenge my father," Rogers said.

"And I only want to protect the Malagasy people from evil puppet masters—which makes you my enemy. However, what would you say if I could give you this Eos pirate named Drummond?"

"Tell me where he can be found, and I will be indebted to you," Rogers added.

"Oh, are you going to be a reasonable man? Why shouldn't I just kill you and go hunt for Drummond myself?"

"Newton only wants to crush his enemies, and the people of Madagascar are not his enemies. Give me the Eos survivors, and I'll use them as proof that the famed Templar colony no longer exists. Let me live, and I'll return to England with only Edward Drummond as my enemy."

THE ALCHEMIST'S RING

Louis-Armand turned to Queen Rehena, "It seems a reasonable plan, but first, I'd like to discuss it with my queen in private."

Once again, Rehena turned to her protector. This time, Andriana nodded.

TO HIS SURPRISE, the Queen entertained him with a large meal. Her hulking brother was nowhere to be seen, and after the meal was finished, even her servants dissipated for a mostly private meeting.

"Did your friend find his home?" she asked.

Benjamin Horne. "Yes, but I do miss my old friend. The people of Abyssinia now know they have a faithful ally here in Madagascar. They also wish to keep the remaining treasures a secret between the two nations."

"And what will you do now that you've fulfilled your promises here?"

Surely, she doesn't expect me to stay? "Another friend of mine awaits my return. He's left behind a woman he truly loves in order to protect her and her people. With my help, he hopes to reach her one more time to make sure she is safe."

"And what if she does not need his protection?"

Are we talking about Wenonah and LeSueur or you and me? "If she no longer needs his protection, then he can retire in peace and quiet. He understands that given all the time that has passed between them that she's likely living her own life by now. He certainly doesn't want to impose himself into her life. Simply knowing that his lost love is safe to raise her children is all that matters to him."

"It is a noble quest," she added. "I hope his lost love understands the sacrifices he's made for the sake of humanity."

"Just as I hope she understands the personal loss he's also experienced," Guerin answered coyly. "What will become of you? Will you remain as Queen Regent here at Foulpointe?"

"My brave son has united the scattered tribes of Madagascar. The Imerina, the Tsikoa clans, the Sakalava, and the Zana-Malata have joined the Betsimisaraka in a pledge to oppose any foreign control or influence. Even if you didn't have to run off to help your noble friend, there would be no place for you here in court."

"What about King Laho? I'd very much like to meet him before I go. He's what…a lad of sixteen?"

"He's twenty," Queen Rehena spoke the lie effortlessly. "Unfortunately, your son is far away from the Priory, Eos, the Jesuits, and even the Periphery. He is with his young bride, Bita, who is pregnant with another child, his future heir."

My grandchildren. Guerin could not hide his disappointment. "You said I'd be allowed to see my son when I returned from Abyssinia."

"Long ago, when we first met, you told me how you were sent to Rome because you were a bastard son of a nobleman. Laho is the rightful heir from my marriage to Thomas Tew. Like your mother, any child conceived outside of the bonds of marriage would not be allowed to rule, and with Thomas dead for twenty years, Laho will remain my only heir. Even if Thomas Tew had given me a second son, what would his lot in life have been?"

"A second son? If his father's estate is wealthy, there are many things he could do. My friend Charlie, for example, left his father's estate in France and made a name for himself on the American frontier. Elder brothers often see the younger brother as a threat."

Queen Rehena nodded. "Yes, and for that reason, you *will* be allowed to see your son."

Why is she toying with me?

Queen Rehena called to her servant, "Bring in Prince Zanahary." Her eyes returned to Louis-Armand as she waited. "In my people's legends, the name Zanahary belonged to a god of the air, and sometimes the soul, who is taken away by the sun."

Instead of a young man of sixteen, a curly haired boy of nine walked beside his much darker-skinned escort, who left him at the side of Rehena. While there were many similarities between the two, Louis-Armand Guerin saw more similarities with himself.

"My brother and I have kept his identity hidden for the past nine years. To the outside world, he is an orphan left behind after the Great War of 1705. Meet your son."

From the age to the appearance, Louis-Armand had no doubts. Both hesitated, and once Rehena pushed the boy forward, Guerin wrapped him in his arms in a sustained embrace.

Rehena explained, "My brother and I must maintain King Laho's line, especially now that he is married. Bringing him here would only raise doubts amongst our enemies. But Zanahary…he knows who his father is."

"You're the one who helped my mother win the war?" Zanahary asked.

Guerin chuckled at the over-simplification. "I did my part. I hope I helped end it. She told you about me?"

The boy nodded.

"You've given me two great treasures," Queen Rehena said. "One I must keep for myself, and the other is yours."

"Mine?"

"You already understand the fate of a second son, especially one without a public birthright. While I wish I could keep him here, it is an uncertain future. I also know that if you leave Madagascar, you will likely never return. My brother and I discussed it and we think it's in the best interest of Zanahary to begin a new life on the far side of the world."

"We're going sailing," the boy said. His son.

CHAPTER 113

Pierre-Charles LeSueur waited patiently as his young crew struggled to lift the anchor. Most were local fools, hired recently from the docks of San Juan and Santo Domingo. He patiently tolerated them taking three times longer than his former crew had done. Despite their incompetence, the *White Zombie* looked as fierce as ever.

Looking north past the busy port along the southern shore of Hispaniola, he saw a dark cloudbank coming from Florida.

A storm is good. It'll only add to the chaos.

"Warship!" The call came down from the crow's nest from a man who he barely knew. "It's small, Captain Johnson, but heavily armed."

"The flag?" LeSueur asked.

"Too far away. It's not slowing down to come into port."

A lone wolf hunting for me.

Let it be Blackbeard.

The anchor lifted and the sails dropped, which allowed LeSueur to pull away from the southern shore of Hispaniola. He knew if he lingered in any neutral port, news would reach Eos. His assumption centered on the idea that the single ship would be a scout instead of a pack of wolves. The large port acted as a public shield against brazen attacks. The only issue would be if half-a-dozen Eos ships descended on him at once.

Three miles after pulling out of the port, LeSueur turned away from the ship to study the billowing black clouds north of Hispaniola. *As black as my heart.* Vengeance hung on the air as the downdrafts filled his sails. He turned east, and the enemy ship veered closer. From watching Father Marquette slowly dying in Michigan to burying the rotting corpse of Manuel Del Torro, LeSueur had allowed the sliver of Eos to fester for too many years, and today, live or die, he meant to begin extracting the infection.

"It's the *Earl Mar*!" the answer came from the crow's nest.

Dalziel. "Has he raised the Dobber?"

"Not yet, but he's tracking toward us, Captain Charlie."

Since the attack on Tortuga, LeSueur had done his research on his enemies. Of all the flags and coats of arms that flew in the Caribbean, Dalziel's was the most unique. According to family legend, their name and coat of arms was earned after Scottish King Kenneth II's kinsman was captured and killed by the rival Picts. The body of the nobleman was stripped naked and hung upon a gallows in view of his men. Incensed, King Kenneth offered a sizable reward to the man who could retrieve his body. Captain Dalziel's ancestor stood up and said, "I dare," which in the old tongue was 'dall zell.' The body was recovered, and the coat of arms flown since that day was a matriculated nude man, which in Captain Dalziel's case, had an enlarged penis, or dobber, for effect.

Any ship that engaged or failed to surrender to the dobber would have their necks tied to their ankles and thrown overboard to be "fucked" by the ocean, as Dalziel put it.

LeSueur wanted Blackbeard, but he'd take Dalziel, the man who raped Emperor Aurangzeb's daughter on the *Ganj-i-Sawai*.

The bow chaser of the *Earl Mar* fired a warning shot, but LeSueur had no intention of turning around for the safety of the port. He angled for a spot along the southern shore twenty miles from the port. With a full crew, he'd have the firepower and maneuverability to deal with the smaller, faster vessel, but he'd taken on the bare minimum.

"They raised the Dobber!"

That's right, come closer. LeSueur had spent his life fighting smaller, quicker men, and now with ships, the same tactics would be used. "Keep us close to shore."

"That storm is pushing us pretty hard," his navigator explained.

Will God foil my plans or aid them? "Raise the Old Zik," LeSueur said to his wide-eyed crew. LeSueur had modified a flag for the *White Zombie,* and on white fabric, he used black ink to draw the menacing figure of the monstrous Alchemist, which the Abyssinians had called Zik'itenya and Wenonah knew as the shape-shifting No Soul. The horned figure held a spear that pierced a bright red heart with seven skulls decorating the edges of the flag.

"Return fire on the starboard side."

Aim didn't matter, for it drew the *Earl Mar* into a more aggressive angle just as they were reaching the cove.

Does he see her?

The *Eurydice* dropped sail and lifted anchor, pulling away from the spot she'd discreetly hidden. The fear in his crew's eyes transformed to confidence. The rat had taken the bait.

"I want my berserkers ready on the port side," LeSueur said, and the five men who'd come from rescued Sylphs reported to the skiff.

"Fire a second volley on the starboard side," LeSueur ordered.

The aim was atrocious.

A moment later, the *Earl Mar* blasted away at the side of the *White Zombie.*

"That's your cue, men," LeSueur said after the noise settled. A dozen men ran for the port side, where skiffs were being readied for evacuation. LeSueur clutched the lead, fur-wrapped bundle dangling at his chest. His ax was strapped to his back, and he had two pistols and two knives ready. His berserkers nodded that they were ready.

"One last volley," LeSueur called out with the *Earl Mar* looming on the starboard side. Three brave souls ran from the readied skiffs and fired off the remaining cannons. These hit wood since Dalziel breathed down on his prey. As soon as the men sprinted back to the port side, LeSueur cranked the wheel into the *Earl Mar.*

Knowing what was about to come, LeSueur abandoned his conspicuous place at the navigation wheel and joined his fierce berserkers at the rear skiff. Then the *Earl Mar* blasted away. From such close range, the cannons ripped gashes into the hull of the aging Indian-built ship. The mast came toppling down just as the

skiffs reached the sheltered water of the port side. Gun crews fired down at the *White Zombie*, hitting nothing.

A mile behind it all, the *Eurydice*, aided by a strong northeasterly wind from the storm that passed over Santo Domingo in the distance, began to move into position.

Even though Athena McCormack wanted to pull up beside the Eos ship and kill as many of her enemies as she could, LeSueur denied the request. She lingered, knowing that the skeleton crew would be at the mercy of the *Earl Mar* guns out on the open water. Only LeSueur's skiff was cut free.

The cannons continued to rip the *White Zombie* in half. *Will Guerin be able to forgive me?* If he ever returned, it meant the new Prussian warships would return also.

The skiff came around the stern of the *White Zombie* with one of his men holding onto the rudder to keep them from drifting off in the rough seas. Ten yards away, the stern of the *Earl Mar* drew closer. The call of "boarding parties" cut through the din.

LeSueur called out softly, "Grappling hook."

His man tossed the hook over the railing above the captain's quarters. A younger man took hold of the rope, scurried up the rear of the ship, and with a free hand, broke out the glass of the cabin. He slipped into the cabin as another climbed up the rope. A moment later, more of the window was broken out and a second rope was dropped down.

My turn.

LeSueur felt every bit of a man approaching 60, and for a moment, he began to wonder if he'd be able to haul his three hundred pounds up the rope. Finally, he stood, huffing and puffing with his other men in the empty cabin.

Outside of the cabin door, he could hear Dalziel still barking out orders between cannon blasts. "I want prisoners," he shouted. "And bring me a damage report."

LeSueur waited for his men to finish chopping out the window and for the others to load their pistols. The cabin door flung open, and LeSueur strode out, wrapped his massive arms around Dalziel's neck, and dragged him backwards before the *Earl Mar*'s navigator could even do a double take. Three shots killed the closest men, but most were distracted by boarding the *White Zombie*.

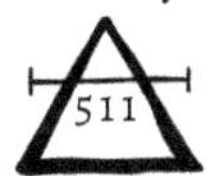

"That ship had no use for me anymore," LeSueur whispered in Dalziel's ears as he dragged him back into the cabin and slammed the door shut. "But it served as bait to draw you into our little trap. Bind Captain Dalziel."

LeSueur's men dropped their hatchets to bind him. LeSueur tossed furniture in front of the doorway just as the nob began to violently jostle.

A pistol shot blew a hole in the door.

LeSueur turned. "Get him out of here before they understand what's happening. Once you're clear, I'll take out the ship."

LeSueur retrieved his ax, just in case. He flexed his hand, including the finger that held Solomon's ring.

The men dragged Dalziel back to the rear window, with two quickly scaling down a rope ladder to two waiting rowboats. Like a sack of potatoes, the men rolled Dalziel from the opening and into the belly of one of the skiffs.

"Good luck, Captain Charlie," the last man said and vanished out the stern.

With the strong wind, the skiff bolted like a startled rabbit from a bush and headed for the distant *Eurydice*, who would pick up their hostage.

LeSueur crushed the small sample of shamir strapped around his neck, spoke the ancient commands, and the green vapor began to devour the *Earl Mar*.

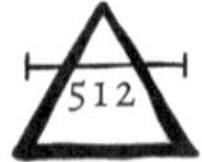

CHAPTER 114

The Island of Hispaniola, now known as Haiti and the Dominican Republic, has an area of over 29,000 square miles. Prior to the arrival of Christopher Columbus, the Taino people lived in five chiefdoms upon the large island. With Columbus came slavery and control by the Spanish Empire. The sugar plantations used slave labor from the Taino, Africans, and enslaved Muslims while the western portion of the island remained empty. French and English pirates on Tortuga eventually expanded control until the 1697 Treaty of Ryswick established two colonies: Haiti in the west and the Dominican Republic in the east.

Located just two miles off the southern coast of Hispaniola and sixty miles east of Santo Domingo, the island of Catalina has only 4 square miles and a highest elevation of only 60 feet. Because of its vulnerability to hurricanes, the island remained wild.

Which was perfect for two men avoiding civilization

Robert Culliford and his partner John Swan spent the past ten years fishing the calm lagoons formed on the northwest shore. With a cabin hidden in the trees of the rocky bluff, where they could spot approaching ships, the partners could stroll down to the beach in the morning, push their rowboat off the white sands, collect a few fresh fish, gather fruit and water on their way back, and spend the day swinging in their hammocks.

But today, John Swan spotted something other than a ship in the waters past the lagoon. "Do you see it?" he asked, pointing.

"Debris, I suppose, from the storm that blew in from the north last night."

"I was thinking the same thing," Swan admitted. "But if I'm not mistaken, it looks like a couple of barrels."

"I've heard full barrels of whiskey float in sea water, and that looks like a flotsam of several barrels bound together, doesn't it?"

John Swan shook his head. "Do you know how long it would take us to drink that much whiskey?"

Culliford winked. "No, but I'd like to find out. Pull up the anchor."

A moment later, John Swan sat with his back to the bow while Robert Culliford navigated the opening in the reef. The western coral reef prevented most pirates from bothering with Catalina Island, especially with its limited resources. After returning from Madagascar in 1705, Culliford and Swan brought their ship and crew to the Bahamas and retired. With Santo Domingo two days away and chests full of treasure buried on the island, they wanted for nothing.

"Is that a corpse?" Culliford asked once the rowboat entered the open waters beyond the reef.

Swan focused on rowing. "So what if it is? We'll pull the whole mess to shore and sort it out there."

I knew I heard cannon fire and not thunder. "I'll be damned, he's alive," Culliford said. After years of living a wild life, Culliford yearned for adventure still, even if it was only a tale of an adventure. *This fellow must have quite a story.* "Hello! Hello!"

The figure wedged between four barrels raised a hand.

"We'll throw you a rope and you grab onto it so we can pull you to shore," Culliford said.

"We're rescuing him?" Swan asked. "He could be crazy. Throw him into the sea and be done with him."

Swan just doesn't want to admit he was wrong about a battle. "If we save him and nurse him back to health, we could trade him to the first slave ship that comes by," Culliford explained. "Besides, by the time we get next to it and find something to tie off, we'll drift a mile downwind. Once we get the rig to shore, we can deal with him then."

As the rowboat neared the four-barrel rig, the figure sat up, caught the rope, and looped it around his arm several times while grasping the barrel rim with his left hand. It took all of John Swan's strength to get the rowboat and rig out of the wind and current. Once he did, they drifted in the lagoon for a spell.

"Are you English?" the marooned man asked. "Where am I?"

"The Island of Catalina, just south of Hispaniola, and yes, I'm from Cornwall originally, and my companion is German, but we are both Catalinan now. What about you?"

"Andre Penicaut," the survivor claimed. "Born in La Rochelle, but from the Louisiana Colony. My ship was sailing to Santo Domingo when a storm came up and sank us."

Curious. Is he lying about the battle? "You've drifted quite a ways from Santo Domingo, Andre. You've floated for almost sixty miles."

"Help me to shore, and I'll make it worth your while," the man called out.

Four barrels of rum, Culliford observed once the boat was back on the beach.

When the survivor took a bit of freshwater and found strength to stand, Swan suddenly looked dwarfed. Like Swan, the man was middle-aged but had another fifty pounds of girth and six more inches in height. *What a monster.*

And he climbed from the wreckage clinging to an ax. *Oh, I've doomed us both.*

But the giant turned out to be gentle. "I will be no burden to you. Could you point me to the direction of the closest port."

"There is no port on Catalina Island."

"If anything, you're standing on it," Swan added. "We have to paddle across the channel to get to civilization, but we have supplies."

"My friends will be looking for me. I will wait here until they come again," Andre said.

"You've been through quite an ordeal," Culliford said. "We have shelter up on the hill, where we can spot friend from foe. We have plenty of food; take a break from the world, friend."

The monster hesitated for a moment, then rotated the ax, using the steel of its head as a hand hold, turning it into a crutch. "I'll

take my chances and give you your space, and the rum is tribute for my rescue. Friend or foe, I'll stay here on the beach and look for rescue."

"Suit yourself," Swan said with a shrug and began to roll one of the barrels.

Not so fast. "You didn't happen to hear a battle? I swear I heard cannons firing right before the storm swept in."

"This again?" Swan muttered.

Culliford shrugged. "We sailed the seas together for decades, from the Caribbean to the Indian Ocean. While he enjoys the quiet life, I still yearn for stories. Stay here. My friend will bring down some food from our camp. All I ask for is a good story. Surely you must've seen the battle?"

The stranger nodded. "Three ships. One appeared to be an Indian Merchant vessel of some sort, and the other two were smaller."

Swan already began to roll the first barrel off the sand and into the jungle. "An Indian merchant vessel? Sounds like a pirate. Did you see the flag?"

Andre shook his head. "We were too far away. Two of the ships became entangled, and that was about the time the storm grew. I was part of a convoy coming from the Louisiana Colony. We turned the corner at the peninsula before Santo Domingo, and a monster wave broadsided us and we rolled."

"You're lucky to be alive," Culliford said. "Did you see what happened to the three ships?"

Andre shook his head. "They were much closer to shore, and the winds blew us out."

Everything seems reasonable. "The Louisiana Colony? I have friends there. Do you happen to know Joseph LeMoyne?"

Andre grinned. "Of course. The two of us go way back. I served beside his brother in the Battle of Quebec, and once the colony was established, I came down the Mississippi with their cousin to avoid those damn cold winters, but those swamps are just as deadly as a Montreal winter."

"What cousin?"

"Marguerite. Pretty little blonde thing. Her mother was a LeMoyne."

Quite convincing. This man appears to be an ally of sorts.
"So I told you my story," Andre began. "Tell me yours."
What's the harm in that?
The guest didn't stay long, and Culliford's tales of the Indian Ocean ended as quickly as they began. Swan hadn't even gotten to the fourth barrel when a small sloop angled toward the small is-land.

CHAPTER 115

Once Pierre-Charles LeSueur reached the top of the Jacob's ladder, he paused. Already, the crew changed sails to depart from Catalina Island, and Captain McCormack stood at the helm to navigate back into deep waters.

In the rowboat below, Robert Culliford tipped his hat and returned the rowboat to the shore. Pistols and rifles were within grasp, but LeSueur didn't act.

Who else still seeks justice?

Benjamin Horne and his gunners had been returned to Abyssinia. Guerin, Jimmy Duke and Drake Murray captained their own ships somewhere between Africa and America. So many others were dead: Manuel Del Torro, Dr. Barrow, Papa Bones, and Naufragio.

Smiling, Navigator Naro Bon stood upon the deck as the final step of the plan was completed. "We thought we'd lost you after the *Earl Mar* sank. The winds swirled so violently we couldn't search for you until this morning."

"I think the storm fed upon the ring's black magic," LeSueur added. He retrieved it from deep in his pockets but put it on a chain around his neck rather than back onto his finger. "Tell me our prisoner is secure."

Bon nodded. "Professor Faero is down there with him."

Faero has no interest in Culliford and Swan. Do I? LeSueur turned around and saw the rowboat reaching the white sands of the lagoon. He'd taken the name of Andre Penicaut and filled Culliford with half-truths just to get through the situation.

"Is something wrong?" Bon asked.

LeSueur shook it off. *Another day. I tire of bloody vengeance.* "Dalziel is in the brig?"

"Captain McCormack said she'll question him once we're in safe waters," Bon added.

"Our ploy worked," LeSueur reviewed. Had the ship been the *Pretender*, would LeSueur's vengeance have ended? Having seen the new destructive power of the ring, LeSueur gave thought to simply tossing it into the sea. "What happened to the *White Zombie?*"

"Once it broke free of the Earl Mar, it capsized. The storm drove it toward the island, which led us to finding you."

"And the skiffs?"

"All of our men have been collected," Bon said. "You were our greatest concern."

Looking up at Athena McCormack at the helm, LeSueur knew Dalziel would soon be spilling his secrets, and LeSueur would have to make sure she didn't go too far in exacting her own revenge. McCormack didn't care about a wise old chief named Gaspar, but LeSueur did.

You once saved me, Gaspar, and I'll do all I can to save you.

CHAPTER 116

Sir Isaac Newton sat down in the chair facing the prison cell where he'd kept Pierre-Charles LeSueur locked up, reviewing the conversation that had given him his first victory against time.

I only have a short time left on this earth; I need to do more.

Bernard Clairval remained standing in the open doorway of the Mint offices. It pained Newton to see his companion of two decades struggling with his health. He knew little of Clairval when the Priory sent him, and now, as he transitioned out of his role, Clairval remained a bit of a mystery. Clairval finally announced, "He's here."

Newton rose from his chair, touching the bars of the cell for perhaps the final time.

My time in power is coming to an end. I've restored the former glory of the Priory of Ormus. I've helped make England a protestant country and have punished the Catholic nations with two decades of war. I must now prepare the next generation to finish what I have started. Lady Columbia is groomed to do my bidding, and now I must finish my shepherding of the Priory of Ormus while I still have breath.

Despite being 72, Newton moved without the crippling burdens most men experienced in life, for his greatest toil had always been intellectual. He joined Clairval at the door. Walking from the gate was Bernard Clairval's replacement, Arnold Germelshausen, sent by unknown powers to recall his aging assistant along with the guest.

All four men gathered at the Royal Mint.

Newton could not help but gasp when he looked upon the face of Woodes Rogers. *Who gets shot in the head and survives?* "It is good to see you again, Captain Rogers."

"Sir Isaac." The captain vigorously shook Newton's hand as Clairval and Germelshausen drifted to the corners of the room. Newton assumed his position at the desk.

Rogers avoided eye contact. "I've come to apologize for my fumbling before Parliament. I clearly overestimated my sway with certain lords. I know how important it was to colonize Madagascar."

The poor fool blames himself when it is I who have changed the focus. "You could not have predicted the death of Queen Anne, or how it would sway political tides. You, like your father, did England a great service. You've cleansed Madagascar of a pestilence, and in doing so, you have honored your father's memory. You are now an independent man, wealthy enough to go wherever you'd like to go."

Rogers scoffed. "My wife has left me, and my petition to colonize Madagascar has been denied. Perhaps you could guide me once again."

"Of course," Newton said with a smile. "When you were sent back to Madagascar, we believed our enemy remained in the fabled Templar colony of Libertalia," Newton paused as he realized he was repeating a narrative created by Baron Lahontan under a pseudonym. "But your reports proved how worthless a Colony in Madagascar would be for England."

"I don't understand," Rogers admitted.

"What did you claim before Parliament? 'The Pirates of Madagascar have gone native.' Those who did have obvious European ancestry signed a petition of clemency to Queen Anne, and those remaining with hostile intentions were sold into slavery. You've brought that chapter of history to a close."

"I failed to find King Ratsimilaho or his Queen Regent mother," Rogers added meekly.

"We've won the war in Madagascar, and it has returned to its wild ways. If you'd found a Queen ruling a court, I'd be concerned, but everything you said to Parliament—an untamed island

with an uncivilized population suitable only for slavery—shows me that my efforts were successful. Eos is no more."

Rogers nodded in affirmation. Granted, he'd made a fool of himself before Parliament, but it proved to Newton the man's truthfulness and sincerity.

"So cheer up, Captain Rogers," Newton said. "I still have great plans for you. Bernard, review for Captain Rogers and Mr. Germelshausen our goals in America."

Clairval first cleared his throat and then coughed for a few seconds before gathering himself. "We had three objectives during the war. England has claimed Hudson Bay, into which a series of rivers connect to the heart of the continent. We also claimed the peninsula of Acadia, which has value far beyond the fertile fishing grounds surrounding it. Yet our final target, the colony of Louisiana, now remains out of reach, lest we want a full fledged war with France to begin anew."

"The LeMoyne brothers," Rogers said as Clairval caught his breath. "Send me and I will discreetly see that the colony falls to ruin."

"One thing at a time," Newton said. "Mr. Germelshausen, explain to Captain Rogers why Catherine is not here with us today."

Unlike Bernard, Arnold was tall and lean with a thick shock of black hair swept to one side and a heavy Walser accent from the mountains of Liechtenstein. "She is rallying support behind King George and his son."

"So that a Catholic monarch never returns to the throne of England," Newton finished. "Long after I die, my plans for England and America will continue. She's fostering relationships with Protestant leaders in New England. Given time, America will rid the continent of French influence for us. To strengthen America, we must deal with a new threat. And what is that Mr. Germelshausen?"

"Many pirates that once existed in the Indian Ocean have taken up residence in the Caribbean."

Always so brief? Newton elaborated. "Life has been cruel to you these past few years, Captain Rogers, so I will be sending you to a tropical paradise, as it is described. But it will not be easy. If the rumors are true, it is currently a hell on earth, a place where thou-

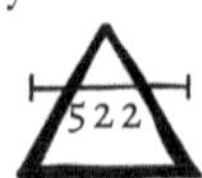

sands of pirates gather to rob, rape, and ravage anything representing civility."

"The Bahamas?" Rogers guessed correctly.

"There you will find Blackbeard, also called Edward Teach, but he's known to us as Edward Drummond, the man who betrayed your father. You will need to plan carefully if you are to attack this nest of vermin, for if you come in too forcefully, they will scatter to other holes. Most are greedy men, who can be purchased and turned. At the heart are men like Drummond, feigning loyalty to the Catholic Pretender, James Francis Edward Stuart—when in reality he serves Eos. With the death of Queen Anne, I fear civil war may once again rekindle here in England, and if it does, men like Drummond will use it to strengthen their hold on the colonies. You must not let this happen. Rid the islands of these men, and I will see that you are appointed governor. Agreed?"

"Governor?" Woodes Rogers smiled. "I will begin preparation at once."

CHAPTER 117

TORTUGA

1715

Pierre-Charles LeSueur felt his own heart breaking as he watched the scene taking place on the *Reinforcer*. He thought of his own children—now adults somewhere in the Louisiana colony. He'd never been able to give them a proper goodbye.

In this regard, he felt jealous of Louis-Armand Guerin, who'd get his happy ending.

For the past two days, Guerin, McCormack, Murray, and Duke met at Tortuga to plan their daring rescue of Chief Gaspar. With five ships flying Spanish flags, no one from Hispaniola bothered them.

Louis-Armand Guerin nodded in affirmation for Zanahary to walk over to the sea hag, Athena McCormack. "She's not as scary as she looks," he added.

The men standing around him muffled their response.

Zanahary looked back over his shoulder. "Your father has to help save an old friend from a very bad man," Guerin paraphrased the situation. "I'll be gone for two weeks. Professor Faero, a good friend of mine, will stay with you."

"I'll keep him safe," Faero said as he stepped closer to McCormack and Guerin's son.

"I'll make sure your father comes back," LeSueur said with a nod.

Why is Guerin even risking this? LeSueur wondered, but he knew the answer. Not only did Gaspar know too much, but Guerin felt responsible for getting him involved in the first place. Killing

Blackbeard motivated all of them, but thoughts of going up the Mississippi River now seemed foolish.

"We'll all make sure he comes back," Jimmy Duke added. Even though they'd returned from Madagascar with all five warships, hundreds of other pirate ships gathered in the Bahamas.

If we don't do this properly, the hornets will swarm the nest.

For that reason, McCormack would linger far behind the others.

Some of the Sylph crewmen who sailed with Vero, Galloway, and Jacobs volunteered for the most dangerous part of the mission: offering the prisoner exchange. They'd enter Nassau, find Blackbeard's men, and offer the return of Patrick Dalziel in exchange for Adario, as they called him.

That tough old muskrat never broke under torture, LeSueur reflected on what Dalziel had told them of Blackbeard's pet.

Dalziel deserved a terrible death, but now, he stood in chains as he smirked about his impending freedom. His foul deeds twenty years earlier had sent the world into a maelstrom that still raged. Henry Avery had paid for his deeds, but Dalziel still breathed.

And I still need to atone for my sins.

Perhaps saving Gaspar will bring closure.

CHAPTER 118

Edward Drummond shook off Charles Vane's suggestion of killing one of the four messengers. *Who would've thought it'd be nice to have Dalziel back?* The previous summer, Dalziel had been sitting with him when news of the *White Zombie* sailing the southern waters of Puerto Rico arrived. Unlike the wild Republic of Pirates, Dalziel had been an Eos man. His loss hurt the cause. By all accounts, the storm that took the *Earl Mar* also sank the famous ship south of Santo Domingo.

"Before I sail off to Bimini Island," Drummond responded to the messengers, "tell me about your commander."

"Monstruosamente grande," the sailor said, and then placed a flattened hand at eye level with Blackbeard and raised it another foot. "No pequeno. Muy grande."

That's LeSueur. Drummond kept his joy internal. "How did you get here? I thought I sank all your ships?"

"We found new allies," one of the four said in French.

"What about that bold female captain?" Drummond asked, remembering how the *Eurydice* had rammed the *Pretender* during the attack on Tortuga. "Is she still alive?"

The men shook their heads.

A lie. She's probably waiting at Bimini already. "Vane, go fetch Adario from the brig so we can show these 'Spaniards' that we're honest men."

His first mate rose slowly, thus displaying the most disrespect the cautious and cruel man dared showed to the menial task. With the Republic of Pirates growing, the two LeMoyne brothers had sailed back to the Gulf.

Old Adario came in, wincing his eyes in the full light of Drummond's cabin. "Good news: these gentlemen have come to our fine port to ransom you in trade for my friend, Patrick Dalziel. I'm going to agree to their terms. I'll approach Bimini with only one ship. We'll anchor, send out our prisoners on skiffs, and return on our merry way. Did I get the details right?"

The messengers nodded.

"Well then, go back to Captain Monstruosamente Grande and let him know I'll see him tomorrow at noon."

The messengers almost looked surprised to be returning alive.

"It seems like a trap," Charles Vane said once they'd left.

Drummond only chuckled. "Bring Adario back to the brig, and then we'll talk about traps."

Drummond looked out his window to the town of Nassau. What once had simply been a landing place had now turned into a pirate city. Surrounded by men of all nationalities, he understood how the plans of Alvorez and Morrison were now coming to life off the shore of America. While the puppet masters pitted empire against empire, Drummond gardened by planting seeds up and down the coast of the continent. While many claimed he sowed terror, Drummond knew he sowed something much simpler—democracy.

If he could prove himself in the days to come, he might be chosen as one of the elect, and in his elder years, he might select the men to preside over a new democratic nation.

Here, in the Bahamas, he'd watched his candidate, Benjamin Hornigold, be democratically elected to the Republic of Pirates. Of course, the man he defeated was another fellow chosen by Drummond, Henry Jennings. Democracy, not the monarchy, would take root here in Nassau and spread to the continent.

The Madagascar experiment is working.

A few minutes later, Charles Vane returned without Adario. "The trap?"

"They're already dead men and they don't even know it. I want a dozen ships to sail south around Andros Island, and then a dozen ships to sail north around Abaco. If those fools think the

isolation of Bimini Island is their ally, they're gravely mistaken. An hour after I set sail, I want you to lead a dozen ships right at Bimini. There will be nowhere for them to run."

This pleased Vane.

He wants to be a king. If I fail, he might usurp the throne.

CHAPTER 119

At only nine square miles, the tiny island of Bimini barely rises twenty feet above sea level. Although the western-most island of the Bahamas, it rests closer to Florida than the most populous island of New Providence. Its name came from the misapplication of the Taino word *Beimini*, which connected to the legendary Fountain of Youth sought after by Juan Ponce de Leon. While the skinny island did not hold the source of immortality, it resides within the mysterious Bermuda Triangle, and just off the northwest coast, a strange road with the appearance of paving stone can be seen under eighteen feet of water leading into the depths of the Atlantic.

For Edward Drummond, the weather—not the island—proved to be the strangest thing about Bimini. Black clouds gathered above the island yet the wind remained strangely calm.

"Do you see what I see?" Drummond asked his quartermaster.

"The big fellow on the shore? I see him."

So did Drummond. A massive figure, likely LeSueur, already waited at the island along with a man whom he assumed to be Dalziel. Drummond pointed to the little cay ten miles south. "I think I can see a few ships hiding behind it."

"Not much of a trap. What do we do?" the quartermaster asked.

"We take our time. Vane and the others will be appearing in an hour. Drop anchor and get Adario ready for the exchange."

"We're giving him up."

"He's served his purpose in getting me the giant. These men can run but they can't hide. We'll play along for an hour. Keep an eye on those ships. Until Vane arrives, we're vulnerable."

"Yes, Captain.

Drummond watched as the skiff was lowered, followed by Adario and two men to row it. Once the skiff hit the water, the big brute on shore pushed away as well and began paddling toward the *Pretender*. Through his looking glass, Drummond visually confirmed that Dalziel was in the rear.

Why would he be so foolish as to bring Dalziel himself? Drummond walked over to his marine sergeant. "Once we get Dalziel on board, shoot that man." Then he thought of all the secrets held by LeSueur. "No. Shoot the boat. I want that man more than I want Dalziel."

"Yessir."

Am I missing something? He's giving me both things that I wanted.

When the skiff reached the *Pretender,* Drummond felt the hair stand on end when LeSueur called out, "Permission to come aboard."

His men turned to him.

"Granted."

So the big monster climbed up the Jacob's ladder.

He's older than I expected. "Who are you?"

"I am Wishwee, sent to rip the dark spirit of No Soul from his cave."

Drummond grinned. "Poetic. You plan to do that with a bottle of rum?"

LeSueur nodded. "The victor gets to drink it."

"Victor?" Drummond mocked loudly. "Do you think I'm going to fight you fairly in a duel?" Patrick Dalziel, bruised and battered but quite alive, came up over the side also, and upon seeing Drummond, rushed to his side.

LeSueur nervously glanced at the skiff carrying Gaspar, who climbed up into the solitary ship. "Are you a coward?" LeSueur asked.

Drummond laughed louder, but Dalziel took hold of his arms. Dalziel showed his tongue had been removed.

"Now this upsets me," Drummond said. "Bring our new prisoner to the brig. Raise the red!"

LeSueur put up no effort, and soon, was dragged below deck.

The quartermaster called out, "Sir, four sails emerging from the cay."

Patrick Dalziel took hold of him, shaking him so vigorously that Drummond pushed him away and drew a cutlass. "Get a hold of yourself."

Dalziel motioned to his finger and then pointed at the big bottle of rum.

"What are you trying to say? The rum is poisoned?" Drummond drew back the cutlass and Dalziel almost tackled him only to be pulled back by the quartermaster. Drummond finished, smacking the bottle hard enough that its contents spilled onto the deck.

It wasn't rum.

What is that stuff?

The answer came in a gasp, and when he turned, Dalziel dove overboard, soliciting a slight chuckle and then absolute panic as the blue-green contents began to sizzle upon the deck. *What have I done?*

Just then, a lightning bolt hit the foremast and the sound and energy that followed knocked most of the men off their feet. Drummond found himself flat against his cabin wall. Looking up, Drummond noticed the black clouds swirled like the eye of a hurricane.

"Get off the ship!" He shouted as the surface of the deck began to disintegrate. A man closest to it found himself caught in the strange web, and when his flesh began to melt, the other men followed Dalziel into the water.

Anger kept Drummond's feet planted as the ship began to rock in the wild sea. When the deck dissolved to reveal the deck below, he spotted Pierre-Charles LeSueur staring up at him.

CHAPTER 120

As soon as Gaspar climbed aboard, Louis-Armand Guerin adjusted the wheel to point the *Reinforcer* toward Blackbeard's *Pretender*.

He almost called out for Duke. "What do we see on the horizon?"

"Sails coming out of Nassau, straight ahead of us," the report came down. "Our ships are coming around the cay."

Whatever Nassau threw at them, Guerin knew his Prussian warships would be able to take that punch and hit back twice as hard. Once past the Republic of Pirates, the port of Nassau would be wide open for attack.

Ignore the wasps and just knock down their nest.

"Sir, we have sails to the west."

"West?" Guerin muttered. He ran to the poop deck where Naro Bon pointed and then handed him the looking glass.

"Spanish?" Guerin asked his own eyes. Eleven ships hugged the Florida coastline. From what he could tell, the eleven ships were about twenty miles away and still heading north. Another ship, French from the looks of it, angled towards Bimini.

Who are they?

He didn't have time for an answer.

A bolt of lightning that came out of the low hanging clouds struck Blackbeard's ship.

"Sir, they're abandoning ship," the lookout in the foremast shouted.

"Fire on them as we pass," he shouted.

"What about LeSueur?" Bon asked quietly.

"He'll stay on that ship until one of them is dead. We'll all be dead if we don't crush this first wave of the ambush."

He took one last glance at the Spanish ships. Even though the Imperial powers of Spain, England, and France were at peace again, the sight of a Spanish Treasure Fleet could be enough to launch a new war. Luckily, the unexpected fleet had no interest in the fight.

The cannons fired and rifles spit lead at the water, but in thirty seconds, they flew past the anchored *Pretender*.

Guerin jogged back down to the helm. "Signal the other ships to trail," Guerin said. "I want the wolves to think they've found an easy meal."

The other ships soon trailed, and the *Reinforcer* passed through the gauntlet at full speed. The shallow waters near the shore were light turquoise, while the channel itself was dark blue, making it easy to maintain the line right to Nassau.

A dozen small sloops appeared from New Providence Island, but they spread out in a wide net. "Catch this wind," Guerin called out. "Get us going as fast as we can."

Behind him, a storm billowed above Bimini Island.

"There it is." The *Marianne*. Captain Dalziel's information had been correct, including the identities of the captains in the Republic of Pirates and Blackbeard's chosen man to operate it—Benjamin Hornigold. Unlike the other rogues hired as part of the Republic of Pirates, Hornigold was educated, came from an aristocratic family, and more likely than not, was an apprentice member of the Order of Eos.

"Target that ship," Guerin said.

With cannons at the ready and marines loaded with sharpened swords and fresh powder, the *Reinforcer* prepared to take out the strongest tooth in the jaws of the trap.

Both ships fearlessly charged at each other, but Guerin knew his other four ships followed tightly on his stern.

The crooked smile on Guerin's face disappeared, not because the *Marianne* loomed, but because beyond it, the horizon blackened with billowing storm clouds seemingly rising from the island of

Bimini like a volcanic explosion. *Control yourself, LeSueur. Kill that bastard Blackbeard, and as old men, we can re-tell the story, again and again.*

Cannons fired on both sides.

"Get down here, Captain!" his quartermaster called out.

Guerin shoved his scope into his vest and began to jog down the stairs to the wheel.

With his third step, however, the stair exploded into splinters, and he found himself falling, head over heel down the remaining stairs until he crashed upon the deck and slid into the support base of the wheel.

He laughed, looking up at the face of Naro Bon and his quartermaster, who both stood over him with wide eyes. "Scabby sea bass, that was close!" He brushed off splintered wood from his chest.

Beyond the wide eyes of Bon and the quartermaster, he found himself distracted again by the dark clouds expanding from Bimini.

What's happening, LeSueur?

He reached out a hand to Bon, "Help me up."

Bon took hold of his outstretched fingers, but instead of jerking him to his feet, he clasped the hand with both of his, and knelt down at his side. "It'll be okay, Captain. It'll be okay."

The fear in Bon's eyes unnerved him. "Fetch Dr. Barrow!"

Dr. Barrow is buried back at Tortuga. Why is he calling for a doctor? I only tripped and fell.

Guerin pushed himself up onto his elbows, giving him a view of the stairs, where a cannon ball had blown a hole right into his cabin. *That was a close call,* he thought attempting to stand, only to have Bon push him back down by the shoulders.

Then the pain arrived along with the red blood that was spurting all over the deck.

Is that my left boot back on the stairs?

He began to scream.

CHAPTER 121

B I M I N I   I S L A N D

1 7 1 5

I *wish I had my ax*, Pierre-Charles LeSueur thought as he climbed up out of the belly of the ship. The vaporous fog flowed around him but also avoided Blackbeard.

I'll hew him down myself!

LeSueur picked up a spare cutlass.

Blackbeard drew a pistol, but by the time he fired, LeSueur ducked behind the mainmast and received only splinters of wood. A second shot fired but whizzed by.

"We can't just sit down and talk?" Drummond called out as he retreated into his cabin.

LeSueur moved from behind the mast and picked up another cutlass near the navigational wheel. The crew had left their captain to his fate.

LeSueur quickly peeked his head into the doorway and pulled it back as a lead ball shattered the doorframe.

He repeated the act as the fourth pistol discharged.

LeSueur filled the cabin doorway.

Blackbeard had gone for a powder horn but dropped it when he saw LeSueur appear. "I'd love to hear the story of how you rose from your grave in Cuba only to ambush me in Madagascar. Although the greater mystery is how you could abandon that beautiful wife of yours."

LeSueur shook his head. "I want to kill you in a fair fight, so what will it be...pistol, knife, cutlass, or hand-to-hand?"

"No storytelling?" Blackbeard cracked a smile. "Then I choose pistol."

Blackbeard's hand swept to his desk, bringing up a pistol.

LeSueur swept his right cutlass in the air to deflect the shot but the bullet struck him in the left shoulder and the second cutlass fell out of his numb fingers and to the ground. Undeterred, LeSueur thrust his remaining cutlass at Blackbeard, who backed up and used the desk as a shield. LeSueur sent it flying with a kick.

Trying to avoid the desk, Blackbeard stumbled and LeSueur thrust again, catching him in the thigh and sending him to the ground.

Blackbeard's feet kicked frantically, and LeSueur aimed his thrust for Blackbeard's chest, but at the moment of impact, he moved away, creating a slice to the side of his ribs. The cutlass stuck in the floorboard, allowing Blackbeard to kick him in the knee and knock him to the floor.

With both men on the ground, the two cutlasses slashed wildly at each other. Each man drew glancing blows but were unable to land a fatal blow. LeSueur drew his dagger.

Blackbeard retreated briefly, just to get to his feet for a better attack, but LeSueur reached out and sunk the dagger into the man's calf.

Blackbeard swung the cutlass, severing LeSueur's hand at the wrist.

He took a breath to bellow in pain but Blackbeard's blade swung for his head, and LeSueur managed to deflect the blow with his own cutlass. Both men rose to their feet. The ship rocked and buckled, adding to the dizziness of blood loss.

An arm strengthened from a life of chopping wood released a blistering assault on Blackbeard, who defensively caught the blade with his own cutlass but steadily lost ground. LeSueur pursued, and with Blackbeard just a stride in front of him, a concussion of energy lifted him off his feet and threw him—along with Black-beard—onto the main deck below.

As he tumbled, tangled with Blackbeard, he noticed that his ears rang with a high-pitched tone but the rest of the world had grown quiet. Before he could even make sense of things, he was engulfed by white fabric.

His strong right fist smashed into the back of Blackbeard, trying to do as much damage as he could before the pirate was out of his reach.

A sail?

A moment later, the fabric lifted to reveal the deck with Blackbeard just a few paces away. The beaten Scot tossed himself over the edge of the railing and into the sea.

LeSueur finally had a moment to take sense of things.

First, he inspected the two white knobs protruding from his wrist, bones from his severed hand. He reached to his waist, ripped out his belt, and tightened it around his forearm with numerous loops that cut off the flow of blood.

Looking back at the cabin, he clearly saw how another bolt of lightning had toppled the rear sail onto the deck.

Then for the briefest of moments, he thought he saw a stairway from heaven appear for him to meet his maker. A pillar of light appeared in the darkness as if illuminating the path of an angel, or for Christ himself, to descend from Heaven to join him in his darkest moment.

No, LeSueur realized, it wasn't light in the darkness, but darkness swirling around the ship. *The ring!*

Somewhere back in the cabin, his severed hand still wore the ring! He tried to crawl back to the cabin, but on three limbs, the movement of the ship kept knocking him back down to his belly.

Finally, he rolled to the main mast, and with rope from the rigging, began to tie himself to the mast like Odysseus approaching the Sirens. The released shamir wouldn't hurt him, but without being in his possession, the ring did whatever it wanted.

CHAPTER 122

Captain Athena McCormack watched the hurricane continue to track north along the Florida coast while the *Eurydice* followed the shoreline to inspect the damage. The shore was littered with corpses and debris from shipwrecks.

You better not have made an orphan of this boy.

Most of the debris came from a Spanish fleet that'd been in the wrong place at the wrong time. They'd found one of the ships—the *Senora Carmen*—still floating with its masts tangled in an underwater reef. A bit further up the shoreline, the *Senora del Rosario* had been tossed entirely onto the beach. Two small campfires burned beside it, and the ten marooned seamen waved to get the captain's attention, but she kept the *Eurydice* moving.

Pirates are coming, you fools. Don't expect a rescue from these vultures.

The previous day, McCormack had witnessed the birth of the hurricane over Bimini Island. The sudden appearance of the storm surprised everyone in the region except for her. She knew where it'd come from, and when it rose up, she lingered behind it. The oblivious Spanish fleet found itself blown ashore like leaves floating on the surface of a pond. The twelfth ship—the fleet's guide ship—narrowly escaped the storm's vengeance.

The French warship the *Griffon* had been part of the attack on the Natchez and Tortuga, and it most likely belonged to Eos. Seeing it in relative isolation made Athena want to raise the sails and pursue. Had she listened to vengeance, she'd likely be hung up on the Florida reefs. The Spanish Fleet took the brunt of the storm, and the lead ship flew ahead of the storm to the north.

The rest of Eos didn't fare so well.

The southern pincer of Blackbeard's trap—almost a dozen ships—capsized in the rough waters. Several others washed up at Bimini, but she didn't do much more than peek, for two ships anchored there to gather up surviving pirates.

"Ship approaching, Captain," the first mate of the *Eurydice* told her. Her glass went to the shore where a scavenger party had gone to look for survivors in the newest wreckage.

I am fast and nimble, she reminded herself as she steered toward danger.

"It's the *Mary Dyer*," the call went out.

Jimmy Duke's ship. Thank God.

AN HOUR LATER, the two captains exchanged information. After sinking a few of the Eos ships coming through the channel, the storm caught them before they could attack Nassau. The others, including the *Reinforcer,* were blown north.

So McCormack and Duke headed north together.

They found several more shipwrecks, including more Spanish and Eos ships, but not who they needed. Young Zanahary and Professor Faero clung to her side each time they found a wreck.

"Sail," her lookout shouted. "And a wreck."

Jimmy Duke's *Mary Dyer* began blasting, and when the ship turned, she also recognized the ship as the *Bersheba.*

"Who is that?" Professor Faero asked as the ship veered sharply toward the east and the Bahamas.

"Captain Henry Jennings—an ally of Blackbeard," she said and turned her scope to the shore. A chill came over her as she saw the wreckage of the *Pretender.*

"Prepare a landing party," she called out.

"Can I come with?" Professor Faero asked.

He fears for LeSueur just like I do.

"Is it my father?" Zanahary asked.

"I don't think so," she said. "I'll go find out."

The *Pretender* lay on its side, with the hull facing the Atlantic and the shattered deck and mast facing the beach. As soon as Athena and her seven men came around the corner, they found a corpse tangled in rope around the center mast.

Professor Faero leapt into the wreckage and stumbled until he reached the mast. Once he touched the corpse, it came to life.

LeSueur lives.

Pale and battered, LeSueur clung to life. As they carried him out of the wreckage, he had a delirious smile upon his face. "Ah! I will vent my wrath on my foes and avenge myself on my enemies."

"We've been avenged, my friend," Faero added. "You've made quite a mess."

A cannon fired.

Athena's heart leapt, knowing they were vulnerable. When she looked up, she saw the *Reinforcer* returning from the north and another ship trailing behind.

LeSueur took up the space of two men in the skiff.

"Get him to your ship's doctor," Faero insisted. "Just leave me behind for now. I'll wait for Bon to pick me up."

"I'll make sure the Reinforcer doesn't leave without you," she promised him.

They lifted LeSueur back inside of the ship using their skiff, and by the time they unloaded LeSueur, the *Reinforcer* sent its own skiff to shore to gather Faero and another to the *Eurydice*. At the helm of the big warship, she saw Naro Bon. In the skiff, she saw a pale Louis-Armand Guerin, whose leg was missing below the knee.

Zanahary gasped when he saw his father, but Louis-Armand smiled and weakly lifted a hand to tussle his hair. "Never try kicking a cannonball, son."

Duke, Bon, and myself, she realized. *I'm the senior captain.*

The fight was over, even though it was impossible to tell who'd won or lost. As much as she wanted to search for the other two ships, continue with the attack on Nassau, or to simply search the wrecks for Spanish gold, she knew her duty.

"We're going back to Tortuga," she said.

CHAPTER 123

Edward Drummond returned to port on another man's ship. With a blanket thrown over his shoulder and his wounds bandaged, he stood grieving the loss of his *Pretender* and his lot in life, at the railing of the *Marianne*. All of his fury and all of his bluster meant nothing without his warship.

I am a toothless lion.

He shivered under the blanket. Loss of blood had left him cold, and infection in his wounds had given him a fever. But if he laid down, he might not ever get up again.

He looked back at Captain Benjamin Hornigold, who stood at the helm as he guided the tattered fleet back into the port. Wanting to make the Bahamas a New Madagascar, he avoided being a tyrant and supported Hornigold's ascent to leadership. *I've lost the advantage. I've created a monster I can't control.*

Hornigold and Vane arrived at Bimini while the storm still raged, scooping up terrified men who'd faced a monster with a magical ring. Dalziel, now without a ship or a tongue, fanned the fires once he'd been given pen and paper.

Drummond had seen the madness firsthand, including the moment the dark clouds and dark spirits seemingly joined forces. *LeSueur's ring.*

Once the ship docked, Hornigold was the only man brave enough to approach him. "Let's get you into a soft bed and let a real doctor tend to your wounds."

"No," Drummond muttered. "I'll stay here until everyone has returned."

"Best not be thinking of stealing my ship and going back out there," Hornigold said in a joking manner that revealed a bit of truth. "I'm your servant to command," he quickly added, "but even you need to rest."

"If I collapse, you can bring me to your doctor. For now, I'll greet the fleet as it returns."

One by one, the tattered Republic of Pirates limped back into port, allowing Drummond to learn the truth. The mysterious warships that scooped up Gaspar and attacked the pirates in the channel—Jennings had seen at least three of them along with the *Eurydice* off the coast of Florida. He'd also found the wreckage of the *Pretender*.

"Cheer up," Jennings added. "With one hand the Lord takes away; with the other hand he returns what was lost. The storm sank a Spanish Treasure fleet. Tomorrow, I'll return with some lads to go scoop it up. We'll rebuild, Edward. Don't worry."

Spanish gold? Yes, that will do. "There is a ring," he began, realizing he suddenly sounded like a crazed fool. "Don't let anyone search the *Pretender* without me being present. Is that clear?"

Even without a weapon, Drummond still could intimidate the average man. Jennings agreed and crawled back to a tavern.

Hour by hour, the news grew worse. He'd unleashed dozens of ships and only a handful came back.

A ship from Bermuda brought back the worst news.

Yes, Joseph LeMoyne and the *Griffon* survived the storm, but after reaching Bermuda to refit along with survivors from the Republic of Pirates, he left for France.

He abandoned me. Who else remains?

Jean-Baptise? Antoine? The Louisiana colony finally was flourishing and had no leadership while the New France colony had old aristocrats blinded by the fortunes of fur trade.

The reason Joseph LeMoyne continued home soon became clear. British ships carried news to Bermuda. The famed circumnavigator Woodes Rogers now had the financial and military support of English Parliament to root out the "nest of infamous rascals" inhabiting the Bahamas and establish order.

THE ALCHEMIST'S RING

Sent by Newton.

The new war was beginning already.

So despite being on death's door, Drummond stood at the prow of the ship and waited, hoping to find Solomon's ring hidden amongst the Spanish treasure.

But can I rebuild everything I lost before Rogers arrives?

CHAPTER 124

Gaspar finished his prayer. Opening his eyes, he looked upon all those who'd had a role in saving his life. They gathered on the hill where the new village had been built. In the harbor below, four ships temporarily anchored.

His oldest friends—LeSueur and Guerin—were now shells of their former selves, dealing with life-changing wounds.

The cruel hag Athena McCormack, who once found joy in torturing captives, now offered maternal care to young Zanahary while his father healed. Her newfound compassion extended to the Huguenot refugees still on the island and those she'd rescued following the destruction of the Sylph fleet.

The crew of the *White Zombie* had blossomed into more than just men—they grew into respectable men. Jimmy Duke and Drake Murray pledged to stay and support the colony, both to guard it and to bring supplies from foreign ports. Duke would captain the *Mary Dyer* and provide a smuggling lifeline to the American colonies. Drake would smuggle religious refugees out of Europe on transatlantic trips.

Naro Bon would replace Guerin as captain of the *Reinforcer*. Like Gaspar, he was in his final stage of life, and after traveling the world and gathering details for his world map, he now wanted to return to the mountains of his home. Professor Faero, tossed around for twenty years, elected to follow and continue his study of Asia as a free man.

Gaspar stood and looked past the familiar faces of his journey and to the other faces who'd shared his harrowing life. The Natchez slaves who'd been used as pawns and were unleashed upon Tortuga island provided him with a new purpose. All across the hemisphere, warriors who were defeated by European colonizers were put in chains and shipped off to remote islands. In his day, he'd captured and sold Iroquois chieftains into slavery, and for his penance, he'd seen the French do the same to his Natchez allies. Now, there were rumors of New Englanders selling the Mi'kmaq into slavery, and the Spanish had a long tradition of hauling off countless slaves to work in their plantations. As long as the Lord permitted, he and the surviving Natchez would find and ferry these people to freedom.

Gaspar stood and embraced Bon and Faero, whose journey would be the longest and more perilous. "By whatever name you call him, may the Creator watch over you on your journey east."

"It seems the Creator has use for both of us old men," Naro Bon grinned his almost toothless smile. "When I look up at the stars, they will be the same stars you see at night. In that way, we are still together."

Gaspar turned to Faero.

"With your earnest prayers," Professor Faero said, "I'm sure he will light our path." Faero turned to LeSueur. "While my search of the wreckage was fruitless, the ring didn't vanish. Remember the pledge. Don't let evil men discover the ring."

LeSueur lifted his stump. "This time, I'm sure the relic is at the bottom of the ocean or in a shark's belly."

Faero and Bon departed.

Gaspar turned to the others mentioned in his prayers, Guerin and LeSueur. "May the Lord preserve you for your final journeys."

Plans to travel up the Mississippi to the Land of the Blue Woman had obviously crumbled, and it would be up to the Jesuits, the Periphery, the Order of Eos, and the Priory of Ormus to find new pieces for the chess board.

"I wish I could linger and see what becomes of the colony," Guerin said to both Gaspar and also to Captain McCormack. His leg had healed, leaving him with a stump below his knee and a pair

of crutches. "But a promise is a promise, and I still have duties to those oaths."

He looked to Captain Drake Murray, who nodded with grim sincerity. Drake and Duke would both help on the initial leg of the next journey.

"The Great Lakes people hold a tradition," Gaspar began. "When a warrior gets home, he stops being a warrior and buries his hatchet. I worry that you will bloody your hatchet and show your son a dark path."

Guerin looked to LeSueur. "The final story I mean to tell will not involve murder. I'll raise my son, and he, in turn, will take care of two cripple old warriors who intend to bury the hatchet."

"Raise him well," Gaspar said of Zanahary. "The future will need good men."

With that, the men went their separate ways.

Captain Naro Bon and Professor Faero departed for the Indian Ocean.

Zanahary left with his father, Pierre-Charles LeSueur, Jimmy Duke, and Drake Murray, to collect an unpaid debt.

Do not let revenge stain your hearts, Gaspar thought silently as the three ships departed.

CHAPTER 125

Louis-Armand Guerin looked down into the clear waters, and caught in the reef, the ruins of the *White Zombie*…the *Adventure Prize*…the *Quedagh Merchant*…gathered barnacles. His former prison and then home for the better part of two decades was no more.

After being dropped off in deep waters, they approached the small island with Pierre-Charles LeSueur in the bow. The long approach finally ended as walls of sharp rock flanked the starboard side of the rowboat.

LeSueur pointed out the lagoon, but Guerin had to pause, exhausted. He braced his wooden leg against the seat in front of him and used his shoulders for most of the rowing. "Son of a bitch," Guerin muttered as he aimed for the center of the opening.

The nose of the rowboat hit the beach with such momentum that it all but beached itself.

With a hook strapped to his maimed forearm, LeSueur fumbled for a moment to climb out of the boat. He took the nose and dragged it the rest of the way out of the water and onto the small beach.

Guerin, out of breath, took a moment before slipping his pistols into his chest holsters and then readjusting his wooden leg onto the healed remainder of his left leg.

How pathetic are we? He accepted LeSueur's good hand to climb out of the boat. They both struggled to lift a chest out of the boat and set it onto the beach in plain sight. "Are you sure they can see us?"

"They should be watching us from that rocky peak," LeSueur again declared. "We'll see how curious they are."

"Then I'm sitting," Guerin said, flopping onto the sand. The trap had been set overnight, and when morning came, Jimmy Duke sailed within a mile of the island, dropped them off, and made a big circle with orders to anchor off shore of the island. On the western side of the island, Drake Murray already anchored the previous night.

Guerin watched as LeSueur adjusted his holstered pistols and a small hatchet. "Are you sure about his plan?"

"Gaspar is right. If we are to be done, we must turn away from killing." *Neither of us can return to civilization without being plagued by assassins. We follow this plan or…what? Open our wrists?*

No, I still have living to do.

"Perhaps they left." LeSueur asked after a few minutes of waiting.

"Should we go knock?" Guerin teased. "Do you ever look down and expect to still find your missing limb?"

"There are times when I still feel like I am wearing the ring and my hand is still attached."

"After this, should we go back and search the beach one more time?" Guerin asked.

"After this, our story is over."

Guerin sat up, looking around the quiet island. He nodded and LeSueur helped him up. The two traveled a few hundred yards from the beach and up the little bluff. Just as LeSueur anticipated, a small cabin had been built just above a clearing of trees. The cabin faced the gentle beaches, the reef, and the only place where large ships could safely land.

Fishing, fruit trees, shelter—all a man could want.

Ahead of them, a balding man wearing pantaloons with suspenders over his graying chest stepped out of the cabin. He yawned and staggered toward the small cliff, urinated off the edge, and with a large scope, studied the ship anchoring offshore.

A larger man of similar age came out of the cabin and immediately went to the campfire and stirred up the coals. He was clothed

in an oversized white shirt, a large, wide-brimmed hat, and shorts that reached to his knees.

I understand what LeSueur meant. They have an uncanny resemblance to us.

When the big fellow reached the man with the scope and both turned to study the approaching ship, LeSueur took out his pistol and stepped forward.

By the time the strangers heard the scrape of his crutch along the ground, it was too late. LeSueur leveled the pistol at their faces with the command, "Sit, now!"

It's them.

The startled men jumped, and seeing the obvious danger, obeyed without question, allowing Guerin to hobble closer. He dropped his crutch, and with rope in hand, quickly tied their hands behind their backs while LeSueur alternated the pistol between their faces.

Then he quickly bound their ankles together.

We got 'em. Breathing a sigh of relief, he leaned back on his palms, just feet in front of his prisoners. LeSueur kept the pistol ready, circling behind them.

In the distance, he saw Drake Murray with a landing party walking up the slope from their hiding place on the western shore.

"It's been a while," Guerin said. "You might recognize my friend from his recent marooning, and because you spared his life, we are going to do everything we can to spare yours. My friends are coming ashore right now, and the captain of that ship has unfinished business, Captain Culliford. Do you remember me?"

"We have money," John Swan, the brute, offered while Culliford tried to figure out the situation.

To help, Guerin flipped up his eye patch and laughed. "We have more wealth than we could spend in a lifetime, just like you. We're here for justice."

The former pirates were perpetual liars. "We've walked away from that life," Swan insisted. "For twenty years, we've been fishermen. We saved your friend. We're not pirates any more."

"Do you remember me?" Guerin asked again. "Eye...remember you."

Realization fluttered in their eyes. "I didn't kill you, did I?" Captain Culliford finally said. "Taking your eye showed our resolve. We had orders."

"I'm glad your cruelty is remembered," Guerin said with a shrug. "The other men joining us are survivors from Captain Kidd's crew. You might have delayed justice, and you might have hoped to avoid it all the way to Judgment Day, but it seems fate wanted you to pay for your crimes."

For the next hour, Guerin made casual small talk with his bound captives, who made more attempts to bribe and plead their case.

Captain Jimmy Duke finally appeared, walking up the hill with a vanguard of ten men, all armed with cutlasses for good effect.

"He's shrunk," Duke scoffed once he stood in front of Culliford.

"He's been living a soft life for a few years," Guerin said, wiggling his pegleg. "But life shrinks all of us, doesn't it?" Drake and Duke didn't even smirk at the joke. Hatred filled their eyes. "Charlie, could you lend a hand?"

The vanguard chuckled even when LeSueur didn't. He almost lifted Guerin off his feet, and his friend found balance upon his good leg.

"Captain Murray, have your men bring Mr. Swan to your ship. I have no business with him. You'll want to stay for this next part."

Still bargaining, John Swan was pulled to his feet and, with a cutlass at his back, was led back down the path toward the *Son of the Sea*.

Guerin stared down at Culliford. "There is a bounty on both of your heads, and if we bring you back alive to London, they'll make a spectacle of hanging you on Executioner's Dock. It's the same place where they hung Captain Kidd. Ironic, isn't it?"

"I had nothing to do with his arrest," Culliford insisted. "You! You betrayed your own captain."

Guerin sighed. "Keep telling yourself that, and perhaps one day it will be true. Kidd was devoured by his master. You're not here because of Captain Kidd. One good deed, like saving a marooned sailor, does not wipe out the rest of your sins, and you and I are

going to set matters straight. Now...where does the old adage come from, Charlie?"

"What adage?"

"An eye for an eye," Guerin said.

LeSueur slipped out a short dagger and handed it to Guerin, all while Culliford began to whimper. "I think Christ said it."

Guerin laughed heartily. "He might have quoted the adage, but he preached mercy, didn't he?"

"Yes, please, mercy," Culliford said.

"Hammurabi," Guerin snapped. "Christ was quoting the old Babylonian code of justice."

LeSueur put his hook under Culliford's chin and his big palm over the man's forehead. "I'd try not to flinch. You can live without an eye, but you won't last a minute with a cut throat."

AN HOUR LATER, LeSueur, Guerin, and Jimmy Duke watched as the one-eyed Culliford joined Swan, bound for a distant port across the Atlantic, on Drake Murray's ship.

"You took his eye," Jimmy Duke said. "But these men deserve death."

"Did I kill Captain Kidd myself? No. I left him to our enemies. Culliford and Swan live for now, but trust me, they'll soon be devoured by our enemies."

"Will Captain Duke actually bring them all the way to London?"

"Oh, no. That was a bit of fiction, but Drake is a man of his word, and he understands that justice comes in all forms. Culliford and Swan will escape obvious justice to serve another kind of justice."

"What kind of justice?" LeSueur asked.

"In the four months it'll take them to sail to England, Captain Murray will visit the brig on a regular basis until it would seem he's an ally. Honestly, do you think the *Son of the Sea* would be safe making port anywhere near London?"

"No, which is why I was surprised you didn't kill them here," Jimmy added.

"Captain Murray has orders to disobey orders, and instead of sailing to London, he will go to Amsterdam, a friendly port with plenty of enemy eyes. At some point in time, Robert Culliford and John Swan will be released, free to do what they want with their life."

"How is that justice?"

"Robert Culliford is from England, and as a wanted pirate, he certainly can't return home, nor does he have any means, or inclination, to return to the Caribbean. Yet John Swan was born Johann Schwan, and by all accounts, he had family in Hanover. Where else would they turn?"

"So you *are* showing mercy?"

"The blood from his eye might have stained my hands, but I'll let fate take care of the rest. A flamboyant one-eyed man and a hulking ogre stepped off the *Son of the Sea,* a ship affiliated with the Flying Sylphs of Tortuga. Louis-Armand de Lom d'Arce, Baron of Lahontan, needs to die. This plan will make sure it happens."

CHAPTER 126

Lady Columbia stood at the doorway of her uncle's chamber and listened for several minutes. She heard him groan as he got out of bed and wince as his gout caused terrible pain with each step. A great sigh meant he'd taken his place at his red couch, which now faced the large window and open yard of their new home in the country.

Marrying John Conduit provided financial stability for her, her Uncle Isaac, and his legacy, something her husband fully understood before agreeing to the arrangement. Even while they transitioned both the man and his works for his pending demise, the seventy-six year-old retired scientist and politician was not finished as a puppet master.

With a box under her arm, Lady Columbia turned the knob and walked into the main level library. "Good morning, how did you sleep?"

He glanced over at the box she set down on the table in front of the couch before climbing into the other corner of the couch. "A bit restless. How do I know for certain that our assassin killed the right man?"

"Michael Sikkar is thorough," she insisted. "After he discovered the publication trail in the Netherlands that connects the Lahontan manuscript with the anonymous works of Adrian Van Broeck, he kept digging. He discovered that the corpse buried in Cuba is not the body of Pierre-Charles LeSueur."

"When was the last time anyone had seen the man?" Newton asked.

"Who? LeSueur or Lahontan?" Newton ignored her counter-question so she answered, "I suppose the last time anyone made a credible sighting of Lahontan was in the bed of the Governor's daughter."

"Twenty-five years ago? After all that time, evading bounty hunters, he just settles in Hanover Germany for his retirement. It doesn't make any sense."

"Lahontan is dead, Uncle. Do you want to meet with Sikkar to get the details?"

"Of course not, nor do I want you questioning his claims, else I find myself poisoned one morning."

Lady Columbia reached over and read the letter about the passing of Baron Lahontan. "At the age of fifty, the American frontiersman, writer, scoundrel, and fugitive settled in Germany following the end of the War of Spanish Succession with his first mate, Johann Schwann. Although the estate was purchased under the name Robert Anruff—"

"Pseudonyms," Newton added. "Am I supposed to believe LeSueur and Lahontan settled together in Hanover?"

"Robert Anruff purchased the estate with Spanish gold, it adds, where the two bachelors lived out their final days together." She looked up from the death notice. "Until our man Michael Sikkar knocked upon their door. Anruff had one eye and wore flamboyant wigs. Johann Schwann, another pseudonym, matches the description of a first mate that towered over his captain. Lahontan is dead, Uncle. LeSueur is dead. Why do you fret? You've won. You're the last one standing."

"Imposters. Sikkar probably killed the wrong men. LeSueur and Lahontan are most likely laughing at me on some tropical island."

"A flamboyant one-eyed man and a giant? What are the odds, Uncle? Ockham's razor dictates that—"

"Then where are the treasures that were stolen from my predecessors? Where is the stolen *Al Marakk* map? Where is the ring? Why didn't we have a party as we burned the ancient maps and texts? What have I accomplished?"

Lady Columbia took a deep breath. "England is now a global power, ruled over by someone other than a Scot or Catholic. The island of Madagascar has been purged of pirates, allowing global trade to continue. The whole of Acadia, which they are now calling Nova Scotia, belongs to England, and despite the truce, New France teeters on collapse, to be gobbled up by England. Perhaps the box will cheer you up."

"What is it? Who sent it?" Newton asked, showing no inclination of leaning forward to retrieve it.

"Our man, Woodes Rogers, shattered the Republic of Pirates set up in the Bahamas. This past summer, he took the town of Nassau, and has turned pirate against pirate. Spain is worried his hunt for pirates is a veiled attempt to claim the entire Caribbean for England."

"What about—"

"Edward Drummond? As the Pirate King, he called himself Edward Teach, or more simply, Blackbeard. He fled from Woodes Rogers, and so did the rest of his ilk, but the reward you placed eventually did the trick. It is believed he was trying to make contact with his Eos contacts in the American colonies when his ship ran aground and he met a violent end at the hands of a Captain Maynard, who earned his reward by bringing this to Governor Rogers."

This will give his paranoid mind ease.

Now her uncle was interested, leaning forward to snatch up the box, which had a simple Latin phrase written upon it—*veritas caput.*

Newton's momentary smile stopped when he slid the top from the ornate box. The stench of death permeated the room. Having inspected it already, Lady Columbia understood the black fabric inside of the box was a flag bearing the Coat of Arms Newton had fashioned for himself, the two crossed thighbones.

Edward Drummond's skull rose from the box with just a few pieces of flesh still holding the infamous black beard.

Newton nodded and dropped the head back in the box. "This…this is evidence of death. But even a severed head does not mean the war is over. Do you remember what I taught you about Eos? If we are to stop the world from coming to an end in 2060, we must stop them from finding the tomb."

Lady Columbia nodded. It had become her legacy over the past few years. One day, Catherine Barton-Conduit would die, and on that day, Lady Columbia would become an immortal—tasked with preventing an ancient alchemist from rising from his grave.

CHAPTER 127

A R U B A

1 7 1 8

Of the 700 islands in the Caribbean, the island of Aruba is one of the southernmost. Although twenty miles long and six miles wide, much of Aruba's eastern shore offered wave-battered inhospitality, which is why pirates ignored it. When the Spanish discovered it in 1500, it was inhabited by the Caquetío, but after a century, the wild horses and livestock outnumbered the sparse population. In the 1600s, the Dutch also took an interest in Aruba, but not for settlement. While the Dutch utilized neighboring Curacao for salt harvesting, Aruba was deemed a "worthless island" to them. Located near the largest tropical rainforest in the world, the small island was mountainous and almost arid despite being so close to the equator.

The perfect place to hide from the civilized world, Captain Jimmy Duke decided. Two years after last visiting Aruba, he now knew where to anchor.

He anchored the *Mary Dyer* almost a mile from shore since reefs protected most of the island. He and a small landing party knew their approach could be seen. It was a three mile hike through shallow cuts and ravines before the volcanic mountain rose from sea level to a height of five-hundred feet. The terrain was steady with few obstructions, allowing Duke to plod along at a relatively quick pace.

Are they still alive?

His answer came a few moments later as the ground began to shake under the thunder of hooves. A herd of Andalusian war-horses crossed the base of the mountain with two saddled horses breaking off from the herd for a closer look.

Jimmy Duke threw his hands up and waited for the two riders to approach. Pierre-Charles LeSueur and Zanahary Guerin galloped up to the small band of men.

"Good to see you old friend," LeSueur greeted. "Trouble?"

"No trouble, but I do bring news. Where is Louis-Armand?"

"My father's tending the corral," Zanahary said. "We were rounding up some of the foals."

"I'm sorry to interrupt," Duke added.

LeSueur and the boy escorted Duke and the others to the simple cabin built along the shade of the mountain. From the view, Duke could see his anchored ship and the beached skiff. Any approaching ship could be seen hours before it could effectively reach shore, allowing the two outlaws half a day to effectively hide.

Which is totally unnecessary now.

A shirtless Louis-Armand Guerin leaned against the gate of the corral where several other horses already waited. He was tan and fit yet still used a crutch to compensate for his wooden leg.

"I've come with bad news," Duke began. "Baron Lahontan died at the age of 48 in Hanover, Germany."

"What was I doing in Hanover?" Louis-Armand asked.

"Hiding from your powerful enemies, apparently. France, England, India, Spain—when these powerful nations want you dead, there aren't many other options to hide. After you were last seen making port in Amsterdam, it didn't take long for your enemies to find you?"

"So who killed me?"

"Unsure, but Hanover has alliances with the current British government, so it is likely that an assassin from the Priory of Ormus did it."

"It upsets me that Newton will go to his grave thinking he's beaten me," Guerin admitted.

"It upsets me that Newton isn't in his grave," LeSueur added.

"Then I might have news to cheer you up," Duke offered. "The Republic of Pirates has been crushed by Governor Woodes Rogers, which allows our efforts to support our refugee colonies. Captains Murray and McCormack haven't fired a cannon in

months, nor have I. Patrick Dalziel was hanged and the scoundrel known as Blackbeard was beheaded. So Newton goes to the grave believing he's defeated Eos as well as the infamous Baron Lahontan."

"And Pierre-Charles LeSueur?" LeSueur asked.

"You died a second death in Hanover. It seems Captain Murray convinced the world when he took the hand off of John Swan. The assassin claimed it matched your likeness."

The two aging men solemnly nodded, understanding they'd be allowed to grow old while raising young Zanahary.

"I have something for you," Louis-Armand Guerin said, and brought all of them to the small house. He went into a room and returned with a small box. "After such a wild life, the simple life felt almost too quiet. So for the past several months, I've been busy on my final work."

Duke opened the lid. Inside, hundreds of pages with handwritten text filled the pages. *A General History of the Robberies and Murders of the Most Notorious Pyrates* by Charles Johnson. "A book?"

"I would greatly appreciate it if in your travels, you could pass it along to Captain Murray. When he makes his seasonal trip to Europe, place it in the hands of my old friends. I'm sure they'll see the humor in publishing such a work."

"What kind of work?" Duke asked.

"I changed some names, left others, and invented much more. Aruba is so dreadfully boring at times. Like my other works, I hope to leave the world with more questions than answers. This will certainly muddy the waters. They have my permission to make adjustments as needed."

LeSueur scoffed and took off the hook to massage his stump. "Charles Johnson?"

"I thought the pseudonym to be a fitting tribute," Guerin smirked.

In the distance, the herd of wild horses settled in an open valley. "Can I go?" Zanahary asked.

"Go, ride like the wind," Louis-Armand said to his son, and the young man spurred his horse and vanished. "He'll soon outgrow this island."

"And knowing the world believes you are both dead…will you stay?"

"Our days of adventure are over," LeSueur admitted. "We'll tend to our little island."

"We've only delayed an inevitable future," Guerin added. "One day, the ring will wash ashore. One day, the Philosopher's Stone will be discovered again. One day, the real white zombie will rise from his tomb. On that day, I can only pray there are others like you who are willing to make the needed sacrifice."

Jimmy Duke winked. "I'll keep an eye out for trouble."

EPILOGUE

M O U N T   K A I L A S H

1 7 1 8

Two old men looked up to behold one of the wonders of the world.

I can't believe we've made it, Naro Bon thought. *Do the gods not know our intentions? Why have they not stopped us?*

For Naro Bon, Mount Kailash existed in the shadows of his home in nearby Kathmandu. After crossing the earth, he and Faero spent a winter at home before continuing on to their destination.

For Professor Josiah Faero, Mount Kailash had been unfinished business. He showed Bon the diagram of the emperor's private examination of the mountain. "Before I was recalled to Bombay, we'd almost finished a complete study of the mountain's base. We need to make sure we're alone before continuing."

"Emperor Aurangzeb is dead," Bon muttered and continued walking, "and the flame of his curiosity had been extinguished."

"And what about you?" Faero asked with a grin. "Are you still curious?"

"I've spent my life traveling the world, pulling the curtains away to see what is hidden underneath," Naro began. "Eos believed they could wake a sleeping god. Is that what we are about to find?"

"LeSueur and Guerin believed an ancient enemy was buried out on the frontier. If they'd been allowed, they would've traveled up the Mississippi River to take a closer look. I think we are as far away from this evil being as we can be," Faero said.

"So what will we find ahead?"

"Confirmation," Faero said and smirked.

Bon shook his head in frustration. "Was the Ark not confirmation? Was the ring not confirmation?"

"When I was taken from my comfortable home, Thomas Tew knew I'd uncovered an ancient language—perhaps the first language—far before the Tower of Babel or the Phoenician alphabet. The Ark and the ring came from our known world in the time of King Solomon. I hope to find proof of the ancient kingdom. It's what Emperor Aurangzeb longed to discover also. We've come too far to turn back now."

Naro Bon shivered under his fur jacket. It wasn't the cold that caused him to shiver. He'd spent the past month growing used to the cold of the Himalayas, and walking caused heat to build up quickly in the space between his body and the thick leather hide of the jacket. Naro Bon shivered because he could see his tomb. "I'm not ready to die."

Faero shrugged and kept walking. "I need to know, regardless of the consequences. We could've gone to Madagascar and sifted through the historical garbage collected over the past four thousand years…or we can peek inside back to the very beginning.

Bon knew what needed to be done, so he moved his feet steadily forward, keeping an eye out for pilgrims. Here, at the navel of the universe, pilgrims like himself came wandering from all directions to worship all sorts of gods.

The last few steps of his journey seemed to take the longest, as he crossed the arid isthmus between two drying lakes.

A crease in the world.

Behind him, the continent of India.

A mile ahead, the continent of Asia.

To his left and to his right, a smooth valley extended in all directions, where the earth slowly buckled. He expected to see armed riders come charging in, but here at the top of the world, no one cared about two old men, who'd begun their final journey by scouring a wreckage upon the sands of a Florida beach.

"Then, my friend," Bon said. "Let's finish the adventure."

Bon and Faero walked around the western slopes of Mount Kailash with relative familiarity. The God of Irony had patted them on the head and handed them a key.

Faero stopped at a natural doorway. The fissure in the earth was closed to mortal man, locking its secrets away.

Naro Bon reached inside of his parka, then inside of his shirt, until his finger felt the leather pouch. Untying the cord, the stench of death wafted up to his nostrils.

A large, skeletal hand, with dried flesh still clung to bone.

"Let me see, my friend. You owe us this," Faero addressed Pierre-Charles LeSueur far away on the other side of the earth. Neither of them dared to put on the ring, but one of them could speak to it.

Josiah Faero uttered the same words he'd taught to LeSueur.

The ring upon the dried finger began to glow unnaturally, and Bon began to feel the hairs on his neck stand on end—not because of fear or premonition, but because the elements around him began to obey.

Is LeSueur dreaming of this mountain? Does the ring still obey its former master?

The fissure opened, and with each step, the passage continued.

I am walking into the heart of the mountain.

The passage was neither manmade or natural, and a blanket of darkness pushed away solid stone as he stepped forward. Faero paused to light a lantern, allowing them to continue.

Like a wet blanket protecting one walking through fire, the song and the ring allowed them to pass through the rocky barrier.

Behind them, the passage closed, cutting off any thought of dying in some local village.

This is where I die.

Their exodus into the mountain continued for a few more moments, until the walls suddenly opened up.

A chamber, Bon realized, looking up at the distant ceiling. Light from the ring and lantern showed him the far wall also, hundreds of feet away.

It's all true.

Ahead of him, he saw a collection of ebony steles—rectangular blocks of stone, blacker than any night he'd ever experienced. If Faero's tales were true, the stones contained the designs of the universe from the tiny fly to the cosmos itself.

The navel of the universe, indeed.

"Thank you, my friend," Faero said to him. "Now let's go learn the mysteries of the universe."

Faero walked ahead, carrying the lantern with him as he approached the closest of the black steles.

Bon felt something move. At first, he worried the hand itself had come to life. Instead, the bony appendage broke off the hand at the knuckle and Pierre-Charles LeSueur's finger fell to the ground.

It bounced once, and then the ring came free, clanking and rolling.

"What happened?" Faero asked, but then the spirits guarding the place, freed from the control of the ring, darkened the light.

THE END

The quest continues
for Joseph Nicollet
in
The Alchemist's Map

Abracadabra—an ancient magic phrase.

Abyssinia—an older term for Ethiopia.

Adario—the fictionalized name of Petun chief Kondiaronk.

Aksum—an ancient city in Ethiopia.

Alamgiri Library—the private collection of Emperor Aurangzeb

Alarie, Andreas—a Canadian doctor.

Alvorez, Marco—Grand Master of the Order of Eos.

Andriana—the brother of Queen Rehena of Madagascar.

Anishinaabe—an indigenous tribe ranging from the Atlantic to the Great Lakes. Also known as the Chippewa and Ojibwe.

Aurangzeb—the leader of the Mughal Empire.

Avery, Henry—a notorious pirate.

Baba, Corgi—the former captain of the *Quedagh Merchant*.

Bakinis—an Anishinaabe chieftain of the Wijigan Clan.

Barrow, Thomas—a ship's doctor.

Barton, Catherine—the niece of Sir Isaac Newton.

Beaumains—a term from Arthurian legend meaning "good hands"

Bellomont, Black Robin—a notorious privateer.

Bennett, Thomas—a notorious privateer.

Benoit, Francois—a Canadian servant.

Betsimisaraka—an eastern tribe in Madagascar.

Bilocci—the Indigenous term for what became Biloxi.

Black Stone—a legendary object associated with creation.

Bon, Naro—a navigator and mapmaker from Nepal.

Boyle, Robert—a scientist and member of the Invisible College.

Bridgeman—Henry Avery's crewman.

Burniston—a British Commander.

Callendar, Augee Peree—a British businessman.

Campbell, Torc—a servant in the Order of Eos.

Cass, Richard—a notorious privateer.

Cathars—a heretical Christian group in western Europe.

Chippewa—see Anishinaabe.

Choquet, Julien—a Canadian servant.

Churchill, George—the English Admiral of the Blue

Clairval, Bernard—a servant in the Priory of Ormus.

Crapeau, Jean—a notorious French pirate.

Culliford, Robert—a notorious pirate.

Daalman, Laurens—a Flying Dutchmen captain of the Moss Maiden.

Darika—a Mughal princess.

de la Salle, Nicholas—a French colonist in Louisiana.

de Lom d'Arcy, Louis-Armand—the Baron of Lahontan.

Del Torro, Manuel—a quartermaster.

Delhut, Etienne—a servant in the Order of Eos.

Dewili—an Ethiopian priest.

Dias, Pedro—a notorious Madagascar pirate.

Dobie, Daerg—a servant in the Order of Eos.

Drummond, Edward—a notorious pirate of uncertain allegiances.

DuBois, Phillip—a servant in the Periphery.

Duke, Jimmy—an anchoring boatswain.

Elixir of Life—a legend involving immortality.

Endura—a suicide rite practiced by the Cathars.

Faero, Josiah—a scholar.

Falcoa, Denis—the vizier of the Madagascar colony.

Farquhar—an Irish dramatist.

Farrington, George—a notorious English privateer.

Firken, Jago—a provisions boatswain.

Foisy, Antoine—a Canadian servant.

Fylgia—a Norse concept for spirit or avatar.

Galiote, Therese—daughter of Louis Joliet.

Galloway, Vincent—a pirate in the Flying Sylphs.

Gaspar—the Christian name for Petun war chief Kondiaronk.

Germelshausen, Arnold—a servant in the Priory of Ormus

Gibson—an English ship captain.

Great Work—a term found in Alchemy.

Guerin, Jeanne—mother of Baron Lahontan.

Hamingja—a Norse concept for a protecting spirit.

Hamr—a Norse concept for the body.

Hornigold, Benjamin—a notorious pirate of the Caribbean.

Huguenots—a group of French Protestant refugees.

Humphreys, Captain—an English ship captain.

Huron Confederacy—an alliance of Great Lakes tribes.

Ibrahim, Muhammad—the captain of the Ganj-i-Sawai.
Imerina—a southwestern region of Madagascar.
Ireland, Ned—a notorious English privateer.

Jacobs, Wart—a captain in the Flying Sylphs
Jennings, Henry—a notorious pirate of the Caribbean.
Johnson, Charles—a pseudonym used by an author on a book about pirates.
Joliet, Claire—the widow of Louis Joliet.
Joliet, Nicholas—the son of Louis Joliet.

Kam, Aqueel—a servant of the Mughal emperor.
Keoxa—a Dakota warrior.
Khātam Sulaymān—an alternate name for Solomon's ring.
Kidd, William—a notorious New England privateer.
Kikkert—a member of the Flying Dutchmen.
King Solomon—the King of Israel in 1000 BC.
Kokebi—an Ethiopian navigator and mapmaker.
Konhoji—a servant of the Mughal emperor.

L'Huillier, Alexander—Farmer General of France.
LaGrande, Gareth—a pseudonym for a notorious pirate.
Lairet, Abraham—a farm manager at Beaupre, Quebec.
LaSalle—Rene-Robert Cavelier, a French nobleman.
Lavasseur, Oliver—a notorious pirate.
LeMoyne, Antoine—a French nobleman (1683-1747)
LeMoyne, Charles—a French nobleman (1626-1685)
LeMoyne, Charles Jr—a French nobleman (1656-1729)
LeMoyne, Francois—a French nobleman (1666-1691)
LeMoyne, Gabriel—a French nobleman.
LeMoyne, Jacques—a French nobleman (1669-1690).
LeMoyne, JC—a French nobleman.
LeMoyne, Jean-Baptiste—Sieur de Bienville and founder of Louisiana (1680-1767).

LeMoyne, Joseph—Sieur de Serigny (1668-?).
LeMoyne, Louis—Sieur de Châteauguay (1676-1694).
LeMoyne, Paul—a French nobleman.
LeMoyne, Pierre—Sieur d'Iberville.
LeMoyne, PLJ—a French nobleman.
LeSueur, Jean-Paul—the son and heir of Pierre-Charles LeSueur.
LeSueur, Louise—daughter of Pierre-Charles LeSueur.
LeSueur, Margaret—daughter of Pierre-Charles LeSueur.
LeSueur, Marguerite—the wife of Pierre-Charles LeSueur.
LeSueur, Mary—daughter of Pierre-Charles LeSueur.
LeSueur, Mary Ann—daughter of Pierre-Charles LeSueur.
LeSueur, Pierre-Charles—a French fur-trader and explorer.

Makeda—the ancient Queen of Sheba.
Marquette, Jacques—a Jesuit priest and explorer.
McCormack, Athena—member of the Flying Sylphs.
Men of the Dawn—an alternate title for the Order of Eos.
Morrison, James—a Presider for the Order of Eos.
Mount Kailash—a sacred mountain in Tibet.
Moore, William—a master gunner.
Mozeemlek—a fictional Indigenous tribe.
Muelles, Francois—an assassin hired by the Order of Eos.
Munz, Johan—a German administrator of the Gold Coast colony.
Murray, Drake—a provisions boatswain.

Naufragio, Giovanni—a ship carpenter.
New Voyages to North America—a book written by Baron Lahontan.
Newton, Isaac—Master of the Mint at the Tower of London.
Norris, John—an English ship captain.

O'Byrne, Admiral—an English naval officer.
Oceti Sakowin—an Indigenous group also known as the Sioux or Dakota.
Odin Stone—a black stone with ancient language written upon it.
Ojibwe—another term for the Anishinaabe.
Order of Eos—an ancient secret society.

Panni, Admiral—a Mughal naval officer.
Papa Bones—a Haitian cook.
Penicaut, Andre—a French ship carpenter and fur-trader.
Petun—an Indigenous tribe of the Great Lakes.
Plantain, James—a notorious Madagascar pirate.
Poiter, Charles—a Canadian servant.
Presider—a democratically elected office within the Order of Eos.
Prince George of Denmark—the husband of Queen Anne of England.
Priory of Ormus—a secret society dating back to 1188.
Pro, John—a notorious Madagascar pirate.

Queen Anne—the English monarch from 1702-1714.

Ramano—a Madagascar tribal leader.
Ratsimilaho—King of Madagascar.
Ravana—a multi-headed evil deity in Hindu mythology.
Rehena—Queen of Madagascar.
Rogers, Woods—owner of a merchant fleet.
Rogers, Woodes—an English captain and explorer.

Samuel, Abraham—an English privateer.
Shah, Imam—a Mughal religious figure.
Shamir—a legendary substance created by King Solomon.
Sheba—an alternative term for Ethiopia.
Shrine of Sheikh Zainuddin—the location of Emperor Aurangzeb's tomb.
Sikkar, Michael—a Priory of Ormus assassin.
Silverthorn, Roger—an English privateer.
St. Clair, Bartolome—an Order of Eos assassin.

Swan, John—a notorious Madagascar pirate.

T'ebaki—an Ethiopian priest.
Tariyy, Abdi—a Mughal ambassador.
Templar Knights—a holy order later deemed heretical and disbanded.
Tew, Thomas—a notorious New England pirate.
The Invisible College—a secret society of intellectuals.
Thomas, Willow—a member of the Flying Sylphs.
Tonpa Shenrab—a legend in the Bon tradition.

Valencourt—a member of the Free States.
Van Broeck, Adrian—a Dutch captain.
Vane, Charles—a notorious Caribbean pirate.
Vero, Archibald—a member of the Flying Sylphs.

Wachter, Burkhard—a servant in the Order of Eos.
Walsh, Robert—a notorious English privateer.
Washa Tekula—an Amharic word for a cave in Rome.
Wenonah—a Dakota woman.
Witenagemot—a Germanic word for gathering.
Wiyipisiw—a warrior from the Wijigan clan of the Anishinaabe.

Yarland, John—a notorious Madagascar pirate.

Zana-Malata—an ethnic group in Madagascar with European and African ancestry.
Zik'itenya—an Ethiopian legend of an ancient sorcerer.

ABOUT THE AUTHOR

Imagine the love child of Rambo and Ma Ingalls. That's Jason Lee Willis. Overly nurtured by his Vietnam War veteran father and Lutheran church secretary mother, he grew up in the fantasy realm of South Dakota before his exodus brought him to mysterious Minnesota for college.

His love of mythology and storytelling led him to a career as a high school English teacher, and now, he works as a journalist and blogger as well as a full-time novelist. As a professional storyteller, he's done historical lectures, book talks, radio segments, podcasts, and a video channel on YouTube, The Minnesota Alchemist.

Willis currently lives in Minnesota, where he lives the life of a hobbit by gardening, writing, walking around barefoot, wearing vests, fishing, and going on adventures with his wife, Julie.

For more stories, visit williswrites.com

(Oh, and if you made it this far, please leave a review).